THE MARIGOLD FIELD is a story of poor, proud, high-spirited people . . . people whose roots were in the farming country of southern England . . . in the bawdy and exuberant streets of the East End.

Jonathan Whitman, his cousin Myra, Anne-Louise Pritchard and the enormous Pritchard clan to which she belonged, saw the changing era and incredible events of a passing age—an age of great poverty and great wealth, of the Boer War and social reform, of straw boaters, feather boas, and the Music Hall. . .

And above all THE MARIGOLD FIELD is a story of one woman's consuming love . . . of a jealous obsession that threatened to destroy the very man she adored. . .

'An exceptionally good read. One of those *comfortable* books you can live in for a while with pleasure.'

MCCALLS MAGAZINE

'When Maxie takes Anne-Louise home on Sunday, when his relations assemble loudly at the meal-table . . . there is an instant of the finest, broadest comedy. . .'

SUNDAY TIMES

Also by Diane Pearson

THE LOOM OF TANCRED

and published by Corgi Books

Diane Pearson

The Marigold Field

CORGI BOOKS
TRANSWORLD PUBLISHERS LTD
A National General Company

THE MARIGOLD FIELD

A Corgi Book 552 08525 1

Originally published in Great Britain
by Macmillan & Co. Ltd.

PRINTING HISTORY
Macmillan edition published 1969
Corgi edition published 1970

This book is set in 10-11 pt. Garamond.

Corgi Books are published by Transworld Publishers Ltd.,
Cavendish House, 57-59 Uxbridge Road,
Ealing, London, W.5.
Made and printed in Great Britain by
Hunt Barnard Printing Ltd., Aylesbury, Bucks.

For Lillian L. Scott—'Joy'
in gratitude and appreciation

One

ANNE-LOUISE always enjoyed serving at the Rectory Hunt Day dinners.

Invariably the Rector was drunk and the dinners were dramatic and full of incident. She wasn't especially shocked or bothered by the Rector's behaviour, merely interested – and also a little contemptuous because she knew that none of the Elders in the Meeting where she worshipped would indulge in this kind of conduct. But she enjoyed the excitement and the general air of tension, the sense that at any moment some unexpected mishap could occur. It made her feel nervous but at the same time very superior and detached.

Mrs Panter, the Rector's wife, was always irritable and fault-finding at dinner parties – Anne knew it was because she resented having to make do with a village parlour-maid instead of a butler – but when the Rector was drunk the necessity of having to conceal his inebriation from the guests made Mrs Panter even more capricious and disagreeable than usual.

On this April day – the last Hunt of the season – Anne recognised all the symptoms of the Rector's disorder – the too-red face and the too-loud voice. More than ten minutes had passed since she had brought in the fourteen-pound goose and placed it before him. It lay resplendent and glistening with apricot sauce, and still the Rector made no attempt to begin carving, occupying himself with a rearranging of the plates and an unnecessary examination of the carvers.

Waiting to serve the vegetables from the sideboard, Anne-Louise debated whether or not she should put down the dish of roast potatoes she was holding. The dish was heavy and she could feel the heat gradually seeping away from the vegetable dish. She sighed and rested her arm against the edge of the sideboard. Mrs Panter heard the sigh, turned, glared at Anne-Louise and said icily, 'I see the gravy tureen is missing, Pritchard. Go and fetch it at once.'

Anne pushed the potato dish spitefully back on to the sideboard, said, 'Yes, m'm', and stumped disagreeably out of the dining-room and along to the kitchen.

The Rectory was a big one, built on a gently sloping hill so that the kitchen and back quarters were below ground level. It was probably about fifty years old, built when the Queen was still a young woman, and although the evidence of Victorian architecture was strongly present, the square windows and high rooms were faintly reminiscent of the Georgian period – except for the servants' quarters which were dark, overcrowded, and full of winding passages covered in brown linoleum that required constant polishing. The kitchen was a good fifty yards away from the dining-room, which meant that the staff had hot meals but no one else did – even on days when the Rector's lapses from sobriety didn't hold up the serving of food.

Anne-Louise crashed the green baize-covered door open and swung crossly into the kitchen.

'Old cat,' she said without rancour to the kitchen maid who was standing on a box by the sink washing dirty saucepans. 'Taking it out on me just because he's too drunk to carve.'

Cook, her efforts for the evening completed with the five dishes of assorted puddings and sweets waiting on the kitchen table, said 'Hmmph' and carried on looking at the pictures in *The Illustrated London News*.

Gracie was a thin, grey little girl who earned three-and-six a week living in. She swished apathetically in the dirty water.

'Are they nearly through the goose?' she asked hopefully, knowing she would have to stay at the sink until the coffee had been drunk and the cups carried out to the kitchen to be washed and dried.

Anne-Louise shrugged. 'Haven't even started. He's really very drunk this time. Can't carve the goose – I think he's frightened of it. Mrs Panter's cross and all the others are pretending not to notice.'

8

She lifted the gravy tureen carefully from the table, twitched the starched muslin bow at the back of her apron, and began a leisurely walk back to the dining-room, pausing to admire herself in the long mirror outside the dining-room door.

She was smart, she thought pleasingly to herself; small, gay, and smart, standing no more than five foot three, yet every inch erect and energetic. She put the gravy tureen down on the polished hall table in order to rearrange her frilled cap over the silky, high-piled hair. Her black silk dress – passed on by Mrs Panter to be worn only when serving at dinner parties – was pulled in as tightly as Anne could manage with the waist bands of her apron. It swirled elegantly around her ankles and she tried to walk so that it swung out sometimes and showed those same ankles that were – she considered – very neat and well shaped.

If only he could see me like this, she thought suddenly. If he could see me in this black silk dress with the tight waist, instead of the horrible old blue Sunday-go-to-Meeting dress, he'd notice me then. Jonathan Whitman would really look at me, really look and see how pretty and smart I am. Everyone else looks at me – even in the drab old blue dress – why doesn't he notice me? Why can't he see I'm pretty and clever?

She pulled irritably at the skirt of the dress, the pleasure in her mirrored reflection dissolving as she thought of Jonathan Whitman. She tweaked again at the apron band, then untied it and held her breath while she pulled it even tighter. 'He ought to see me in this,' she murmured to herself, and then added determinedly, 'He *must* see me like this.'

She stared blankly at herself in the mirror, trying to see a way of slipping out one evening when she was dressed for a Rectory party and could contrive a casual meeting with Jonathan Whitman. Her mind, feverishly working at times and coincidences, clung fervently to the knowledge that once he had seen her looking elegant and beautiful he would be as adoring and besotted as she wanted him to be.

There was a sudden crash and a shout from the dining-room – a small stifled scream from Mrs Panter, and a murmur of embarrassed voices trying to hide a social mishap with

9

conversation.

Anne scooped up the tureen, turned the handle of the door and quickly slipped inside.

The Rector, who had at last managed to sever a leg from the goose, had apparently pressed too hard. The angle of the carvers had been miscalculated and the goose, congealing in its glazing of sauce, had skidded from the dish and settled in the crimson, silk-covered lap of Mrs Panter.

Anne-Louise always enjoyed an emergency. Some untapped source of dramatic talent provided her with sufficient verve and dash to cope with the unexpected. Before Mrs Panter had time to gasp again, she had in one swift action, darted forward, put down the gravy tureen, and scooped the goose out of the lap and back on to the dish.

'I'm sorry, ma'am,' she said soothingly. 'I told Cook she'd put too much glazing on. She's made it impossible to carve.'

Mrs Panter began to wipe the front of her dress with her table-napkin.

'Shall I take the goose to the sideboard, ma'am?' asked Anne kindly. 'The master will be able to carve better there.'

The Rector's wife darted a look of malevolent gratitude at Anne-Louise. She knew and Anne knew, that once the Rector was at the sideboard, Anne could direct the serving of the bird without robbing the Rector of either dignity or authority.

'Perhaps that would be best, Pritchard,' said Mrs Panter tonelessly. The carving dish was removed and the Rector followed Anne to the sideboard. Dreamily he allowed her to dismember and distribute the meat. She was quick and efficient, and at the back of her mind gnawed the tiny thought again, 'He should have seen the way I handled that. How everyone did what I wanted them to. He should have seen me like that. Jonathan should have seen me.'

There was only one further emergency during the evening, when the Rector gradually slumped forward over his plate and was about to fall into his untouched portion of Queen Anne pudding. Anne-Louise hurriedly dropped a glass dish of nuts on the floor – she chose nuts as being the easiest to clear up – and was rewarded by seeing the Rector's head jerk swiftly up again.

'Sorry, ma'am,' she said serenely to Mrs Panter. 'I'll clear them up at once.'

'Do that,' said Mrs Panter rigidly. She was furious because the large grease stain on her lap was soaking through to her taffeta and poplin petticoats. The dress was ruined, and she also bitterly resented being in debt to Anne-Louise. The girl had saved Hunt Day dinners before, but this time both she and the Rector had excelled themselves.

On her way to the kitchen Anne hummed a little tune. She was pleased with herself, pleased with the way she had shone at the dining-table – and pleased because, at the back of her mind, she was beginning to think of a way of letting Jonathan see her in the silk dress.

Gracie was leaning over the sink with her eyes closed. She was thirteen and sometimes found it difficult to stay awake on dinner party nights.

'Finished?' she asked hopefully.

Anne shook her head and pulled a piece of meat daintily from the carcase of the goose.

'She's furious with me. I had to break a dish to keep him awake and she hates having to rely on me to keep him going for the evening. Her dress is spoilt – the red silk – all covered in grease. I don't suppose she'll wear it any more.'

Gracie closed her eyes again and leaned against the wall. 'I'm tired,' she said. 'I wish they'd finish so that I could go to bed.'

Anne-Louise put the piece of uneaten meat back on to the dish and stared speculatively at Gracie.

'Gracie,' she said slowly, 'if I help you with the washing-up tonight, will you do something for me next time there's a dinner?'

'What?' asked Gracie warily. She was uneasily aware that in bargains with Anne-Louise she didn't always profit.

'Set the table for me. Get the wine up from the cellar – I'll tell you which one to get. And try not to let Mrs Panter know I'm missing for a few moments.'

11

'Why? Where will you be?' asked Gracie nervously.

Anne twisted away so that the dress swung coquettishly out into the air.

'I want to pop out for a few moments to see someone.'

Gracie looked at the pile of cutlery still to be dried, and thought of the pudding plates, finger bowls, spoons, forks, port glasses, coffee cups and brandy glasses still to come out of the dining-room.

'All right,' she said tiredly. 'When do you want me to do it?'

'I'll tell you. Next time there's a dinner.'

Gracie nodded and swished. Whatever Anne-Louise had in mind, she wasn't really interested. Washing-up and bed seemed the only important things that anyone could possibly think about. She nodded again and thrust a vegetable spoon into the water.

It was over a month – at the beginning of May – before Anne's opportunity came. She instructed Gracie carefully in the laying of the table and fetching up of wines and then she hurried into Cook's small cubicle at the end of the pantry and put the black silk dress on. It was hot, unusually hot for May, and she felt the silk begin to stick to her ribs almost as soon as she had dressed.

Outside the Rectory she had to hurry, partly because she didn't want Mrs Panter to see her, but mostly because if she wanted to meet Jonathan on his way home from work, she would have to be at the top of long meadow in a very short space of time.

'Don't let me miss him,' she breathed. 'Please. Don't let him be gone already!'

And then she saw him, and the relief was so great she felt a fresh wave of heat break and swell over her body. He was lying face down on the grass, his head pillowed on his folded arms and a large red book resting close beside him. His body was strong and powerfully built, and his well-shaped smooth neck made her feel sick and happy at the same time.

She slowed her walk, smoothed her hands quickly against

12

the sides of her dress and began to tread softly towards him. He doesn't know I'm here, she thought. He'll look up, not expecting anyone, and he'll see me in the silk dress.

She walked right up close to stand over him, and still he didn't move, so she pulled a piece of grass and lightly touched the back of his neck.

'You're asleep, Jonathan Whitman,' she said brightly.

The man on the grass turned and looked up into the small, thin face giggling down at him. Then he quickly stood up, because when Anne-Louise stared at him like that he felt somehow at a disadvantage. As soon as he was standing she came closer to him. She had a sharp, fidgety way of darting her eyes up and down over his body and it made him feel uncomfortable.

'Hullo, Anne,' he said politely.

She twisted on one foot and swished her skirt. She had knotted her black hair very high on the crown of her head. It gave her an added height and she felt rather elegant and regal.

'How surprising! Seeing you here, I mean.'

He didn't answer. He bent down and picked up the book and she laughingly reached out and snatched it away from him.

'*Jude the Obscure*,' she read slowly. 'Thomas Hardy. Now what kind of a book is that?'

'Be careful with that, Anne,' he said nervously. 'It's not my book. You know that. It belongs to Mr Fawcett.'

'You still take the books from his study? Without him knowing?'

Jonathan shrugged. 'They don't even know what books they have there. I don't think either of them has ever read one of the books on those shelves. And, Anne you should see the books they have, hundreds and hundreds. And they still keep coming down from London every week.'

'Do you understand them?' she asked curiously. Jonathan's reading, like his quiet, secretive smile, like his air of knowing something that no one else knew was part of the enigma, the fascination of him. She wanted to know what he thought and felt and why he read books that he 'borrowed' from the Fawcett house.

He flushed and said stiffly, 'Some of them. I understand some of them.'

He had learned to do many things. He could farm and garden and rear bees. He could – and had – soldiered, he could build, and he could ride a horse. But his schooling – that had ended at twelve – had given him only the same amount of reading that everyone else in the village had – enough to write gossipy family letters from county to county, to read the Bible and the hymn on Sundays, to recite proudly extracts from *Pilgrim's Progress*, which most people in the village had won, at some time or another, as a Sunday School prize.

He had come to work on the Fawcett estate – and there, in a soft, dark room that was devoted entirely to books – he had discovered how to read. He was starved, thirsty for words and ideas. He gorged himself on anything and everything he could, good and bad reading were consumed with the same avidity. *The Monk*, *The Mysteries of Udolpho*, Dickens, Walpole, Mrs Gaskell, he had read them indiscriminately and without wit. He had not understood them all. The words were long, the sentences strange, but the sounds they made were beautiful. And with each book read his understanding became a little clearer, his ability to select and discard a little more adept Once he had found an author he enjoyed he worked his way solidly through the line of books in the exact order in which they stood. It made for thorough, if confused reading. Of *Jude the Obscure* he knew nothing save that it was the tenth Hardy on the shelf and he had just quietly replaced the ninth. He resented Anne-Louise's question because a brief look at *Jude* had made him wonder if he was going to understand this one.

'You weren't at Meeting on Sunday,' she said, suddenly losing interest in the book.

'No.'

She waited for an explanation that didn't come. She stood looking at him with a proprietary air, both demanding and

14

questioning, as though she had a right to know his business.

Jonathan felt irritation surge afresh in him, not only with brothers and sisters. In-laws, vague distant connections of the Pritchard family. They were a huge tribe of garrulous, inquisitive extroverts who spread throughout the village with the efficacy of established bindweed. They were noisy, generous, practical to the point of ugliness, and considered that the life and conscience of the village was theirs. They were many and vigorous in number, for the Pritchards never decreased in size – every time a Pritchard married the new member was absorbed into the family network and very often the new member's family as well. No member of the clan was ever allowed to lose contact. Fifth cousins twice removed were accorded the same affection, the same sense of family responsibility, as brothers and sisters. In-laws, vague distant connections of the family found their identities completely submerged until they too were Pritchards.

And the vast amoeba of the family spread into every household and farm in the community. Every piece of news, each scandal, death, sickness and birth was relayed back from Pritchard kitchen-maids, housekeepers, dressmakers, shop assistants, to the centre of the family. Sometimes, in the first rebellion of growing up, a Pritchard would turn from the family and try to get away, or at least to keep a secret from the rest of the tribe. A few had left the village, gone to work in other towns, other parts of the country. But always after a few years, they were drawn back, sucked into the comforting part of belonging to an enormous safe unit which grew from life and death and birth.

In fairer moments Jonathan admitted that the Pritchards were the strength of the village. Superstitious, gossiping, domineering, yet they were the standard of wholesomeness against which the village was measured. They were the ones who laid out the dead, who delivered at births, who knew which house it was safe to put a young girl to service in. They served good meals, believed cleanliness *was* godliness, and in spite of their lack of spiritual grace provided an innate sense of honesty among their neighbours.

15

Jonathan, while recognising their goodness, found their inquisitiveness, their sense of self-appointed leadership, frustrating, and particularly he found Anne-Louise frustrating. He stared down at her, trying to fathom why he could not like her. The only reason that came to him clearly was that she was not his cousin Myra. And he had little time for any woman who was not his cousin Myra.

Anne-Louise watched him, saw the changing moods of his mind reflected on his face, and wished she could understand, wished she knew what he thought, what made him smile sometimes when he thought no one was looking at him. She wished she knew whether he liked her or not.

The heat of the afternoon and the frantic speed with which she had hurried up the hill to meet him had made her perspire and she was conscious of the rings of sweat that stood out around the sleeves of her dress. Her face was hot and sticky and the fine covering of black down on her upper lip was beaded and moist.

'I'm on my way back to the Rectory,' she said carelessly. 'Will you walk me that way?'

He could do nothing else. It was, as she very well knew, the way he was going himself. With resigned ill-humour he shortened his stride to hers. He tried to think of something impersonal to talk about, something that would not lead to the web of coquetry he usually became involved in when talking to her.

'When is your sister marrying her sailor?'

She turned.

'Of course, I forgot. That's what I wanted to ask. The wedding's on Whit Monday and Betsy wants you to come. There's a party in the evening and she said especially that you and your sister were to come. There's no need to bring a gift. Just come.'

She couldn't understand why his face went still, couldn't see that she should not have made the remark about the gift. Jonathan could afford a gift as little as anyone else in the village, but to ask him as a free guest was insulting and tactless.

16

'I don't think I shall be free on Whit Monday.'

'But you must come,' she said angrily. 'Why can't you come? Mr Fawcett isn't expecting you to work on Whit Monday. Why, even Gracie's got the day off.'

'I have some private work to do,' he answered, stiff with anger and polite good manners. 'And now, here is where I leave you.'

He leaned across her to open the gate, and he smelled of honey and blood and earth. The warm animal scent of his body made her legs weak and the skin tighten across her breasts. Overwhelming longing smote her, a desire to press the length of her body against his, to grip her hands around the smoothness of his neck and sob. Eyes half-closed, she swayed towards him. He was waiting politely, holding the gate open for her with a courteous and gentle smile, and the desire in her throat turned to spite at the sensed rejection. She looped the folds of black silk up in her right hand, filled with a need to hurt him.

'Perhaps it's as well you can't come. My brothers all have suits to wear.'

She said no more, but looked pointedly at Jonathan's corded trousers and braid jacket.

'Good-bye, Anne-Louise.' His face was tight, devoid of everything, even good manners. He took one step through the gate and vanished down the lane, leaving her sick with unhappiness, tears of angry frustration standing out in her eyes.

She wanted Jonathan, wanted him because she could not understand him, because there was a part of his mind she could not touch. Twice he had walked her home, mostly because she had contrived a situation where he could do nothing else. She had done her best to provoke and attract him, chattering gaily, twisting her hands in the air to illustrate an item of gossip and holding her head well back to show her neck which was extremely white and slender and considered one of her best features. He had hardly spoken, just smiled and nodded and taken no notice when her arm accidentally dropped against his.

Never once had he asked to partner her. He never refused if she engendered a meeting, but he never asked her himself,

17

and she was, in turn, miserable and infuriated. She wasn't beautiful, but she knew she had vivacity and her figure was excellent. When she became excited – and she could stimulate excitement whenever she wished – she sparkled and glowed with animation. Now, determination lifted her small chin and sent her hurrying back down the hill to the Rectory.

'I'll get him to Betsy's wedding somehow,' she said. 'Somehow I'll make him come.'

She was half-way back when the sick realisation about the dress hit her. He hadn't even noticed she was wearing silk.

The kitchen door was open and Jonathan went straight in and put *Jude the Obscure* in the rough-wood desk that stood in the corner. His sister was bending over the black kitchen range that belched out heat from a wood fire. Sometimes, when the day was hot, he wished Emily would leave the fire and let them just have milk or water for their tea. But Tuesday was baking day, whatever the weather, and in consequence the small room was turned into a furnace. He felt stickiness break out afresh beneath his arms as the waves of heat beat across the room towards him, but Emily was as coldly immaculate as though she were dressed for Meeting, her steel-grey hair drawn back into its bun so tightly that the skin on her hair-line was raised into tiny bumps. A print apron covered her brown calico dress, the same type of dress he had seen her wearing for all of his twenty-two years. She didn't look at him, just lifted the big black kettle and began to fill the teapot. When he came in she nodded and said, 'Tea's ready, best go outside and wash.'

He came back from the pump, his hair flattened and wet and she was already seated at the head of the table waiting for him to say the grace. Hands resting in her lap she bowed her head as he repeated, 'Oh God, our Father, we give thanks for this, thy food, mercifully vouchsafed to these, thy servants. Amen.'

The teapot clattered; hot brown liquid filled the blue cups and Jonathan cut himself a thick wedge of the freshly baked bread, trying hard not to notice Emily's sigh at the indelicate size of the piece he was cutting and spreading with honey. She ate nothing – she rarely did – but sipped her milky tea and

18

then poured out another.

'A message from father.'

'Yes?' He accidentally slurped his tea; and Emily glared at him. 'Sorry,' he mumbled into the cup. Emily's lips curled distastefully, but she made no comment.

'He's well. But he won't be coming up for the holiday. The sheep can't be left and one of the dogs has gone lame.'

Her voice held a slightly accusatory note and Jonathan was correspondingly aware of guilt, knowing that it was his fault that his father was shepherding down on Romney Marshes instead of living comfortably in the village. The story was an old one, and Emily never directly referred to it, but whenever she spoke of their father there was an implied rebuke in her manner that never failed to make him aware of his filial responsibility.

Emily was the eldest of her family, Jonathan the youngest, and between them were eleven brothers, now all either dead or dispersed about the country. One had emigrated to Australia and, as he could neither read nor write, they had never heard from him again. Two died of tuberculosis – of neglect rather than the disease – another from meningitis. Three had married into other villages and one had made a good match with the daughter of a publican in London. The rest worked around the two counties as gardeners or farm-hands and turned up for Christmas or to visit their mother's grave from time to time.

Jonathan, at twelve, had been put to work on Brigadier Fawcett's estate, a position he had no very strong feeling about one way or another. Most of the farms around the village belonged to the Fawcett estate and all the work that was available was through the auspices of the Brigadier, a rather choleric gentleman groomed in the best traditions of the Indian Army and given to violent, curry-tinted rages. Not everyone in the village was dependent on the Brigadier's good will. It was the 1880s and Britain was no longer a feudal community. The village shopkeeper, the postmaster, the dressmaker and one or two small farmers were independent in name, but, such was the economy of the village, none could really afford to cross the man who lived at the Big House.

19

By the time he was fifteen Jonathan was a slender but strong youth capable of working twelve or fourteen hours a day on any task around the estate. He was well liked by the bailiff – a man called Walters, who was detested by the Brigadier because of his 'radical' views, but who was so efficient that the Brigadier could not manage without him – and was ignored by Brigadier Fawcett, which was a good sign in itself.

Often he found himself working with the oldest farmhand on the estate, a labourer called Ted MacPherson, seventy-three years old, arthritic and in constant terror of losing his job and cottage and being separated from his wife in the Union Poorhouse. He had made the grave mistake of having no children in an era when children were not only a blessing but an insurance against a destitute old age, and his conversation tended to deteriorate at times into a whimpering fear.

He could still manage a little hedging, and Bailiff Walters (radical that he was) got into the habit of putting Jonathan, the youngest and strongest, to work with the old man, hoping that Jonathan would be able to cover MacPherson's work with his own. They managed for several months, the old man pushing a hoe or trimming the hedges while Jonathan forked the heavy clay soil at a frantic speed. At hay-making Jonathan would heave the bales up into the stack and the old man would try to look busy gleaning the odd strands that fell and tidying them into the stack. In time the old man and the boy became expert at turning out the work of two men during the day. And then one morning, just as the old man had paused for a second to ease his crippled hands, Brigadier Fawcett, seated heavily astride his brown gelding, had noticed MacPherson.

He glared across at the old man and then turned to Bailiff Walters.

'What's that old fool doing here. Get rid of him. Take a new man on.'

The words hung clipped and icy in the morning air. To Jonathan they meant little except a rather detached sympathy for Ted MacPherson and he was hardly prepared for the outburst from the old man beside him.

He felt, rather than saw, the old man throw himself forward

and clutch the reins of the Brigadier's horse. He was babbling
incoherently, words fighting in a jumbled effort that would
convince the Brigadier that he was a man still capable of holding his job. With a growing sense of disgust Jonathan heard
the confusion of sounds pouring from his mouth.

'No! Not the Union. No, sir, Brigadier, sir. Kitchen work,
yes that's it. I'll do kitchen work. Not the Union. No, sir,
please. Not the Union, not the Union. Don't send me away.
For God's sake, don't send me away.'

He was sobbing and his hat had fallen back into the road,
leaving his shiny scalp exposed. His face was streaked with
mud, and Jonathan and the bailiff looked away from his
pleading, unable to witness the sickening humiliation on the
old man's face.

Foolishly Jonathan pretended not to know what was happening and dug more fiercely into the ditch with the big dredging
shovel. MacPherson was pulling on the reins and the horse
began to stir restlessly against the erratic pressure. Desperation
had given MacPherson strength and also an abandonment of
reverence for the sacrosanct person of the Brigadier. With a
surprising speed for one so old and crippled he snatched
Fawcett's hand. He was now so agitated and choked it was
difficult to hear what he said, but at last the words, repeated
again and again, became clearer.

'Not the Union, not the Union! Please, dear Jesus, not the
Union!'

Fawcett wrenched his hand away from the old man's grasp
and lifted his riding crop high in the air.

'How dare you!' he breathed murderously. 'How dare you.'
His face was crimson and throbbing. Jonathan watched him
swing the crop back into the air and, as he did so, the boy
suddenly felt a small cord snap somewhere at the back of his
throat. A moment of pure magic, a feeling of wild exhilaration
and release swept his whole body. He felt his face whiten
with temper and it was a glorious emotion, an emotion
prompted by something he didn't quite understand. Certainly
it wasn't solely because of Ted MacPherson grovelling helplessly on the ground; in actual fact he didn't really like the

old man very much. It was something in the way the Brigadier held the whip, the way he sat the horse and spoke and behaved. It was something that demanded Jonathan should challenge him.

He leapt from the ditch with the shovel held high over his head and stood in front of the big, brown horse, his eyes glittering and the skin over his cheekbones taut and transparent like that of an old man. The words came from his mouth and surprised him with the noise they made.

'You hit him and I'll kill you.'

MacPherson was a sodden heap of clothing lying weeping on the ground and neither the bailiff nor the Brigadier were aware of him, both compelled to stillness by the figure of the white-faced boy standing legs apart and holding the huge shovel over his head. Fawcett was unable to move. Years of telling men what to do had given him an authority he didn't even consciously exert. He started to order the boy away and then stopped uneasily. Horrified, he realised that the young man *would* kill him, batter him from his horse with the iron dredger. He tried to stare Jonathan down, but the boy curled his mouth into a derisive snarl and moved a step closer to the horse.

Fawcett swallowed once and without a word turned his horse and rode back to the house.

The field was strangely quiet, the stillness broken only by the frightened ramblings of the old man kneeling on the grass. Jonathan slowly let the shovel fall to the earth, the white heat of temper evaporating and leaving in its place a sticky fear. He looked at the bailiff. Walters was as startled and white as he was himself, and Jonathan noticed, in a queer, disconnected way, that his hands were trembling. The enormity of what he had done began to pierce the clouded atmosphere of the morning.

'I'll have to run. Get out right now.' His voice had broken a couple of years back, but now his words ended on a quavering, high-pitched note.

Walters nodded. 'He'll have you before the magistrates. Threatened assault.'

The young, white face stared up at the bailiff, both of them admitting that the outcome of that action was inevitable. The Brigadier was himself one of the magistrates and the others were all members of the same hunt. Clemency would be non-existent. His mind began to rotate alarmingly, seeking for a way out.

'Can you get to my father before he does?' He nodded in the direction of the house, and when the bailiff nodded he said, 'Tell my father to say I've always been disobedient and wild and he washes his hands of me, wants nothing more to do with me. If he can convince the Brigadier he's even more angry with me, there's a chance he won't be put out of the cottage. I daren't go home. Someone's sure to see me and tell Fawcett.'

'Where will you go?'

The boy tried to look jaunty.

'I'll walk to Tonbridge. It shouldn't take me more than a couple of days, and he'll never think of looking for me in that direction. I'll join the army.' His face brightened at the sudden inspiration. 'That's what I'll do, I'll join the army. I'll tell them I'm a year older than I am. They're not fussy.'

Walters pulled a coin from his purse.

'Here's a sixpence. You'll need to buy some food if you're going that far.' He waved Jonathan's protests aside and said:

'Get off, now, quick as you can. As soon as he realises he was bested by a lad he'll be a raging devil until he catches you.'

Jonathan had looked back once to wave to the bailiff and then taken a skirting route round the estate and cross country towards the Kent border. The exhilaration of subduing Brigadier Fawcett had completely dispersed and he was beset with a constant fear, both for his father and for himself.

It had taken him five days to reach Tonbridge, and without the bailiff's sixpence he couldn't have managed. He had bought bread and a slice of cheese at a village on the second day and eked it out with some onions he stole from a field. There was plenty of water to drink, and when he began to feel really tired an old woman had given him a pennyworth of

23

milk; a great quart jug of warm, frothy liquid that had kept his legs moving for the rest of that day. On the outskirts of Tonbridge he tried to wash and smarten himself by a stream, but it was a tattered, white-faced youth who walked into the recruiting centre, to the resplendence of a glossy sergeant seated in front of coloured posters depicting all the glamour and patriotism of life in the Queen's regiments.

Jonathan studied the posters as carefully as his gurgling stomach and aching legs would permit, and then he had plumped for the Hussars, partly because he liked the picture of the good-looking man astride a thoroughbred mare, but mostly because his feet hurt and he felt he would like to spend the rest of his life on horseback rather than walk. And a small germ of youthful vanity made him reflect that he would probably look quite a fine fellow on a horse.

Two days after he had entered barracks he received a message from Bailiff Walters. The ruse to divert Brigadier Fawcett's wrath away from his family had failed. His father had been dismissed from the estate and consequently evicted from his cottage. He, Emily and the three brothers still residing at home were frantically trying to find some new means of livelihood. For Emily the situation was not so severe. She was a strong, capable woman who had brought up twelve younger brothers and she was invited to move in with a cousin and assist in the rearing of a further eight children. The boys moved to other farms, other villages, and Jonathan's father, too old to move to another large estate, reverted to his boyhood task of shepherding, following the flocks down to Romney Marshes in the summer and bringing them back for the winter months.

Jonathan's years of soldiery – during which time he never even mounted a horse, but only washed them, cleaned out stables, and polished the officers' leathers – were made more miserable by the knowledge that he and he alone had engendered the shattering of their family. Guilt kept him separate from his father and his sister, and he was, in addition, constantly aware that he was an anomaly among the other men in the regiment. His companions at arms recognised with

24

delight what they had among them and spent the next six years trying to entice Jonathan into a brothel or persuade him to get drunk so that they could indulge in some of the more offensive forms of horseplay. Eventually they gave up. The boy was quiet and refused to be drawn, and they ignored him as the harmless oddity that he was.

In the fifth year of his service the regiment passed through the village and Jonathan went to see his sister and learned that the Brigadier was dead. A heavy dinner, a surfeit of jugged hare and port, followed by one of the Brigadier's choleric rages had induced a stroke, and the estate was now awaiting the arrival of the younger Fawcett brother from India. With relief Jonathan finished his term of soldiery and returned to the village, the Fawcett estate and the assembling of a fresh home. Fear and an iron sense of self-discipline had kept him out of trouble in the army, but he knew he could not have tolerated the arrogant stupidity of meaningless orders and the stomach-turning habits of the other men much longer.

He waited for his father to come back and live in the new cottage, and then was astounded when the old man refused, saying that he was too old to change his trade again and he would stay following the flocks. Again Jonathan was aware of guilt, self-reproach at his violence, which made his father wander over the face of two counties like a homeless nomad.

In actual fact old Peter Whitman was, for the first time he could remember, enjoying the complete freedom and solitude that had been denied to him in a lifetime of marriage and too many children in too small a cottage. He found he no longer needed or wanted his children, and sometimes, accompanied only by the two dogs, he would spend several days deliberately away from the company of other men. He had no idea of Jonathan's guilt and probably would have cared little even had he known. His daughter and son were there in the village if he needed them, but while he could roam the hills at will he had no intention of returning to live with them.

Jonathan atoned as best he could by endeavouring, in every possible way, to placate his sister, Emily bearing with her severity, her constant reminder of his bad habits and objectionable masculine ways. Mealtimes were a trial almost beyond his strength, but he bore with them and with the continual admonitory tuts that came from Emily's lips every time he committed some small social misdemeanour. When, as now, he allowed a tiny rivulet of honey to trickle on to the oil-cloth, he was already tensed and waiting for her irritated 'Jonathan!'

'Sorry, Em.' He wiped the honey up with his finger and licked it, then realised he had, once again, done the wrong thing. He tried not to notice Em's face, but thought instead, with a smug glow of anticipation, of the book in the desk. Later, when the lamps were lit, he would spread the book carefully open on the table and read, holding each page tenderly between thumb and forefinger so as not to damage the spine.

Emily put her cup down. 'Cousin Myra's been round.'

The food in his mouth congealed into a large sawdust ball that impeded his breathing. Before he could speak Emily went on, 'She wanted to know if we were going to Betsy Pritchard's wedding. Mrs Pritchard's asked us all, and Myra would like to come with us.'

'We're going aren't we?' He was talking with his mouth full, but Emily's glare didn't even impinge on his consciousness. He was frantic in case Em had already declined the invitation.

'Well . . .' Em considered disagreeably for a moment. 'I suppose we should. You haven't a suit, but your Sunday jacket is quite tidy.' She stirred her tea reflectively. 'There is the matter of the gift, of course.'

'Take my egg money. You go into Grinstead tomorrow and get something.' He had been saving to buy a copy of *Westward Ho!* but now the prose of Charles Kingsley faded into miserable obscurity beside the opportunity of escorting Myra, beautiful, soft Cousin Myra, to the wedding. Emily looked sourly acquiescent.

'If you're sure?'

'Would there be enough for a new collar, Em?'

'I'll see.' She rose abruptly from the table, signifying that both tea and the conversation were ended, and Jonathan pushed back his chair and began to help her clear the things away. He was unable to control the wild tightness of his heart any longer, the excitement threatened to burst from him in a boisterous shout and he sang three verses of 'Jesus bids me Shine with a Clear Pure Light', before Emily tutted him into silence.

He couldn't read. *Jude the Obscure*, was, indeed, obscure, and outside the night was cool and and huge. He stood by the hen-run and looked up at the sky through the browning blossoms of a late pear-tree. One of the heavy branches hung low, and he grasped it with his hands and pulled his body up into the air in a violent excess of energy. The flowers fell on his head and one of the hens clucked sleepily.

'Myra. Oh, Myra!' he said softly into the night, and a scavenging night owl answered him.

When Anne got back to the Rectory, Gracie was waiting for her in the servants' passage.

'She's been asking for you,' she said, white-faced and frightened. 'She came down just after you'd left and said you was to go up to her room immediately you came in.'

'Did she ask where I'd gone?'

Grace shook her head and swallowed. 'Just you're to go up at once.'

Mrs Panter was seated at her dressing-table. Her hair was already dressed in the rather ugly flattened braids that she favoured. A poplin wrapper round her shoulders partially concealed the sallow, stringy skin on her neck, and she was in the process of lightly brushing a hare's foot across her forehead and cheeks.

'Come in, Pritchard,' she said serenely in answer to Anne-Louise's defiant drumming on the door.

Anne came forward, then stood and looked down at the dress that was lying on the bed. It was the crimson silk, the one the goose had sat on, and the front of the skirt, spread out over the feather quilt, was covered in alternate streaks of white and a dark, discoloured red.

'You're not wearing that dress this evening, are you,

ma'am?' she faltered.

Mrs Panter smiled.

'Of course not, Pritchard. I am wearing the grey grosgrain. I left the dress there because – you see, Pritchard – I thought you might like to try it on and see if it suited.'

'The red silk, ma'am?' She couldn't believe what Mrs Panter was saying, couldn't accept that Mrs Panter was about to give her the dress. And even while she didn't believe it, her mind was working out the best way of getting the grease out.

'You may have the dress, Pritchard, providing it looks suitable on you.'

'I'm sure it will fit, ma'am!' she said quickly. Betsy would know how to get the grease stain out. Betsy would know how to wash it carefully so that the silk came up fresh and soft again.

'You must try it on now, Anne-Louise. I shall want to see if it's suitable for you.' Mrs Panter had her face turned away from the mirror, and Anne couldn't see her properly. But suddenly she felt embarrassed about trying the dress on in front of her. She didn't want Mrs Panter looking at her in her chemise – which was clean but old – and watching her struggle in and out of dresses and getting hot and untidy.

'Shall I go downstairs and put it on, ma'am?'

Mrs Panter smiled, 'Put it on here, Pritchard.'

Anne hesitated, then looked at the dress lying on the bed and began to unbutton the black silk. She turned her back before she took it off and quickly dropped it round her feet. The red dress was sticky and smelt horrible, but when she turned round and looked in the mirror she forgot the smell.

'Oh!' she said, twisting and turning at her reflection. 'I *do* look nice.'

The red was dramatic and striking on her. It made her black hair even blacker, and her erect figure and small waist even more noticeable. She realised now how ordinary the black dress was, how very dull and plain. And she had thought Jonathan would notice her in it. How stupid and ridiculous she was. The black dress was nothing. But this one, this shimmering column of glowing silk, this was the dress he should see her in. This made her beautiful – more than beautiful.

'It's lovely, ma'am!'

She would wear it to Betsy's wedding. She could get the grease out by then, and she could wear it to the wedding. Jonathan – she dismissed his refusal of the invitation, knowing that once she had devised a way of getting him there, he would come – would be startled when he saw her like this. No one in the village had a dress like this. And she deserved it too. It was she, after all, who had saved the dinner-party, who had rescued the goose from Mrs Panter's lap. The dress was hers by right. It belonged to her.

'What a pity,' said Mrs Panter, still smiling. 'It doesn't fit you. I shall have to send it along to the Union House. They can probably do something with it there.'

Anne-Louse stared disbelievingly at her.

'I thought it might just be right for you. But, of course, now you've tried it on, I can see it is most unsuitable.' The smile on Mrs Panter's face didn't change. It was smooth and pleasant and controlled.

'But it does fit, ma'am. It fits beautifully!'

'Oh, no, Pritchard,' she answered quietly. 'You're quite wrong. It doesn't fit at all, not at all. You had better take it off and put the black on at once.'

'But, ma'am . . . ' She was angry, so angry she thought she was going to cry. 'It does fit me. It's a lovely dress. I like it very much and it fits me!'

'Take it off, Pritchard.' Mrs Panter put down the hare's foot and rose from her dressing-chair. 'Please hurry, I shall want dinner served without any mishap this evening – no dropping dishes of nuts please, Pritchard. Hurry now. You haven't long to get ready – I gather Gracie had to set the table, so you will need to check that – and your hair needs tidying.'

With furious, shaking hands, Anne unbuttoned the dress and threw it in a heap on to the bed. She rubbed her hands carelessly over her hair, not bothering to look in the mirror, but glaring venomously at Mrs Panter all the while. And Mrs Panter just smiled and nodded pleasantly at her.

'That's right, Pritchard. Hurry now.'

At the door Anne turned and looked back, unable to control the rage in her breast any more. 'You can do what you like with it, ma'am,' she said savagely. 'But I shall have a red dress just the same. I'll have a red and you won't be able to stop me wearing it when I want to.'

She shut the door – even in her rage she didn't quite have the courage to slam it – and ran down the stairs, frustration lending speed to her furious body. 'I'll get a red dress for Betsy's wedding,' she said aloud to herself. 'I'll not let anyone stop me. I'll have a red dress if it's the last thing I do.'

When the bell rang for the first guest of the evening, she was able to answer the door with a pert, lively face. She smiled at the guests – at the male guests in a different way from female – and served the dinner without a mishap. And all the while her brain was working on the way – the way to get the crimson silk.

Two

THE VILLAGE, as most rural communities, consisted of a curious structure of isolated groups which touched very briefly at interlocking points. It had the common bond of stubbornness possessed by all Englishmen who live by the land, but particularly by those living in the south-eastern corner of the country.

Some kind of erratic wind seems to blow across from the Continent and imbue the otherwise solid and terse Englishman with a ridiculous contrariness. Perhaps the geography of the land, or the history, or both, had produced the defiant community that was typical of the village. It was a land invaded by Vikings, Romans and Normans. Centuries had seen messengers, kings, ministers and refugees hurrying between London and the rest of Europe, dropping random pieces of disquiet along the ditch-lined roads; news of wars and dynastic marriages, rebellions and religious strife, torture, rape and carnage. For five hundred years they had lived in dread of France, then Spain, then once more France. The years had subjected them to a heavy stream of thoughts and ideas, which resulted in a curious mixture of fear and ideological rebellion.

They had joined whole-heartedly in throwing off the restrictions of Rome and the pope, taking savage pride in being the only part of the country that was entirely protestant, and then, when the tide of events had swung and the persecutions commenced, they would not recant, but bore their suffering with a terrified self-righteousness that was both foolish and courageous.

And now, when the Established Church of the country was comfortable and respected, when it was easy and demanded little to join in the universal standards that all were using, they turned their backs on the illegitimate child of Rome and worshipped in a new, austere and uncomfortable way. It was not entirely ideological. The Established Church, in keeping with most established customs, favoured the 'haves' rather than the 'have-nots'. All who rode to hunt, who employed, who lived rather than worked on the land, followed the easy, well-designed pattern of worship. In the village it meant attending the square twelfth-century church once on Sunday and listening half-heartedly to the Rector – decorously sober – offering a respectful sermon to his betters.

They – the estate-owners, the magistrates, the retired military – did not worry unduly if their villagers were there or not, but if they were they expected them to regulate their presence with the same deference that tempered the rest of the week.

And the stiff-necked villagers saw no reason why they should bow to their employers when it was Sunday.

The families of the village had no special meeting-place. They worshipped three times on Sunday in one or other of their homes, the hymns accompanied by a creaking, foot-pumped harmonium or not accompanied at all. Prayer was extempore, sometimes funny, many times illiterate, but nearly always sincere. Being outside the accepted conformity of faith gave them a sense of unity that extended beyond the parlour walls of the Sunday Meeting. Their worship reflected, without sophistication, the life of the village. They prayed for health, because sickness meant they could not work or eat. They prayed for the protection of their children because most families lost two or even three children in infancy. They prayed for their wives who died in childbirth and they prayed for their gardens because it was the produce they grew themselves that supplemented their living standards. On Sundays they were independent of their employers and believed, rightly or wrongly, that they were better. They regarded the Church and the Rector with a good-humoured condescension that verged on the impertinent, and they bitterly resented the fact that there were occasions when they were forced to ask for the services of the Church.

For the Church was needed. To obtain the legal signature of the State, without which neither marriage nor death was blessed, they had to defer to the Church. They used the legality of altar and cross with courtesy, but without reverence, and, once the ceremony of wedding or burial was over, they returned to their own communal parlour and participated in a meeting of blessing or grief – whichever was applicable – a meeting that they considered far transcended the elaborate service of the Church.

On Whit Monday, the day of Betsy Pritchard's wedding, they filed into the church with an air of amused toleration at the 'goings-on' in which they were forced to participate. The women wore their Sunday dresses with fresh pieces of lace at neck and wrists, one or two sported new hats, but most were content with a different ribbon or an extra flower stitched on to the brim of the old one. The men, black-coated in many cases, held hats of straw or soft felt between sore-scrubbed hands and, among the older men, these who were losing their hair, the uncovered whiteness of a scalp gleamed vividly against the contrast of weather-stained necks and faces.

The church was old and dark. In the side recesses the stone replicas of ancient crusaders lay dimly on their tombs, the faces broken and chipped, the stone dogs at their feet worn smooth by six hundred years of children reaching up to touch them. Candlesticks gleamed dully back from shadowy corners and, against their own beliefs and reasoning, the villagers found themselves reduced to a dull uneasiness, a kind of hereditary fear of episcopal power that was tenuously linked with mysticism and witchcraft. At last someone propped the big doors open and, with the permanent presence of sunlight and noises coming in from outside, their superstition lifted a little, their condescension returned.

Mrs Pritchard, seated in the front pew, scarcely noticed the opening of the doors, and she alone had been unaffected by the sombre presence of the church. She was shaking, angrily and uncontrollably, with a fury that increased at every moment, a fury directed at her second daughter, at self-willed, spoiled Anne-Louise Pritchard. Dimly Mrs Pritchard was aware of the curious glances about her, of the sly faces of the women staring when they thought they were unobserved, and she tried to compose her face into a smooth smile, a smile that would carry her through the service, through the Meeting to follow, and through the rest of the long, unutterably strained festivities of the day. 'I must try not to think about it,' she told herself. 'Try to put it to the back of my mind. Try to remember that this is Betsy's day, the day my Betsy gets married.' And then a surge of furious resentment bore down on her and her self-homily turned into, 'And the day that Anne-Louise has ruined! A day like all the others that she has spoiled with her consuming selfishness!'

Somehow she had dragged herself to church, forced herself to leave the cottage, the bedroom where bride, bridesmaid and brother were raging at each other.

Betsy, who was a homely, uncomplicated daughter, had begun by quite enjoying her day. She was as excitable and garrulous as the rest of the Pritchards, and the importance of using her mother's bedroom, of relatives and friends rushing in and out, causing a deliberate confusion that added to the difference of the day, had made colour infuse her face with an unnatural brightness.

The small room was in turmoil, the rose-patterned wash-hand-set was filled with cold soapy water – for on this special day Betsy had been accorded the privilege of washing in the bedroom instead of the scullery – a bottle of toilet water had accidentally been overturned on the marble stand and everyone who came in dabbled their handkerchiefs in the fragrant puddle. Hair-pins were scattered profusely across the bed as Betsy, clad in her lawn petticoat, brushed and rebrushed her hair, the thick, dark-brown curly hair that was the only beauty poor Betsy possessed. As soon as she had fixed it up in a thick coil on the crown of her head, glossy tendrils sprang forward over her forehead and neck. Her Sunday dress of serviceable dark-blue poplin had been carefully washed and pressed with heavy flat-irons. Her hat was new, twenty-four inches from brim to brim and so covered in pink roses and a silk bow that the brim was completely invisible when viewed from the top.

When she was ready, the dress fastened, the hat firmly secured with five large pins, Mrs Pritchard had stared hard at

Betsy, tried to see her with the eyes of a stranger, as just a young girl going to her wedding. She found it impossible, and as she looked away she felt pity pricking at the back of her throat, a pity that was strengthened undeniably with love for this, her favourite daughter. Betsy was not beautiful. She had no grace or brightness of spirit like Anne-Louise. But she had a wholesome honesty about her, an ability to tackle any task, however dreary and back-breaking, and see it through to the end. It was Betsy who had assisted in rearing the five younger children, contributing everything she could towards the family budget. Betsy, even at twelve, was the one the Fawcetts sent for when there was rough scrubbing or spring-cleaning to be done at the big house. Betsy was called upon when old people were sick and needed special attention. She coped with unpleasant, dirty tasks and, providing she felt she was an integral part of the family, she made no demur.

Mrs Pritchard kissed her. God, she prayed irreverently, please, please make Betsy look pretty on just this one day. Give her just one day when everyone admires her, one day to remember for the rest of her life. For it never occurred to Mrs Pritchard, or to anyone else, that Betsy's lot would be anything other than toil and hard work.

'You look very pretty, dear,' she said, hoping that the lie would form the basis to a truth. Will came into the room, in his hand a small posy of flowers that he had picked from the garden. He handed them to his sister, and Mrs Pritchard noticed that he had taken the trouble to tie a ribbon round the stalks.

'Thought you'd like to hold these, Bets,' he said uncomfortably. Betsy, unused either to compliments or flowers, flushed even brighter, and the miracle nearly happened. Her eyes began to shine with unaccustomed vivacity, her face, already flushed, blended delicately into tones of pink and white beneath the glossy hair and the big hat. Mrs Pritchard watched her daughter's face, watched the first outward signs of a faint beauty creep into the dull worthy countenance of her eldest daughter.

And then Anne-Louise had come into the room, and the

35

beauty had become still-born.

There were still several friends and relatives in the room and, at first, they were all so astonished they could not speak. A shocked stillness fell across the excited chattering, the noisy expostulations. Every head turned to look at Anne-Louise, and Mrs Pritchard heard the quick indrawing of breath as a dozen frilled neck-pieces moved and fluttered in surprise. Then Betsy's voice, muffled and unhappy, broke the silence.

'She's wearing a new dress.'

Mrs Pritchard darted one look at Anne-Louise's defiant, bright eyes, and with sinking heart realised she was going to have to cope with one of Anne's self-willed tantrums. Quickly, with a practised skill that deceived no one, she tried to clear the room of all but Betsy, Will and Anne-Louise.

'Would you like to wait downstairs, Madge? Florrie, perhaps you'd check the table in the kitchen. I don't remember covering the trifle. Vicky, dear, I think it's time you started walking your mother to church. You know how long it takes her.' She eased them reluctantly from the room, each one of them longing to remain and witness the scene that would erupt the moment the door was closed. Good manners forced them to leave, and when the door was shut Mrs Pritchard turned back into the room, trying to control the mounting anger in her breasts.

'Well, Anne,' she said quietly. 'Where do you think you're going in that dress?'

Anne-Louise stood erect and defiant and smiled at her mother, at Betsy, and at Will. 'Why, Mother, you know very well where I'm going. I'm going to church to be bridesmaid to Betsy. Don't you think I look well?'

She thrust her small, bony chin forward in a stubborn dare and, even while Mrs Pritchard fought the desire to strike her across the face, a tiny, deep-seated pride in her daughter made her admit that Anne-Louise did look well.

The dress was not cotton or lawn or even *crêpe*. It was silk, and not the black silk of a renovated maid's dress, but a rich crimson silk embroidered with loop-daisies of the same colour. The neck, slashed to a deep vee at the waist, was filled with

36

row upon row of butter-coloured lace frills, and the dress was so tightly moulded to her well-shaped waist that it was obvious that it had not been passed on from one of the Rectory ladies. She had a hat to match, maroon-dyed osprey feather and a double-bow of grosgrain. She stood, hat poised carefully on the mounted black hair and her bright, fanatically blue eyes defied her mother to do anything, anything at all. Mrs Pritchard's temper began to fray.

'You can go to your bedroom,' she said crisply. 'You can take the dress off and put your Sunday one on, the same as Betsy.' Her voice shook and ended louder than she meant it to. Anne-Louise's mouth firmed into a straight line.

'I'm wearing this or I'm not going. And if I don't go I shall wear it to Meeting on Sunday, or I won't go to that either.'

Mrs Pritchard's temper suddenly snapped and her hand shot out and slapped the girl noisily across the face. Anne's head recoiled from the blow and immediately swung back to face her mother, her eyes glowing with delighted disobedience. The two women glared at one another, young alert face trying to stare down the faded older one. Betsy was crying quietly in a corner, and Will, a stiff, uncomfortable arm about her shoulders, was staring sullenly at the floor.

'Where did you get the dress?' he asked suddenly and turned to his mother. 'You know she can't sew a sheet seam, let alone make a frock like that. And we'd have known if Myra Whitman was making it for her.'

Anne-Louise twisted to face him, turning abruptly so that the folds of crimson silk swung smoothly out into the air with a rustle.

'I bought it,' she said jeeringly. 'I went into Grinstead and I bought it ready made.'

'Where did you get the money?' asked Mrs Pritchard slowly. A sick nervous dread burned dully at the back of her throat, a suspicion, a dreadful premonition of where Anne-Louise had got the money. The girl didn't answer, just tossed her head and sniffed, and then the suspicion flared into certainty in Mrs Pritchard's mind.

She pushed Anne roughly to one side and ran from the

room, down the stairs and into the kitchen. The babble of voices was deafening and she could hear fragments of excited noise – 'red silk!' – 'wants a good slapping!' – 'needed a father's firm hand'. The news of the dress had spread, giving an added enjoyment, an extra vivacity to the day. She noticed them looking curiously at her and she wondered if she was crying, but she was really too agitated to care. She crossed to the dresser and lifted down the blue jar with the stone lid.

It was empty. For a moment she thought she was going to be sick.

'She's taken it,' she thought dully. 'She's taken all the money for Betsy's wedding gift and bought herself a dress.' The jar suddenly became tremendously, unaccountably heavy in her hands, but she didn't put it down. She carried it carefully back through the kitchen and up the stairs to the bedroom. She wanted to cry, but pride held her tears back and she managed to smile and nod as she walked up the stairs. When she got inside the bedroom she sank tiredly on to the bed, staring down at the empty blue jar.

'How could you do it, Annie?' she asked quietly. 'How could you take the money we'd saved for Betsy and Math?' Not knowing what she did, she stroked the round curves of the blue jar, finding some kind of comfort in its smooth, heavy shape. 'You know how long it took us to save it. And you know that if anyone had had a new dress it should have been Betsy.'

Anne twisted uncomfortably. Her mother's temper and sharp rebuke she could delight in defying, but faced with this tired resignation she felt a tiny shaft of guilt. Quickly, in order to drown the shame, she said loudly, 'What does she need a new dress for? She's got a husband. She doesn't need to look nice!'

Betsy suddenly wrenched herself away from her brother's arms.

'It's Jonathan Whitman,' she shouted. 'That's why she's done it. She thinks if he sees her like that he's going to fall in love with her. Well, he won't!' Her round, good-natured face, used to bearing anything without resentment, was distorted with unhappiness and shock. 'You could wear silk every day!' she sobbed. 'You could wear silk every day and he still wouldn't notice you while his cousin Myra's around.'

Anne's face drained of colour. 'Liar,' she breathed softly. 'You liar, you liar . . . ' Mrs Pritchard found she was, after all, able to move. She rose quickly from the bed and stood between the two girls.

'I've had enough,' she said firmly. 'Quite enough. Anne, you've done your best to ruin the day for Betsy, but what can be saved is going to be. Will,' she turned to her son, 'take your sisters to church. You'll lead Betsy to the altar, and Anne-Louise, you will walk behind your sister without any fuss and without drawing attention to yourself.' Even as she said it she knew how ridiculous it was. Anne-Louise had won. The day was hers.

Betsy was crying again. 'Mother,' she said chokingly. 'What shall I tell Math? About the money. He knew there was going to be a gift.'

Mrs Pritchard's anger, her resignation, her sorrow were suddenly all submerged in the anxiety of presenting a solid family front before the village. She felt humiliated as she realised how it would appear, a family who blessed their daughter without a gift. The money, frugally saved over the past two years, had been spent on Betsy's new hat and the magnificent tea waiting downstairs. What remained had been intended to start Betsy's home when Mathew retired from the sea. Now there was nothing left, and with Betsy married there was one wage-earner less. It would take years to save the money again. Will cleared his throat.

'I'll talk to Math.'

Mrs Pritchard stared across at Anne-Louise. The girl was slumped by the window and looked faintly abashed. She had enjoyed the excitement of the quarrel, the feeling that she had made herself the centre of a family feud and that she had won, beaten her mother in the matter of the dress. But now, reflecting on the way the family would appear before the village, mean and tardy, she was aware of a slight uneasiness. Outshining Betsy at her wedding was daring and dramatic, but having people sniggering at the Pritchards because they were too mean to give their daughter a gift was unsettling.

'I'll pay it back,' she said sullenly.

'How?' snapped her mother. 'Tell me how, when only you and Will will be earning for six of us.' She pulled her gloves on to her fingers and buttoned them angrily.

'Will, I'm going to church and I shall expect to see the three of you in ten minutes.' She would have liked to kiss Betsy, but the room was too charged with emotion to permit even the slightest show of affection. She opened the door.

'Ten minutes,' she said menacingly, and was gone.

It had taken some stiff-necked pride to walk to her seat in the front of the church, knowing that the news of the red dress was simmering along every pew. She prayed that Betsy would get through the service without crying again. Then she heard the footsteps at the back of the church and she stood up, pulling young Frankie to his feet beside her. Mathew, his navy sailor-suit newly pressed, waited at the altar. He turned once and smiled at her, then didn't look round again.

The sound of three pairs of stoutly clad feet on a stone floor hammered loudly through the church. There was no music to soften the noise, to deaden the walk to the altar, for music, even if it could have been afforded, was an affectation, a manifestation of idolatry.

Will took Betsy by the arm, whispered, 'You look fine, Betsy,' and began to walk forward. Anne-Louise, following, felt magnificent. She knew Jonathan was looking at her, knew that she had his undivided attention. She knew because everyone in the church was looking at her, all eyes were following the glorious crimson-clad figure following and completely overshadowing the insipid, swollen-eyed Betsy.

The Rector, who bitterly resented having to marry – or bury – the villagers of the Meeting, assimilated the strangeness of the small group approaching him up the long stone aisle, but was not sufficiently interested to waste time thinking about it. He disliked these assemblies so much it was almost more than he could manage to conduct the services with a degree of civility. He was well aware that the villagers managed for most of the time without him and his services and that they looked upon him as no more than a government clerk. They were polite but evasive when he questioned them in the village, and they paid him none of the deference that he felt his cloth entitled him to. When conducting a service for them he hurried through his duties as quickly and unpleasantly as he could.

'Dearly Beloved,' he snapped, and the service began.

Five hours later the wedding was over, the parlour blessings had been said, the gargantuan tea of bloater-paste and sardine sandwiches, lettuce, tomatoes and cold beef, trifle and seven different kinds of cake had been consumed and Betsy and Mathew had been sent on their way to the station, on the first lap of their journey to Portsmouth.

In the back kitchen, hats had been removed and coats taken off. The old people – and that included any of the company who were married – sat packed into the room around a big, black teapot. The wedding meal had been enjoyable and tea had been served at that repast, but about this relaxed and less ceremonial cup of tea there was an intimacy that allowed for frank and uninhibited discussion. And on this special day there was much to be discussed.

In the parlour the young ones were playing party games and giving an impromptu entertainment. Gracie, not quite so thin and sallow as she was when working in the Rectory kitchen, recited a poem about a little boy who died of starvation in an attic, and the poem was all the more enjoyable because they had just eaten such a very good tea. Someone else sang a hymn, and then Will brought out the package for musical parcels and everyone got excited because they knew that for an occasion like this – a wedding – there would be real prizes inside. Annie-Louise won a packet of pins and someone else an enamel brooch and then, as the evening progressed and the little ones went home, Anne suggested they should play Postman's Knock.

She had become steadily more discontented throughout the evening. At first the party had been just as she had wished. Betsy had left and she had been the most important one in the room, flashing everywhere in the red dress and telling them

41

what to do and where to go. She had made them sit down and talk for a while so that she could play hostess and pass more sandwiches and cakes round, although they were all so replete they didn't want any more. Then they had played Jenny's-a-Weeping and when it was her turn to stand in the middle and choose a partner she had held her hand out to Jonathan, waiting for him to come into the circle and kiss her. Whenever anyone had a party and older folk were present, the kiss was always just a brief contact of lips against cheek, but sometimes, when they were left on their own and no one was watching, the kisses were different – on the mouth and longer – so that the room was filled with a nervous excitement.

She had held her face up to Jonathan, her mouth as close to his as she could reach, waiting, willing him to kiss her properly. He had barely touched her cheek with his mouth before turning to join in the song once more. When it was his turn to choose he had held both hands towards Myra and, when she came smiling into the ring, he had kissed her for such a long time that the others had shouted at them.

Postman's Knock meant kissing outside the door, just the two of them. And if Jonathan was alone with her she would *make* him kiss her properly. And once he had kissed her he wouldn't ever want his cousin Myra again. Not when he could have Anne-Louise.

They numbered off, giggling and teasing. Will said he would be postman and he began to call the numbers and see that no one stayed too long outside the door. She thought she would scream because her number wasn't called. Each time Will came into the room and said a new one, she was ready to jump up and go outside, and every time it was someone else. At last Will called her and it was Billy Tyne who was waiting for her. When he tried to kiss her she pushed him and said slightingly, 'You mouth is so *wet*.' Billy, who was sixteen, blushed miserably and fumbled for the door handle, anxious to get back into the room away from the scathing presence of Anne-Louise Pritchard. And then Will stuck his head round the door and said, 'Number please.'

'What's Jonathan's number?' she whispered.

Will stared at her, stared at the crimson dress and then said coldly, 'I'm not allowed to tell the numbers.'

'Don't be stupid,' she hissed. 'Tell me his number.'

Will, who was an undemonstrative boy, unable to convey his affection to his family, but aware, nonetheless, of the misery of his sister Betsy, fumbled for the words that had been seething in his mind all day.

'Jonathan Whitman doesn't want you, Annie, so stop making a spectacle of yourself.'

He turned his back on her. 'Choose when you're ready,' he said abruptly and went into the room, exhausted with the effort of fighting Anne-Louise with words.

Gracie came out from the kitchen. She had left the game to go to the privy and Anne caught hold of her, gripping her thin shoulder tightly between her fingers.

'What's Jonathan Whitman's number?' she asked.

Gracie wriggled and tried to free herself from Anne's rigid fingers.

'You're hurting my shoulder.'

Anne shook her roughly. 'What's his number?'

'I don't remember.' She wriggled again, then became nervous at the tenseness of Anne-Louise's face.

'You remember,' said Anne-Louise. 'If you don't remember I'll make you walk through Piggotty's yard at midnight.'

'You can't make me,' said Gracie anxiously. 'You can't make me.'

Anne-Louise bent down so that her face was level with Gracie's, and her sharp blue eyes bore down into Gracie's dull grey ones.

'Yes, I can,' she whispered softly. 'I can make you do anything I want.' She waited for a moment, waited for Gracie to swallow hard and try to pull away from her. 'And if you do tell me Jonathan's number,' she continued, 'I'll give you the pins I won in the parcel game.'

Gracie wriggled again and tried to look away, but Anne held her face firmly in one hand.

'It's seven!' blurted Gracie suddenly, and Anne smiled and let go of her. 'Thank you, Gracie,' she said sweetly. 'You shall have the pins as I promised.' Gracie darted quickly through the door and Anne smoothed her hair and pulled the skirts of her dress out in a bell about her. Then she knocked on the door and said to Will, 'I'll have number seven, Will.'

Will smiled. For the first time in a long, miserable day he felt really pleased. 'You can't have seven,' he said happily. 'Seven was Jonathan, and he's just gone out of the other door to take his cousin Myra home.'

Gracie, her fear suddenly forgotten with the remembrance of the bribe, stuck her thin face underneath Will's.

'Anne, can I have the pins now?'

Anne turned on her, vitriolic frustration boiling in her because she did not know whom to vent her anger upon.

'No you can't!' she spat, and slapped Gracie hard across the face.

It was still not quite dark outside. Both the sun and the crescent of a moon were present in the indigo sky. To the west, against the black line of Tyler's woods, huge streamers of rose-and-silver cloud tore the evening into vivid colour and one or two late birds chattered quietly before bedding down under their feathers for the night. It was the deceptive, intimate hour before darkness.

Jonathan moved slowly beside Myra, not touching her, but walking as close as he dared. Sometimes they bumped gently against one another, at first whispering a muffled 'sorry', but then, when the soft collisions ceased to be accidental, saying nothing at all.

They could tell, from the scent of the gardens, whose cottages they were passing; Madge Parker's, thick with the cloying perfume of rambler roses; Mrs Tyne's mint and then the heady, overpowering smell of night-scented stock gone wild as they passed the completely overgrown and neglected garden of the weird Misses Vincent. The scent of the flowers suddenly became too much for Jonathan. He ran back to Madge Parker's garden and tore off several of her prize blooms. Then he walked back to Myra and handed them to her with a sheepish grin. She laughed, took off her hat and tucked one of

44

the flowers into the neck of her dress so that the overpowering scent was even closer, even heavier than it had been before. Jonathan swallowed hard and then said, 'Would you like to hold my arm, Myra?'

She pushed her hand through his looped arm. They walked stiffly and self-consciously together for a little way, and then Myra slowly relaxed and he felt her lean warmly into his side. When they reached the bend of the lane, to where Miss Cotterell's lavender beds came nearly on to the road, Jonathan could bear it no longer. He swung her round to face him and said frantically, 'I've got to kiss you, Myra! I've just got to!'

He snatched her impatiently round the waist with one long arm and held the back of her head in his other hand in case she should try to run away. When he brought his mouth down on to hers he expected her to struggle, but he didn't care whether she did or not. He wasn't going to let her go until he had kissed her the way he wanted to. He was faintly surprised when he realised Myra wasn't struggling, and if she was shocked or startled she seemed to be giving no outward sign. Once he had begun, he found he couldn't stop, and at last Myra, trying to draw breath, pulled her face away from his.

'Oh, Myra, don't,' he groaned. He pulled her head back again, rubbing his hands round her throat and moving his mouth softly over her cheek and hair. He found himself wanting to do a whole lot of other things – things he knew were done, but which he had never done himself. He wondered if he dared go any further.

For one glorious second he felt Myra's soft, warm breast against his hands, moving, full, beating with a life of its own. Then a violent push caught him off balance and sent him toppling back into the hedge.

'Jonathan Whitman! How dare you!'

He had never seen Myra so angry, in fact he had never seen Myra angry at all. Her hair was untidy where he had been touching it and her breast – he swallowed hard – was moving splendidly in her rage. He pulled himself out of the hedge, beginning to feel appalled at what he had done. Myra was his cousin, his respectable, well-beloved cousin. As children they had played together, and on Sundays they worshipped in the same houses, praying for comfort and the forgiveness of sins. He doubted whether any number of Sundays would bring him forgiveness for what he had just done.

'Oh, Lord,' he thought, 'what a miserable sinner I am!'

He reflected on his sin and, as he thought about it, he found to his horror that he wanted to sin again.

Myra, with shaking hands, was trying to tidy her hair and fasten her hat back on. She had dropped her gloves and Jonathan picked them up and began to hurry alongside her.

'Myra, please!' She did not look at him, but she quickened her pace until she was nearly running.

'Please, Myra, listen to me. I'm sorry. I didn't mean to, truly I didn't.' He held the gloves towards her and she ignored him and his outstretched hand.

'Oh, Myra, please listen to me! I didn't even mean to kiss you, not this time. Just walk arm in arm and ask if I could take you to the Meeting on Sunday.' She paused for a second and anxiety made his voice choke a little.

'It's just . . . you're so beautiful, Myra . . .'

She stopped. They were at the gate of her home and he could think of nothing else to say. A solitary cricket threaded somewhere in the grass. Myra's thick curled lashes moved slightly and then her huge, soft, hazel eyes were turned directly on to his face.

'Don't you ever do that again, Jonathan Whitman.'

'Oh no, Myra, I won't,' he said fervently.

She smiled suddenly, and a fantastic notion that she wasn't as angry as she had pretended to be flashed across his mind to disappear as soon as it had come.

'And, Myra,' he gulped, 'you won't let it make any difference. I mean . . .'

'If you want to take me to Meeting on Sunday, you can,' she said slowly. The colour flamed in her face as she spoke, as she admitted and acknowledged the rules of elaborate courtship that were now beginning. Nothing would be said by them, or anyone else, for some considerable time; it would be even longer, much longer, before any mention of marriage was made, but Jonathan's request and her acceptance meant that they were matched, that Jonathan and Myra Whitman were walking out.

With a gentle, awkward movement he reached out and took her hand in his, then he raised her fingers to his mouth and kissed them. 'Can I kiss you again, Myra?' he asked, anxious to take no further chances. She nodded. 'Just kiss me,' she said warningly.

He leaned forward. Young mouth met young mouth, held, and broke before the danger point was reached.

'I love you, Myra.'

'Ssh, Jonathan. It's too soon for that.' She put a hand up to his face and stroked his cheek.

'Good night.'

'Good night.'

He watched her vanish into the doorway and then he turned back into the lane, wondering if he would ever be more happy than he was at this one sharp moment. He started to run, alongside the hedgerow and up through Tyler's fields, waving his arms in the air and leaping over the ditches until he reached the stile.

'My – ra!' he shouted at the moon. Then he climbed down from the stile and began to walk home, reckoning soberly how long it would be and how much money he would need before he could, once again, reach out to touch Myra's soft breast with his hands.

Betsy had managed to get through the rest of the day without crying. Once the shock of seeing Anne-Louise in the silk dress had passed, her unhappiness had dulled to a gentle pain, a pain she didn't fully understand, but that, every now and again, rose to hit her across the back of the eyes. It wasn't that she especially wanted a silk dress, it wasn't that Anne-Louise was prettier. That had always been the way. And somehow it wasn't, either, the knowledge that Mathew would have to be told about the money. Every so often, amid the congratulations, the kisses, the prayers and the big tea, she tried to think why it was the pain hurt so much. But she couldn't see why, couldn't understand why Anne-Louise in the red silk dress had hurt her more than the occasion deserved. Whenever she felt tears standing at the back of her eyes, she would remember that her mother was watching, and that her mother was badly upset about the day's events. She knew that if she cried again it would hurt her mother, so she laughed and chattered and pretended that she had forgotten all about the dress and Anne-Louise and the money. It helped that so many people were present and she didn't have time to talk to her mother or to Math, alone. Sometime she would have to bring the subject up in front of Mathew, but not yet, she thought, not yet.

Just before they left for the station, Will had pulled her quickly to one side.

'I've told him,' he said awkwardly. 'I've told Math about the money.'

The stupid, irritating tears threatened again. She swallowed.

'Didn't tell him everything, did you, Will?' she said briskly.

Will looked unhappy and tapped her shoulder with his hand. From Will it was a sign of both affection and distress.

'Said there'd been an emergency and mother had had to use it for the family.'

Betsy nodded. 'That's right. That's what you should have said, Will.' She paused and looked down at the ground. 'Did he . . . I mean, did he seem surprised?'

Will tapped her shoulder again. 'Didn't seem to be very interested,' he said slowly. 'You know how quiet Math is, you never know what he's thinking. He just said he hadn't thought there would be anything left after the tea and all the things to be paid for.'

Betsy felt the pain ease a little, not much, but just a little. When her mother came up to kiss her good-bye she was able to force a big smile across her face, and then look back and wave at everyone as they walked across the station fields.

And then, when they got on to the train to take them to London, the misery descended even heavier on her heart. She sat watching the steam float past the carriage window, blinking back tears and hoping that Math wouldn't look at her. He hadn't spoken since they left the village. He stared out of the

48

window, whistling a little tune at the back of his throat and nodding in time to the music. When the train began to pull into London he leaned across the carriage.

'Better?' he said. She smiled, and after that he didn't speak again, partly because he was a man who spoke very little anyway, and partly because they came into the station and he was lifting their bags from the rack and passing them down to Betsy.

She was confused and frightened at the size of the station. She had been to London only twice before. Once, when she was thirteen years old, just after her father had died, her mother had brought her up to London to see an aunt who lived in Camberwell. The aunt, a sister of Betsy's father, was believed to have some property, and, indeed, she was obviously a very wealthy lady, living in a large double-fronted house with a sign in the window that said 'Gentlemen Boarders'. Betsy remembered only that her mother had been ashamed and that the aunt had made them wait in the scullery until she could see them. She couldn't recall what her mother had said, but she remembered the aunt taking a half-sovereign out of a box and throwing it down on the table. When Betsy had seen her mother's face she had angrily picked up the money and hurled it back at the old woman. She had reflected since that she had no right to indulge in such a gesture of pride; probably her mother had needed the money very badly to go asking for charity.

She had come to London again with her mother two years ago, applying for a post as housekeeper – a position that seemed to offer a salary that would make everything come right for the family. She had written in answer to an advertisement, not expecting that anyone her age would be taken seriously. When she had received a reply, Mrs Pritchard had said firmly that she had no intention of allowing Betsy to go until she had examined the post for herself. Her caution proved worth while. The prospective employer was a widower of fifty-eight who was unnaturally eager to have a seventeen-year-old housekeeper. Mrs Pritchard had led Betsy home with an air of outraged indignation, having first had a private and

49

animated discussion with the elderly widower.

Now, walking up the platform behind Math, she felt the familiar twinge of excitement that London had given her on those other two occasions, a sense of adventure, of going somewhere to new worlds and sensations. She caught sight of herself suddenly in a train window and, when Math had given up their tickets, she asked shyly if he would excuse her while she tidied herself in the cloakroom.

The cloakroom was rather magnificent, marble and brown leather and a big dark-green rubber-plant standing on a side-table. She dabbed her handkerchief in cold water and held it against her eyes, trying to make the puffy, red look go away from them. When she rejoined Math she felt better, excited and caught up into the mystery of London. Math smiled at her and nodded, as if to say, that's better.

'To Waterloo now, Math?'

Again he nodded. Math never spoke when a nod or a shake would serve as well. He led her out of the station, through the grandeur of the arched roof and cathedral-like entrance and suddenly she realised he wasn't carrying the bags.

'Mathew! the bags.' He grinned again, his neat, little sailor's grin, and said quickly, 'In the hansom, Betsy. In the hansom.'

'A cab! A hansom cab! Mathew . . .'

'Ssh,' he whispered, opening the carriage door. 'Up we go then.'

'But Math, the money?'

'He'll hear you,' said Math, pointing to the cabby in his top hat and cape-coat.

The lamplighters were out, swinging their poles high into the air and making little beacons of lights as they moved along the road. Everywhere people, cabs, horses, milled into a confusion of colour and noise – and she, Betsy, was part of it.

When they came to Waterloo she tried not to look and see how much Mathew gave the cabby, she tried to stand waiting on the curb looking unconcerned and as though she always rode across London in a hansom. Math picked up the bags and she followed him through a pair of swing-glass doors, and then she stopped.

'Math!' she shrilled in horror. 'It's a public house!'

Math put the bags down and led her over to a small recess. 'Not a public house,' he said. 'A hotel.' He pushed her gently down on to a plush and tasselled chair and she drew well back into the shadows of the alcove, trying not to be there, but conscious all the time of a growing and delicious sense of abandoned sin. The waiter, white-aproned and with the largest moustache she had ever seen, came over, and Math said neatly, 'Two cherry brandies, please.'

When they came she took a disapproving sip, and then realised how very, very delicious it was, and how very, very warming. The dull pain at the back of her neck – nearly gone, but not quite – disappeared completely. She stretched her feet out beneath the blue poplin dress and coat and looked around her. Of course, now she could see that it wasn't a public house, not like the one in the village. It was a very elegant establishment with gold-fringed curtains hanging over every alcove and potted plants in brass stands on every table. There were other ladies present, ladies with leg-of-mutton sleeves and velvet revers, ladies with veils over their hats that they lifted daintily when they wished to sip from their glasses. Betsy reached out for hers and found it empty.

'Oh,' she said bleakly. 'It's all gone.'

Mathew stood up and went to collect the bags, and Betsy, feeling better than she had done all day, followed him out of the hotel and into the station, down the platform and on to the train.

The first half of the journey passed in a pleasant cloudy haze of sleep and cherry-brandy relaxation. Whenever she opened her eyes Math was looking at her, smiling and watching her. At first she didn't mind, and then she began to feel a little uncomfortable, wondering why he was smiling, what he was thinking.

Suddenly she sat up and straightened her hat, feeling oddly nervous and wondering how long it would be before they got to Portsmouth and their furnished lodgings near the dock.

'You're sure the lodgings are all right?' she asked, more because she wanted something to say than because she was concerned about the rooms. Mathew patted her knee.

'Don't you worry. You and Mrs Bunts'll get along famously. She's a sailor's wife too. She'll know how to look after you.'

Betsy swallowed. The pat on the knee had reminded her that, later on this evening, something would be expected of her, something she was a trifle hazy about, having only the vaguest idea what she was supposed to do. She began to worry again.

It was raining when they pulled into Portsmouth and they had to walk to the lodgings, the lateness of the hour prohibiting the use of a cab. The pink hat began to wilt in the damp, Math didn't say a word, and the pain in her head came back. At last he stopped in front of a tall, narrow house and dumped the bags down on the step.

'Not long now,' he said cheerfully, and Betsy wondered nervously what he meant. He pulled the bell and waited. Nothing happened, and then, dimly from inside, Betsy caught the faint sound of someone singing jerkily and slightly off-key. Math pulled the bell again and hammered on the door, and this time they were answered by footsteps hurrying towards them down a hallway. The door was abruptly flung wide and a plump, round-faced woman in a night-wrapper stood before them with a candle in her hand.

'Hello, Mrs Bunts,' said Mathew.

Mrs Bunts stretched her arms wide to welcome them with a tragic and dramatic gesture. 'You poor dears,' she cried loudly, then turned to Math. 'Your sailing orders have come. You're to leave in the morning.'

Betsy burst into tears. All the while Math and Mrs Bunts were leading her into the front parlour and removing her hat and gloves she was sobbing. Splintered fragments of speech fell out in a confusion of sound and her misery ended with the words, 'I want to go home.'

'Well, now,' said the over-stout, good natured Mrs Bunts. 'You shall go home in the morning if that's what you want. But, bless me, you'll get used to him coming and going. Why

I've been married to Bunts for seventeen years and I hardly notice he's gone before he's back again.'

Betsy's sobs dulled to a few muffled gasps. Mrs Bunts patted her shoulder.

'That's it. You'll feel better when you've had a nice cup of tea. And then up to bed and in the morning it will all seem different.'

Betsy doubted it, and the mention of bed brought the other depressing matter back to her mind. Mrs Bunts turned to open a door of the huge, mahogany sideboard.

'Before you have some tea, we must toast the bride and groom,' she said jovially. 'I've saved some of my home-made sloe-gin especially for the occasion.'

It was a dark red, much deeper in colour than the cherry brandy, but really just as nice to taste. And, naturally, home-made wines weren't really intoxicants at all.

Mrs Bunts sipped and leaned across to refill Betsy's glass.

'You'll excuse Mr Bunts not coming down, dear,' she said. 'He's a bit indisposed at the moment. The damp weather's inclined to upset him.'

The singing, coming from somewhere at the back of the house, was still going on. Actually it was rather gay, Betsy decided. It had a cheering, enjoyable note about it.

When she stood up to go to bed she felt most curious and, climbing the stairs, she had an overpowering urge to join in singing with the invisible Mr Bunts. She contented herself with a gentle humming as she followed Mrs Bunts up the stairs and into the bedroom. She sat on the bed while Mrs Bunts put her things away in the closet, and when the stout lady had gone she began to undress, finding the fastenings of her dress difficult and giggling when the buttons wouldn't come undone. The candle made a funny pattern on the ceiling, and when she had climbed between the sheets she lay flat on her back and squinted up at the shadow with one eye closed.

Math's small, dark, well-formed head came round the door and he smiled at her, his small, tidy, sailor's smile. He blew the candle out and then she heard him undressing and felt the bed go down on one side when he climbed in.

And really, she thought later through a pleasant haze of warmth and sloe-gin, there wasn't any need to worry. It was, after all, quite simple.

Her tongue felt nasty when she woke up, thick and rather unpleasant, like when she'd had the measles. For a moment she couldn't recall where she was, and then she rolled over and saw with embarrassment, that her nightdress was lying on the floor. The rest of the bed was empty and smooth except for a small, round dent in the other pillow where Math's head had been. She reached out and picked up her nightdress, feeling much better when she had put it on and pulled it well down round her feet. Then she heard Mrs Bunts' voice from the other side of the door.

'Are you awake, dear? I've brought you some tea.'

She came in, beaming conspiratorially, and Betsy wondered why she had looked different, then realised it was because Mrs Bunts' broad bosom and buttocks were encased in a shiny, bombazine dress instead of last night's wrapper. Betsy sat up and looked at the tray of tea. She could never remember having tea in bed before.

'Where's Math?' she asked timidly.

'They've sailed, love. Gone on the morning tide. Now, don't you get upset, dear,' she added hastily as Betsy's eyes began to fill with tears again. 'You drink your tea, and when you're up we'll have a look round the town.' She patted Betsy's shoulder and went to the door.

'He was up in time to get to the shops,' she added mysteriously, and then she closed the door.

The tea was hot and sweet. Betsy drank appreciatively. The sun streamed through the window directly on to the bed and she could smell the sea. She began to feel excited at the thought of staying at the sea for a long, long time. And she would only have her lodgings to keep clean and only herself to look after – and Math, when he came home. She would sew for extra money, but it wouldn't be like working in other people's houses and helping to bring up the younger brothers and sisters. She finished the tea and lay back in the soft feather mattress, stretching her toes out to try and touch the bottom of the bed. When she moved she caught a faint, familiar smell, and then realised it was the scent of Math, of soap and rough skin. She felt warm and nice when she put her face close to Math's pillow, and then wished sadly that he hadn't gone away so quickly. She reached out and touched something in the bed, something lying on Math's side beneath the sheets, a large brown-paper parcel printed with the name of a Portsmouth draper. It had her name – BETSY – printed carefully on it in Math's small writing, and she opened it carefully, anxious not to tear the place where Math had written.

It lay, soft and gleaming, carefully wrapped in tissue. And even while excitement and delight made her sit up abruptly in the bed, she was conscious of anxiety – worry that Math had spent too much money and maybe even the money they needed for the first month's lodging and food. And she was conscious, too, of the fact that it wouldn't really suit her – not like it suited Anne-Louise – it was seven yards of crimson, loop-embroidered silk.

Three

EIGHTEEN months later, on Christmas Day, Jonathan Whitman married his cousin Myra and brought her home to the cottage to live. The marriage had taken place earlier than Jonathan had thought possible because, to his surprise, neither Em nor Myra seemed to mind sharing the cottage with the other. Jonathan, thinking he would have to try to find an extra home for Myra and himself, had been surprised when Emily had suggested that Myra should live with them.

'Wouldn't you mind, Em?' he asked cautiously, and was astonished when Em said, somewhat peremptorily, 'Of course not. She can carry on with her dressmaking and lend a hand when I need her.'

At first Jonathan wondered if it was wise, having Em and Myra together, but he wanted so desperately to marry Myra that he pushed all objections to the back of his mind, swept aside Myra's tentative protests, and hurried her into marriage before either she or Emily could change their minds.

It wasn't the gregarious occasion that Betsy Pritchard's had been eighteen months before. There was no money for a big tea. Myra's parents were dead, and the aunt with whom she lived intended to waste no money on the marriage of a mere niece. When Jonathan arrived at the church there was only Em, two of his brothers and Myra's aunt waiting to see them married.

Half-way through the service he heard someone moving at the back of the church and, later, when he looked round, he saw the wild, slightly bizarre figure of his father, old Peter Whitman, sitting at the back of the church. He was pleased, strangely and unaccountably pleased, that the old man had come to his wedding. When they left the church Peter was sitting on a tombstone in the graveyard, his long-haired, weather-cleaned dogs leaning up close to his legs and a long skein of sheep's wool wound round his battered hat.

'God's blessing, son,' he mumbled. 'And a good life for you.'

Jonathan leaned forward and kissed his father's cheek. The skin smelt good, of salt and dry hill-grass.

'Why don't you come home for a spell, father?' he said, but Peter shook his head.

'I like to go with the sheep,' he muttered. 'I like the sheep.' The air was frosty and the ground hard and Jonathan wondered where his father wandered to, what houses and farms the old shepherd drifted upon while he waited for the moving of the spring flocks and the lambing to begin.

'Come back to eat with us then.' Jonathan placed his hand on old Peter's shoulder and one of the dogs suddenly sat up and whimpered.

'Away now, away,' answered the old man. He went to his other two sons and looked them up and down. He was a small man, round, stocky and, in his strange clothes and trimmings of sheep's wool, he reminded Jonathan of one of the small fairy-tale men in the stories of the Brothers Grimm. He nodded at his sons, his three tall, strong sons, and then he stood before Emily and said, inexplicably, 'Poor Em, poor Em.' He whistled to the dogs, waved back, and then clumped his way across the churchyard and into the wood, leaving the six of them standing sadly in the December cold. Myra shivered.

'Shall we go home?'

Jonathan turned and smiled at her cold-pinched cheeks, forgetting the solitude of his father in the delight of knowing that now Myra was his, belonged to him for the rest of his life, was there to hold fast and be with him when he was happy.

'Come along,' said Emily impatiently. 'Let's get home and I'll make a cooked tea.'

Sometimes, when he was working in the Fawcett gardens, he worried about marrying Myra and bringing her to live with his sister. He worried so much that he ran all the way home to see that they weren't quarrelling, or that Em wasn't bullying Myra the way she had bullied him and his brothers when they were small. But usually Em was bending over the big, black kettle, just the way she always did, and Myra was sitting sewing, making dresses and coats for Mrs Panter or the doctor's wife or one of the village women.

It was cold that January and February, bitterly, unbelievably cold. When he went for the milk in the morning it was frozen by the time he had walked the three miles back to the cottage, but still he delighted in getting this task done early so that he could have the stove lit and the first tea boiled for the day. If he managed to do all this without waking Myra there was the infinite pleasure of taking her tea to her, seeing her braided head poke out from the blankets and her breath turn to mist in the icy air.

In the morning, first thing, she was soft and pliable, forgetting to be shy with him and only anxious to curl into his body away from the cold. That was when he loved her best, when she gripped her arms round him, trying to draw warmth from his body and pulling against him when he teased her and went to move away. She hated the cold, hated getting out of bed into the icy bedroom and shivering her way down the stairs to the kitchen and ash-choked stove. He would bend right down and put his mouth into the smooth fold of her neck and face.

'The stove's alight. The kitchen's warm and there's tea ready.'

She would smile slowly and yawn and then climb out of bed and wrap a blanket round her to see her down the stairs. He had an overpowering urge to lift her, wrapped tightly in the blanket, and carry her to the fire, hold her tightly in his arms all the way to the kitchen. But he never did, because he thought Em might see them, and he didn't want Emily to know the way he felt about Myra.

Towards the end of February it grew a little warmer. In a sheltered corner of the Fawcett gardens, behind the gazebo, he came across a small clump of aconites, pushing their yellow, buttercup heads above the frosty ground. Usually he couldn't bear to pick the first of the spring flowers, they died so quickly, but he knew he must show them to Myra and he stopped and picked them, taking care not to break the stalks off too low so that the plant would die.

He hurried back across the fields, anxious that Myra should see the aconites before they lost their first freshness. He pushed the door of the kitchen open, calling to Myra as he went, and then he stopped, feeling foolish and awkward when he saw that Myra and Emily were not alone. He closed the door, wondering just how ridiculous he looked with the pathetic clump of flowers in his hand.

'Hullo, Jonathan,' said Anne-Louise, turning in her chair to look at him. 'Whatever are you holding?' She giggled suddenly. 'Don't tell me you've been in the woods picking flowers at this time of year.'

He put the aconites quickly down on the desk. Anne-Louise was sitting in the best chair they had, the chair that Myra usually sat in, and now she – Myra – was standing by the table over a large bolt of blue serge cloth.

'Myra's going to make my dress,' said Anne gaily. 'She's going to do it quickly, before I go away.'

'Anne-Louise is going to work in London, Jonathan. As parlour-maid in a house in Lambeth. Isn't it exciting?'

Myra's face was flushed and her hair was untidy where she had been running her hands through it as she moved over the cloth, pulling it straight and measuring the pattern pieces across it.

'She's going in two weeks, so we must hurry. You won't mind me working in the evenings, Jonathan?'

'No, of course not,' said Jonathan, without enthusiasm. He was aware that he was not being polite to Anne-Louise.

'A good position?' he asked, without interest. Anne-Louise shrugged.

'It will suit me very well,' she said deprecatingly. 'It's a big house, seven servants and twenty-four pounds a year.' Jonathan heard Myra gasp over by the table. Twenty-four pounds a year was quite exceptional for a living-in parlour-maid.

'They seem quite nice,' continued Anne coolly. 'The mistress sent me the serge and two ready-made coveralls before I've even started there. I'm to have all Sundays and one evening a week off.'

Jonathan saw that Myra had put the scissors down on the table. She was sitting on the kitchen stool with her chin resting in her hands, gazing at Anne-Louise.

'London,' she said dreamily. 'Just imagine working in London. I've never even been to London.'

Anne shrugged. 'Well, it's very different, of course, everyone is a whole lot smarter than here, and more clever and fashionable. So you see, Myra, it's rather important that I have the dress to take with me.' She drummed her fingers impatiently on the table and lay back elegantly in the chair. 'I shall probably go out quite a lot and need more dresses than we have here.'

'I promise. It will be ready before you go!' Hastily Myra stood up and picked up the scissors. She looked untidy and harassed, and suddenly Jonathan hated Anne-Louise Pritchard, hated her because he couldn't afford to buy Myra a length of blue serge or take her to London or buy her presents. All he could give her was a bunch of aconites from someone else's garden. Anne-Louise stood up and fastened her coat buttons.

'I'll come tomorrow for a fitting,' she said grandly. 'Will that be all right?' Myra nodded and hurried to open the door for her. When Anne was half-way through, she suddenly turned back into the room.

'So sorry,' she said loudly. 'With all the excitement and all, I completely forgot to wish you happiness and so on. I meant to come before, just after the wedding, but there's been so much to do. And with Betsy gone to Portsmouth . . . ' She waved her hand excitedly in the air and then vanished into the darkness. Jonathan heard her feet clopping quickly down the brick path, and he closed the door to shut out the sound. Myra was bending frenziedly over the blue cloth. He couldn't bear to see her working on Anne-Louise's dress.

'Put that to one side and let us have our tea,' he said curtly. Emily, who had not spoken since he came into the room, clattered the kettle on the stove.

'We can eat from the side-table,' she snapped. 'Sewing is money, and from what I learn today you're going to need it.'

Myra suddenly grew still over her cutting.

'Em,' she whispered. Emily, her mouth in a fixed straight line, poured boiling water on to the tea leaves.

'Some people don't know when things are going well,' she spat furiously. 'Some people can't leave well alone. They have to change things.'

'Please, Em.'

Jonathan watched the colour across the back of his wife's neck beneath her upswept hair, turn to an angry red. He began to feel afraid of something, something to do with Myra.

'Who's changed things?' he asked warily.

'You,' snapped Emily. 'You. A man. Always men have to change things, interfere and meddle and dirty everything.'

He heard Myra give a muffled cry, and he was aware of anger, curt, abrupt anger towards his sister.

'Stop!' he shouted. 'Stop saying things like that. You say things and tell me I've changed everything. What? Tell me what I've changed.'

Emily crashed the kettle back on to the stove. Water shot out from the spout and hissed on the black range.

'Ask her.' She pointed to Myra. Shocked, Jonathan saw that Myra was crying. 'Ask her how things have changed,' continued Emily. 'We were comfortable here, just the two of us and you only here in the evenings. We could bear with that. And now it's going to be like it was with mother all over again. Every year the house getting smaller and noisier, and every year less money and more work.' Emily's face was white, not the white of rage or pain, but the dead, dull white of a body drained of pleasure. Myra had suddenly grown quiet and now she stood up slowly from the table.

'You had no right to say that, Emily,' she said softly. 'You had no right to speak for me to my husband. It was my duty and my wish to tell him.'

He knew what he had been told, what Emily and Myra between them had said. He supposed he should have felt pleased and perhaps, if Emily had not been there, he would have been. Now all he could think of was wanting to go to Myra and hold her because Em had made her cry.

'You said you didn't mind us living here. You said you wanted to live with your family. What is it that makes you hate us now? It is still your family. The child will be mine and Myra's, still your family.'

'No,' said Emily. 'No more family. Not like that. Not children, hundreds of children always needing food or clothes or washing. Not like that.'

Jonathan felt everything was unreal. He didn't care what Em thought any more and he moved round the table and put his arm round Myra's shoulder.

'If you feel like that, Em,' he said, 'we'll go. We'll try and find another place and we'll go.'

The enormity of the decision appalled him, but he knew it had to be done. Somehow he had to find another cottage and get some furniture inside before the child was born. He worried frantically for a moment, and then Emily said, 'There's no need. I've already made my arrangements. I went to see the Misses Vincent this morning. I'm moving in with them at Eastertide.'

'The Vincents!'

Jonathan wasn't sure whether to laugh or whether to accuse his sister of making a joke of the whole affair. 'Don't be ridiculous, Em. You know you can't live with the Vincents.'

'Why not?' Emily had returned to her customary non-committal calmness. She arranged the cups on the side-table and began to pour.

'Well . . . well you just can't, Em. Everyone knows they're mad. You can't go and live with those two old women.'

Emily straightened her back and looked at him.

'In fact,' she said, 'the Misses Vincent are only a little older than I. They are not mad. They are considered to be so because they do not like people and prefer to live alone. I do not like people. I shall enjoy living with the Misses Vincent.'

Until she said it, she had not realised just how much she would enjoy living with the strange women in the isolated cottage. She had sought refuge there because, with the news of

Myra's pregnancy, she had to go somewhere, somewhere away from the start of a new life, from the noise and the work and the confusion that children would bring. For it was not people that Emily disliked, it was men, men and the children that the presence of men always produced.

Jonathan could not understand her, and Myra, although dimly perceiving something of the events that had formed Emily's life, did not truly understand either. Emily had assisted in the rearing of twelve younger brothers. The experience had left her with neither the desire nor the inclination to marry. She considered she had had a sufficiency of men and male company. When Jonathan had run away and the family had been evicted, she had been forced to live on the charity of a cousin, and the charity had been earned by caring for yet another eight children, five of them boys. She disliked children, especially boy children, and she loathed men. Generally, she considered them dirty, unpleasant creatures who had to be watched continually and washed forcibly, otherwise they degenerated into a standard only a little above that of swine. Their table manners were disgusting. They belched, scratched and broke wind whenever they felt like it, and sometimes forgot to fasten their trousers before leaving the privy. They married women, frail, soft, delicate women, and turned them into faded shrews, or killed them in childbirth. They made cottages asylums of shrieking noise and heat and work. At best they were irritating, at worst bestial.

She had welcomed Myra to the cottage because, for the first time in her life, it meant she lived in a house where the women outnumbered the men. All day there was just the two of them and, as she had said, she could bear with Jonathan in the evenings, for Jonathan was the least irritating and offensive of all the men she had yet encountered. Somehow, because he was her youngest brother, because his manners and his ways were not too degrading, too offensive, she had thought this time it would be different. Almost she had considered Myra another sister in the house, as though Myra had chosen to come and live with her, Emily, and that Jonathan was there purely as an accident. And now the round of work, of dirt, of noise was to start again.

All her life she had dreamed, without hope, of a home entirely devoid of men, a house with delicate china that was never broken and small dainty chairs that only women sat upon. She dwelt lovingly on the thought of frilled, wispy curtains and little pots of flowers standing on tiny ledges and window-sills. She imagined the meals she would have, little trays of thin bread and butter, and weak tea, sometimes a boiled egg or a fillet of steamed fish, but never, never the great mounds of boiled potatoes and bacon pudding that she had seen her brothers shovelling into gaping mouths ever since she could remember; the bowls of thick pea soup, the treacle pudding served on thick, clumsy china, great revolting servings of coarse, indigestible food.

And the first time she had entered the Misses Vincent's cottage, the house that she had expected to be dirty and strange, she had discovered that this was the place she had imagined as her own.

They were not, as she had said, really mad. One hundred years earlier they would have been called witches, because they lived alone and because they housed a weird family of seven cats. But in fact they were self-sufficient, eccentric, perhaps a little distorted in their way of living. But certainly not mad.

The garden of their cottage was completely overgrown. Night-scented stock, bindweed, marigolds, moon-daisies, blackberries and nettles fought and tangled in a confusion of neglected vegetation. People passing were startled to see the occasional face of one of the cats lurking in the undergrowth, and the Misses Vincent were only seen on their way to fetch milk from the farm or in the village shop or at night calling to the cats. At one time, many years ago, there had been a father, a Sergeant Vincent, a heavy bull-necked man who shouted and thrashed his daughters with a hogskin belt. When he died they had become, almost at once, the strange, withdrawn Misses Vincent in the isolated cottage at the end of the lane.

Emily, passing the cottage one day, had noticed one of the sisters standing at the window. She was fidgeting nervously with the curtain, staring back into the room and then out again, into the garden. Emily walked on and then paused, sensing something in the movement of the woman at the window, something that needed help.

She didn't go into the garden. She stood at the gate and looked at the strange woman wavering at the window. She nodded interrogatively at Miss Vincent, a movement that said, 'What is wrong? Do you need help?'

Suddenly Miss Vincent had disappeared and then the door opened and she called, nervously, but with a note of desperation in her voice.

'Please!' she called. 'Could you come. My sister . . .'

Emily threaded her way slowly up the path, between the tentacles of brambles and thorns that reached out to grasp her skirt. A cat darted from the undergrowth and shot across the path in front of her. When she reached the door she stopped.

'Yes?' she asked.

The woman beckoned into the room behind. 'It's Thalia,' she said, and Emily was startled at the queerness of the name. 'It's Thalia. She's lying on the floor and cannot move.'

Emily followed her into the cottage and then stopped. It was not like the garden, not at all. It was clean and small and pink. A piano with brass candlesticks stood against one wall and a cat was sitting on the top of it. There were flowers, marigolds mostly, and frills and dainty china painted with a pattern of mauve and blue pansies. A silver jug stood on the mantelpiece, a good silver jug, and it gleamed with regular cleaning and polishing with a soft cloth. Emily stood and gazed upon the room she had always wanted to live in. A clean well-ordered room that was quiet and never changed.

'Here, here,' said the strange little Miss Vincent. 'Over here.'

Emily followed her round to the back of a hide and brass-studded sofa. The other Miss Vincent was lying on the floor, and at the corners of her mouth small specks of foam moved in her breath. Emily recognised the symptom.

'She's had a fit,' she said bluntly. 'You must know what it is. She's had them before, hasn't she?'

Miss Vincent nodded. 'Poor Thalia. She goes like it some-

times, ever since we were little girls, ever since Papa . . . '
She stopped as an unpleasant memory reasserted itself. 'But
she hasn't spoken for half an hour. Before she was only like it
for a minute. I can't make her speak.'

'Help me lift her up.' Emily put her hands behind Miss
Vincent's shoulders and between them they managed to lift
her on to the sofa. 'Best get a blanket and keep her warm,'
she said.

The little woman hurried away and returned, in a moment,
with a woollen crocheted blanket. It was beautiful. Soft and
coloured and clean. Emily stroked it.

'It's a beautiful blanket,' she murmured. Miss Vincent
smiled.

'Thalia made it. Thalia is clever. She can do anything. She
plays the piano, and she paints. See.' She waved her hand to
the walls and Emily noticed small drawings of flowers and
trees. 'I can only sew,' said Miss Vincent. 'But I cook, just
cakes and things, and small biscuits.'

The room was quiet. A gilt-and-ormolu clock clicked softly
into the air and Emily peacefully resigned herself to the calm.
She looked at the woman lying on the sofa and was startled to
see that her eyes were open and that she was staring at her.

Emily swallowed, and suddenly the woman sat up, throwing
off the blanket and then picking it up, folding it and laying
it carefully on one side.

'Some tea, Aleen,' she said tersely. 'Some tea for Miss Whitman.'

The first Miss Vincent fluttered out of the room and Emily
heard the sounds of a teapot and kettle.

'Why did you come?' Miss Thalia's voice was very strong,
almost harsh in texture.

'You were very ill. Your sister asked me to come in.'

Miss Thalia nodded. 'Aleen is not strong, not strong,' she
said hoarsely, as though that explained everything.

She said no more, and Emily, after one or two slight
attempts at ordinary conversation, gave up and relapsed into
a similar silence. She felt no discomfort in the presence of
the strange woman. They sat without speaking. It was quiet

66

and Emily liked it, she liked the room, and she liked Miss Thalia.

The other one came back, the one called Miss Aleen, and she carried a tray with a tiny pot of tea and a silver milk-jug and sugar bowl. She carried it to the table and filled one of the pansy-patterned cups for Emily.

'Aren't you having any?' asked Emily, surprised.

Miss Thalia shook her head and smiled. She got up suddenly and went to the piano. She touched the head of the large black cat gently with her forefinger, then she sat down and began to play. The music was so soft that when it stopped it seemed to Emily that it had just evaporated into the air. She paused – and waited, then began to play again. Miss Aileen took the teapot and the cup back to the kitchen and Emily sat on the soft little armchair and listened.

When the ormolu clock chimed she realised that she had been there for more than an hour and she hurriedly got up to leave. Miss Aleen opened the door for her and as she was stepping through she heard the other Miss Vincent say, 'Come again. Please come again.'

She had gone again, lots of times, until at last she was going every day. Often she was able to help Miss Aleen lift her sister, frothing and rigid, on to the sofa, and she didn't mind because Miss Aleen was a woman and Miss Thalia was a woman and so was she, Emily. Sometimes she would take her sewing there, and once, when Miss Aleen was ill, she went in and helped Miss Thalia clean and cook, finding it was easy to absorb herself into the strange, calm household.

This morning, when she had heard Myra being sick in the privy for the fifth consecutive morning, she had gone to see Miss Thalia. And Miss Thalia had known at once that something was wrong. Emily told her, tried to explain, in a way she could not understand herself, the horror of Myra and the baby.

'Come here,' said Miss Thalia simply. 'Come and live here.'

At first Emily was disconcerted. She liked the Vincent house, she liked the quiet and the pinkness and Miss Thalia. But for so long had she thought, like everyone else in the

67

village, of the two queer Misses Vincent that she could not perceive how she could live there.

And then Myra and Anne-Louise and Jonathan had filled the cottage kitchen and it was untidy and noisy and Myra was crying because she was going to have a child; she was going to have lots of children, one every year, all crying and needing food and comfort. And Emily thought of the haven of the Vincents' cottage and decided, suddenly, that it was the only place she wanted to be. The more Jonathan and Myra railed against it, the more she wanted to go there.

'The cats,' said Jonathan, using the last argument he could think of. 'The cats will make everything smell. You know how you can't bear anything to smell bad, Em. You know how you hate it.'

'They don't.'

'But if there's all those cats, it will smell, Em.'

'It doesn't.'

It didn't. In some odd way the huge, sleek beasts that lived at the Vincents' didn't smell. They were silent and soft and strange, like Miss Thalia and Miss Aleen.

Myra came over to Em and touched her arm.

'Please, Emily,' she said. 'Please stay here. I'll try not to let the baby cry, and you needn't have anything to do with it.'

'I want to go to the Vincents',' said Emily stubbornly, and Jonathan remembered his father saying something vaguely similar on the day of his, Jonathan's, wedding. And he recalled his father saying, 'Poor Em, poor Em.' Faintly he saw why old Peter had said 'Poor Em'. Dimly he began to understand and feel a pity for his sister, not for the years she had had to work – they all had to work like that at something – but because she lacked grace, because she had no compassion in her heart to make her happy.

'Yes, Em,' he said quietly. 'Go if you must. You're a good woman. You'll be all right.'

He wished that, as well as pity, he didn't feel a very small desire to laugh, a deep-hidden chuckle when he thought of the three ladies and the seven cats living together in the cottage.

'I'll stay until Easter.'

'As long as you like.'

Emily began to feel excited. It was like planning for a holiday that she had never had. For the very first time in her life she experienced pleasure and a sense of anticipation.

During March she began to take her things across, one by one, a few at a time. Vaguely she was aware that Anne-Louise was at the cottage a lot, having fittings and standing around until well into the evening when Jonathan came home.

She said good-bye to Anne-Louise when the girl came the day before leaving for London, and if Anne seemed strange and shrilly vivacious, well that was the way of Anne-Louise Pritchard, but she, Emily, would not have to put up with her or Jonathan or Myra much longer. And on Easter Saturday she moved into the weird household of the Misses Vincent.

Jonathan helped her carry the last of her things across. He was sad and worried because, again, an action of his had precipitated the disruption of the family. She wouldn't let him come to the front door. She took her bag at the gate and said, 'Don't come in, Jonathan. We don't want you there.' He noticed that already she included herself with Miss Thalia and Miss Aleen.

'Good-bye, Em.' He reached forward to brush her cheek with his lips, but already she was gone, hurrying up the tangled path and through the door that was opened from behind so that Jonathan could not see who was there.

When the door was closed he felt released, happy and free for the first time since his return from the army. On his way home he stopped at the village shop and bought Myra a bar of chocolate and a packet of needles, knowing that now he could give them to her when he liked, and where he liked, without waiting for a time when Em was not there.

It was the best summer he had ever known. They were alone together, the weather was warm, and Mr Fawcett held a harvest supper in the kitchen of the Fawcett house for the servants and groundsmen. Jonathan was pleased because Myra was different from everyone else there. She was quiet and beautiful, and Jonathan liked the way the others looked at her, the way Mr Fawcett strutted and preened in front of her and called her 'my dear'.

He didn't think very much about the child. It was enough that he had Myra to himself, and now, too, he had someone to share the books with in the evenings. He would come in and Myra would try to pull the calico parcel from under his arm.

'What book is it, Jonathan? What book did you bring tonight?'

Perversely he wouldn't let her see, holding the book in the air and making her reach for it. After supper she would sit on his lap while he read aloud, fumbling over the words that he knew how to think but not how to say. She liked the Brontës, but when he began to read *The Vicar of Wakefield* she leaned her head against his shoulder and went to sleep.

She was still shy with him. She still hurried upstairs every night and undressed quickly before he came in. Once, when he went up at the same time as she did, she undressed in bed beneath the blankets.

When September drew near he knew he was going to need more money, and he bought himself a last and a sheet of leather and began to make and mend the boots in the village. He practised first on stiff paper and one day walked over to Quinchurch to watch the bootmaker there. The first pair he made for himself. They were not quite right, but the next pair were fine and they were for Mr Tyler, who paid him money. It meant he had to rise two hours earlier if he wanted to make boots and go to Fawcett's just the same – but the money grew and he set some of it aside to buy Myra a present when the child was born.

Now he could no longer ignore the presence of the child. Myra was big, and at night he felt her turning restlessly beside him. He caught her, when she thought he wasn't watching, placing her hand in the small of her back and biting her lips as she straightened up or tried to ease the pain. And although she was shy she spoke to him about the birth, telling him that he must fetch Mrs Pritchard when the time came, and make up the fire, and then go out of the house until it was all over.

'And Jonathan,' she said nervously. 'We shall need newspapers, lots of newspapers. Can you get some from Fawcetts'?'

There were always newspapers in the Fawcett kitchen, newspapers for cleaning or wrapping and, when they first came down from upstairs, Jonathan read what he could before they were snatched away from him. He felt a little uneasy about bringing them home. One book 'borrowed' from the library was permissible – he could not quite work out why, but he felt it was. Walking off every day with a bundle of newspapers made him feel both beggardly and dishonest. He resolved to ask Mr Fawcett before taking them.

He waited until Mr Fawcett was following him round the garden one day. He was an irritating, pretentious little man who was not really much good at anything. He annoyed his wife, who consequently sent him out into the garden and grounds whenever she could. There he annoyed his staff, who could do nothing about it. Jonathan, who was taking cuttings from the chrysanthemums on this particular day, bore with his employer's fatuous condescension with a mixture part pity and part knowledge that he wanted a favour from the man.

It had rained the night before, and Fawcett had to keep stopping and wiping the mud from his two-colour kidskin shoes.

'Over here, Whitman,' he said imperiously. 'Over here. This yellow one. I want several cuttings from this one.'

Jonathan finished what he was doing and then went and studied the yellow chrysanthemum.

'It's a sound plant,' he agreed. He wiped the knife on the back of his trousers and carefully took three joints from the plant, grooved and pinned them, then pressed them firmly into the box of soil.

'And this one. And this one.' Mr Fawcett had snapped off a couple of shoots himself and, imitating Jonathan's movements, he tried to groove and pin. They were not budding shoots, but obediently Jonathan pressed them into the soil, knowing that they would die within ten days. When they came to the end of the bed, Jonathan looked at Mr Fawcett and broached the subject of the newspapers. Fawcett was surprised.

'Newspapers, Whitman? Our newspapers?'

'Yes, sir. The old ones; when you've finished and they come down to the kitchen. I should like to take one or two of them home.'

Mr Fawcett looked slightly amused.

'Well, well, Whitman. This is a surprise. Are you learning to read?'

'I can read, sir.'

The smile faded from Mr Fawcett's face. He seemed annoyed.

'My word. And what kind of things do you read, Whitman?'

'Books, sir. And the Bible on Sundays.' He was treading on dangerous ground. Anxiously he waited for Mr Fawcett to ask where he got the books. Fawcett, however, was intent on trying to categorise this new information – a gardener who read. He didn't approve of education among servants. It made them restless and discontented and gave them ideas that they should have the same things that were possessed by their employers. He studied his gardener carefully. Jonathan, instinctively knowing what part he should play, slumped his shoulders a little and twisted his hat round between his hands. Then, to make it more realistic, he scratched stupidly at his head.

'What do you like to read in the papers?' Mr Fawcett asked.

'About the Queen, sir. And the texts are nice,' answered Jonathan, astutely selecting the things he felt sure Fawcett would approve of.

Suddenly Mr Fawcett perceived what a wonderful anecdote it would make. A gardener, a labourer, painstakingly spelling his way through the announcements in *The Times*, letter by letter, and pronouncing it all wrong.

'Well yes, Whitman,' he said benevolently. 'By all means take them whenever you wish.'

He wiped some more mud from his shoes and then padded towards the house. Jonathan, watching, carefully held back the shout of laughter threatening inside him. In fact he had forgotten why he wanted the newspapers, he was so delighted at his easy victory.

He took three that night and didn't bother about a book. Myra was as excited as he, and after supper she brought the lamp over to the table and they spread the sheets carefully page by page. The world swam before their eyes.

'Mr Chamberlain is bothered about the situation in South Africa.'

'The Princess of Wales received at a Drawing Room wearing a lace tea-gown backed with lavender sateen.'

'The Kaiser has sent a squadron of warships to China to punish them for killing the missionaries.'

'Where's China?' asked Myra suddenly.

'It's . . . ' He was conscious of his ignorance and felt irritated and frustrated because he did not know where China was. He did not understand the article about strategic trade or commercial expansion. He could not follow Mr Chamberlain's comments about South Africa or Kruger or the Jameson Raid.

'I don't know where China is,' he said. Myra did not appear to be unduly shocked. 'Bring a map home tomorrow, instead of a book,' she said briefly, turning to another page.

They read everything, even the advertisements. The Queen's laundress gave an unqualified testimonial for Glenfield's Starch. Carter's Little Liver Pills promised relief from almost everything. Someone called Marie Rose — 'Who's she?' — stated that the Y and N corset was far superior to all other corsets. An Aeolian harp could be purchased for only £1 11s. 6d.

'And see this,' said Jonathan incredulously. ' "In consequence of spurious imitation of Lea & Perrins Sauce, calculated to deceive the public, Lea & Perrins have adopted a new label." '

Myra was silent and he looked up to see that her face was crimson and her eyes fixed on an offensive advertisement further down that read, 'Thin Busts Perfected'. Hurriedly Jonathan turned over the page.

'Oh, Jonathan! Look! "A lady's home should have a sewing-machine. For the home-maker and lady of fashion. A small sum paid weekly under conditions of the utmost secrecy, ensures the long and instant use of this valuable article." '

She had shared a sewing-machine with her aunt for the dressmaking. Now, if she wanted to seam in a hurry, she had to go back and borrow it for a while.

'Do you want one?' Jonathan felt the godlike glow of distributing pleasure run through his veins. Myra finished reading the advertisement and then was quiet.

'No,' she said. 'No, I don't.'

She said no, but Jonathan knew she meant yes. She said no because the baby was coming and they needed the money. She said no because Jonathan had to get up two hours earlier every morning and make boots. She said no because she was Myra.

And the next morning Jonathan counted to see how much money he had from the boot business, to see if he had enough for the first payment – under conditions of the utmost secrecy. He thought about the sewing machine almost constantly during the next month, and then he had a form and a letter which was difficult to understand, but he read every word of it in case there was something he ought to know. Every day he wondered if it would come, every day he thought about the machine, about Myra's face when she saw it.

He was thinking about it when he saw Betsy coming across the Fawcett meadow towards him. He was thinking so hard about the machine that he forgot that Betsy was supposed to be in Portsmouth.

'Hullo, Betsy,' he said distantly.

'You're to come home, Jonathan. Mother's with Myra now and says you'd better come home.'

Jonathan felt his throat suddenly go dry.

'I was coming home anyway,' he said. 'She's all right, isn't she?'

Betsy looked sideways at him, a look that was uneasy and nervous.

'She's all right. But mother says you'd better come.'

He began to stride, Betsy trying to keep up with him and finally breaking into a little run alongside him.

'It's all right,' she said again, panting with the effort of running and talking at the same time. 'It's all right. Just that mother said you'd better come.'

He didn't listen and his pace grew faster and faster. Betsy's hair began to fall and she felt a pain in her side.

'Please wait, Jonathan!' she cried. 'I can't keep up with you and there's nothing you can do at home anyway. I was just sent to fetch you, that's all. You can't do anything when you get there. And I've such a pain with running!'

He stopped, halted by the urgency in her voice, and waited for her to catch up. Her face was red and her hair had come right down at the back. One hand was trying to hold it up and the other was pressed into her side.

'Sorry,' he muttered. 'Sorry, wasn't thinking.'

He let her struggle with her hair, and then he realised that she was supposed to be in Portsmouth, not helping her mother with a lying-in.

'Why, Betsy,' he said slowly. 'What are you doing here? Where's Math?'

'At sea,' said Betsy curtly. 'He's been at sea for three months this time, and while I'm paying for lodgings there I might just as well come home. And mother's finding it hard without Anne-Louise, but she would go to London, she would go. So I thought I'd come home for a spell.'

Jonathan felt uncomfortable in the face of Betsy's obvious discontent. He knew she had seen Mathew only four times since their marriage; the rest of the time he had been at sea and Betsy had worked as outside help in a Portsmouth hotel. And now she was, apparently, needed once more to help with the family. When he considered his time with Myra he felt ashamed.

'It's nice to see you back, Betsy. I'm glad you're here to help Myra. She always liked you better . . . ' Embarrassed, he realised he had been on the point of mentioning Anne-Louise. Betsy took no notice.

'Yes, well,' she said bluntly, 'I suppose I'm useful in the village.'

Awkwardly he patted her hand, wishing he could comfort her because he liked her and felt sorry for her.

Mrs Pritchard was heating a bucket of water on the range when he went in.

'I shall want a lot more wood,' she said importantly. 'And you can help by keeping the buckets filled. It'll save me running outside to the pump all the time. But don't get in the way. And I shall want some bricks.'

Humbly he nodded, feeling useless and somehow guilty. 'Is she all right?'

'Yes.' Mrs Pritchard's face was turned away as she lifted the bucket from the stove.

'Can I see her?'

'Don't stay up there long.'

Myra was lying with her eyes closed, her face looked thin and yellow compared with the gross swell of the sheet over her body. Her hair was wispy and clung in little strands close to her damp forehead, and her wrists, sticking out from the long-sleeved nightdress, looked unusually thin and helpless.

'Myra?'

Her eyes opened and she smiled, the movement of her lips showed just how colourless they were.

'Help Mrs Pritchard, Jonathan.'

'I will, Myra. I will.'

She closed her eyes again and he thought she had gone to sleep. Then, as she moved slightly in the bed she realised she was hiding her discomfort from him.

'Have you been . . . ill for long, Myra?'

She didn't answer, just kept her eyes closed and her body still. He waited until she was ready and could look at him again.

'Since this morning, when you left.'

He nodded. 'Shall I go?'

She smiled at him again, like a child, a small pale child, and he wanted to cry. She raised her hand to take his and he was aware of just how fragile her hand was, and how the forefinger was rough with the marks of a needle.

'Look after Mrs Pritchard.'

'I will, Myra.'

'And Betsy. Poor Betsy. Make a cup of tea for Betsy.'

76

Again she closed her eyes and he watched colour drain from her face until she looked like the wax figure of an old woman. He couldn't stand it any more and he got up and went softly from the room.

'She's all right, isn't she?' he asked Mrs Pritchard in the kitchen.

'Of course. Betsy's going to get your supper, and then you'll have to sleep on the sofa in case I need you to get more wood for me.'

They sat and ate together, he and Betsy, and the room had never seemed so silent. Betsy was lost in some private thoughts of her own, but when she remembered him she darted a quick uncomfortable look towards him, and then stared hard into the fire. There was no sound from upstairs, only the soft murmur of Mrs Pritchard's voice and the sound of her footsteps over the ceiling.

Towards the early hours of the morning he heard Myra moan. It was the first sound she had made, and a hard, terrible knot formed inside his stomach, a knot that clenched, and turned, and then rose up to his throat. He got up and went outside to get more wood, although there was plenty already on the fire. When he came back, Betsy was downstairs and she looked tired and drawn.

'I'm going back home for a while,' she said wearily. 'Just to see if the children are all right. I'll be back before you go to fetch the milk.'

He nodded and she lifted the latch on the kitchen door and went out into the pale light. He followed her and watched her trudging up the lane, pulling her thin coat round her and shivering in the morning air. He waited until she was out of sight, then went into the shed and began to fit leather over the boot-last and wax the thread for stitching.

Betsy was back before he left for the milk and to go to Fawcetts'. He'd made tea and porridge for her and Mrs Pritchard and then he said good-bye. Betsy at last had reached out from her unhappiness and was aware of his strained misery.

'Don't worry, Jonathan,' she said kindly. 'I'll come and fetch you the minute it's necessary.'

He grinned and nodded. 'I'll be home midday.'

Mr Fawcett wouldn't leave him alone that morning. He was especially irritating, which, no doubt, was why his wife had sent him into the garden. Jonathan, usually able to temper his impatience with humour and caution found himself wanting to tell the little man to go away, to leave him alone and pursue his vanities and his fatuous pretensions elsewhere.

At midday the child had still not been born and he could hear Myra crying, not screaming, but crying, and again the knot rose, twisted and hurt him.

That evening, when he returned, Mrs Pritchard was waiting in the kitchen. Her eyes were circled with blue shadows and the round curves of her face hung in sagging lines.

'Can you afford the doctor, Jonathan?'

He wasn't surprised. All the time he had known that something was going to happen, something terrible that would bring an end to the good things between him and Myra. The knot was there all the time now, sick and heavy in the pit of his stomach.

'She's bad, isn't she?'

Mrs Pritchard closed her eyes for a second. 'If you can afford it, I think the doctor should come.'

They sent Betsy. Perhaps he should have gone himself, but he was frightened to leave in case Myra died while he was gone. Mrs Pritchard leaned heavily against the door and then began to walk slowly up the stairs.

'Can I see her?' Jonathan asked, and she nodded.

There was newspaper – Mr Fawcett's newspaper – spread all round the bed and two bricks were jammed under the bottom legs of the bedstead. The sheet was screwed and untidy, completely untucked from the mattress all the way round. Myra's feet stuck out from the bottom. They didn't look any different, they were white and small and just like her feet always looked.

On the tallboy was a piece of torn sheeting with scissors and a bowl and some other things. A bucket stood by the head of the bed and, as he waited by the door, Myra suddenly turned and retched uselessly into the bucket. When she saw him she took no notice at all, she moaned once and lay back against the pillow. She wasn't pretty any more. Her cheeks had sunk to the shape of a skull and her hair, the soft, brown hair, was wet and putty coloured. Her eyes were blind and unseeing, glazed and sunk deeply back into her head.

'Can't I do anything, Myra?' he asked, agonised. She didn't answer, and her feet suddenly twisted at the foot of the bed. Wetness splashed down on to his hands.

'Please don't die, Myra.' She couldn't hear him, but he had to say it, because it might make a difference, the fact that he had said it out loud. When she turned over towards the bucket again, he left the room.

Mrs Pritchard was sitting on the sofa with her head resting on the table, and when he saw how tired she was, and how she admitted – by her request for the doctor – that she could do nothing more for Myra, his fear grew big again, huge and agonised inside his breast.

'Is she going to die?'

'Wait for the doctor,' she said wearily, too tired to pretend with him, too tired to lie and comfort him.

Silently they waited, not speaking, for there was nothing to say. The water hissed and steamed on the stove and, from above their heads, came the intermittent sound of Myra's agony. Through Jonathan's head, like a litany, ran the names of the women who had died in childbirth over the last five years. 'Maud Payne, her fifth child. Elizabeth Johnson, seventeen years old, her first. Mrs Wrexham, forty-two, her ninth. Mrs Caine, her first.' The names jumbled and confused themselves in Jonathan's mind. He tried to remember the faces of the women, but they were blurred and confused, and finally they all converged into the face of Myra, lying on the bed upstairs.

'Maud Payne,' he muttered. 'She was fair, yes, she was fair. Mrs Caine was thin and walked with a limp. No. That was another one, not Mrs Caine.'

He saw that Mrs Pritchard was staring at him, but now it had become terribly important to remember what the women looked like. If he could remember, then Myra would not die.

'Maud Payne, Elizabeth Johnson, Alice Caine . . .'

'Stop it, Jonathan,' said Mrs Pritchard suddenly.

'Mary Wrexham, Elizabeth Johnson, Maud . . .'

'Stop it!' He didn't really hear what she said, nothing impinged on his consciousness until he felt the blow on the side of his head. Mrs Pritchard stood over him angrily.

'There's enough to do upstairs without this. Stop it because you're not helping. You're not helping me or Myra.'

Her good-natured face registered irritation and common sense. He felt ashamed of himself. 'I'll make some tea,' he muttered. 'I'll make some tea for Betsy and the doctor.'

The doctor didn't stop in the kitchen. Whatever Betsy had told him on the way across the fields made him walk straight past Jonathan and hurry up the stairs in front of Mrs Pritchard. They were gone a long time, and when he came down his coat was off and so was his collar. He poured some of the hot water into the basin and washed his hands.

'It's a forceps delivery,' he said bluntly. 'And I don't think we can save the child.'

'What about Myra? What about my wife?'

'I'll do the best I can.' He paused and stared hard at Jonathan. 'You should have called me yesterday. You stiff-necked villagers make me angry. You can turn your back on the Church if you like, be your own theologians if you must. But when will you learn that you can't be your own doctors?'

He wanted to hit the doctor. To punch him hard in the mouth so that his teeth cracked, to knock him down on to the floor and stand over him shouting that it was money, not stiff-necked pride, that killed the women. His frustration and contempt boiled to danger point, all the resentment he had for Fawcett and the Rector and the magistrates who had made him run to join the army boiled into a huge bursting sore of resentment. They didn't know, and most of them didn't care. They said the women died because of dirt or ignorance or stupidity. They never admitted it might be poverty that killed them. And when they were called in at the end, to watch and help the women die, they sent their bills in just the same. They took the money as their right for being present and legitimatising the death.

The doctor turned his back and dropped a metal instrument into the boiling water. He was thin and severe, with long side-whiskers and a lantern jaw. Jonathan hated him.

The doctor told him to carry the bucket upstairs and then said impatiently, 'That's all. You can go now.' He took the bucket from Jonathan and closed the bedroom door.

Again he sat and waited. It was nearly eleven at night and Myra had been in labour for forty-two hours. Betsy had gone upstairs with her mother. He was alone.

He was alone when Myra screamed, not the hysterical, jerky scream of a frightened woman or a silly one. Just one long terrible scream that reminded him of a fox before the dogs close in. The scream faded thinly away and was swallowed in the low rumble of the doctor's voice. He heard a child cry and then that too abruptly ceased. Ten minutes later Betsy came into the room with something in her arms.

'It's a little girl, Jonathan,' she said gently.

'What's he done to Myra?'

'She's still alive. He thinks she'll be all right.' She held the child towards him. 'And the little girl is all right too. She's badly hurt at the moment, but he managed to keep her alive.' She reached across and placed the baby in his hands.

He looked at the child and felt nothing, only a vague surprise that this small, bruised, helpless shape should have caused Myra so much pain, so much agony.

'Can I see Myra?'

'Not now, dear. The doctor hasn't finished.'

Dully he handed the child back to her, not knowing, not really caring that it was his. Betsy took it in her arms and crooned softly to the small damaged face. Through his apathy and tired concern he was aware, once more, of pity for Betsy. She stopped talking to the baby, remembering something she had to tell him.

'I forgot, Jonathan, a box came yesterday afternoon, just when Myra was getting bad. I told the men to put it in the shed.'

It was the sewing-machine. The present for Myra. He wondered why he could not feel excited about it any more.

When the letter came for Anne-Louise she knew what it was about, she recognised Betsy's large, round childish print and she knew that Jonathan's child had been born. Florrie, the other parlour-maid, looked at her curiously as she stood with the letter in her hand, frightened to open it.

'Who's yer letter from?' Florrie was insensitive and blatantly bad-mannered.

'My sister.'

'Ain't yer going to open it then?'

'Not now.' Florrie sniffed and turned away offended.

'All right then. Have yer secrets. I don't care.' She began to flounce out of the pantry where they were cleaning the silver. 'By the by,' she added spitefully, 'the mistress saw the table-cloth where you spilled the port last night and I had to tell her it was you that done it.' She slammed the pantry door and Anne-Louise waited to see if she would come back. When five minutes had elapsed she tore the letter open. There was a lot of uninteresting preamble, about her mother and Will and Frankie. Some more about Betsy herself that Anne threw impatiently on to the table. Then she saw Jonathan's name leap from the page.

. . . a poor little girl they are calling Harriet. Myra is still very sickly and has to have someone in every day. Jonathan asked his sister to help, but she has got odd since she went to live with the Vincents and said No, and wouldn't even let him come into the house. She said the sight of him would make Miss Thalia have another epileptic. So I am helping out there every day for as long as I can. I might just as well as Mathew won't be home for a long spell again. I suppose I shall go back to Portsmouth when the ship docks, but I don't never want to live with the Bunts again. Mr Bunts drank and though I never told Math or Mother, he was horrible when he was drunk. That was why I went as a daily, so as not to be in the house with him during the day.

Jonathan is working in Major Finch's garden every evening after he's left Fawcetts', to get the money for the doctor. He bought Myra a sewing-machine, but he won't send it back, even though it would pay the bills. He is very quiet and doesn't listen to what mother and I say. He keeps looking at those newspapers Mr Fawcett gives him and don't talk much, at least not while I am there. The baby is small and quiet too. I wish she was mine.

Your loving sister,
Betsy

Resentment, bitter, acid resentment rose slowly in her throat and spread sourly throughout her body. She reread the last page of the letter, the part about the sewing-machine, and her resentment turned to rage, rage that made her sweep her hand across the table violently and send the silver, the spoons, the forks, the epergne, crashing to the floor. The noise relieved nothing of her fury, and she stood abruptly and kicked the heap of cutlery so that it scattered about the floor.

'I hate them! I hate them!' she hissed. 'Why couldn't she die? Why didn't mother let her die so that I could go home to him?'

Tears of self-pity flooded into her eyes and and she slumped back on to her chair and leaned her head on the table to cry, finding a temporary outlet in the loud and extravagant sobbing to which she abandoned herself.

She heard Florrie's footsteps racing along the passage and then the door burst open and Florrie, fair-complexioned and large-featured, put her foot into a small pile of forks just inside the door.

'Gawd! Whatever was that crash? Mistress nearly went mad. She's got company and . . . ' She was always slow to absorb things, and it took her some time to notice that Anne-Louise was crying, noisily and dramatically.

'Here. What's the matter then?' she finished feebly. Anne did not answer. Having an audience made her grief all the sadder, and her loneliness more poignant. Florrie looked uncomfortable.

'You're not crying because I told the Mistress about spilling the port, are yer?'

Anne-Louise stopped long enough to snap, 'Of course not. I wouldn't get upset over a stupid thing like that.' She began to cry again, but the strength of her paroxysm had gone and she contented herself with a gentle, occasional sob. Florrie suddenly caught sight of the letter on the table.

'Oh, Gawd!' she gasped, clapping her hand over her mouth. 'It ain't your folks, is it? I mean you ain't lost your ma or anything, 'ave yer?'

'No.' She had a sudden twinge of conscience for what she had just thought about Myra. Naturally, she didn't *really* wish Myra, or anyone, dead. If Myra had died she would have been as sorry as everybody else. And she'd have gone home to attend the burial and to tell Jonathan how sorry she was and how she and Myra had always liked one another.

'No, my mother is all right.'

'Then what . . . 'ere, it's a feller. That's why you're upset. It's a feller. He's gone and let yer down, ain't 'e?' Florrie, who was slow in most things, was not slow when it came to grasping the habits and wiles of the opposite sex. As Anne-Louise recommenced her orgy of self-pity she gave a smug, self-satisfied nod.

'Ain't they all alike, the bastards?' she said fatalistically. Anne was so shocked that she stopped crying and stared at Florrie.

'Well, they are,' said Florrie sheepishly. 'They're all the same, every one of them. 'Ere,' Her eyes brightened suddenly. 'Come out with me this evening and cheer yerself up.'

'No, thank you,' sniffed Anne-Louise.

'Oh, come on. There's a smashing programme at the Brixton Empress. Kate Carney's on, and Datas the memory man. Come on out and 'ave a good time.'

'I couldn't!' said Anne, appalled.

She knew that Florrie went to such places, of course, but then Florrie was worldly and given to a life of immorality, attending music-halls and, on one occasion, going into a public house.

'Chaa!' shrugged Florrie disparagingly. 'You never go anywhere. You've been here two months and the only place you go is that old Meeting you 'ave on Sundays. All that religion 'asn't done you no good neither. You've lost yer feller, ain't yer? Take my advice.' She leaned against the door and folded her arms in a superior, irritating kind of way. 'You take my advice and go out a bit. Fellers don't like a girl what's always praying and going to Meetings and things. They like someone with a bit of life. 'Struth! I don't know 'ow you stick it 'ere with the old girl so mean and the food so rotten. It's only me days off that keeps me alive in this miserable hole.'

It *was* a miserable hole, and Anne's habitual discontent was not improved by the condition of the household in which she found herself. Because, all her life, she had got what she wanted provided she put her mind to it, she was the more dismayed because in one year she had lost both Jonathan and a good position in service.

When Jonathan had married she had determined to prove to the village that she had never wanted him, that she wanted no man who was a gardener, who was unsophisticated and a countryman. And indeed, once the idea had taken hold, it became more than a show of strength against Jonathan. She became obsessed with the idea that London was the place to which she was suited, the place where quick wits and smart people would recognise her as more than a village girl, more than a rectory parlour-maid.

She had, with her usual tenacity of purpose, set about finding herself a position in London. With impertinent daring she had visited her aunt, the one who lived in Camberwell and to whom Betsy, as a child, had proudly returned the half-sovereign. She had demanded assistance in seeking a London post and, because she always got her way, because she was strong and violent in character and it was difficult to stand against her, the old woman had done her best and found her a position.

She had lasted six months. Her quick, neat appearance and her sharp ways had at first pleased the new mistress. Subsequently she found Anne-Louise irritating in her superiority and, finally, impertinent. Parlour-maids were plentiful and, for a good house, it was possible to take one's pick of several suitable girls. Anne-Louise was kindly told that she would do better elsewhere, that she would be given a reference praising her work and cleanliness, and that there were several acquaintances who were looking for maids and who would be prepared to give her a trial. Anne-Louise's temper had refused the introductions, and for two anxious weeks she had endeavoured to find a situation for herself. She had succeeded, thanks to the recommendation of one of the members of the London Meeting, but the house was a mean one, mean at least so far as the servants were concerned. The wages were only just enough, the time off a little less than normal, and the food sparse and extremely poor in quality.

Anne-Louise was astonished on her first afternoon to see Florrie cutting up the cake to take into the drawing-room. As she cut each slice she then pared off a wafer-thin piece which she stuffed into her mouth. She did it all along the cake which was loaf-shaped, taking a sliver of the gateau between each piece and then carefully arranging the rest on a plate with a small gap between the slices. Florrie had looked at Anne-Louise and grinned.

'It's the only way you'll get anything to eat,' she said cheerfully. 'But, mind, you can only do it with long cakes, not round ones. I tried it with round ones and the old girl pushed the pieces together when she got it in the drawing-room and that did it. She saw the cake didn't fit properly.'

Anne-Louise, at first scornful, had quickly learned how to supplement their diet. She learned, with Florrie, to throw a spoonful of the 'kitchen jam' – the pips and skins sieved from making blackberry jelly that was boiled up with more sugar for the kitchen staff – away into the dustbin each morning so that the mistress would think they were eating it and therefore not be so observant of the falling level of the household jars. She learned to take the minced meat from a shepherd's pie, replace it with carrot and breadcrumbs, and use the stolen meat to fry up a rissole that she and Florrie would share between them in the evening. She was at first astounded, then disgusted, for whatever her personal faults she was, like the majority of country people – however poor – contemptuous of those who were ungenerous with food. She had never, even in a family living only just above the line of bare existence, eaten quite so badly.

When she came into the kitchen that evening, the evening after the letter had arrived, Florrie was standing at the stove unwrapping a small newspaper parcel. She stood by Florrie and watched to see what was inside. There were two kippers.

'Gawd,' said Florrie vehemently. 'A kipper each for our dinner, and she said we're to give the cat what's left.'

The cat, a lean scarecrow of an animal, tried to claw at the kippers.

'Poor devil,' said Florrie without pity. 'He'll 'ave to manage without again, I'm afraid. I can't give 'im none of mine.'

The kippers were small, not worth dirtying the plate for, and the two girls sat picking the scraps of flesh off the bones.

'Oh, come on,' said Florrie suddenly. 'Come to the Brixton Empress. At least it's warm there and I might see a feller I know who'll buy us a baked potato outside.'

'I'm not allowed to go to those places,' said Anne-Louise without conviction in her voice.

'Who's to know?'

'Is it very wicked inside?'

Florrie shrugged and rolled her eyes to the ceiling. 'Well, it's a bit more lively than 'ere. Oh, come on.' She nudged Anne in the side with her elbow. 'Kate Carney's smashing, sings lovely songs, she does. I think she's better than Marie Lloyd.'

The desire to live wickedly smote Anne-Louise in full strength. After all, she *was* different from the rest of her family, she was different from the other girls in the village. Life was there to be embraced in all its glorious, evil splendour. And hanging over the temptation to sin lurked the shape of a baked potato.

'All right. I'll come,' she said decisively. 'What shall I wear?'

Florrie, animated by the thought of an unexpected evening

out, fell at once into a mood of festivity.

'Let's dress up and make a pop of it. I'll put me ostrich-feather dress on and me black jet hat. Shall I lend you something of mine? You 'aven't got anything nice, 'ave you?'

'I've got a red silk dress,' said Anne slowly.

Florrie looked disconcerted, then envious. 'You never showed me,' she said accusingly. 'You could've offered to lend it to me, couldn't you?'

'It's a special dress.' She remembered how special it was, not the bad part about taking Betsy's money. She'd forgotten that already, but she remembered walking up the church with Jonathan looking at her.

'Well, it's a special evening,' said Florrie, recovering her exuberance quickly. 'So wear it.'

She threw the plates into the sink and left them with a muttered, 'We'll do them when we come home', and then she was off up the stairs. Anne heard her voice disappearing in the distance.

'Oh, Mr Porter, what shall I do . . . '

When Anne came down in the crimson silk dress Florrie's lower jaw dropped. 'Blimey,' she said unflatteringly. 'You ain't 'alf bad-looking when you're dressed up. You won't 'ave no bother getting a feller. Come on now, it's quite a walk if we want to make the first house.'

They sneaked quietly out of the back door and up the area steps and then Florrie stepped out briskly towards the Brixton Empress. Anne-Louise felt better almost at once. A couple of passing mashers looked back and winked at the girls. Florrie giggled and Anne-Louise tossed her head regally, feeling delighted at the attention. When they got to the Empress, years of obedience to the worship of a God who forbade the entering of music-halls, theatres and public houses made her grow suddenly weak in the legs. A brief terror made her consider the possibility that, if she went inside, the Lord would punish her by sending the roof crashing down on her sinful head. She held back for just a second, but it was too late. Florrie had plumped herself at the end of a queue formed mostly of small, ragged boys and pairs of young men and women, all eyeing each other disdainfully but speculatively. Anne pulled the skirt of her dress out of the way of three unpleasantly dirty urchins.

'It's all right inside, isn't it?' she asked nervously.

'Oh, stop worrying, do!' Florrie was sizing up a young man in front of them in a blue jacket with a velvet collar. The young man turned round suddenly and was seen to have a squint in his right eye. Florrie immediately lost interest.

'Course it's all right,' she said enthusiastically. ' 'Ere, watch out now, they're opening the window.'

There was a sudden, fantastic surge from all round. The queue swept forward and Anne and Florrie with it. The gaggle of small boys suddenly hurled themselves past the ticket window and up the stone stairs to the gallery in a solid, menacing tidal wave. The doorman shouted and managed to catch a couple, who were promptly booted out into the street. The rest had escaped and mingled with the legitimate ticket-buyers. Anne found herself bowling up the stairs at an incredible speed. She was frightened, out of breath, and concerned that her dress might be dirtied or torn. When they reached the gallery she was hastily pushed down on to one of the wooden planks stretching across stone struts.

'Grab yer seat and stay on it,' said Florrie hoarsely. Anne sat rigidly on the hard plank. She was terrified to move in case she should draw attention to herself by her ignorance of what happened. The place was full, every plush row downstairs and every wooden row upstairs was packed with osprey-feather hats, boas, leg-of-mutton sleeves, high stiff collars, check waistcoats and gold watchchains. The noise was deafening, and in front of her, stretching up from the gallery rail to the ceiling, was a network of wire mesh. She felt as though she were in a bird cage hanging from the roof.

'What's the wire for?' she whispered to Florrie.

'So as the ginger beer bottles can't be thrown at the stage,' said Florrie bluntly. 'And the kids drop cow-heel into the pit as well, if they get half a chance.'

Through the wire she could see, hanging from the centre dome, a glowing, vibrant, shimmering chandelier, moving slowly in a haze of heat and strong smells. At the front, on a canvas curtain, was depicted a garden and a rose-covered bower.

There was music, loud thumping music, and she had to lean forward to see who was making the music. Seven black-coated gentlemen were sitting in a hole just in front of the stage. The music ascended, thumped, jollied itself up and down. Feet began to tap, voices began to sing the familiar tune, a tune that Anne-Louise had never heard before.

'How do they *know?*' she whispered. 'How do they know what the orchestra will play?' Florrie sniffed.

'They always play the same old things,' she said disparagingly

'But it's wonderful!'

Florrie grinned smugly.

'You wait,' she said. 'You 'aven't seen nothing yet.'

Someone sitting in the row in front, a few seats along, turned and stared at the girls. Florrie kicked furtively at Anne-Louise's foot.

' 'E keeps looking at us, that feller in the check waistcoat. Wonder if it's you or me 'e fancies.'

Anne-Louise darted a quick look along the row; a blond head with very elegant sideboards showed over an exceptionally high starched collar. The profile turned and stared at Anne-Louise. He had a fancy yellow waistcoat and a Prince Albert moustache. He stared at Anne-Louise, then raised one hand and stroked the long silky whiskers adorning his upper lip.

'It's you!' nudged Florrie. 'You're the one 'e's got 'is eye on. See, 'e's turning round again. Bet 'e speaks to you in the interval.'

Anne-Louise sat haughtily upright, holding her white neck as high as she could and imperiously ignoring the man in the yellow waistcoat, who, now that he had caught her attention, made no secret of the fact that he was blatantly staring at her. Now and again Anne darted a keen, quick look at him and then lowered her eyes disparagingly. She began to talk loudly and with animation to Florrie.

When the curtain went up she was so amazed, so stupefied and swept into a strange dazzling world, that she forgot all about the masher with the Prince Albert moustache.

The Ten Terpischoreans, clad in satin ball gowns with incredible low neck-lines performed a graceful and intricate dance. Anne-Louise considered it most ladylike (apart from the neck-lines) and was startled and hurt when the gentlemen of the audience shouted and whistled at the girls. They did the same for the baritone who sang, 'Why should we wait for tomorrow, when you're queen of my heart tonight?', and then Anne saw the value of the mesh-wire wall separating the gallery from the rest of the theatre. A shower of orange peel, stone bottles and old bones aimed at the baritone rebounded off the wire and spattered the front rows of the gallery. There was shouting from the pit below as some of the smaller items slipped through the mesh. The baritone was pulled hastily from the stage and, as the sketch came on, the audience quieted to at thrill of anticipatory tension.

The sketch was brilliant and breathtaking and concerned the fate of a young bride married to a killer who was trying to strangle her on her wedding night. It was most realistic, and when, at the end, the villain leapt from a cupboard and pulled a purple scarf over his young bride's face, Anne-Louise, together with a large part of the rest of the audience, screamed. The curtain came down, hats were straightened, glasses refilled with stout or Guinness or porter. The masher in the front row was suddenly in front of them, leaning over the back of the seat towards them.

'Could I get you ladies something to drink?' he asked silkily.

Anne-Louise stared straight ahead, then she lifted her right hand and casually fluffed up the ruffles of cream lace at the neck of her dress.

'A small glass of port, perhaps?' persevered the masher.

Anne-Louise didn't answer. Florrie giggled.

'Sooner 'ave a glass of stout, meself,' she said.

'And your friend?' Silky Whiskers raised an interrogative eyebrow at Anne-Louise, who faltered slightly and wondered what her next move should be.

'She'll 'ave the same,' said Florrie quickly, before Anne could protest.

The masher moved into instant action. 'Right,' he said, having won the first round, and speedily disappeared along the row.

'I don't drink!' said Anne-Louise.

'That don't matter. Just 'old it in your 'and and give a sip now and again. Wait 'til 'e's got the drinks and then perhaps 'e'll ask us if we want something to eat.'

'Should we offer to pay?'

Alarm registered in Florrie's face. 'Don't be daft! 'E knows what 'e's doing. 'E didn't 'ave to buy us nothing, did 'e?'

The masher returned bearing two glasses and accompanied by a 'friend', a stocky, dark young man in a check suit and a green tie.

'This is my friend 'Erbert,' said Yellow Waistcoat. 'And my name is Maxie.' He waited and stared at Anne-Louise, who accepted her glass of stout and sat holding it uneasily between her two hands.

'I'm Florrie.' Florrie giggled again and looked at the stocky young man in the green tie. Maxie waited for Anne-Louise. When she didn't answer he said, 'Bet your name's Topsy.'

'It's Anne-Louise!' she answered, insulted into replying.

'That's pretty. I like your hat.'

She raised her hands and dabbed at the hat, refixing the pins and smoothing back the feathers.

'You're not drinking your stout.'

She took a sip and managed not to grimace. It was thick and very bitter and she wondered how she was going to get rid of it.

'Like the acts?'

'It's wonderful!' said Anne, forgetting her superior airs with the masher in the enthusiasm of the evening. 'I liked the memory man. He was ever so clever.'

'And I nearly died in the sketch,' said Florrie. 'You know, when 'e got 'is long, boney 'ands round 'er neck from be'ind. All that suspense made me feel quite 'ungry.'

The masher knew when the ball had been tossed into his court.

'Bert,' he said to Check suit, 'nip outside and get a couple of pig's trotters for the ladies.' He fished in his pockets and, with a flourish, handed Bert a coin. Anne-Louise couldn't help noticing it was a florin.

'You come from far, then?' asked Maxie.

'Kennington.'

'We come that way ourselves. On yer own, aren't yer?'

'We came together,' said Anne haughtily.

The orchestra filed out into the pit again and this time Anne-Louise was able to recognise the music as the same tune they had played at the beginning. Bert came in with two hot paper parcels just as the curtain went up on Captain Joe Woodward and his performing seals. Maxie thrust one of the packets at each of them, hissed, 'See you at the end, then,' and went back to his seat.

Anne, her glass of stout tucked neatly under her seat, chewed greasily at the trotter. There wasn't a lot of meat on it but, compared with the way she had been eating over the past few weeks, it resembled a full-scale meal. She paid as much attention as she could to the seals and the comedian that followed and then the acrobats, and was conscious of Florrie noisily sucking her trotter bones beside her. By the time they reached the top of the bill, the fabulous Kate Carney herself, they had both deposited greasy packets of bones underneath their seats.

When the star performer came on to the stage the audience roared. Dressed in a coster's suit with mother-of-pearl buttons and coloured feathers, she strutted the stage, singing and turning before the audience, taking their praise, their adulation, their applause. Anne leaned forward in her seat, straining every muscle in her arms and legs with the fantastic woman on the stage. She saw how wonderful it would be to have everyone looking at you, everyone cheering and clapping for you, everyone admiring you. She listened and watched the singer, intently, passionately, until finally she *was* Kate Carney. She was the one they all admired. The one who was the centre of attention and the one who could do no wrong.

Kate Carney took off her hat and sang again, but this time it was a quieter song, a very sad song that was answered by a small boy clad in rags that were realistically rent in inoffensive places . . . 'Mother, I love you, I can work for two. Don't let those tears roll down your cheek. I'll bring my wages every week. Mother, I love you. What more could a loving son do? You've worked for me a long, long time. So now I can work for you. . . .'

The audience were hushed and Anne felt a big sad lump in her throat. The small boys in the gallery wriggled uncomfortably, torn between derision and honest emotion. The lady on Anne's right pulled out a dirty handkerchief and loudly blew her nose. When the song was finished, a small rustle of gratified synthetic grief ran through the theatre and then Kate went into her last rousing song, gave a final twirl to her feather hat, took six curtains, and the evening was over.

When the curtain finally fell for the last time Anne-Louise could not move. She felt she had lived a whole life since she and Florrie had left the kitchen three hours earlier. She sat in her seat, numb and adrift with glorious dreams of appearing on a music-hall and having all the men call and shout for her. She felt Florrie poke her violently in the side.

' 'Urry up. Those fellers are waiting at the end of the row.'

Maxie and Bert were leaning against the wall and letting the people push round and past them. When Anne and Florrie eased into the gangway, Maxie said, 'Ah, there you are then,' as though it had all been arranged. In pairs they filed out of the theatre, milling on to the pavement in a huge spill of sweat and noise. Maxie took Anne's arm and guided her through the crowd.

'What about 'aving a drink?' he said when they were joined by Florrie and Bert.

'Oh, no!' She blurted the words out before she could stop herself, and then was furious because she knew it made her look silly and inexperienced. To her surprise Florrie backed her up.

'We'd better get home,' she said moodily. 'We're not supposed to be out anyway, and there'll be a right old set-to if we're caught.'

'We'll walk you home then,' said Maxie. He still had hold of Anne's arm, and she was nervously aware of his sweaty hand gripping her arm tightly against his side.

They began walking. Two well-spaced couples just out of listening distance.

'You in service?'

'That's right.'

'You're from the country, aren't you?'

She was annoyed because, from the tone of his voice, he obviously thought her an overawed bumpkin up in the city.

'Oh, I've been in London some time now,' she said airily. 'Course, it's not as exciting as working in the country. I was in an estate house, you see, and they were always having receptions and balls and so on. There's nothing like that much in London.'

Maxie stared impersonally at her for a moment and then said, 'I work in the market, in Billingsgate. Bert's my mate there.'

She wasn't sure where or what Billingsgate was, but she shrugged as though it was of no consequence.

'You're different from your friend,' he said suddenly. 'You've got quite a bit of style about you. Your friend's all right, but she's quite ordinary really.'

'Oh, she's not my friend,' said Anne hastily, anxious that the impression left by the vulgar Florrie should not be in any way associated with her. 'We just work together, that's all.'

There were plenty of hansoms about and quite a few young men on bicycles. They walked in silence for some way before turning off the main road into a side street. Anne-Louise looked back to see if Florrie and Bert were following and was alarmed to see they had disappeared.

'We'd better wait for the others,' she said uneasily.

Maxie laughed. 'Don't be a daisy. Come on, they know what they're about.' He squeezed her hand and pulled her into his side for a moment, so that she caught a sudden whiff of something vaguely unpleasant, but she couldn't say quite what it was. He let go of her arm, but before she had time to feel relieved he had dropped his hand round her waist and pressed her even closer to him.

'I don't think you'd better do that,' she said nervously.

'You've not 'alf got a bad figure. Better than your friend.'

'I go up here,' she said, turning quickly round into the street where she worked, feeling glad that they had arrived home and ignoring what he said about her figure. 'The third house.'

At the top of the area steps she pulled away and held her hand out towards him. 'Thank you for walking me home,' she said. 'And the drink and the trotter and everything. And I'll say good night now.'

'All right, love.' She opened the gate and walked down the steps. She was horrified when he followed her.

'You can't come down here,' she whispered. 'The mistress'll go mad if she sees you here.'

'That's all right,' he said heavily. 'I'm going in a minute.'

Down in the area he stood close because there was hardly any room and she realised how very big he was. She hadn't realised before. She tried to open the door quietly and he put his hand out and held it shut.

'Just a minute.'

'I've got to go in.' The smell was closer now and she decided she definitely didn't like him. In the theatre it had been fun, having him staring at her and saying her name was pretty, but here, with his hand pressing on her shoulder and his face so close, she could feel his breath. It was unpleasant and slightly frightening.

'Come on, then,' he said, moving closer and slipping his arm round her back.

'I've got to go in.' She pulled away from him and, as though it was that he had been waiting for, he suddenly pressed right up close to her and pushed his mouth against hers. She struggled and tried to pull her arms out from the circle of his, but he had her jammed hard against the door.

'Come on, come on.' He was breathing noisily, so noisily she

96

began to worry that the mistress might hear. She tried to pull away again, quietly and without fuss.

With a horrified sense of violation she suddenly felt his hands move from her back and squeeze her breasts.

'Let me go! Let me go!'

Roughly he pulled her round to the small area of brick wall that bridged the gap between the door and the window. She found she was pushed up hard against the brickwork, held fast by the tight pressure of his body. His hands squeezed again and as he pushed his legs close to her, something large and unpleasant moved against her dress.

'Let me go! I'll shout if you don't let me go!' She began to struggle violently now, the concern of concealing her presence from her mistress swallowed up in the greater fear of the large, fumbling man who had her pinned against the wall.

'You didn't scream when you were drinking the stout, did you? Or when I said I'd walk you home?' he demanded hoarsely. His hands were moving over her body with a curious, greedy movement. Quickly she brought her foot up and kicked him hard on the shin.

'Chaa! You bitch! You high and mighty little bitch!'

Her hat came off and she was really frightened because the kick had unleashed his temper. He pounded her body so hard with his hands that her shoulders recoiled from the wall. He tried to pull her skirt up and she beat her fists uselessly against him, shouting and crying at him to stop. Again she was able to kick, hard and violently, in the groin. At the same time he reached his hand to the cream ruffles, tearing the bodice of her dress in one furious movement.

Through her humiliation and fear she heard the sound of running feet and then Florrie's voice at the top of the area steps in a terrified stage whisper.

'Gawd! What do you think you two are doing? For Gawd's sake stop shouting will yer?'

She ran down the steps and tried to pull the panting figure of Max away. Anne was crying.

'If the mistress 'ears any of this we'll all be out. And I'll reckon she'll 'ave the police 'ere as well.' Maxie suddenly quieted. 'You get 'ome!' she spat at him. 'You dirty bastard, clear off!'

He looked at Anne, and then at Florrie, his face distorted with male frustration and rage.

'Go on,' hissed Florrie. 'Clear off, or I'll get the police meself.'

'Tarts!' he shouted. 'That's what you are, tarts!' He ran up the steps, avoiding Florrie's arm, which swung round to hit him across the side of the head.

'Tarts!' They heard his footsteps running away down the street until it was all silent. Trembling, the two girls waited, listening for the sound to come from inside, the sound of an infuriated woman opening the kitchen door to see what had happened. The minute stretched into five and everything was quiet. Florrie slowly released her breath.

'I don't know 'ow it 'appened,' she whispered, 'but somehow we've got away with it. Come on, let's get upstairs quick before anything else goes wrong.'

She led the way into the kitchen and up the stairs to their attic bedrooms. Anne-Louise began to feel sick, and when she reached her room she sat down on the bed and began to retch.

Her dress was ripped right down the neck on one side. It was ruined and the frills were filthy from the rough, dirty hands of the masher. Her body felt filthy too, dirty and bruised. She lay back on the bed, stuffing the pillow in her mouth to stop herself from screaming, from crying and screaming all at the same time, and she let the convulsive sobs that shook her body muffle their way into the pillow.

And finally, when the crying had stopped, when the initial sense of disgust and shame had passed, a deep furious anger began to seep through her, an anger for the people who had started the horrible adventure, who had made her the victim of Maxie and his pushing body. She felt nothing for Maxie, her anger turned from him, and from Florrie who had taken her to where Maxie was. The cold, deep fury was turned back to her village, to Myra and Jonathan Whitman, who had sentenced her to a miserable house in London, to a mean mistress and a common, vulgar working companion.

The tears, self-pitying and spiteful, began to fall once more into her pillow.

'I'll never forgive them,' she sobbed. 'I'll never forgive Jonathan Whitman. And I'll get even with them somehow. I'll pay them back one day. I'll pay them back. . . .'

Four

It was the golden age of Britain, the age of splendour, of the Diamond Jubilee, of the seventy-hour, six-day week. It was the age of electricity and Oscar Wilde, of Aubrey Beardsley, of Kipling and of George Bernard Shaw (undoubtedly a very clever man, but what a pity he's a socialist).

Kaiser Wilhelm continued to make the German navy uncomfortably powerful, gold had been unearthed in South Africa, and the French experimented with the submarine – which was exactly the foolish kind of thing one would expect the French to do.

In public the Londoner could take his daughters on the underground railway or in a motor car – released from the frustrations of the red flag – or to see one of the delightful entertainments by Mr Gilbert and Mr Sullivan. In private he could chastise his daughter as he wished, censor her books, her friends, her clothes, and choose her husband for her when the time came.

Darwin had died – leaving a few uneasy questions not answered. General William Booth and his band of uniformed followers, after ten years of persecution by street gangs, marched militantly through the streets and gave succour to 'the unfit, the criminal, the unwashed and the very scum and dregs of the race'. Shop assistants still stood – there was nowhere to sit – for ten hours a day, but children under twelve were no longer accepted as employees – at least, not officially. The railway train delighted in such niceties as the corridor and the restaurant car. Public baths were opened and the Londoners hurried to be clean – and then on to have their vaccination. The Cockneys – those who could afford it – went on a day trip to Boulogne to see if the 'Froggies' were as peculiar as everyone had believed for the last nine hundred years.

The bicycle craze had arrived, and had succeeded at last in helping to rid women of at least some of the fifteen-pounds-weight of clothes they had been wearing for sixty years. Curiously they began to wonder why they were permitted to work in mills and factories, to have children at the rate of one each year, to nurse the diseased and wounded – which no one else wanted to do anyway – but had no real rights or status in society.

It was the age of wealth, of vast unbounded riches. And it was the age when the majority of the population lived – and not all of them lived – just above the line that divides poverty from famine. Mass education – to a very elementary stage it is true, but still education – had brought them awareness of their inferiority, but not offered any solution. It had given them pride that made them ashamed when they saw how they lived. Dignity and independence were the only things they could – sometimes – afford, and they clung to these with a tenacity that was ridiculous in view of their living standards.

It was the age of universal peace. Apart from that little upset in the Crimea, no one had seriously challenged the Imperial might since 1815. And if one or two were bothered by the news of a Johannesburg boilermaker being shot by four Boer policemen, it would surely all be settled very soon.

And Jonathan, quietly and with a greater facility reading Mr Fawcett's cast-out newspapers, began to worry about what was happening six thousand miles away in the Transvaal. His concern was not entirely altruistic. He had been a soldier only a short time ago. He was on the reserve, the immediate reserve, and he had no special desire to participate once more in the communal life of brutalised manhood doomed to regular soldiery. He recalled, without relish, the horseplay, the stupidity, the lack of privacy and the wide variety of unpleasant and disgusting habits that men living together tolerated. He felt no fear at the thought of fighting, he had never fought in a war and therefore could not imagine the sequence of blood and death that would make him afraid. He disliked the army because his companions in the ranks were mostly louts, and his officers incompetent bluffers who reminded him both of the late Brigadier Fawcett and of the present Mr Fawcett. He had resigned himself before to six years of service because he had no alternative and because he needed a place to hide. Now, older and with a wife and child, he doubted his ability to accept the useless futility of army life. And all the time, at the back of his mind, was Myra, not the child, but Myra, whom he could not bear to leave. Soft, quiet, smiling Myra, whose presence was now such a part of his life that he could hardly recall the way he had lived when she was not there.

Sometimes, watching her bending over the stone copper, pulling out the steaming clothes on a wooden stick, or seeing her frown over the sewing-machine or the silent child who was their daughter, he would feel such an agonised ache in his breast that he had to jump up and busy himself with a task outside, the bees or the hens or the fruit-trees. When the pain of loving her became unbearable he would reach out and touch her hand or neck, hoping that the contact of flesh would ease the silent tears in his heart. For he had nearly lost Myra. Myra had nearly died. Ten, twenty times a day he said this to himself. At night, lying awake and tormented by the needs of his body, needs that he dared not indulge, he relived the day and the night and the day when he had thought she would die. Every clear, pin-bright event of those hours was scoured into his heart, every fear, every glimpse of her pain-dragged face was indelibly etched across his brain.

The relived terror struck him violently when he thought he had forgotten. On the estate grafting trees and shrubs, absorbed in what he was doing, the thought would sear suddenly into his mind. 'Myra! She nearly died. I nearly lost her.' He would have to stand upright for a moment and swallow hard to rid himself of the fear in his throat.

Once, when he reached out to grip her hand and reassure himself that she was still there, she turned and smiled at him, lifting his white-knuckled fist to her cheek and holding it smoothly there for a second. 'It's all right, Jonathan,' she said softly. 'I'm here. And so is Harry.'

He didn't really care about Harriet. He tried because he

knew Myra wanted him to love the child and enter into the intimacy that she shared with the frail, bruised baby. He held the little girl and washed her, but still could feel nothing except surprise that she was part of him and part of Myra. He wondered if he would have felt differently if the child had been a boy, but the speculation was too remote for him to dwell on. He doubted that he would ever have a son. His fear of losing Myra made him sublimate the desire she roused in him. His need of her was terrible, but he could not countenance the thought of a future without her presence.

She had a dress, a faded, rough blue dress that she wore about the house to work in. It was plain and worn and had no collar, just a round banded neck with buttons to the waist, and when she was washing or baking bread she would roll the sleeves of the dress up high and throw open the top two buttons on the neck so that he could see the soft swell of her throat and breast. His body would become an agony to him, an agony confused with love he could not express other than with that same body. Reaching out for her, unable to quell his love, he would suddenly recall her face, yellow and drawn in pain, and his desire would instantly vanish, absorbed into the tearing anxiety that beset most of his waking hours.

In April he at last had enough to pay the doctor's bill and felt himself free to ease the racking programme of work necessitated by Myra's confinement and the payments on the sewing-machine. There had been little time for the Fawcett books during his trial of deadening, intensive labour, but now, once more, he felt free to sit with Myra in the evenings, poring over the borrowed words with a sense of renewed enthusiasm. Occasionally Jonathan would bring home the Fawcett atlas and they would bend over the pages, studying far countries and distant seas, using the Fawcett *Times* to stimulate their curiosity. The far-away continents held the greatest charm, European countries seeming to lack the hazy excitement of China, of the Americas, of Australia. And again and again – in accordance with the columns of *The Times* – they found themselves with the double-page spread of South Africa open before them. Myra, unaware of the disquiet that the Boers aroused in Jonathan, tried to assimilate the reading she had missed.

'Is it the gold?' she asked Jonathan. 'Or the religion? Or is it the farming land they want?'

Fumbling, not fully understanding himself, Jonathan tried to define his worry.

'None of those. I think none of those,' he said slowly. 'It's the English who live there. They want to vote or something. I think they want to vote.'

'Then why don't they let them vote?' She was impatient, seeing the problem with uncomplicated feminine logic. Jonathan paused.

'If they let them vote, the country will become English.'

'Of course it will. Why shouldn't it?'

He knew she was right, of course. England was master of the world, queen of the seas, a gracious, guiding, generous being. He wondered why he was still uneasy about the Uit-lander's demand for freedom to the Queen, and he wished the confusion of ideas and opinions, of statements and reports in the newspapers were more concise in their content.

'What will happen if they don't get the vote?' Myra had put down her flat-iron and was staring at him, sensing some-thing of his personal concern. 'It couldn't mean war. It couldn't mean that, could it, Jonathan?'

He didn't answer, not because he didn't want to allay her fears, but because he knew he would have to answer yes, and the word lodged unhappily in his throat. Across the room their eyes met and held, each knowing the fear of life without the other, although this had been something he had lived with for more than six months. A cuckoo suddenly called from deep in the woods, the silly, meaningless sound waking them from their dread.

'Put the iron away, Myra,' he said briskly. 'Let's take Harry and walk in the woods for a bit.'

'It's late,' she said hesitatingly. 'Nearly dark. And Harry's asleep.'

He leaned over the table and took the flat-iron gently out of her hands.

'Harry won't waken. You know how quiet she is, and the evening's warm outside. Come on, Myra. Let's get out and walk for a bit.'

She smoothed her hands back across her ears, tucking away the wisps and chaff-like pieces of hair that had escaped from her bun, and then went up the stairs to fetch the baby. When she came back Harry was wound about with a grey shawl and Myra had a wrapper across her own shoulders. Jonathan took the child from her and Harriet stirred a little before curling acqiescently against his shoulder and sleeping again.

It was warm and fragrant in the lane, a soft, browsing, anticipatory April evening full of gentle noises and invisible scents. When they came to the stile, Jonathan stopped and held Myra's arm quickly so that she didn't move. Two young rabbits were perched up on their long back legs in the field beyond the stile. They stared interestedly about them, studying the grass and young dandelion shoots that showed dimly in the declining light. One lifted his tiny front paws and polished rapidly at his muzzle and whiskers.

'Boo!' said Jonathan, and they were gone, vanished in a blur of grey fluff and thumping paws. Myra laughed and took the baby from Jonathan while he climbed over the stile.

'Will Pritchard says there's Romanies at the far end of Tyler's woods. He saw them making their fire early this morning when he went to get the milk.' She was, like most of the villagers, curious and a little fascinated by the country nomads who roamed silently through the woods and fields, the gipsies, the true Romanies, who were not to be confused with the tinkers who stole and trespassed and smart-talked the housewives into bargains that were not bargains at all. The Romanies were seldom seen, they rarely begged and seemed to live from the land without actually taking anything. Usually they were no more than a brief brown glimpse through the trees, or a family on a cart pulled by a thin donkey. But they were, by the way they looked – round-headed and smooth-cheeked – by the manner in which they moved, striding leanly beside their wagons, easily recognised and separated from the itinerant tinkers and peg-sellers who came around the cottages.

'Let's walk up and see them,' said Myra, refusing with a shake of her head to hand back the baby to him.

He stepped ahead of her and led a path through the woods, his feet accidentally crushing on primroses and wild daffodils. The scent of bruised wood violets and speedwell hung elusively in the air, making them both restless with the clean, promising smell of spring. Up the slope, covered in thick trees, budding and in some cases already bearing small, uncurled leaves. Insects and soft night animals rustled in the undergrowth, resenting the intrusion of booted feet across their hunting grounds.

The smell of smoking apple-wood and the noise of snapping cinders mingled distantly with the other smells and sounds of night. They moved carefully to the top of the hill, inching warily to the clearing where the smoke from the Romany fire could be seen.

'Don't go any nearer,' said Myra suddenly. 'Stay here in the trees. We can see the fire from here.' She realised that it would be impolite to go any further and stare at the gipsies, as though someone had walked uninvited into the cottage one evening and sat watching her and Jonathan.

They could see a woman by the fire, a Romany woman, and she leaned forward and put more wood on the flames so that the fire leapt brilliantly to lick at the iron kettle hanging from a tripod and metal chain. A pony grazed at the edge of the clearing, pulling roughly at the young spring grass growing into the borders of the wood. The Romanies had built a small cone-shaped shelter from branches, and blankets were draped over the sticks. As the fire flared up again, Jonathan could see, even from a distance, that the blankets were woven in brilliant colours, reds and greens and purples that matched the colours of the shawl round the woman's neck.

She was vivid and quick-limbed, still young and with thick, black hair hanging in a mane over her shoulders, shining greasily in the glow of the fire. The bodice of her upper garment – it did not seem to be a dress – was open, and a child cradled in her left arm sucked at her breast. He should have been shocked and embarrassed at the sight. He had never seen

106

a woman unclothed before, and had certainly never seen Myra
when she was feeding Harriet, but the woman and the fire
drew him so that he took a few paces away from the wood and
into the clearing, compelled to move into the night scene, the
moon, the flames on the naked breast, the thick dark hair of
the woman.

The Romany looked up, raising her head slowly, and he saw
dark eyes flash briefly, the whites turning away into the flames.
If she saw him she gave no sign. She turned her head back
and stared hard into the centre of the fire, pulling her shawl
up again as it slipped down from her shoulders. He knew he
ought to make some sign to the woman, either move forward
and speak, give her a greeting and perhaps an apology, or else
leave the wood altogether and restore the clearing to its rightful
owner. He knew all this and yet he could not move, nor could
he take his eyes from the woman by the fire.

From the opposite side of the clearing, the side where the
brook ran, a figure walked out from the trees, a man swarthy,
powerful, shaking his bare shoulders and head free of the
brook water glistening on him. He stopped quietly when he
was a little way into the encampment and faced Jonathan
across the grass. Jonathan could not tell if the man was looking at him or not.

Then the Romany moved over to his wife and put his hand
on her shoulder, sliding the shawl and her bodice off at the
same time. The gesture was aggressive and, at the same time,
beautiful, indicating his possession, his brutality and pride in
the woman.

She sat with her neck and breast gleaming bare in the fire
below and the moon above. Then they both looked across the
fire and into Jonathan's face.

He heard a quick indrawing of breath beside him and knew
that Myra was there, drawn out of the woods by the Romany
couple, forced, as he had been, to come into the strange pulsing
circle of the fire. He could not stop staring at the woman, at
the brown swell of her breast, the line of shoulder and neck
partially concealed by her hair, and especially he stared at the
wet hand of the Romany resting against the copper skin. His

eyes moved to the man's face, wondering if he would witness anger or jealousy or fear, but the man did not see him. The man was staring at Myra, and Jonathan turned his head to look quickly at his wife.

She held the baby, their baby, Harriet, in the same way that the gipsy woman held hers, cradled under her left breast. The line of the neck was the same, the outline of her shoulder beneath the blue dress identical. Myra's hair was combed back into a tight coil, but the flames turned the wispy tendrils to a dark amber and gave it the same glowing life that burned in the gipsy woman's hair. He saw the Romany's face, the hand on the naked flesh, and suddenly he saw Myra as though she were the woman, with her breast and throat bare, with the faded dress open to the waist and nothing to stop the smooth skin of her neck flowing voluptuously down into heaviness. He put his hand on Myra's shoulder, reflecting the gesture of the man and, as though the dress were not there, he felt skin and pulsing flesh beneath his hand.

The two men, two women, studied each other, watched in the firelight, saw many things, desired one another until they were no longer sure which hand rested on which shoulder, which woman belonged to the damp, half-clothed Romany and which to Jonathan. The Romany's hand slid down to encompass the swell of the woman's breast and Jonathan's did the same, and he did not know if it were Myra or the gipsy he touched. He stepped, in a swift, coil-like movement to stand close to Myra, pressing against her, gripping her round the waist with his other arm so that he was supporting the weight of Harriet. The Romany bent over his wife and copied the movement, looking up at Myra and smiling, his teeth showing white in the bronze face. He pulled his wife up beside him and, for a second, stood watching Jonathan and Myra, then he turned the woman round to face the wood and pushed her gently away from the clearing. They disappeared swiftly among the trees, leaving the wood suddenly desolate and still, with only the small, rough-haired donkey moving about the grass verges.

Jonathan turned and led the way back down the path, not

looking behind, but knowing that Myra followed him. They did not speak, and when they reached the cottage she went straight up, the sleeping Harriet folded in her arms. He heard her moving in the bedroom and waited to see if she would come down again. When the sounds of movement ceased he went upstairs and into their room. He saw, for the first time, the soft, naked body of his wife lying across the bed, lit only by the brilliance of the moon beaming down through the window.

There was no escape from the avalanche of events that moved faster and uncompromisingly in the Transvaal, in Natal and in the Orange Free State. In May, Oom Paul Kruger and Sir Alfred Milner sat, one each side of a Bloemfontein conference table, and tried to divert the coming clash. It was no use. There was no contact between the squat, God-fearing patriarch of the Afrikaaners and the fastidious, over-cultured British diplomat. The meeting ended with doomed misunderstanding, each thankful to be away from the presence of the other.

On 2 October 1899 the Volksraad approved the motion of war against the invincible, the mighty, the undefeated motherland, and on 10 October, when the war commenced, Jonathan Whitman knew the unhappy despair of fear once more. Because of the war. And because his wife was again expecting a child.

Five

SAYING good-bye was the bad part. Not just to Myra, but to everyone in the village. Even Emily, withdrawn and aloof in the isolated refuge of the Vincents' cottage, made him feel bad when he said good-bye.

He stood, as was his custom, at the gate of their cottage and waited for Emily to see him from the window and come out. The only time he had gone to the front door there had been a wild, erratic scuffling from inside and then Emily, flushed and angry, had come out of the door and shut it behind her.

'Don't ever come to the door again!' She was furious and pushed him away, down the path to the gate.

'Don't be silly, Em. How am I going to see you if I can't come to the door?' He was annoyed, justifiably so. He had come to give Em a little money because, even committed as he was to a wife and child, he still considered Em his responsibility. Had she continued to live with him and Myra, he could have supported her without too much extra strain on his thin income. Her decision to separate herself from the family meant an extra drain on his resources, but one to which he was morally bound. The half-crown he set aside for her every week was not always given with a loving heart. He had to work hard to surrender it without a pang of frustration. And when Emily didn't even seem bothered about accepting the money, treating him as a stupid intruder when he tried to see her, his unadmitted grudge flared into irritation.

'If you want to stay shut away from everybody in there,' he gestured impatiently to the silent, withdrawn cottage, 'then that's your business. But if you want to continue seeing your family, then stop behaving like those two crazy old women. Otherwise the village will think you're mad too.'

'I don't care what they think!' she snapped. 'Just don't come up to the house. Wait at the gate until I come down.'

His dignity rebelled at the thought of hanging about among the tangled weeds and cats until she saw him from the window.

'I haven't got time to wait until you see me,' he said impatiently. 'I'll leave your money under the brick here, unless I want to speak to you particularly.'

Em nodded without interest, seeming to hardly hear him. She kept darting quick backward glances towards the blank windows of the cottage.

'It wouldn't hurt you to go and see Myra some days,' he said, drawn into a fresh surge of indignation at her apathy.

'I might,' she said vaguely. 'As your baby is a girl, I might.'

He didn't understand and he was tired. Emily had gone too far for him to try and make any last attempt at a family contact. He turned and swung impatiently down the lane, determining that he would leave her half-crown as she wished, and not even try to venture into the twilight world of the Vincents' house.

But when the time came to leave the village he wanted to see Em again, to say good-bye, to ask her to help with Myra and the child.

He waited at the gate and the door opened and Emily hurried down the path. She looked no different. Her hair was exactly the same, iron-neat as though it were made out of lacquered paint. The dress, the brown calico dress, covered by a print apron was identical with the one she had always worn. Her face was stiff and withdrawn, the expression he remembered as most clearly belonging to Em.

'Leave it under the brick, the brick,' she said testily, pointing to the place just inside the wooden gate-post where he always left the half-crown.

'I've come to say good-bye, Em.'

She blinked at him. 'Good-bye?'

'There's a war, Em. In South Africa. I've been called to the reserves.'

'Oh, yes,' she said casually. 'We heard about the war.'

'I'm sailing for South Africa, Em, and I've come to say good-bye.'

'All right then.' For one insane moment he thought that was to be the end of their conversation, with Em uncaringly turning back into the house. But some remnant of family concern must have stirred at the back of her mind.

'Take care, then. We'll soon have them beat, I've no doubt, and you'll be back before very long. Wash regularly and don't drink any water without boiling it first.' The years of disciplining a family briefly asserted themselves for a moment. Foolishly Jonathan felt a faint pricking at the back of his eyes.

'I'm afraid there won't be any more money for a while, Em. Myra's going to find it a struggle as it is. I've got five shillings here for you, that's all I could manage.' He put the money into Em's hand and she stared down at it uncomprehendingly.

'And Em, could you . . . would you go and see Myra? Make sure she's all right and that. Perhaps help out when you can.' He hesitated nervously, remembering how the news of Harriet's expected arrival had sent Emily into an inexplicable rage.

'She's expecting again, Emily. She's going to have another child in January, and I won't be here to know what's happened. I won't know whether she dies or if she's bad like last time. I've got to go away and I won't know if she'll be all right . . . ' He wasn't talking to Em, he was just talking because he couldn't say any of it to Myra. He had to pretend it would be all fine. That she would have the baby without any trouble and he would come home from the war in a few months and nothing would be wrong. The nightmare of anxiety that kept him awake at night had to be carefully disguised during the day with confident allusions to 'Old Kruger' and how well Myra felt and how the second baby would be no bother at all. He never admitted his consuming worry to Myra and she never spoke of the war as one of death and blood, only of patriotic duty. If either of them had confessed their inward, frantic fears, they would not have got through the last few days together.

Emily stared coldly at him. 'You should have thought of

112

that before, shouldn't you? You should have thought before making her like that and then gadding off to fight the Boers. If she dies it will be your fault, no one else's. You nearly killed her last time, didn't you? But you don't care, you're a man, you don't care.'

He let her talk because it was a relief to have the words spoken openly, the words that sung in his head several times a day, words that were accusing but true.

'You'll help her, won't you, Em? You'll go to see her and help with the child. You'll stay with her when she's ill, won't you, Em?'

Emily began to walk back up the path.

'Perhaps,' she called softly. 'I'll see. Perhaps if Miss Thalia doesn't need me, I'll call. We'll see. We'll see.'

The door closed upon her vague promise of help. She was gone, swallowed into the weirdness of the house. Grief and frustration struggled violently within him and he wanted to run after her, to pound on the door and then break into the implacable, silent house, shouting and demanding that Em would help.

'Oh, God! What can I do?'

He went to see Mrs Pritchard, assuring himself that she would help Myra with the second birth and giving her instructions to call the doctor the moment she thought necessary and then sell the sewing-machine to pay the bill. She was blandly, comfortably unruffled.

'Don't worry, lad. I doubt very much if there'll be trouble this time. The second's usually all right.' She patted his shoulder busily and then put her hands back into the soapy water. She was doing the Rector's washing and wanted to have it dry and ironed to take back that same evening because she needed the ninepence. He said good-bye, knowing she had no time to waste in useless speculations on the future. Betsy, coming into the kitchen door as he was going out, turned round and followed him back into the garden.

'Try not to worry too much, Jonathan. I'll go and see her when I can and give a hand. I know your sister's . . . busy and can't help.'

113

Betsy had grown thinner in the last six months, her hitherto round, good-natured face lengthening into quiet, resigned lines. Twice since the birth of Harriet she had hurried off to Portsmouth to see Math, had stayed a month or so, working at hotels and guest houses in the hope that he would soon be back. Her return to the village was usually rendered necessary from economic reasons. Jonathan, used like everyone else to see her sturdy, drudge-like figure plodding across the fields to help at lying-ins or spring-cleanings or scrub-days, realised, out of the depths of his own concern and worry, how much he took her for granted, and how he had never really spoken to her.

'You're a good woman, Betsy,' he said suddenly. 'You're a better woman than your mother and you're a damn sight finer than a great many in the village. I hope your Mathew comes home soon.'

She flushed and then the meaning of his words penetrated her embarrassment. The mention of Mathew made tears smart suddenly into her eyes.

'He's going on the China run,' she said miserably. 'I don't suppose he'll be home for at least a couple of years.'

He realised how, for Betsy, it was always like it was, only now, for Myra and himself. Consumed in his worry of going away and leaving his wife, he had never thought of Betsy, continually saying good-bye, continually wondering if she would see her husband again. Impulsively he leaned forward and kissed her on the cheek.

'Good-bye, Betsy. You're a good friend. You deserve better. Why don't you get Anne-Louise to come home and give a hand?'

'She's courting,' Betsy said fatalistically. 'A fish porter or something, I don't know. She hasn't brought him home yet.' His kiss didn't disconcert her as his unexpected compliment had. Later, she would treasure the memory of his thanks, the gratitude that very seldom came her way.

'Good-bye then, Jonathan. Don't worry. You'll soon have old Kruger licked and be home. Perhaps even before the baby's born.'

114

They neither of them believed it, but it meant they parted on lighter, more jovial tones, the note that was generally accepted as the pattern for saying good-bye all round the village.

Mr Fawcett was patriotic and gallant, courageously sacrificing his gardener and bee-man to the Cause.

'Don't forget, Whitman,' he said jauntily. 'When you return from teaching them a lesson there's a place waiting for you on the estate.'

A sense of changing fortunes stirred in Jonathan's heart. Beneath the worry of Myra, the possibility of death in the war, or a thousand other things, he felt the first stirrings of something moving in the pattern that had governed his life for so long. The future was uncharted, but he was aware of a growing conviction that, whatever happened, he would not work as Fawcett's gardener again.

'Thank you, sir.' He touched his hat, in a meaningless gesture of deference.

He never actually said good-bye to Myra, he couldn't. He collected the milk as usual that morning, tramping the three miles to the farm and seeing every tree, every hill and ditch with a new, penetrating clearness. The pale-blue autumn sky banked with distant clouds, the yellow leaves on the hedgerows falling rapidly to a thick dusty carpet in the ditches, the rutted, mud-filled cart-tracks along the lane, the great stretch of meadow before he came to the wooden bridge over the stream rustling wetly along between the banks of bullrushes and loosestrife.

When he came home he lit the stove and put the water on, but Myra was already up, he could hear her talking softly to Harriet in the room above. They ate together, talking practically of last-minute facts and details.

'You've got socks and writing paper, haven't you, dear? And I've put some Beecham's in your bag because they're always useful. And some bread and cheese and apples. I expect it will be a muddle today and there won't be a chance to eat. Write when you can, but don't worry if you're busy or haven't the time. Just a note when you can to tell us you're well.'

He nodded, sensibly making notes of everything she said because he was sure it would be useful.

'I've left what money I can, and I'll try and find a way of getting some back to you.'

'We'll be fine,' she said confidently. 'There's my sewing, and the village will help.'

'You're sure you can manage the hens?'

'Of course. I see to them mostly now, don't I?'

'And Will Pritchard has promised to give an eye to the garden and the bees. Everything's dug over and the bees have more or less finished, so there won't be too much to do.'

Neither of them spoke of the fact that he might still be gone when the summer came, when the garden and the bees needed more than just 'an eye'. When the money he had saved and borrowed had come to an end.

Myra stood up and collected the dirty plates, scraping the uneaten food into the hen-bucket.

'Better get along, dear. You don't want to miss the train.'

He went upstairs and collected his bag. When he came down she was standing at the tub, her back to him, washing the breakfast things.

'Off you go,' she said, not turning round, her hands busy in the soapy water.

He lifted the latch of the door, not trusting himself to speak, unable to look at her in case he should submit to the misery in his heart. Half out of the door he heard her give a breathless, strangled cry.

'Jonathan!'

She was across the kitchen, gripped tight to his aching body, her soapy hands holding his shoulders and the last comforting warmth of her body held alongside him. Then they separated and he ran away from the kitchen, down the path as quickly as he could, because he didn't want to hear her, or see her, sobbing into the sink of dirty washing-up water.

Black Week – December 1899, when the might of the British

Empire trembled before three major defeats inflicted by a civilian army of scouts and horsemen.

Black Week – when Germany and France openly gloated over the crumbling power of Great Britain, the largest shareholder in the foreign territories they had carved up between them.

Black Week – when Russia waited for the final defeat so that she could march her armies in and take possession of India, when the Irish section of the United States urged the President to take action against the British.

The Battle of Kissieberg; confusion and incompetence and a surge of fusiliers attacking a hill held by a handful of Boers – and being shot to pieces by their own heavy artillery. Magersfontein: another of those cursed kopjes where the Scottish Infantry never even got close enough to mount the hill. The Boers had dug in at the foot, hidden among the scrub and brush and mowed the Black Watch and Seaforths into the ground, and this time it wasn't only the ranks who died. Andy Wauchope – Major-General Andy Wauchope – beloved and adored by clansmen and troops alike and lauded in his native Scotland was mown down with the rest. The army stirred uneasily, doubting its invincibility and wondering where the fault lay.

Colenso: the artillery pushed so far forward that, when the ambush came, there was no way to escape and guns, men and horses lay screaming together in the dust. Black Week – when Oom Paul Kruger gave thanks to the Lord, who fought on the side of right, the side of the Boers.

Jonathan, trekking tiredly in the long thin line of cavalry across the veld, stared with dull dislike at the back of Finch's neck. It was the sixth day he had stared at the back of Finch's neck, and he knew every red, inflamed swelling that showed beneath the helmet. Finch, more than most of them, was inclined to boils and carbuncles, a complaint which poor food and insanitary conditions aggravated. At Kimberley a huge and painful abscess had slowly swelled up on the back of Finch's neck, so painful that he had been unable to turn his head or

117

wear his helmet, and one of the troopers, an old sweat who had seen service in the Matabele wars, suggested that they helped Finch by giving him the bottle treatment. Finch, driven by pain to attempt anything that would ease his misery, agreed, and over the fire that night Jonathan and the old trooper had held a bottle over the steam from a billy. Finch, lying face down groaning at them to hurry and get rid of the bloody thing for him, braced himself when the bottle was full of steam and Jonathan shouted, 'Now!'

Neither Jonathan nor the old trooper were prepared for Finch's reaction when they clapped the hot neck of the bottle over the violent swelling on his neck. Finch had screamed and leapt into the air – it seemed to Jonathan – straight from his prone position without using legs or arms. Wrenched away from their hands, the bottle, surprisingly, had not dropped away from Finch's neck, but had stuck out like a broken-off lance while Finch capered screaming over the camp site. Jonathan tried to catch him before the lieutenant came to investigate the noise, but Finch was uncatchable and a good ten minutes elapsed before he sank whimpering and swearing on to the ground again. Jonathan and the old trooper bent over Finch and the trooper pulled at the bottle.

'Ah,' he said satisfied. 'That's done it. I knew it would. There's no better cure than a bottle of steam for breaking a boil. He won't have no trouble with that one now.'

Finch's neck was still swollen and to Jonathan's eye looked worse than before they had clapped the bottle on. But the old trooper knew his stuff and Jonathan had to admit that at least the abscess was broken even though it was also scalded and raw.

The next day they had started the scorching, midsummer ride to try and cut off the escaping besiegers of the town, a useless, futile campaign that had failed because the men and the horses were exhausted and because there was no water for miles ahead. The ride back to Kimberley had been a test of dragging, dust-soaked endurance and their reception had been the news that they must ride out again in pursuit of Cronje's convoy.

Too many campaigns, too little water, too much bad food, for horses as well as men, had meant that only a thousand of the troop were able to ride out again, and Jonathan, his sense of personal involvement with the war reduced to a hatred of the back of Finch's neck, had wanted to burst into tears when he knew Finch was still fit enough to ride and could take his place ahead of him in the column.

On the rare occasions when he had eaten a good meal and was rested, he could view the war with the horror that his battle encounters had fostered. But tired, thirsty and aware of the flagging pace of the worn-out animal beneath him, his war degenerated into the petty irritation of the moment, leaving no thought or pity for the blood and death that was soaking into the veld.

Finch's horses stumbled and he saw the man's head jerk up quickly, waking from the heat-induced daze that gripped them all. Finch looked round and grinned at Jonathan, his teeth baring in the dirty blur of his face. Jonathan forced himself to grin back, hating Finch, hating General French, who had ordered the new expedition, hating Cronje, and above all hating the back of Finch's neck.

On the distant line of sky a small cloud of dust formed, moved and grew slowly bigger and the cavalry line stirred, men pulling themselves from their lethargy and reaching nervously for their rifles. The line was halted and a thousand pairs of strained eyes screwed themselves into pinpoints of observation. The dust ball grew bigger and the line relaxed, seeing the threatened Boer attack disperse into three cavalry scouts and a Zulu guide.

The scouts were even filthier and more exhausted than the rest of the line, but they had information that fostered a temporary enthusiasm, giving them a brief, illusory confidence that vanished once they had conveyed their news to General French. The information, fed along the lines of officers and ranks, brought the first, uneasy fear, a familiar fear that most of them knew would be followed by battle fever, when guns and smoke and screaming men would drive the fear away from them and lead them screaming and mad into a frenzy of killing.

Finch turned round again. 'Old Cronje's up ahead,' he said, grinning quickly. 'He's camped by the Modder. We're going to attack.'

'Without waiting for the infantry?' said Jonathan, wondering why he should still be surprised at the incompetence of the command. 'Without waiting for Kitchener? They reckon there's ten thousand in Old Cronje's convoy. There's only a thousand of us.'

Finch grinned foolishly and nodded. The column in front of him began to move forward again, and Finch turned back to face front and jerked his heels into the side of his horse. The back of Finch's neck no longer aggravated Jonathan. Now he and the rest of the troop sat nervously waiting the onslaught that would hit them at any moment. They were used to sniping Boers, but every time they went into action there was the same sick looseness in the pit of every man's stomach. The officer ahead signalled the trot and weary men spurred wearier horses into a speed neither of them were fit to take. A hill, coming up to the south, made the line slow down again and they knew, the entire line knew, that Cronje's army lay behind the hill.

'God! Surely not.' He spoke the words aloud, softly but aloud, still refusing to believe that French would send a thousand exhausted men into an attack against the Boer army. No one took any notice of his protest. If they heard they were too busy thinking themselves and wondering if they were advancing into an ambush like the Scottish infantry at Magersfontein.

The hill grew closer, the line moved to one side of the slope. Men licked dust from their mouths and tried to ease the cloth from sweating armpits.

'Troop at the ready!'

Jonathan swallowed and looked hard at Finch's neck wishing it could arouse the same concentration of hate in him that it had before.

'Once round the slope, dismount and fire from the rocks!'

The horses rustled uneasily, catching fear from the men. If

they stayed much longer, the noise of the animals would alert the Boers.

'Troop! Char . . . ge!'

The engulfing tide of flesh and steel surged up over the slope and into the scrubby rocks leading down to the river. Rifle fire, screaming men and pounding hooves threw the midday calm into shrieking panic. A few shots were flung wildly back from the Boer encampment. Through the noise and nightmare screams Jonathan saw small figures, some human, some animal, break camp and run for the river-banks. Over his head whined the first of the shells from the horse-drawn guns, smashing into the bank of the river and sending up a column of red and yellow earth.

'Dismount! Troop dismount and fire from the ground.'

He was flung from his horse, who reared suddenly at the whine of another shell, and he rolled over until he felt the comfort of a small decline beneath his body. He felt wetness against his leg and wondered idly if he was bleeding. When he looked and saw that his canteen of water was leaking, running away into the dust, he wished it had been blood, for blood was less important than water in the veld. Finch was lying against a rock two feet away, firing rapidly into the Boer encampment. He took time off to shout at Jonathan, 'We've caught them with their trousers down. They're panicking.'

They were panicking. The surprise attack from the hill when they were tired and watering their oxen and horses had caught the convoy completely off guard. Belatedly they tried to form a defence line, marshalling into small groups that set out to dislodge the invisible troopers shooting from the rocks. The mounted guns and the massed rifle-fire from the dismounted troopers threw them back.

Scorching sun bore down into the afternoon. Brief, spasmodic outbursts of gunfire broke the hot, dust-drenched air from time to time, and Jonathan, his tongue growing huge with thirst, stared down at the River Modder gleaming in the sun. He tried not to look when Finch unstopped his canteen and held it to his lips. Mercifully, a thin stream of saliva trickled into Jonathan's mouth as Finch drank. The saliva was hot and sticky and vanished as soon as Finch stopped up the canteen.

'What now?' said Finch cheerfully. 'Suppose we wait for the infantry to arrive.'

Jonathan, lying stomach down against the clay-coloured rock, turned his eyes from the river to the distant sky-line, hoping vainly to see the huge cloud of dust that would precede the arrival of Kitchener and the infantry. He and every dismounted trooper lying with rifle cocked knew that the possibility of survival without reinforcements was hopeless. Cronje, taken by surprise, was on the defensive. Once he had estimated the size of the cavalry line he would be able to take it in one attack.

The afternoon, leaded with yellow heat, pressed thickly on trooper and Boer alike. Finch drank from his canteen, and the noise made Jonathan retch as the back of his tongue touched his throat. Finch looked across and wiped the back of his mouth with his hand, then, seeing Jonathan's face he said slowly, 'Why aren't you drinking, mate?'

Jonathan grinned wryly and held the smashed canteen up for Finch to see. A Boer bullet screamed suddenly across the veld and splacked its way into the metal.

'Keep down there! You men on the left! Keep down!'

The brief flurry of rifle fire lulled again into deadening heat. Finch pushed his canteen along the ground to Jonathan.

'You should've said, mate. Should've asked me for the canteen.'

Jonathan unscrewed the cap and took a very small mouthful, holding it carefully on his tongue and then allowing it to trickle down his throat. He replaced the stopper and pushed it carefully back to Finch.

'Thanks.'

Finch wiped sweat from his face, leaving a damp band across the expanse of dirt and moisture.

'This is the worst I've had,' he said unashamed. 'I don't mind the fighting, but lying in this bleeding sun is more than I can stand.'

'It's like Spion Kop,' said Jonathan, without thinking. It was the first time he had mentioned Spion Kop to Finch. He tried not to think of Spion Kop, especially when he was lying on the verge of another battle.

'Gawd!' said Finch disgustedly. 'That was a lot that was.'

'They couldn't help at all there,' said Jonathan slowly. 'They had to let us die there. Most of the wounded bled to death . . . some died because of thirst. There wasn't anything they could do, you see.'

Finch looked uncomfortable. 'Never mind, mate,' he said reassuringly. 'You come out all right didn't you? Not like the other poor bleeders.'

Jonathan didn't answer. He had seen, on the horizon, a small, thin wide-stretching line of dust, a line that could be Kitchener and the infantry or could be Boer reinforcements.

'Look, Finch, on the horizon. Is it the infantry?'

The dust moved, closer and higher into the white sky. Somewhere at the back an officer with field-glasses shouted, 'It's Kitchener!'

They were too exhausted to do more than move slightly against the rocks, easing themselves into positions that signified a slight relaxation of tension. The arrival of the infantry didn't mean they could be relieved from their stronghold. Kitchener was on the far side of the river, the other side of the Boer encampment and separated from the cavalry by the river and by Cronje's army. But now Kitchener would divert some of the Boer attention away from French's cavalry.

Jonathan watched the dust line grow huge, stop and settle in on the far side of the river. The sky turned suddenly to red and purple, making the scrub and rocks of the veld appear unnaturally dark. Then the sun, huge-balled and red, dropped swiftly below the skyline.

Finch shared his water with Jonathan that night and during the following morning. They had hard-tack in their kit-bags, but their mouths were too dry and sore to eat. Just before noon the relief troop line, restored after a rest in Kimberley, rode up behind the hill and took over from the dismounted cavalry men.

Jonathan, Finch and a thousand sick men moved to the back of the hill, watered the nearly-dying horses, and then dropped exhausted on to the ground.

He came to hate that hill on the Modder river. Sometimes it seemed he had lived his whole life there, watching the spouts of lyddite fumes leap into the air, seeing boulders hurled fifty feet and shrapnel sizzling into the ground. On the fourth day, during a mounted attack, he saw Finch lean forward in the saddle with a spume of blood shooting from his mouth and soaking down into his khaki uniform. When the attack retreated he tried to look for Finch among the horses and bodies, but an officer hit him across the shoulders with his reins as he rode past.

'Mount, man, mount! At the gallop!'

Later, when they truced with the Boers to bring in the wounded, he looked for Finch, hoping that every red, swollen neck he saw would be the lacerated bottle-scarred flesh of Finch. He must have died. He wasn't brought in and they dared not stop to look at the faces of the dead.

On the sixth day it rained, warm, pelting, drenching rain that meant they could wash their faces if they lay face up on the ground. Carcasses from the besieged Boer camp began to wash away down the rising river and the cavalry troop, now lying in advanced positions away from the hill and well towards the area of the Boer camp, found, after a few hours of the flooding rain, that they were lying in mud. The mud turned almost at once into a thick, warm, clinging quagmire, and Jonathan found he was, incredibly, still thirsty, even while lying in the seeping mud.

The old trooper, the one who had helped put the bottle on Finch's neck, crawled over to Jonathan, leaving a long gully in the ground like a snake would leave in the sand.

'Oi,' he said pantingly to Jonathan. 'Old glossy-whiskers back there says we're detailed to do a detour round and down-stream and get fresh water from the river. There's a cart back there for us.'

He wanted to laugh. For six days they had lain on the burning veld eking out a tiny ration of water. Now, with the rain drenching down and soaking everyone and everything, they were to fetch water from the river.

'I'm not thirsty,' he said blithely. 'I've just had a nice drink of rain, thanks.'

'Maybe you ain't,' said the old sweat. 'But the horses are, and you and me is detailed for water fetching. So git up and move.'

They slithered back over the mud to where a convoy of four water-carts waited. Each cart, accompanied by five troopers, started in a wide detour, trying to hit the river at a place where the Boers could not reach.

The banks of the river were bitten deep into the soft soil of the veld. They were like cliffs, steep and perpendicular with a narrow shore of sand and rock shelf at the bottom. Here and there prickly mimosa scrub gave the river an illusion of vegetation, but for the most part it was wet rock and steep uncompromising sides.

They rolled the carts down about three miles before they found a break in the bank, a declivity that enabled them to push the carts down to the water's edge and fill the drums. Jonathan and the trooper heaved a drum together and dragged it down to the water.

He saw it first, before the trooper. It was washing gently against the bank, caught into the side against a jutting rock by the rising river level. Jonathan, accustomed to seeing the dead, the lacerated, the bodies of men with faces blown away and chests ripped open, suddenly felt sick because the body, floating gently on the surface of the water, was bloated and gaseous. Mercifully he was spared from seeing the face, the body floated front down, but the hands, fingers sausage-like in their distortion, made him turn suddenly away from the water.

'God!' said the old man. 'Look, the river's full of them.'

Across the stretch of water bobbed the lifeless, balloon-swelled carcasses of the massacred Boers. Besieged in their river encampment, refusing to surrender, they had no outlet for their dead except the river. Like a liquid cortège, the bodies of Cronje's army flowed silently along downstream.

'Where to?' thought Jonathan. 'Probably down to the Orange River and out to the Atlantic.' He recoiled from the passing thought that before they reached the Atlantic, the crocodiles and scavengers of the river would consume the bloated bodies.

'Poor sods,' said the trooper slowly. 'We think it's bad. God knows what it's like in that camp.'

The macabre procession of dead drifted along, the old man fascinated by the sight, Jonathan not looking until he felt his arm grasped urgently by the old man.

'God Almighty! There's a woman!'

He looked, seeing the same bloated shape as before, but this time held in a wide sweep of skirt that should, by right, be waterlogged enough to pull her mercifully to the bottom.

'There's women in that camp! And children, like enough. I don't want to fight no women! It ain't right! It ain't right!'

The old man, used to killing savages, used to unceasing fire and cannon was unnerved at the sight of the woman. Jonathan, who had seen the worst of the war at Spion Kop, felt only a dull surprise at the sight of the woman. He no longer believed that there were any barriers of horror that this war would not encompass.

'Fill the drums,' he said dully. 'We won't be able to drink it, but fill the drums like the officer said.'

On the eighth day the stench from Cronje's camp stretched across the sun-drying veld to the British lines. The smell, abominably vile, was of excrement and decaying dead. The river, polluted and undrinkable downstream, provided no means of getting water, and they began to send the carts upstream. When, on the ninth day, the infantry brought up four howitzers and began to bombard the camp, sending up debris and utterly destroying the bridge the Boers had built, the old trooper told Jonathan he would fight no more.

'I ain't fighting women,' he said vehemently. 'I tell you, I ain't mounting no more charges and I ain't firing this rifle again!'

'They said the women could go,' said Jonathan wearily.

'Roberts gave them safe conduct as soon as he knew they were there.'

'I ain't fighting women.'

'They refused to leave.'

'I ain't fighting.'

He didn't have to. On the following day the broken, filthy figure of General Cronje surrendered to Lord Roberts, Imperial representative for Her Majesty, the Queen.

It was on the relief ride to Bloemfontein that Jonathan first began to feel ill, aware of something wrong that was more than just the usual battle fatigue and hunger. After leaving the Modder, which the whole troop, sick of fighting women and the pathetic remnant of Cronje's army, had been glad to do, there had been more forced marches and useless forays against the Boers, who seemed capable of disappearing into the putty-coloured landscape as though they were themselves made of rock and scrub. At Abraham's Kraal the line had seen vicious and repetitive cavalry action which had killed four hundred of their troopers and Jonathan had felt the fifth of his horses drop screaming and torn into the dust. He had become adept at jumping quickly off a mount that rolled and squealed on the ground in pain. The first horse he had lost — a shell splinter impaled in its stomach — had made him shout, and then sob with the frustration of an action that murdered gentle, uncaring beasts. Now, dulled by blood and no longer capable of anything except a grim determination to bear anything, he was able to look at the horse, put a bullet through its head, and quickly unstrap the saddle and harness and run to the flank line as quickly as he could. The action ended, as most of Jonathan's forays into battle did, with the arrival of Roberts and the infantry.

Since then there had been two more gruelling, midday forced rides and a last desperate attempt to reach Bloemfontein before the supplies and the water gave out completely.

And Jonathan, after a campaign on hard-tack and dried meat, after days when rations dropped to one and a half biscuits per day, suddenly found he was no longer hungry, that the thought of the generous supplies awaiting them in the relieved city of Bloemfontein brought a vague feeling of nausea to his throat.

For the seventh time he dismounted and went to crouch behind a rock, feeling the scalding pain of his stomach dropping out on to the parched ground. His distress was all the more acute because he had not previously suffered from the stomach disorders that beset the rest of the line. The youngest of the troop, probably the hardiest, he had been regarded with envy by his fellow troopers because of his resistance to regional complaints.

If he had felt like this after Paardeberg, he could have understood why. The first few days after the surrender of Cronje had seen the cavalry completely cut off from their supply-lines. Food, reduced to one biscuit a day, had fostered a dreamy lethargy in the men that no amount of shouted instructions and disciplinary measures could alter. The lethargy had flared into a resentful mutiny when a rumour passed through the ranks that the officers were eating butter. If they had not been so crazed with fatigue and thirst they would probably not have believed the tale, and indeed Jonathan still was not certain if the rumour had been true or no more than the fevered imaginings of tired men. That night, when the bivouac had been called, he and Partridge had crawled to the site of supply horses and stolen a tin of what they supposed to be butter. Furtively and in the darkness the men had spread the purloined grease over the inch-thick grey biscuits and, within half an hour, had hurried away from the fire to vomit the stolen butter back into the desert. Jonathan, feeling no ill effects of what he took to be unaccustomed richness, was the only one who did not succumb to the orgy or regurgitate biscuit and butter. The morning had seen the reason for the outbreak. The tin, snatched hurriedly in the night, proved to be not butter, but zinc ointment. Interested in spite of their lethargy, the men had waited for Jonathan to die, and felt a little indignant when he continued to show no ill effect.

Two weeks had elapsed since then. Jonathan, convinced that it was not the stolen 'butter' that caused his present discomfort, wondered if he could make it to Bloemfontein without dismounting from his horse again.

By noon his head and back ached with an excruciating pain. Continual movement in the saddle had chafed the inside of his legs to sand-paper soreness. The veld became a blur of yellow and brown blacked out with frequent dark patches that seemed to come from somewhere inside his head. Added to his stomach and bowel discomfort was a growing desire to be sick, a sickness that would be futile in view of the fact that his inside was drained of food.

When the sun was at its highest, the order to dismount was called and thankfully he slid on to the ground, trying to ease his back against a low rock and tilting his hat forward to cover his eyes. Partridge, who had helped him steal the zinc ointment, came and stood over him, making a welcome barrier between Jonathan and the sun.

'Reckon we'll be in Bloemfontein by nightfall. A message just come by the heliograph. Roberts and the advance cavalry are going in that direction.'

'Good,' said Jonathan without conviction. Partridge screwed his eyes up against the sun and squinted down at Jonathan.

'What's up, mate? You got sunstroke?'

Jonathan shook his head, wondering bleakly how he was going to sit the horse until nightfall. He sipped gingerly at the tepid water in his canteen and a sudden vision of Sandy Bottom, cool and sparkling as he had seen it on his last day in the village, sprang to his mind. The veld, dotted here and there with scrub-covered kopjes, shimmered in front of his eyes, and the lukewarm water he had just drunk leapt back into his mouth and out on to the sand.

When the next order to dismount came, the afternoon one, he didn't dare to risk it, knowing that once off the horse, he would never get on again. He slumped forward along the neck of the beast, sensing the animal's weariness, but feeling too ill to consider any kind of pity for it. He began to shiver, a cold uncontrollable shiver that contrasted foolishly with the heat of his sun-baked skin and when he looked over the veld the black patches had become bigger and darker.

Two miles outside Bloemfontein, with the trees and the buildings of the city in view, he realised he wasn't going to make it. Partridge pulled his horse up alongside Jonathan and leaned over him.

'You all right, old man?'

Jonathan shook his head and the pain behind his eyes jolted viciously with the movement. Partridge leaned over and took the reins, pushing anxiously at Jonathan's swaying body.

'Hold on if you can mate. I'll lead the horse. Just hold on if you can.'

Through a mist of shivering nausea he heard the Troop Captain shouting at him, or maybe it was Partridge he was shouting at. Hooves and voices sounded very loudly by his head and he wished they would go away and leave him to concentrate on holding tightly to the horse's neck. The voices stopped, all except Partridge's, which kept repeating the words, 'Hold on. Hold on, mate. It ain't far now. We're nearly at the town.'

He sensed the change of surface terrain beneath his animal. The horse was moving easily, on level ground that was firm and hard unlittered with scrub. Voices, not the voices of cavalry men, but the soft hum of civilian throats that included women, buzzed faintly in his ears. When he opened his eyes he saw buildings, solid buildings, and houses with gardens and flowers. Thick crowds of people – well-dressed people – blurred and receded before his gaze. He heard Partridge say, 'It's O.K., mate, you've made it,' and then, unable to grip his legs and arms round the horse any longer, he fell unconscious to the ground.

Six

ANNE-LOUISE was enjoying the war. It gave the city a taut, excited air that she grew and thrived on – an air of wild, barely controlled hysteria that culminated in the dramatic fury of Mafeking night.

Since the outbreak of hostilities London had been a teeming cauldron of shouting newsboys, of marching men, of people – strangers – calling out to each other in the streets (and they were always readier to call out to a good-looking girl like Anne-Louise than they were to male passers-by), of patriotic songs and the passing of the hat during the 'Give, Give, Give' appeal at the end of the music-hall. Anne-Louise had felt the suspense thrill through her veins, reviving her, giving her sparkling vivacity an upward thrust. Sometimes, when Maxie was jealously protecting her from the admiring cat-calls of a passing troop of soldiery, she felt that the war was being fought for her alone; that the conflict, the tension, was so that she could be provided with a brittle, clear-cut background that admirably suited her sharp, spiteful attractiveness.

On Mafeking night Maxie came round to the house and tapped on the window of the basement kitchen.

'Come on out for an hour,' he whispered urgently. 'Come on up West. There's a fine time going on, flags and lights, the lot.'

She hesitated, torn between caution and the desire to participate in yet another glittering evening.

'It's not my evening off,' she said doubtfully. 'They've gone to the theatre.' She jerked her head back towards the subterranean depths of the house, signifying who 'they' were. 'Florrie's out too.'

'Well, come on then!' He walked to the foot of the basement steps and invited her to listen to the noise. It was distant, a vague thunder of cheering and music, but the message was clear. London was celebrating. London was heady with its own frantic success.

'Come on, Annie!' he said impatiently.

He looked very smart, a real masher, and she noticed that he had a new suit, a double-breasted, high-lapelled tan suit that was piped in green. His bullet-shaped blond head was crowned by a green-banded straw boater and his jacket sported a pink carnation.

She decided.

'Won't be a minute.' She flashed through the kitchen and ran up the five flights of stairs to her room, anxious to change and live up to the dapper, Maxie-style of the evening.

'We'll have to walk,' said Maxie when she returned. 'The streets are so crowded up West that the cabs and omnibuses can't get through. We'll try and get to the Circus. There's sure to be something going on there.'

Kennington was deserted, every inhabitant had disappeared into the night in the direction of the Circus or Mansion House or the Square. A four-wheeler suddenly bowled round the corner. It seemed to be bulging with men all hanging out from it at the peril of their lives and shouting, 'Hurrah for the Queen! Our Tommies have done it! Hurrah for Baden-Powell! Hurrah for the Queen!'

As the four-wheeler hurtled past, one of the men leaned out and was suddenly sick. The stream of port-smelling bile shot past Anne-Louise and splashed on to her dress.

'Pigs!' she spat. 'Filthy pigs that drink too much and don't know how to behave.' Her mood of brittle elation was instantly transformed into a grudge – that it should be her dress, Anne-Louise's dress that was soiled! The four-wheeler had vanished, taking the alcoholic offender with it and leaving Anne-Louise with no one on whom to vent her wrath. Angrily she turned to Maxie, the only person in sight.

'Why can't you walk on the outside like a gentleman? You're uncouth and crude. If you'd been on the outside it wouldn't have happened.'

Maxie gazed at her admiringly.

'It would 'ave gone over me then, wouldn't it?' he said reasonably. He ducked as her hand came out to box him across the face.

'You've a right spirit on you, Annie. It's a treat to see you when you're nasty; look a real peach you do.' When she tried to kick his shin he burst out laughing and held her away with one hand.

'Stop it now! Or I'll wallop you one.'

She hesitated, because she knew he would wallop her. He had done so once before. He had caught her walking in Kennington gardens with a corporal who was sailing for Cape Town on the following day. He had felled the unfortunate soldier to the ground and then pulled Anne-Louise unceremoniously back to the house. Going down the area steps ahead of him, she had felt his hands rise and fall briskly over her behind. It hadn't hurt – she had too many petticoats for that – but her indignation had nearly made her scream at his impertinence. At the kitchen door he had given her one last swipe, a hard one that had really hurt, and suddenly, behind her fury, she had known a tiny shaft of fear coupled with an even tinier shaft of respect.

She paused now and eyed Maxie warily. Then she flounced her skirt out, trying to flick the offending unpleasantness on to the road, and marched swiftly ahead of Maxie, throwing her head well back and letting him see how she despised him.

'I have no further wish to walk with you – on this or on any other occasion.'

'All right,' said Maxie mildly. 'Good-bye.' He turned round and walked back, then vanished round a corner. For a while she took no notice, marching stiffly on, every curve and muscle of her body denoting arrogant dislike.

When she reached the Cut, she looked back to see if Maxie was following and just how far away he was. The street behind, now scattered with a few celebration-seekers, showed no fair-haired figure in a green-banded boater and a tan suit. She walked back a little way, looking down side-streets in case he was hiding. There was no sign of him at all.

'Maxie,' she called coolly, having no intention of letting

him see she was concerned. The streets remained empty.

'Maxie!'

A couple walking past, arm in arm, sniggered at her and turned whispering to each other.

A worrying, depressing thought niggled at the back of her mind; the thought that Maxie might have taken her at her word and was no longer interested in 'walking out' with her. She felt hurt and martyred, seeing the whole affair as his fault and herself as an innocent abandoned in a London street. Then the full implication of what his desertion would mean dawned on her; no more nights at the Empress with fish suppers to follow; no more jaunts down Petticoat Lane with Maxie buying her things – whatever she took a fancy to – off the stalls. No more presents, chocolates, gloves, scarves, brooches. And after all, no more flattering adoration, no more constant wooing and courtship making her feel she was the most exciting, vibrant, brilliant young woman that Maxie had ever met. For that was the real attraction of Maxie – the fact that he considered her utterly desirable and utterly unique – the very centre of his admiring eyes. Of course, she admitted to herself, he wasn't much really, a fish porter and uncouth and not at all what she considered to be a gentleman. She could, and would, do a lot better for herself, but in the meantime it was difficult, very difficult, to resist the battery of attention and flattery with which Maxie surrounded her. Indeed, it was that very flattery, the adoration and the continual insistence that she should accept his homage that had resulted in her finally accepting the apology for his disastrous behaviour on the occasion of their first meeting.

She still, in the rare moments when she thought dispassionately about that first horrible evening, found it hard to associate the Maxie of then, the vile, thrusting, panting Maxie, with the blatant, somewhat common, but always generous Maxie who wooed her now. The transformation was due entirely to Maxie's perseverance in the face of six months of insults, rebuffs and haughty disdain from Anne-Louise.

Two days after the terrible fight in the basement area – when she was still angry, still humiliated and fighting a sense

134

of personal defilement — Florrie had called her to the kitchen door.

'There's a feller to see you.' She was a little resentful and, at the same time, uneasy. Anne-Louise wondered at both.

'What sort of fellow?'

Florrie pursed her mouth up and shrugged to show she didn't care.

'Well, if you must know, it's one of the fellers we met the other night. Not yours,' she added quickly when she saw Anne's face suddenly drain of colour. 'It's the other one. My one. The one called Bert.'

'Why should he want me?' asked Anne nervously.

Florrie turned sulkily away. 'I dunno. But he want to see you and not me.'

'I'm not coming. Tell him I don't want to see him or his horrible friend. Tell him to stay right away from this house or I'll have the police on them!' She was trembling and she leaned against the pantry door to steady herself. The nightmare of the evening with Maxie was recurring with the visit from his innocuous friend. Florrie walked the length of the cavernous kitchen and disappeared through the kitchen door. She returned almost at once.

' 'E says 'e's sorry, but 'e must speak to you. It's very important and 'e can't leave till 'e does.'

'You sure the other one's not there?'

'It's Bert,' said Florrie crossly. 'And 'e's on 'is own.'

'All right. I'll talk to him. But you come too.'

Florrie, who had had no intention of missing whatever confidences were to be exchanged, once again led the way through the length of the basement.

When Anne opened the kitchen door, Bert was standing on the bottom of the area steps, poised as though ready to leap away at the first sign of agitation. Anne-Louise stared amazed, not recognising the check-suited young masher of the other evening. He was clad in a long, enveloping white canvas smock, and had a curious flat-topped leather hat on his head. The smock was damp and stained across the shoulders and down the front, and there was a faint but unmistakable smell of fish wafting across from him. Anne-Louise wrinkled her nose distastefully, recognising the smell as similar to the one on Maxie two evenings ago.'

'O . . . er . . . 'ullo,' he said lamely. Anne-Louise didn't answer. She stared angrily at a point somewhere over his left shoulder.

'I . . . er . . . that is . . . '

'What do you want?'

The unfortunate Bert flushed at the iciness in her voice. He fidgeted his feet on the bottom step and passed a large newspaper parcel from his left hand to his right.

'I . . . er. Well . . . it's like this, you see . . . As a matter o' fact, Maxie asked me to come.' Having spoken the offending name he rushed on to complete the speech before Anne-Louise could either scream or rush back into the house, slamming the door in his face.

' 'E asked me to come, like. 'E was going to come 'eself, but fought you might really go for 'im. So 'e says, Bert, 'e says. You get along there to that little smasher. And you tell 'er that Maxie is real sorry for what 'e done the other evening, for tearing 'er dress and swearing, and calling 'er names, not to mention the other thing what 'e nearly done.' Bert coughed and stared hard at the ground. 'And 'e says you tell 'er, 'e says, that it was on account of 'ow you met. 'E made a mistake, you see. Not realising you was a lady on account of 'ow you met.' There was an indignant and ruffled, 'Well, really!' from Florrie, but Bert was now in full stride and didn't stop.

' 'E says 'e realises *now* what a lady you are, as well as being a proper little smasher. And 'e says, tell 'er Bert, 'e says, tell 'er that Maxie Dance is real sorry. And will she tell 'im 'ow much it costs to mend 'er dress. And please to accept this from 'im.' Bert suddenly thrust the newspaper parcel into Anne's hand. Stunned by his flow of rhetoric, she accepted the package without quite realising the significance of the gift. The parcel was heavy and flabby. When she felt the damp on her hands, she just as quickly thrust it back at Bert.

'Well, you tell your friend,' she whispered murderously, 'you tell your friend that I want nothing more to do with him.

136

And I don't want his apologies or his horrible presents. You just tell him that.' She was angry. She meant what she said because the memory of the other evening, the humiliation and the sense of disgust, was still remarkably fresh in her mind. But she couldn't help making a special note of some of the things Bert had said : 'a real little smasher' and 'a lady'. They were not enough to cancel the disgust of the fight with Maxie, but they were things to be remembered later, to be taken out and examined at leisure.

Bert, his face now almost purple with combination of effort and embarrassment, carefully put the parcel on the kitchen window-sill.

'I shall 'ave to leave it,' he explained doggedly. 'Maxie, 'e says to me, Bert, 'e says, you bring that parcel back wiv you and I'll bash your bleeding 'ead in. Very quick tempered is Maxie,' finished Bert apologetically. ''E gets cross very easy wiv fings like that. And if I take the fish back again 'e *will* bash my 'ead in.'

The magic word 'fish' had galvanised Florrie into instant action. She swept the parcel off the sill and held it well away from Anne-Louise, against the possibility of another dignified – but unrealistic – refusal.

'We'll take the fish,' she said graciously. 'Because your friend did wrong and behaved very badly.' Bert nodded vehemently. 'Tell 'im we don't want to see 'im no more. But we accepts the fish as 'e sent it to show 'e's sorry. What sort of fish is it?' she queried critically.

' 'Alibut,' Bert said a little more cheerfully. He felt happy when speaking on a subject that he knew, and one moreover that did not demand emotional pleas to an icy, irate young woman. 'It's a fresh 'alibut. A nice size and Maxie made sure it's fresh and came from a good catch. You do it wiv a bit of white sauce and a spot of pickled cucumber, and it'll go down a real treat.'

Anne-Louise tried to take the parcel from Florrie, who held it well away from her. 'Give it back,' she said stonily to Florrie.

'Oh, don't be daft! You won't see 'im no more. And it's the

least 'e can do. When all's said and done, 'e did ruin your dress.' She stood well away from Anne, but held the parcel up for her to see. 'And look at the size of that fish! Just think what a feed we can 'ave. Even the poor ole cat'll get something tonight!'

Anne-Louise, about to render a haughtily dramatic reply, suddenly had a vision of the halibut, cooked and golden and surrounded with parsley sauce. In the same way that the promise of a baked potato had sent her – abandoning religion and upbringing – to the Brixton Empress, so the halibut made her waver from her principles of not being under any kind of obligation to the loathsome Maxie.

'I don't want him coming round here,' she said feebly. Florrie saw the spirit weakening and pressed her advantage as hard as she could.

'Course 'e won't,' she said confidently, and turned to the unhappy Bert. ' 'E won't come round, will 'e?'

'No.' Bert spoke without conviction, knowing the ways of his friend and the strength of his unruly enthusiasms.

'There!' Florrie was triumphant. 'You're shot of 'im, and we've got a decent supper to make up for the other night.'

Bert, hoping the matter was now at an end, edged his way gingerly up the area steps. 'Got to get back,' he mumbled. 'Just nipped out between loads so I'd better get back now.'

She knew she ought to snatch the fish from Florrie's hand and throw it after the retreating Bert, but, weakly, she echoed Florrie's words to herself. 'It's just an apology. And I shan't see him any more.'

Unfortunately there was no parsley sauce. The mistress kept the flour locked and measured out what was needed first thing every morning, and a careful note was kept of how much milk was used in the kitchen. But the halibut, cleaned and scaled and steamed over the fish-kettle was nonetheless delicious. Two large portions remained for the following day, and the scraggy black cat wrestled happily with the head and tail.

Three days later Bert was back. With another parcel.

'It's Maxie again,' he said apologetically to Anne's stony

face. ' 'E began to worry about whether that 'alibut was fresh or not. Bert, 'e says, what'll that young lady fink if the 'alibut was a bit off. Bes get round and see if it was all right – and take these dover soles in case it wasn't. We're very touchy about our fish,' Bert explained earnestly. 'Reflects on us like, if a nice bit of 'alibut ain't all it should be – we being experts like.'

'The halibut was very nice,' Anne was reasonably polite. 'But that's the end of it. I don't wan't any more messages from your friend, and I don't want any more fish.'

A hitherto unconsidered worry wrinkled Bert's face. ' 'Ere. You do *like* fish, don't you?'

'Of course.' The idea of anyone who worked in that house having likes and dislikes about food was too ridiculous to contemplate. 'It's just that I don't wish to have any further contact with your friend.' Somehow she could not bring herself to mention the hateful Maxie by name. The reference, 'your friend', helped to preserve the anonymity. Bert was relieved.

'That's all right then.'

'So I don't want the soles.'

Bert sighed. 'Look,' he said patiently, 'you might just as well take 'em. If you don't, I shall throw 'em away in the street. You don't know Maxie when 'e's in a temper. If I take them fish back 'e'll lead off at me for days, 'e will.' Firmly Bert put the parcel on the sill and walked up the steps.

The time for dramatic hurling of newspaper parcels of fish was past. If it was going to be done at all, it should have been done at the time of the halibut. She wouldn't bring the parcel inside though, disdaining to openly accept the gift. It was Florrie who took the parcel in, cleaned the soles and cooked them. Anne-Louise helped eat them.

On Monday Bert was back with a cut of salmon, a delicacy that Anne had never tasted before. The argument about acceptance was purely token and was quickly dismissed before Bert came into the kitchen – invited by a sociable Florrie – to instruct them on the cooking of fresh Scotch salmon.

Life became decidedly richer. Mondays, Thursdays and

Saturdays saw Bert with his newspaper parcels of fish, and not always fish, sometimes Maxie sent along an offering of poultry. The household cat grew fatter, and Anne-Louise found that the image of Maxie, the rapist, was dimming in the new guise of Maxie, the sender of fish dinners. Florrie, unashamedly partaking in the wages of Anne's distressing experience, was openly choosy and complained to Bert if the same variety of fish turned up twice in one week.

At the end of the month Maxie himself came.

Anne heard the familiar clatter of the fish-porter's boots coming down the steps and caught a glimpse of the white smock. When she opened the door the nearly forgotten figure of Maxie stood there, blond sideboards and glossy Prince Albert whiskers bringing back an embarrassing wealth of detail to her mind. Maxie's face was untroubled.

'Bert couldn't get along today, so I've 'ad to bring it meself.'

He spoke as though the whole thing was perfectly normal, as though he was a tradesman who had to arrange for the tiresome business of delivering their free gifts of fish. Anne-Louise was unable to speak. She stood holding hard to the kitchen door with colour slowly mounting in her face.

'Was the cod all right, then?' he demanded of the last delivery.

Anne nodded, wishing she could tell him just what she thought of him, but aware, heavily aware, of nearly six weeks of free fish resting in her stomach.

'Came out of my dad's delivery, that did,' he explained. 'He having his own site in the market like.' He carefully unwrapped his parcel, which was large and cumbersome. 'Thought you'd like to try a lobster. Freshly boiled, it is. You try it with some tomatoes and bread and butter. Very nice, very nice indeed.'

Dumbly she accepted the red, scaly monster. Maxie's gay chatter suddenly ceased. She looked up and saw he was staring absently at the frame of the door. 'By the way,' he said casually, 'you never told Bert about your dress, about how much it cost to mend. You'd better tell me and I'll see about it.'

His oblique reference to the terrible night of the music-hall succeeded where his physical presence had failed. Her tongue-tied embarrassment was suddenly released in a sharp tirade.

'Florrie's mended it for me, no thanks to you! How you've got the cheek to call round here after the things you did and the things you said! I wish the mistress *had* caught you, and I wish the police had come and locked you up! That's what you deserve, you disgusting pig you!'

Maxie's gaze never wandered from the door frame, but a telling change of colour crept slowly up from the collar of his shirt.

'And just because I've eaten your old fish, don't think I've forgotten! I shan't ever forget! Every time I eat a piece of your fish I remember what you did that night!'

'I'd better not send such big pieces then.' He was dismayed, but undaunted, and his cheeky back-chat suddenly sent Anne's temper soaring. She swung the lobster high up into the air and brought it down hard on Maxie's head. A claw chipped off and hit the brickwork over her head. Maxie's gaze left the door frame and moved to Anne-Louise.

'You're a right little smasher!' he said admiringly, and moved quickly back up the steps to avoid another swipe from the lobster. 'Bye-bye now, I'll be back on Thursday – probably bring plaice. Good plaice deliveries on Thursdays.'

His large booted feet nipped quickly up the steps out of Anne's reach and she heard him clumping down the street. When she went in, Florrie was sitting at the table, giggling. She didn't ask why. She knew it was because she had demeaned herself, hitting Maxie over the head with the lobster.

When he came on Thursday she refused to go out, letting Florrie say what she wanted to and take the fish if she wished. Florrie came in carrying a different-shaped package, a smaller, neater one.

' 'E was ever so upset,' she said seriously. 'I think you ought to forgive 'im. 'E really does seem gone on you.' She paused and added practically, 'You know 'ow much they earn, them porters at Billingsgate, don't you? They get five pounds . . . a week!'

141

'How much?' gasped Anne-Louise, stung into replying by sheer astonishment.

Florrie looked smug. 'I thought you didn't know. They earn more than anyone else in London – in England, I shouldn't wonder. And 'e's ever so sorry, really sorry. 'E asked me what 'e could do to put things right so as you'd not think so badly of 'im. And 'ere,' she put the package down in front of Anne-Louise. 'This is for you special. Not fish, that's for both of us. This is just for you.' She watched enviously while Anne unwrapped the package

Inside was a large wrapped tablet of soap marked with the luxury stamp of 'Pears'. A glance at the printed leaflet inside revealed that the tablet was 'scented with Otto of roses'. Florrie's mouth pushed into a circle of disbelief.

'That's two and sixpence, that cost! I know, I saw it in Grimshaw's last week. Two and sixpence! On a piece of soap!'

Anne raised it to her nostrils and sniffed. It was fragrant and delicious and the most expensive, unnecessary gift she had ever received.

'If that was me,' said Florrie greedily, 'I wouldn't ever say anything nasty to 'im again. Not about what he tried to do, or calling us tarts, or anything!'

Anne-Louise stiffened and pushed the soap away from her. That vulgar Florrie should suggest how she should behave was both impertinent and audacious.

'I shall return the soap to him on Saturday,' she said.

On Saturday, he not only refused to take back the soap – by throwing it past her into the kitchen – but handed her a bottle of lavender water, the three-shilling size from S. Sainsbury in the Strand. The lavender water was hurled after him and smashed against the steps, making the area smell delicious for several days. Florrie wept at the abundant waste, and Maxie laughed and shouted down, 'I shan't give you another bottle.'

For two months he brought presents, hung about outside the kitchen door, and persuaded Florrie to ask him into the kitchen when the mistress was out. Then he discovered when

Anne's afternoon off was and waited, dressed, shaved and smelling of gentleman's lemon toilet water, until she was ready to go out.

And at the end of six months she gave up, pressed by his admiration, his undoubted determination to redeem herself, and his unbounded generosity. It seemed she could do no wrong in his eyes. He ignored her snubs and insults. He answered her back cheekily when she lost her temper. The thing he never did was ignore her – he might fight her back, but he never, never let his attention move from Anne-Louise, the central figure in both their lives.

She thought she knew him as well as she knew anyone, and thought she could manipulate him as well as she could manipulate everyone else. The incident with the corporal had made her uneasy because she sensed, vaguely, that perhaps Maxie could not always be handled. The incident now, when he had left her, walked off and ignored her, made her uneasiness return again. She liked Maxie to be subservient, not doing unexpected, self-initiated things.

She wandered back down the road towards Kennington, peering up side streets and down into area basements to see if Maxie was hiding. At last, miserably, she gave up, admitting that Maxie had gone and wondering if he really had taken her at her word.

She arrived back at the house. Maxie was sitting on the bottom step down in the area.

'Got over your sulks?' he asked cheerfully.

'How dare you leave me alone like that!'

He pulled her towards him and wagged a large, stained forefinger under her nose. 'Don't start again, Anne, cos I've decided, if you do, I'm going to clout you.'

'You just dare!' she screeched.

He did.

She was so shattered she could hardly move. Tears started to her eyes, partly self-pity, partly because the blow round the ear had hurt. Maxie had *hit* her. Maxie, who spoiled and pampered and adored her, had clumped her round the ear. Her temper evaporated instantly, leaving her in a welter of pathetic weeping. She felt small and helpless and badly used. Maxie put his arm round her shoulder and tenderly patted her with his huge, rough hand.

'That's right, Annie,' he said kindly. 'You have a good cry and then we'll start out again for the Circus. The celebrations are still going on.'

'It's too late to go now,' she sobbed.

'Not if we walk quickly. Come on now.'

He pushed her up the steps, slipped an arm round her waist and began to walk her briskly along the road. Slowly her sobs died away. She was surprised to find she bore Maxie no grudge at all, she felt quite rested and calm.

'That's better.' Maxie grinned jauntily. 'Put your hat straight. We might see some of me mates and they all know what a smasher I've got. Bert's told 'em. I don't want them to see you with your hat like that.'

She straightened it, not feeling at all insulted. She was the most attractive, the most outstanding, the most remarkable girl that any of the market men knew. She appreciated Maxie's vanity in her.

Over Waterloo Bridge the crowds began to thicken and, once in the Strand, pushing among the crowds became violent. She clung tightly to Maxie's arm, sheltering behind the lee of his great shoulder. Excitement, generated by the mass of people, began to warm her blood. Flags were hanging from windows, a small group of people standing on the steps of St Martin's suddenly began to cheer and wave hats, scarves, handkerchiefs and boas in the air. A thin, cadaverous-faced man standing next to Maxie suddenly snatched Maxie's green-banded boater and flung it high over the heads of the crowd. Maxie turned and began a shouted argument with the man, which finished abruptly when a sudden surge of the crowd bore them away from each other.

The evening was London at its warmest, at its most exciting and passionate. It was noisy, vigorous, alive! Carriages, omnibuses, four-wheelers were jam-packed all the way into the Circus. People, masses, crowds, a density of people surged in no definite direction. Pictures of the Queen – God bless her –

of the Prince and Princess of Wales, of Baden-Powell waved
dangerously on long poles over the heads of the milling crowd.
When they got to the Circus everyone was singing 'Dolly
Gray', and then a rival group on the other side of Piccadilly
began 'Duke's son, cook's son, son of a millionaire'. The singing ended in another burst of wild cheering, cheering that was
hysterical, over-emotional, frantic. A man a few feet away in
the crowd suddenly shouted over to them.

'Hey, Maxie! Maxie Dance! Who you got there then?
Who's that little gel you're toting?'

Maxie grinned and put his arm possessively round her
shoulder.

'Let's have a look at her then. Put 'er where we can see 'er.'

Before she knew what was happening, Maxie had hoisted
her into the air and she was sitting on his shoulders. The
crowd cheered her. Fragments of shouts and calls echoed up
from the babel of sound. 'What a smasher! A real darling!
That's what the boys have been fighting for! A peach of a
girl, a real peach of a girl!'

She was elated. Brittle and taut with passionate excitement,
she smiled and laughed at the crowd, waving at her admirers,
blowing kisses, then singing the first line of 'Dolly Gray'
again, so that the song was taken up by the people around her
and then swelled out to fill the whole of the Circus. And they
were all looking at her, cheering her, envying her. It was
Mafeking night. It was Anne-Louise's night.

When Maxie lifted her down, his face was flushed and
eager. A thin film of sweat hung over his forehead and across
the broad cheek-bones.

'Anne!' he shouted above the roaring of the crowd. 'Next
Sunday you're coming home to meet my ma!'

Knowing what the invitation meant, fully recognising the
significance of Maxie's ordered request, but heady with the
success of the evening and the adoration of the crowd, Anne-
Louise accepted.

Enteric fever, contracted from the polluted river at Paardeberg,
spread savagely through the military and civilian population of

Bloemfontein. Of the two, the civilians stood the disease better than the troops. Several months of atrocious living, of thirst, starvation, heat and enforced gruelling marches had turned the flower of the British army into a wasted, tattered scarecrow group of men who had no resistance to the virulent, scalding disease that decimated their ranks. Bloemfontein, a pleasant city of buildings and trees, was turned into a fever camp, every school and city building stinking with men dying in crowded, insanitary wards – insanitary because there was no room to isolate those who were at the violent diarrhetic stage of the fever.

Eventually he came not to notice the smell. It was so much a part of the ward around him, of the men who lay close on each side and indeed of his own body that it no longer offended him. There were one or two women nursing, but mostly male orderlies tried to cope with the overwhelming task of keeping an army of feverish, bowel-loose men clean and in some kind of comfort. During the day he tried to convince himself that he would not be one of the ones to die, that having survived Spion Kop and Paardeberg and Abraham's Kraal he would not, could not, possibly die of something so unchivalrous as enteric fever. But at night, when the smell and the noises of the feverish sick rose to a crescendo, he could think of nothing but Finch, slumping forward in the saddle with a plume of blood spouting over his khaki shirt.

At last, when the hot weather abated with the beginning of the African winter, the tide of fever ebbed slightly. Later it was to surge virulently back again, but for the moment the fever eased and the hard-pressed people of Bloemfontein had a chance to bury the dead and improve the conditions of the men still in fever. The mail, delayed from home for several months, caught up at last with the troop and Jonathan learned, with a remote sense of unreality, that Myra had borne him a son more than seven months earlier. Her letters, there were nine of them, spoke of things and people so vague, so distant and far away that he found it hard to visualise the village as it was. Even harder to contemplate was the existence of another child, born it appeared without undue difficulty, or so Myra said.

And as though to set his fears at rest there was a note from Betsy, the inveterate letter-writer of the village, who occupied her lonely hours in sending communications to friends and relatives alike.

My dear Jonathan,

Myra has a little boy she is calling Peter, after your old father. She is writing, but I thought I would tell you that she is alright, not like when Harriet was born. We didn't have to fetch the doctor as Mother and me managed and Myra is relieved as she didn't want to part with the sewing-machine, the money from the dressmaking being very handy. Your sister Em came down but when she heard it was a boy she left at once and Myra hasnt seen her again. A fine old carry-on and no mistake.

We are all well. Frankie starts work at Fawcetts next week and Anne-Louise writes from London about the fine beau she has. He works in Billingsgate it seems, but she doesnt seem to answer when we ask where she met him. Mother is bothered in case he is not a Christian and is leading Anne into worldly ways.

Dont worry about Myra. Will gets the milk for her every morning. Its no bother as he has to go for us. Mr Tyler has ploughed up Hill Meadow, but we still use it to short-cut to the shop, only it being that it takes longer now as we have to walk round the edge. I expect youll soon have old Kruger beat and be home before the blossoms are out. God be with you. We pray for you at Sunday Meetings.

Betsy

Suddenly Betsy's practical, well-meaning letter succeeded where all of Myra's had failed. The village, secure in its stronghold of faith and poverty, leapt bright and clear to his brain. He recalled Will Pritchard, inarticulate, honest, and unable to accept thanks or to offer them. Emily, rapidly becoming another oddity at the Vincent *ménage*. Fawcett, pompous, irritating and pathetic. For a moment the veld, the fever ward in Bloemfontein, the memory of the killing and the heat receded, gave way to the village and the green of damp lush countryside. He didn't have to remember Myra. His nights on the veld belonged to Myra, the times when he wasn't too tired or hungry or exhausted, they were the times he thought of Myra. Sometimes he tried to imagine going home, to the cottage and Myra and the two children, but he was unable to encompass the idea. When he thought of Myra it was as though she would still be exactly the same as when he left, with just the quiet, unsmiling Harriet upstairs, no older or noisier, and he and Myra in the kitchen reading the books. When he was well enough he sat and wrote to Myra and to Betsy. He gathered that none of his letters had been received, probably destroyed in a Boer ambush or still in a supply-wagon diverted somewhere over the sandy wastes. He told them he was well, that a slight upset had let him off duty, but that now he would be back and riding with his troop. He found no reason to mention that he weighed six and a half stone and could hardly lift a cup without his hand shaking.

In September he left the hospital and joined a scouting raid. Within three weeks he was back at Bloemfontein, back in the hospital, in the smells and the heat of a rapidly approaching spring. Again he left – and again returned – shaking with ague like an old man of sixty. This time they kept him there for two months, and when at last he went out again he felt that, this time, he was really cured.

The regiment had passed on and left him. He hung apathetically around company headquarters waiting for a troop to be formed, or at least for sufficient of his old company to warrant a special expedition to catch up with the main troop. Finally he was ordered to a temporary attachment with the Intelligence Corps, to be deployed scouting across the veld trying to catch the tiny remnants of guerrilla Boers who were fighting a losing but undaunted action. He accepted the posting with no feelings one way or the other. Enteric fever had drained all animation from body and mind alike.

He was given a fresh mount, a Lee-Metford rifle and a pair of field-glasses. A silent Zulu scout waited for him outside field headquarters and he was handed a map, told where to find the signal stations, and then sent – his old uniform hanging flapping from his emaciated shoulders – with the Zulu boy out into the veld.

He called the boy Sambo, partly because everyone else at field headquarters called him Sambo, but mostly because he couldn't pronounce the Zulu sound that was his proper name. The boy, clad in some kind of spotted animal skin held in place by a worn Sam Browne, rode behind on a rough-coated pony. When he spoke to Jonathan he called him *baas*, but mostly he was silent, following Jonathan slowly across the veld, sometimes raising a coal-black arm to point to a movement on the landscape that Jonathan could not see. Their first expeditions were unfruitful. They found nothing except a blurred track too old to read, and Sambo, crouching over the ground, stared hard at them and then said, 'Naa, *baas*. Treks naa good, *baas*.'

He tried to talk to Sambo, finding the boy's mixed Zulu dialect and Mission English hard to understand, but still in spite of this fascinated by his pagan appearance, and the knowledge that, like himself, Sambo was a male of the species and therefore there must be some mutual link between them. Sambo was so completely unlike the figures in *Uncle Tom's Cabin* – and even more unlike the missionary descriptions of African warriors – that he found it almost impossible to find a topic on which he could talk with the Zulu. He asked him if he had a wife and Sambo answered, 'Yaa, *baas*. Much wife. Over big country,' and extended his hand slowly towards the last, standing tall and silent against the high white sky of early afternoon. He never asked Jonathan any questions either about himself, or about the work they were presently engaged upon. He seemed content to ride silently along behind Jonathan with his slender arms and neck swaying reed-like on the pony.

Jonathan, at first conscious and a little puzzled by his companion, came to accept the silence, the withdrawn aspect of the man and, in time, when Sambo was standing quite still looking over the horizon or was loping buck-like over the sand, he felt

149

a vivid awareness of the man's beauty. An aloof, enigmatic beauty that he did not understand, a beauty that in some odd way reminded him and afforded him the same satisfaction that he got from watching a swarm of bees filing into a new hive. At night, alone on the great sandy scrub wastes with Sambo, the dry scent of cooling earth in his nostrils, he felt he was on the edge of a great knowledge, a knowledge of . . . what? Not life, or God. They were words too confining for the experience he knew must happen. Not love, although in some way it was confused with love. A dream perhaps, a dream that would have the delicate fantasy of a night vision, but one that did not vanish when the morning came. At these times he knew that an awareness of a great mystery was enhanced by the presence of the silent Zulu sitting watching the night sky.

The veld, the place he had associated until now with thirst and blood and spirit-breaking fatigue, changed and was huge and golden, a great space of openness and changing sky, white, red, purple, black. Birds wheeling overhead reflected the soaring quality of the desert, startled herds of springbok leaping wildly away gave it a cleanness it had not had before.

Sambo, uncommunicative, belonging to the soil, knew the veld as though it were profusely studded with trees and landmarks. On one occasion, when their water had run low and they were still three hours from the heliograph post, he led the horses to a small outcropping of rock and then carefully lifted a flat stone to reveal a shallow pit of khaki-coloured water. When they and the horses had drunk, Sambo carefully replaced the stone, and Jonathan, looking back as they rode away, wondered how the boy could tell which of the many identical stones it was that hid the spring.

They had been out for two days on a trek when they sighted the troop of Boer horsemen riding across their line of vision. They were sheltering from the violent part of the day, just after noon, on the incline of a small kopje, lulled by the heat into a sense of profound unreality. Sambo suddenly crouched up on one knee, his huge, long-boned hands reaching down to rest on the ground at each side of him.

'Hau, *baas*! Soldiers!'

Jonathan swung round on to his stomach and fumbled for his field-glasses. He scanned the horizon, but, until he put the glasses to his eyes, he could not see the Boer troop-line at all.

'Many soldiers, *baas*. Many hands – soldiers.' He held up both hands, fingers splayed wide to denote the numbers.

Jonathan squinted down the glasses and tried to count. There were about a hundred so far as he could tell and they were riding in a south-easterly direction, coming closer to the kopje, but, if they maintained their line of travel, not actually meeting it. He kept the line in the glasses until they became imperceptibly larger, holding his hand over the top of the lens to minimise the risk of sun-flashes on the glass.

'We go, *baas*? Go message hill?'

Jonathan nodded, wondering if it would be wise to send Sambo alone and for him to remain here, plotting the route of the column, then decided against it in view of his limited line of vision.

Crouching low, they scrambled to the other side of the hill and mounted, not daring to gallop in case they set up a dust disturbance, but hurrying as quickly as they could.

They were passing another outcrop of rock, about a mile from the kopje, when Sambo suddenly stiffened on his pony.

'*Bass* . . . something bad . . . *baas* . . .'

Jonathan brought his horse to a standstill and scanned the outcrop of rock and the surrounding veld with his fieldglasses. There was nothing moving, nothing in sight.

'Bad *baas* . . . bad . . .' Sambo's face was strained upwards, the nostrils flared and the whites of his eyes flickering slightly. Jonathan's horse moved restlessly, and then Jonathan caught the unease himself, the sense of something wrong about them. Sambo moved his head slowly to face the outcropping of rock. The black body was taut, and Jonathan waited for him to indicate, by a widening of the eyes, by a small movement of the hand, where the danger lay.

'There, *baas* . . . over there . . . bad . . .'

The crack of a rifle shot suddenly smashed the stillness into a sharp scream. Incredulously, Jonathan saw Sambo stiffen again, violently and uncontrollably, then slowly topple forward from his saddle – no sign of blood, no sign of a severed limb – and slump in an odd crumpled heap on the sand.

'Sambo?'

He dismounted and bent over the boy. A small round, seeping hole shone in the centre of the black forehead.

'Sambo?'

It had happened so swiftly he felt there had been a mistake, a foolish silly mistake that should immediately be put right again. He stared about him, bewildered and wondering how and why it had all happened so quickly. He still couldn't see anything, but then a second shot divided the air, a shot that narrowly missed his shoulder and sent him flat against the ground with his rifle against his shoulder.

The outcrop of rock was no more than a hundred feet across, bumpy, irregular and giving excellent cover to the Boer scout who must be lying there. Angrily, Jonathan realised that while they had been watching the column, the Boer scout had been watching them, waiting for them to pass his hiding place so that he could intercept and prevent the message from going to headquarters.

He wriggled forward a few yards, reaching the first rock and slipping quickly into its inadequate cover. Another shot sniped viciously into a rock on Jonathan's right. He heard a frightened whinny behind him and then realised that the Zulu pony had stampeded, frightened by the noise and the dead man lying at its feet into a hasty, terrified flight.

Jonathan unlatched his rifle and waited. Quiet slunk back round the rocks and hung in the air. Tentatively he moved his foot out a little and withdrew it sharply as the Boer rifle sang again. This time he had made a careful note of the direction. It came from the left, from the highest part of the rock, an almost impossible eyrie to scale.

There was a deceptive period of calm, minutes that mounted into half an hour with the sun shimmering iridescently over the rocks. The silence became so heavy that Jonathan imagined he could hear the heavy breathing of the Boer scout. He moved his foot again and, surprisingly, nothing happened. He slithered round the other side of the rock, the side farthest from the Boer rifle and tried to swing up a little behind one of the bigger rocks. The rifle fire prohibited further venture, but this time Jonathan had a swift glimpse of a dun-coloured figure and a black beard. He fired quickly, knowing he would miss, but anxious to attack instead of defend.

There was silence again, a long, sun-drenched silence that soaked into the afternoon. Once he nearly called out to the Boer because the close proximity, the sharing of the rocks, gave him a peculiar sense of comradeship with the invisible man, as though they were friends waiting together, instead of enemies. Then he looked back – to the body of the Zulu boy. It was covered in flies, clustering thickly over the hole in Sambo's head. Two large, crow-like birds wheeled high overhead waiting for the violence on the outcrop to settle.

He felt the pain in his head almost before he heard the shot, a sharp, searing pain along the left side of his brow and temple and then something sticky and warm flowing down the side of his face. Incredibly the Boer was standing, a heavy, bearded man, whose patience and concentration had been greater than Jonathan's. He had stepped out from his shelter the moment Jonathan's attention had wandered, taken careful aim – and had not missed.

Dazed, Jonathan looked at the man, assimilated the bush-shirt, the bandolier of cartridges stretching across the deep chest, and at the same time saw the Boer raise his rifle for a second shot, a more efficient shot.

He rolled sideways – and fired.

The bullet from the Boer rifle spat harmlessly into the ground. The Boer stared wide-eyed at Jonathan, wide-eyed and unseeing. Then he sank slowly to his knees, coughed, and suddenly tumbled forward on to the ground.

The birds hovering in the air were joined by a third. They made no sound, as though they knew noise would not precipitate their coming repast. They just hung blandly overhead, waiting patiently for what hereditary instinct told them they could shortly claim.

Jonathan stepped slowly over the rocks and looked down at

the body of the Boer. He wasn't a young man, his face was tired and middle-aged, and his hands were the rough, stained hands of a farmer. A pair of spectacles stuck out from his breast pocket and there were papers of some kind behind the spectacles. The birds overhead came lower and finally perched on the rock a little way away.

He felt suddenly weary and sick, and he couldn't bear the thought of the vultures tearing the tired, middle-aged body to pieces. He fire at the birds and missed, sending them screaming up into the air.

Blood, flowing down the side of his face, began to run under the collar of his shirt. It was sticky and hot and it dried very quickly into a stiff, powdery crust that was swiftly overlaid with a fresh run of blood. He took his handkerchief from his pocket and held it against the burning pain at the side of his head. It came away drenched.

The birds wheeled low again, great ungainly wings lifting greedily into the still air. There were five of them now. When he looked back to Sambo's body one was crouching a few feet away on the ground, its body quivering with expectation. He began to pull some of the smaller rocks aside, sweating and growing increasingly nervous, not because he was afraid of the Boer troop-line passing across the veld some miles away, but because he was obsessed with the idea of beating the dark birds, of depriving them of their gloating feast. He tried to dig a pit with the butt of his rifle, hauling away at the hard earth in an attempt to make a hollow in which to lay the bodies. It was hopeless, the ground was baked hard, and when he looked over his shoulder again at Sambo, he saw it was already too late.

He took the Boer's water canteen and then rolled the body into what slight depression he had made, covering it inadequately with rocks. It afforded little protection, but it gave him the illusion that the man was lying in a grave. He stood up and closed his eyes, saying, 'O Lord, receive this thy servant into the gates of Heaven. Amen.'

The Boer had killed. He, Jonathan, had killed, and he knew he had no right to pray – a prayer from a killer – for a killer.

But this was a personal death, touching him, Jonathan, because the man had shared the afternoon with him, because he was middle-aged, and mostly because he had a pair of spectacles in his shirt pocket. The idea came to him that this was not the first time he had killed. He had probably killed at Spion Kop. He had certainly helped to kill at the siege of Paardeberg, if not by rifle, then by his mere presence, which stopped the trapped men and women from getting out of their disease-ridden camp. He looked down at the funeral mound of the Boer and, as he looked, saw that the shoulder of his shirt was red with blood running from his head.

He found the Boer horse, and then, leading it behind his own, began the trek back to headquarters – the trek that had taken two days coming out, two days with Sambo knowing the desert and with the rough-coated Zulu pony carrying spare water and supplies.

He had ridden only a little way when the veld began to turn to scarlet and black, the sun burning its huge ellipse into a molten ball. When it gave a last vivid flare of light across the sky, and then dropped below the landscape, Jonathan paused, not knowing whether to camp for the night or to continue a night trek.

He rode on for three hours, keeping the Southern Cross behind him. The bleeding from the side of his head had stopped, congealed into a sticky mess over a wound that hurt every time he moved his head even slightly. At the end of three hours he knew he must rest, and he knew the horses must rest too. He lifted the saddles off, rolled his pack under the right side of his head and tried to sleep in spite of the pain and in spite of the fireless cold of the veld night.

The next day he covered good ground although his head was worse, stiff and extremely painful. In the afternoon the horses began to flag, needing water and rest badly. He urged them on, 'Tomorrow you'll have water,' he said hoarsely. 'Stick it out. Tomorrow you'll be at the field centre.'

He dared not go on that night after sundown, the beasts were too exhausted, and he was afraid if he pushed them too far they wouldn't be able to manage the final stretch across the veld. He chewed half-heartedly on a biscuit, and then, having drunk a little of his water, he soaked a piece of his shirt in the water from the Boer canteen and placed it, turn by turn, in the mouths of the two beasts. His head began to ache again.

The following night found him anxious, but still hoping, hoping that the reason he hadn't reached the station was that he had been going slower than he thought. 'Tomorrow,' he muttered dryly. 'Tomorrow we'll be there.' He tried to eat a lump of hard-tack, and failed. It was too dry and solid to digest or even bite into pieces. He cut down on his water ration, unconsciously admitting the possibility that he might be lost.

On the afternoon of the following day the Boer pony lay down in the sand, its eyes blurred and the tongue lolling out from its mouth. He shot it, and then went on foot, leading his own horse, hoping to save it from a similar fate. The pain in his head was so bad that he wanted to scream. He dared not touch the wound because he was frightened at what he might feel, but from time to time the bleeding began again, not much, but enough to run in a thin trickle down the side of his neck. The next morning his horse went the way of the Boer pony.

He was lost. He had two alternatives – to stay where he was and hope a patrol would find him, or to continue walking north knowing that some time he must hit a camp of some kind. He decided to walk – in the morning and evening, saving his strength and water for the time of the day when it was coolest.

He tried, but he couldn't remember what day it was. 'It was Tuesday when we left, so Thursday when we saw the patrol. It must be Sunday – no – longer than that – six days?' It worried him until the worry became a consuming anxiety. He *must* remember what day it was – remember how many days he had been lost – walking – sipping the water in the canteen – looking at the huge-balled sun dropping below the horizon.

His head had ceased to tear him with pain. It had settled into a dull, permanent throb, a thud-thud, thud-thud, that compelled him to walk in time with it, each foot moving at the same beat as the pulsing ache that now had spread down into his neck – the thud-thud, thud-thud – the left-right, left-right. He threw the canteen away. There was no use carrying it when it was empty. Then he realised how foolish it was because he still had lots of biscuits left and if he met someone who had water, but no biscuits, he could exchange his spare biscuits for some water to be poured into his canteen. When he saw how reckless he had been, throwing the canteen aside, he began to cry, then stopped and turned round to go back and look for it.

The thud-thud, thud-thud went on, even when he was lying on the ground it went on, and now it had spread to his tongue and his throat. When he tried to speak the throbbing burnt the words out of his mouth before he could say them.

He saw Sambo – standing by an outcrop of rock and pointing to the ground, at the flat stones that covered the small well of water. He hurried across and pulled the stones away, but there wasn't any water there, only the body of the Boer farmer nestling by the side of a black bird.

He noticed that the left side of the veld was darker than the right, very black and misty, but when he turned round the two sides of the veld cunningly switched about so that the dark side was still on his left. He tried to catch it, turning quickly when it wasn't expecting it, but the black side still moved and the jarring of his body made him fall again.

Suddenly he couldn't see at all, only through a haze – and only the heat and the sky. Everything was yellow, the air, the sun, the landscape – all yellow turning to brown and all shadowed with mist and haze, the right side as well as the left. The only time the haze went away was when he lay with his face buried into his arm – then it vanished. Lying face down on the baked earth he felt at peace, soothed and remote. He heard the sounds of the veld, the sounds that were not sounds, the noises of dust and scrub and the heavy gong of the sun. Then he heard another sound. A tiny rustling sound that continued and whispered into the air. A noise that moved along the floor of the veld and under him – past him – away from him. A sibilant noise, a gentle tumbling noise, a water noise.

It was nice; pleasing and comforting, a reassuring, loving

sound that pulled him forward – not far – just a few feet so that he could lie and listen to it better – and a few feet more because it was a little louder now. He stood up – miraculously he could see again, clearly and properly without the dazed blur or the black patches over the landscape. He walked forward. He fell and stood again.

He saw the tiny river running between sandy banks. He saw marigolds, sheets upon sheets of bright orange marigolds stretching down to the water's edge, jumping over the narrow band of water, growing thickly – profusely – up the other side – up – up to the rise of a slope leading into the sun with the marigolds making a carpet to the horizon – promising . . . something, something beautiful and wild over the top of the hill, something ancient and vivid and huge. It was a golden ante-chamber of flowers before he came to the ultimate beauty – the final answer to the unknown question. Beyond the hill would be more marigolds, brighter, thicker – a field of marigolds – pagan and glowing – leading him to the agony of a beauty he would at last understand.

Just before he reached out to the water he saw Myra walking towards him. She was wearing the faded blue dress with the sleeves rolled up and the button undone at the neck. And the hem was stained with a thick band of marigold dust.

Seven

MAXIE'S ma, together with his pa, six brothers and eight sisters, lived in a three-storied terraced house in Lambeth. Below ground-level was a kitchen and scullery, above that a formal parlour and the bedchamber of Maxie's ma and pa, and right at the top of the house the two bedrooms, or dormitories, that slept and separated the girls from the boys.

Anne-Louise, on her first visit to Maxie's ma, was ushered straight into the parlour and ceremoniously seated on a horse-hair settee covered in moroccan leather. Maxie's ma was large, very large, fair-haired and possessed of a high, somewhat florid complexion. In her youth she had undoubtedly been attractive, and her skin would have been the clear-toned pink and white of those who are naturally blonde. Fifteen children, an abundance of hard work, rich food and Guinness had turned the English rose into an English bulldog, gross, wheezing and inclined to cough at the least exertion. Maxie's sisters were all like Maxie and their ma, big, blonde, handsome and bulging with noisy life. They clustered round Anne-Louise like a litter of healthy piglets at a feeding trough.

'What a lovely little darlin'.'

'Our Maxie knows 'ow to choose 'em.'

'Ever so tiny, ain't she?'

'Real black, 'er 'air is, real black!'

For a second she was overwhelmed, feeling herself smothered in a surge of plump female bodies covered in purple and yellow and pink – Maxie's sisters favoured bright colours – and only vaguely aware of Maxie's ma sitting heavily beside her on the horsehair settee and patting her hand with her own thick-fingered, heavily ringed one. Maxie, standing behind the settee and glowing with self-importance, placed a possessive hand on Anne-Louise's shoulder.

'She's all right, ain't she?' he said smugly. 'Different from us, like. Looks like a canary in a cage of pigeons wiv all you lot.'

His sisters, in an odd way, seemed to feel no insult, but to delight in his rude frankness, and to delight in the tininess, the neatness and the darkness of Anne-Louise.

'Lovely!'

'Like a little doll!'

'Ever so nicely dressed, ever so nicely!'

Ma Dance wheezed, coughed and held up a restraining hand to quell the noise.

'Maxie!' she breathed. 'You done well. She's got *class*!'

The girls all nodded, happily, sweatily. They patted and stroked Anne-Louise, agreeing that she had indeed got class. And as this was exactly what Anne herself felt, she saw no reason to deny it. She just laughed and shrugged her shoulders at the blondeness all about her.

'Moreover,' Maxie's ma had apparently not finished speaking, but only paused to indulge a wild orgy of coughing. 'Moreover it's a treat to look at someone who ain't huge-bosomed and tow-haired.'

The girls nodded again, stroking their bosoms and their hair to emphasise the difference – in Anne-Louise's favour – between them and her.

'Talks nice, too, she does,' added Maxie informatively. 'And behaves real nice when she's out. Like a lady she is.'

Mrs Dance wagged her pendulous chin wisely. 'That's what you need, Maxie, my boy. That's what you need, a lady!'

The door burst open and a fresh avalanche of blond giants – and even the youngest and smallest were giants – tumbled into the room, surrounding her, smothering her, examining her.

'Right smasher, Maxie!'

'Got a sister, then? Do for me?'

'Lovely little peach, lovely!'

She should have felt suffocated, overwhelmed in the room filled to saturation point with huge, sweaty Saxons. She should have felt insulted and shocked at their rude, coarse behaviour, but she was neither. She was aware – she could see quite plainly – that she *was* different, that she shone among them because of her size against theirs, because of her black hair against their yellow, because of her bright blue eyes against their rather colourless grey ones.

'Well then, dear,' wheezed Maxie's ma. 'Well, 'ow did you meet our Maxie, then?'

'At the Brixton Empress,' she turned to watch Maxie's face colour a little at the reference.

'But it was six months afore she come out wiv me,' said Maxie quickly, ignoring the unpleasant reference to that first incident.

'You in service, dear?' asked one of the bosomy creatures clustering round her. She nodded.

'Good place?' asked another, and Anne-Louise grimaced.

'It's all right, I suppose. But the old gir – the mistress is mean with the food. And the wages aren't much.'

'Right!' Mrs Dance made a mighty convolution upon the settee and heaved herself into an upright position. 'Right girls, is the tea ready?'

'Yes, ma!' chorused eight voices aged from five to twenty-two.

'Then let's give the pore little soul a good feed.'

She swept across the room, a towering column of bright-blue bombazine and jet ear-rings. The girls, pushing Anne-Louise before them, formed into a feeding line and hurried down the stairs after Maxie's ma.

The kitchen, boiling hot with kitchen-range and steaming kettles, was mostly filled by a huge table seating six on the two sides and three at each end. Plates of mounded bread and butter, basins of jam, preserves, potted meats, shrimps, hams, tomatoes and strawberries, jostled each other for room on the table. In each place was a plate steaming with a large fillet of haddock crowned with two poached eggs. Half-pint cups of tea waited to be gulped in a single draught, refilled and emptied again.

Anne-Louise was led forward to a place at the head of the

table, by the side of a gargantuan mound of a man, bald, red-faced and already munching his way through the best part of a whole haddock.

'Hullo, Maxie's pa!' said Anne cheekily. 'I've been eating your fish for over a year now, so I thought I'd come and tell you what I think of it.'

Maxie's pa stopped in the middle of a rotary mastication and stared at her. Then he brought his hand down on to the table and guffawed.

'Cheeky little shrimp!' he bellowed. 'What about that then, ma! What'd yer think of that?'

He impaled a quarter of a haddock upon his fork, swept it into his cavernous mouth and followed it by a whole slice of bread. Then he patted the chair by his side.

'Sit down then, girl, sit down. You look as though a feed would do you good.'

She sat down, picked up her knife and fork, then realised, aghast, that no grace had been asked. She stared round the table: jaws were chomping, hands reaching out for slabs of yellow bread and butter, voices busy with 'Pass the cruet, Maisie', 'Another bit of bread up this end, Clarence', and 'I'll 'ave some of that chutney when you've done, Fred.'

It was like a vast ant-colony, with plates coming and going and cups emptying and refilling, hands moving urgently, carrying food from receptacle to depository. Everywhere was flurry and business-like efficiency concerned with the organisation of eating. Maxie's pa turned and stared at her.

'Come on, gel, don't sit there dreaming. It'll all be gone. Get stuck into your grub then.'

It was obvious that grace was not going to be asked. She took a piece of bread and butter, feeling strangely guilty as she did so, and commenced to eat.

Mr Dance, the table finally emptied of food, leaned back in his chair and belched.

'That will do very nicely, ma,' he said appreciatively. 'Very nicely indeed until supper time.' He rose, belched again and made his way heavily upstairs. Maxie's ma swilled back the last of her cup of tea.

162

'Mr Dance always 'as a lie-down after 'is Sunday tea,' she explained. 'And so do I, if that's all right with you. Girls, you take Maxie's Annie up to your room in case she wants to tidy up.'

Replete, rosy and hot with food, she was led amidst the fat giantesses up two flight of stairs. The door, nicely done with rose-enamelled finger-plates, opened to reveal a biggish room containing three double-beds, two mahogany wardrobes and a tallboy.

'Sit down, do!'

'Have some of my toilet water!'

'Do you use powder? Ma won't let us try rouge, but Maisie's got some powder.'

They surrounded her, admired her, asked nothing more than to assist her in caring for her delightful, different appearance. Maisie went to one of the wardrobes and pulled out a long feather boa, at least seven feet of it.

'This is for you,' she said enthusiastically. 'It's right for someone like you. Doesn't look nice on us, does it, girls?'

They chorused agreement. Another, a larger and blonder one, handed her a string of amber. 'And this, you take this. I want you to have it.'

She was pressed with gifts, fans, jewellery, gloves, from all sides. The girls, not knowing envy, protected by a lifetime of material comforts and security, were ignorant of jealousy or female rivalry. They gloried in Anne-Louise's individuality, her style and vivacity, seeing in her association with their family a cause for pride and clanmanship.

She left their house that night carrying gifts, food as well as what the girls had given her, and assured that she must come whenever and as often as she could. Maxie, glowing with pride, walked her back to Kennington and kissed her good-bye with an air of respectful propriety.

At least one Sunday a month after that she went to the bulging house at Lambeth, and if, at times, she was faintly bothered because she didn't attend the Sunday Meeting as often as she should, or because the Dances were so obviously not good Christians, she smothered the guilt in the enjoyment, the great teeming generosity of Maxie's ma and pa and the warren of his brothers and sisters. At Christmas, instead of going home to the village, as she knew she ought, she wrote to Betsy and her mother saying that the mistress expected her to work over the holiday. Then she put on the red silk dress, the black boa and a new black coat – a made-over present from one of Maxie's sisters – and hurried off to join the Christmas party at the Dance house.

The upstairs parlour was festooned with paper-chains – made by the girls – coloured lanterns, a tree, tinsel ribbons and silver globes painted with angels. The walnut piano, boasting a fretwork panel set over a piece of ivory brocade and lit by two bracketed candlesticks, was open and heaped high with music. Brass bowls of tangerines, oranges, Cox's pippins and walnuts, covered every surface of the room, and under the side-table in the corner lurked a large crate of bottled stout.

For Anne-Louise, however, Pa Dance had purchased a bottle of cherry brandy, not expecting such a neat little thing to help wallop back the stout on which the rest of the family thrived.

The tea over – cold turkey, goose, pork, pickled onions and plum cake – there was a galvanised upward surge to the parlour and the festivities began. Sister after sister took seat at the piano, each rendering a piece that was played gustily if unmusically. Pa Dance, after several draughts of bottled stout, stood suddenly and boomed out the entire verse and chorus of 'Asleep in the Deep', giving an attempted *sotto voce* when he came to the tender 'there on the decks see two lovers stand, heart-to-heart beating and hand-in-hand'. The offering was greeted with loud applause and 'Good old pa!'

Clarence played the flute. Maisie sang, 'I love the Sun', (cries of '*whose* son, Mais?') and Anne-Louise, emboldened by three glasses of cherry brandy, suddenly stood up and asked Maisie to accompany her in 'Oh, Mr Porter'.

She was perfect. She had watched Marie Lloyd – at Maxie's expense – too many times to make a mistake. She had the mannerisms, the gestures, the winks. She flourished the feather boa in the way that Marie did, she placed her hands on her

164

hips and laughed in exactly the way the great Marie laughed. When she finished, the family roared. Maxie's pa kissed her, so did Maxie, so did Maxie's six brothers and the three young gentlemen present who were courting Maisie, Gladys and Ivy. She gave them 'Good-bye, Dolly Gray', 'Champagne Charlie', and 'The Dark Girl Dressed in Blue'. She danced, she sang, she twisted and laughed until the family were hoarse with cheers and praise. She drank some stout because she was thirsty, ate a tangerine and then sang again. Maxie hugged her, Maxie kissed her, Maxie asked everyone to see what a little peach he had. And, sitting on the settee beside him, cradled into the angle of his arm, she felt him bend and whisper.

"'Ere, Annie. What about you and me gettin' married?'

She looked up at Maxie, seeing the broad face, the pink-and-white skin that would one day turn florid and fat, the silky, golden hair that would disappear and leave a bald pate, the generosity that would never change, and the admiration and zest he felt for her, Anne-Louise Pritchard. And she saw — briefly — the strong, withdrawn figure of Jonathan Whitman, the smiling face with the hazel eyes that always seemed to know more than anyone else; the isolated dreamer, the man who appeared to know the secret of happiness, but who had refused to share it with her. The man who was married to his cousin and was now the father of two children.

She gazed up at Maxie and wondered why she always had such a good time with him — and why she still could not forget Jonathan Whitman.

'Perhaps,' she said guardedly. 'I'll think about it and we'll decide later.'

'When?' asked Maxie urgently. She paused.

'In the summer — no — when the war ends. We'll get married — perhaps — when the war ends.'

And for a moment she wondered if anything would happen before the war finished to make her change her plans.

That winter was a bad one in the village. Thick blizzards blew down slush that froze into a treacherous grey mantle over the

165

ground and was then covered by fresh layers of snow. The ice settled in early, towards the beginning of December, and there was no sign of a thaw, only heavier and heavier falls of snow that finally covered hedgerow and ditch in one steep white hill. One of the Misses Vincents' fat cats froze to death and the foxes began to come in from the hills to raid the hen runs. Privies froze, taps and pumps froze, milk froze. It was too cold to wash and it was almost too cold to work anywhere other than a kitchen where an iron range sent out a glow of heat. It was miserable going up to bed – even with a hot brick – and it was worse getting up in the morning, in a room where the temperature was far below freezing and the window was opaque with whorls and designs of frost. At the beginning of the winter Myra's aunt, the village dressmaker and the last of her immediate relatives, died. Myra only had time to grieve a little. The old lady had been the fortunate recipient of a tiny private income and she had, since Jonathan's departure, helped Myra with a little money from time to time. The income died with her and Myra was left with what she could earn from sewing and the food vouchers that were handed out from the Soldiers' and Sailors' Families Association. She managed until December practising economies where she had thought it was impossible. The dressmaking began to get less and less as the severity and economic pressure of the winter pressed poverty harder into the village. At last, in December, at the insistence of Mrs Pritchard, Betsy, Fawcett's cook and everyone in the village who knew of her living standard, she choked back pride and decided to ask the Parish for help.

She lay for two nights fighting humiliation and shame, trying not to imagine the faces of Mrs Panter, the Rector and the local magistrate staring at her and assessing her worth as a creature of charity, trying to devise some other way of supporting herself and the children, of keeping the cottage for when Jonathan came home. There was no other way. She had done everything that could be done. She had sewn, mended, washed and cleaned, but there were too many poor women in the village doing the same thing, and there were not enough people who wanted sewing, washing and cleaning done for them.

On Friday, Parish day, she heated water in the stone copper and poured it, bucket by bucket into the tin bath standing on the scullery floor. Stony-faced, she bathed, carefully brushed and pinned up her hair, cleaned her boots and pressed her Sunday dress with the flat-iron. When she put the dress on – the first time for several months – it hung loose and dropping straight from her gaunt shoulders and she had to take it off again and dart it quickly on the sewing-machine so that it fitted her. She pinned her blue hat with daisies and forget-me-nots round the brim firmly on to her head, and then, sick with humiliation and self-disgust, she walked towards the village, dragging Harriet and Peter, one on each arm.

At the Parish house she nearly turned back, but the sight of Harriet's thin, pinched face pushed her grimly through the door. The hall was high-ceilinged, stone-floored and cold. There was a wooden bench to sit down upon and it was placed in such a way that a constant draught blew directly on to their feet.

She waited for two hours, her shame turning slowly to indignation. She could hear them inside the committee-room, she could hear Mrs Panter's shrill voice and the booming laugh of the Magistrate, none of them caring that she was waiting in a cold passage with two small children. Finally she stopped feeling humble and beggarly and was aware only of fury that they should treat her with so little courtesy, with so much open contempt. When she was at last called in there were two high spots of colour on her cheeks and her back was rigid with suppressed anger.

There was a chair on the near side of the table. They did not ask her to sit down and she stood stiffly to attention facing them across the table. Magistrate Wilkins fumbled through some papers and Mrs Panter stared hard at her hat with the daisies and forget-me-nots round the brim.

'You've applied for Parish Relief, Mrs Whitman?'

She nodded, because she could not trust herself to speak. Magistrate Wilkins consulted the papers on the table. 'You have two children. Your husband is in South Africa.' He paused and then said slightingly, 'Did he go without leaving you funds to live on during his absence?' He exchanged glances with the Rector and with Mrs Panter, a look that Myra interpreted as disparagement for a man who did not have the foresight to save money for an eventuality such as war.

'He left what he could . . . sir. He's been gone for over two years. What he left has been spent.'

Again Mrs Panter stared significantly at Myra's hat, at her Sunday dress and her black gloves.

'Have you tried to get work?' she demanded.

'I do work at home, sewing and anything else I can get.'

'How much do you earn at this . . . sewing?'

She told them. Mrs Panter's mouth curled slightingly and Myra suddenly realised that it was Mrs Panter she resented and disliked, not Magistrate Wilkins or the Rector, but Mrs Panter.

'What is your rent?'

'What do you spend on food?'

'What kind of food do you buy in one week?'

She answered as best she could, trying to make her day-by-day budgeting sound as business-like as she could and endevouring to hide her mounting fury under an exterior of humility. Mrs Panter's eyes didn't move from her hat.

'Is there nothing you can sell?' she asked suddenly.

'No, ma'am. There is not.'

The Rector leaned forward across the table.

'Of course,' he said chidingly, 'you people in the Meeting are all the same. You don't want to come to church, but when it's relief you need, it's us you ask, isn't it?'

Suddenly she could take no more. She felt unclean, undressed. Magistrate Wilkins was staring at her as though he could see what she was wearing beneath her dress and how much it was worth. She turned quickly and went to the door.

'I won't trouble you any more,' she said bitterly. She looked back at them and directly into Mrs Panter's face, hating the woman and knowing it was she who had proved the final scourge to her humiliation. Temper, confined too long under hunger, cold and worry about Jonathan, burst hotly from her.

'If you would like to buy my hat, Mrs Panter — for I see you so openly admire it – I shall be pleased to sell it to you for sixpence. My family and I will be able to feed well for one day and you will be happy with the possession of my hat.' She stooped to grip the hands of Harriet and Peter more tightly in her own. 'Good afternoon to you. I am obliged for your time and kind attention.'

She had the satisfaction of seeing a slight flash of discomfort on Magistrate Wilkins's face, then she closed the door and left them.

Returning home she walked so quickly that the children found it hard to keep up with her. When she got indoors she was trembling, a mixture of rage, pain and cold.

'We'll manage!' she said fiercely to herself. 'We'll manage without asking for charity.' But she was aware that she had been taking charity all along, from Betsy and the Pritchards, from Jonathan's two brothers in the next county, who had sent her money from time to time, from her aunt until she died, and from anyone in the village who gave her clothes, or asked her in to have a dinner. Without charity she could not have survived.

Two days after Christmas, economic disaster struck at the Pritchards, a disaster that monetarily crippled them for two years, that threw them right back into their poorest and most worrying days, and had far-reaching repercussions throughout the village. Will Pritchard, the main wage-earner of the family, slipped on a covered ice-patch and broke his leg.

Will, terrified that his injury might prevent him from working, tried to stand upright and pretend that the agonising pain was nothing more than a sprain. He hopped and dragged himself for a few paces – making the leg far worse – and then crumpled in a moaning heap on the snow. He was pulled inside by Betsy, his mother and young Frankie, and heaved himself, with their aid, on to the kitchen sofa.

Mrs Pritchard had helped in too many houses of sickness not to know that her son was badly injured. Frankie was sent for the doctor and she and Betsy cut the boot from Will's foot and tried to ease his trousers from the distorted leg. When the doctor came – at the end of eight hours – he confirmed what Mrs Pritchard already knew, that Will's leg was broken, that he would not be able to walk for several weeks, that the doctor would have to pay several visits. Will, lying flat on the scrubbed kitchen table, bore the setting of his leg with white-faced stoicism, and added to his physical misery the knowledge that the fall would set the family back at least a year in doctor's bills.

The family of Pritchards, cousins, nieces, uncles, in-laws, swarmed through the snow with pies and preserves, most of them leaving a little money, not much, but as much as they could afford. They gave because it was 'family', but what they gave was not enough to replace Will's earnings, or provide for the financial burden of medical attention. Betsy wrote to Anne-Louise, swallowing her pride in their present need and asking if Anne – who had ceased sending money without any explanation whatsoever – could help. For a little while Anne sent a few shillings, then the money dwindled and finally stopped altogether. Betsy could not bring herself to ask again.

She came, on the third day after the accident, to see Myra, trudging knee-deep through the snow and holding her hands, swollen with chilblains, wrapped in a fold of her scarf. Myra winced when Betsy took her hands out of the scarf.

'Betsy! Your poor hands! You must try and keep them warm. I'll make you a pair of gloves as soon as I can.'

Betsy screwed her mouth in pain as she tried to straighten her inflamed fingers. 'I can't get them on. I've tried. It's putting my hands in water all the time. They just don't get better.'

'How's Will?'

'Worried to death because of the money. We've told him, mother and me, that we'll manage somehow, and we will. Worrying won't make it right.'

Myra hesitated, then went to the dresser and took a coin out of a spotless teapot. 'Give this to your mother. I'd like to give more but . . . with Jonathan away . . .' She thought for one dreadful moment that Betsy was going to cry. She watched the round face crumple a bit and then saw Betsy swallow hard.

'Will was worried about you too, Myra. Him not being able to get the milk and that. And not looking in to see you're all right.'

Myra nodded confidently. 'I can manage. Tell him I can manage.'

'I'll come when I can, but it won't be often.'

It was left unsaid that Betsy would need to spend every spare moment trying to earn extra money; that not only would Will be unable to fetch the milk, but that the Pritchards would probably be able to afford milk only once a week. Economies would have to be made, stringent economies.

Betsy nervously chewed her lip and stared hard at Myra. 'I was wondering if you could get Jonathan's sister to come and help.'

'If I need her, I'll ask,' said Myra calmly. 'Now you get home and stop worrying. How's Math?' she asked as an after-thought.

'Still at sea.'

Again she thought Betsy was going to cry, but instead she got up and folded her hands back in the scarf. The skirt of her dress was soaked where she had pushed through the snow.

'Thank you for coming, Betsy.' She reached forward and touched Betsy on the shoulder, then unlatched the kitchen door and watched the stocky figure wade through the snow. Betsy looked back and she waved happily, trying to pretend a confidence she did not feel.

When Betsy had disappeared round a slope of snow she went back and sat at the kitchen table, wondering bleakly how she was going to manage. Not only because of Will, but because Betsy too had helped when she could. The mornings since Will's accident she had risen early and gone the three miles, there and back, for the milk, worrying all the time she was gone that Harriet and Peter might not be all right. Will Pritchard had helped her to drag the logs in from outside, to thaw the pump and get water, to patch boots that leaked and let in the snow. He had set up a scare to try and keep the foxes

171

away from the hens. It had worked for a while, but two nights ago she had heard the hens crying and in the morning there were dog tracks round the side of the run. Without Will Pritchard she knew it would only be a matter of time before the hens began to go.

'Fire's going out, mumma.'

Harriet prodded her hip and pointed to the stove.

'Peter's cold.'

Myra put her hands inside the small, woolly clothes of her son. He was glowing with heat and comfort. She looked at Harriet and knew that the child had used Peter to express her own misery, a habit she had developed when she first began to talk.

'All right, Harry, mumma will make the room warm again.'

She piled logs on to the stove, then hitched her skirt into her apron band and went outside to bring in fresh wood. It was frozen and covered in snow. When she piled the logs in the scullery a wet puddle began to form on the stone floor.

She managed for a week, not daring to leave the children for long, because somehow Harry made her nervous, the thought of Harry alone frightened her more than Peter. Finally she went up to the Vincents' cottage, taking Harriet with her, but leaving Peter alone in the cottage – because he was a boy and would not be allowed in. Emily answered the door, her face registering alarm and then, when she saw it was only Myra and Harriet, distaste.

'Oh.' She stood with the door open as narrowly as her face would permit. Myra pulled her shawl up round her neck and shivered.

'Could I come in and talk to you, Em?'

Emily frowned. 'This is not my house, you know. It belongs to Miss Thalia and Miss Aleen.'

'Just for a little while, Em. I want to talk to you.'

Emily hesitated and then grudgingly held the door back.

'For a few minutes, then, no longer. And wipe your feet, little girl, wipe your feet.'

Myra felt Harriet's small hand grip tightly on her fingers.

'I'm cold, mumma,' she whispered. Her breath made a tiny

cloud of mist in the air.

Myra followed Emily through the door and then stopped, amazed as Emily had been on her first visit at the pinkness, the neatness, the demureness of the room.

By a china cabinet in the corner sat one of the Misses Vincent, a bowl of soapy water at her side. She was carefully removing the china ornaments from the cabinet and rinsing them with a damp cloth. A fire in a grate – not a kitchen range, but a proper fireplace – burned with coal instead of wood, and the heat made the whole room glow with warmth.

'Well, what do you want?' Emily did not suggest that Myra should sit, and she made no attempt to sit herself. She stood between Myra and the Miss Vincent at the cabinet. It was as though she were protecting Miss Vincent from the vulgar intrusion of the outside world.

'You've heard about Will Pritchard, Em?'

Emily shrugged. 'Done something to himself. No matter, no matter.'

Myra cleared her throat.

'He's been coming to help me, Em, he and Betsy, and, of course, now they can't come.' The expression on Emily's face changed suddenly, the apathy and indifference turning to cautious suspicion. Myra hurried on, 'Could you help me, Em. Just a little. Come down in the morning and stay with the children while I get the outside things done. Not for long. Just till I get the milk and see to the wood and hens. Then you could come back here and needn't move out until the next morning. I hate to ask you, Em . . . '

'Then don't,' interrupted Emily curtly. 'Then don't ask me, for I won't come. You got yourself married, I didn't. They're your children, not mine, and I want no part of them.'

'But, Emily . . . '

Emily suddenly swung round as though she had been stung. Harriet, fascinated by the china figures in the cabinet, had moved away from Myra and was standing by Miss Aleen, watching her soap and clean them. Emily was immediately beside the odd little Miss Vincent. She wrenched Harriet's shoulder away and spun her back to Myra.

'Keep away, little girl! You're a very bad, wicked little girl! If you were mine you would be punished!'

'But she's not yours!' snapped Myra. 'You just told me she's not yours and you want no part of her.'

She was ashamed of having asked Emily for help, ashamed because Emily made even the asking seem like begging. She took Harriet's hand in hers and moved towards the door. She could feel Harriet was trembling. At the door she stopped and looked back. 'You're a cruel woman, Emily. I'm sorry for you, but you're cruel and hard.'

On the way back to the cottage she tried not to cry because she knew it would upset Harriet. Once, when the only letters she had received from Jonathan arrived, she had cried, and Harry had rocked to and fro screaming and weeping and refusing to be comforted. It was worse from Harriet because she was usually so quiet.

'Peter wouldn't like it in that house, mumma.'

'We won't go there again, dear.'

Peter was all right when they got back, chortling to himself and trundling round the kitchen on his woolly behind. Peter was usually all right. It was Harry she worried about.

She managed again, sometimes with Betsy's help, and sometimes a member of the Pritchard tribe would come in and chop wood. But mostly the village was shrouded in silent trouble, each house coping with its own problems of sickness and cold and food that the winter had shrunk to a minimum. The vegetables dug before Christmas were eaten, the stores raided and finally gone, and still the ground was covered and there was no way of digging out the late crop of turnips and swedes.

Harriet became ill, not seriously ill, but bad enough to lie on the sofa staring into the fire and not wanting to eat. For two days Myra dared not leave the child, the milk ran out, and there were only eggs and potatoes left in the house. On the third day the still, dark weather broke in another fierce blizzard, a blizzard that kept the sky dark all day and made Myra light the lamps at two o'clock in the afternoon. Harry whimpered slightly and then was quiet on the sofa.

The following morning the snow still swung furiously in

the morning air, but it was lighter and Harry seemed a little better. Myra took the milk-pail from the scullery and packed paper into the soles of her boots.

'Be still, Harry, until I come back. If Peter cries, just talk to him and tell him I'll be back soon with some milk.'

Harry stared up at her, withdrawn and quiet, giving no sign that she had heard.

Myra stepped into the lane and was immediately buffeted by the icy, snow-filled wind. Her face and shoulders were covered within a few minutes, and almost at once she stepped into a waist-high drift that stretched across the width of the lane. By the time she had struggled through the drift and out to the other side, she was panting and aware of a narrow stream of sweat running down the small of her back. She pushed as hard and as fast as she could, blinded by snow and using the hay-ricks as landmarks because the rest of the landscape was one huge blur of white and grey.

When she reached the woods it was easier for a little while, the trees giving a tiny shelter and the snow not quite so thick underneath. But she began to worry about the open fields beyond the wood, the meadow that led to Sandy Bottom and down to the farm-track.

She came out of the trees into a gale that tore her scarf away from her head and filled her nose, mouth and eyes with blinding snow. Her dress was so wet that every step was a conscious, dragging effort involving pulling yards of sodden wool along in the blizzard. A pain in her chest, partly cold and partly caused by hurrying, burned and made her cough. She groped her way across the meadow, hoping she was in the right direction, but no longer able to see – and the cold, the pain, the misery of fighting her way across the freezing fields suddenly burst from her in a gasping, choking sob. A sob that shook the frame of her thin body and was followed by another and another, until she was crying not because of the snow and the wind, but because she was tired, so desperately tired of fighting, tired of pretending that she had enough to eat, or could manage the work and the children, tired of not admitting that Jonathan might be dead, that he might never come home again

175

and she would have to go on fighting for the rest of her life.

Her body began to shake with tears and with cold. Now, away from Harriet, she could abandon herself to a frenzy of grief that she had never indulged in before.

'Dear God!' she moaned. 'How much longer? How many more winters without him? How many more springs and summers?'

She swayed back and forth in the gale, rocking her body to and fro and hugging her thin arms tightly round her waist. The cold and the snow gave release to her pain, her agony. In its bitter, searing ice it reflected her life, her blank, desperate life without Jonathan. Her pride was torn away into the shrieking wind, swallowed up in two and a half years of gnawing torment, the knowledge that he might already be dead, have been dead for months, years, and she not knowing. The agony broke from her in a wild scream, a despair, a cry that rose above a lull in the wind and sounded through the cold.

'How much longer? Dear God, how much longer?'

Tears flooded her face, her throat, her breast. The pain in her chest swelled into more tears, raining down, pouring unchecked from her eyes until they froze on her cheeks and coat. Uncaring, she brushed her mittened hand across her face and felt ice scrape on her skin, and still she wept.

Like a creature without purpose or intent she stumbled forward across the wastes of drifts and banked snow. Hours – years – later the weeping stopped, leaving her with a dull despair that throbbed meaninglessly in her mind. She did not know where she was for the sky had turned black again, but she pushed forward, falling in drifts and standing upright to push forward a few more paces, dragging the wet dress round her legs, and falling again – pushing herself on to get the milk – because there was nothing else she could do.

It was two days before they found her. She was lying in a drift seven miles from the farm. The features of her face were thickened with frost into the face of a monster and her hand was frozen so securely to the milk-pail that they had to break the handle before they could take it away and bury her.

Eight

IF MATHEW, home from the China seas, was surprised to see his wife on the Portsmouth quay with a small boy tugging at her right hand, his face gave no indication of any inward concern. He came down the seaman's runway, balancing neatly on his small dancer's feet and holding his seaman's chest and the canvas ditty-bag under one arm. He looked so much like the picture *'Home from the Sea'* that Betsy nervously wondered why he wasn't carrying a cage with a parrot in his other hand.

A light breeze was blowing from across the Solent, lifting the lawn ruffles on the front of her starched shirt-waist and making the tendrils of hair round her ears wisp up and touch the brim of her hat. She was uncomfortable and embarrassed, wondering what on earth she would have to say to Math, and he to her, after a separation of two years and ten months. Peter, pulling excitedly at her arm, kept pointing to the sailors as they stepped on to the quay.

'Is *that* Uncle Math? Well is *that* Uncle Math?'

She had arranged to leave Peter with Mrs Bunts when she knew Math's ship was coming in, but at the last moment had changed her mind because she felt Peter might help to dispel some of the strangeness of meeting Math again. Now, with the small boy hopping up and down and pointing to the sailors, she began to wish she had left him at the lodgings as planned.

'Well, is *that* Uncle Math then, Auntie Bets?'

'No. That's not Uncle Math. This is Uncle Math now, with the wooden box and the canvas bag.' She watched him coming ashore, seeing him both as a stranger, and as a familiar, intimate figure. Neat, quiet, composed, he was her husband and yet not really a husband. He grinned, came over to her, looked at Peter, said 'Hmm,' and then kissed her gently on the cheek.

'How you been, old girl?'

Suddenly she didn't feel uncomfortable any more, only terribly, terribly choked with tears that filled the back of her throat and stopped her from answering. Mathew put his free arm round her shoulder and pulled her into his side and she realised how tired she was – not tired with her body – but tired with years and nights of worry, about money, about Will, about Anne-Louise, about Myra and Jonathan Whitman and, right at the back of her mind, about Mathew.

'You crying then, love?'

She shook her head, and indeed she wasn't crying. She had learned, since her marriage, not to cry. Too many people who depended on her were disconcerted when they saw her cry.

'I've got some things in my box for you.'

He squeezed her shoulder, gently and then again more boisterously and tried to kiss her mouth. The wind flapped the brim of her hat down and caught him across the bridge of her nose.

'Can't get at you under that perishin' hat.'

'It's the same one I got married in.'

'Well, I was too nervous to kiss you then, wasn't I?'

He grinned again, his narrow, navy-blue eyes crinkling up into dark lines in his pointed face, and the newness of him, the feeling that she was meeting a stranger vanished, leaving her with a warm ache somewhere around her breastbone, an ache that was partly joy because he was home and partly the anguish of knowing he would soon be sailing off again.

'How long have you got, Math?'

'Quite a while, love. Quite a while.' He stared down at Peter, who was hanging back behind Betsy's skirt with one finger stuck in his mouth.

'Hullo, young-un.'

Peter took his finger out of his mouth, said, 'Hullo, Uncle Math,' and put the finger back in again.

'This is Myra Whitman's boy,' said Betsy hastily. 'I wrote

you about her passing away in January. She's up with Jesus and the angels now.' She added the last sentence quickly because Peter was staring warily at her. She knew it was silly that a little boy of two and half would remember much about his mother, but she was anxious not to let the ugly side of Myra's death penetrate his mind.

'Ah ha!' Math grinned again. 'I saw him from the ship, I did. Thought for a moment you'd left something out of your letters that I should have known about.'

Betsy stared hard out to sea, pretending not to understand. A faint flush crept up her neck, a flush that was discomfort and unhappiness and guilt. Because she had left something out of her letters to Math. She had kept secret from everyone, except the vulgar, good-natured, bucolic Mrs Bunts, the news of the child that had not been a child. Mrs Bunts had helped her. Mrs Bunts had seen her through the pain of losing the child, through the agony of grief that had been swallowed up in the more lasting worries of money and Will's illness. She pushed the memory of the time away from her and watched two seagulls lifting and dropping in the currents of wind.

'I booked us back at the Buntses',' she said. 'Mr Bunts is bedridden now. He can't drink as much as he used to, so it's quieter there.'

'That's fine then. Come on, young-un!' He hoisted Peter up on to his shoulder and then began to walk along the quay, balancing the chest beneath his arm and the boy on his shoulder perfectly against each other. Betsy took the canvas bag and walked beside them.

'Would you like to come along-a-me and see the Fleet lit up for the coronation, young Peter?'

Peter glowed and held tightly to the round sailor hat that was swaying gently beneath him.

'It's all right, isn't it Math? Having Peter with me. I can't leave him with ma. She and the family are working every minute they can to pay Will's leg money. I keep Peter with me and Jonathan pays me three shillings a week.'

Mathew stopped, put down the chest and swung Peter

round to his other shoulder. 'Who's looking after the little girl?'

'Emily. I took the children to her after Myra fro – after Myra went to live with Jesus. She went quite funny when she saw Peter, very white and odd, just like the old Vincent women. Said she couldn't have the children in the house under any circumstances. They weren't hers and she didn't want them. She shouted at me and tried to push me out of the door and the children started to cry. Oh, Math! It was awful! I wanted to help, but didn't know what to do. Will was flat on his back and ma and me was frantic with not knowing how to get the doctor's money. Finally she agreed to take the little girl. She had one of those funny old women down and made Harriet sit on the settee while she walked round her and stared and stared at her. Harry just sat there, all white and still. She never even cried when I went out of the door with Peter. Just sat on that settee of theirs, with her feet not touching the floor. I thought when Jonathan came back he'd try to get someone else to take her. But he doesn't seem to know properly what he's doing. He gives Em three shillings a week, and me three shillings a week, and then he's away down to Romney Marshes, herding sheep with his father.'

Mathew nodded, as though it were all quite straightforward, and then she realised that she was shouting, or at least speaking much too loudly. Anxiety and a bad winter had drawn her tension to a sharp, unrelieved pitch. The news about the village, news she had planned to tell Math in concise, well-spaced-out detail, poured from her lips in a confusion of jumbled sound.

'He's so strange, Math! Jonathan's so strange! He won't talk to anyone, and when he comes home he shuts himself in their cottage and reads, and won't come to Meeting or anything. And he looks at the children so oddly. As though they aren't his at all. I get so worried about him, Math. And about Harriet in that funny old house with the three old ladies. And . . . '

Mathew stopped again and put the box and the little boy down on the ground. He placed his two hands on her shoulders.

'You worry too much, Betsy James.'

She never thought of herself as Betsy James, only as Betsy Pritchard. In the village no one ever called her Mrs James. It was always 'Grace Pritchard's eldest girl' or 'That Betsy who's so handy for the rough work'. She remembered that Mathew was home on leave, that he hadn't seen her for nearly three years, and that she ought to try and be entertaining company for him.

'Sorry, Math,' she mumbled. 'And I meant to be so cheerful when you came ashore. If it was Annie now, she'd have had you laughing before you even set foot on the quay.'

'Ah, yes,' said Math mysteriously. 'Our Annie's a different story altogether.'

She darted a quick look at him, wondering what he meant. Sometimes she had the feeling he didn't like Anne-Louise very much, or maybe he did like her, but, being Math, he never said. He never spoke at all about what he thought – only about things – facts – that had actually occurred.

'Well now, Betsy. We'll go to Buntses' and have a piece of tea. Then we'll see what's in the chest. Then we'll take young whatsit here to see the Fleet lit up.'

She began to feel the little tremor of excitement that came every time Math was home, the sense of a holiday, of new un-expected things to look forward to. She wanted to ask him again how long it would be before he must sail, but she de-cided not to spoil the pleasure of this first day with him. Once she knew the day he was leaving, she would begin to count, and then the excitement would be tempered with misery.

'How's Will?'

'He's working again.'

They turned the corner of the street and she took the key out of her purse to unlock the door. There was no need. As they arrived at the step, the door was dramatically flung open to reveal the stout outline of Mrs Bunts.

'Home from the sea!' she shrieked, and flung herself into Mathew's arms. Over the top of her puffed, highly curled and padded black hair, Mathew winked at Betsy and she giggled. When Mathew came home everything was all right.

When they opened the box Betsy was astounded. He always brought her something back, a brooch, or a piece of lace from Gibraltar, a wooden carving from an African port, some sweets, and once a coconut that had been so long on board all the milk had dried out from the inside. But this time, when he opened the box, he lifted something wrapped in a piece of calico, carefully unfolded the cloth, and stood the contents on the table. It was a cup of egg-shell delicacy, pale blue and painted with tiny figures in tones of ivory and mauve. When he held the cup up to the light you could see right through the bottom. He went back to the chest and produced more calico-wrapped packages, unwrapping each one carefully and setting it out on the table until the full tea-set stood there – even a teapot – everything blue and ivory and lavender.

'Oh, Math!' She picked a cup off the table and stroked it. It felt like the shell of a thrush's egg.

'Nice, ain't it?'

She imagined herself sitting at a table filling the delicate porcelain cups from the transparent teapot – perhaps when Mrs Fawcett ventured out from the big house on one of her charity visits. Then she remembered that she was Betsy Pritchard and had no place in which to put a china tea-service, except in a box under her bed at home.

'It's beautiful, Math. Thank you very much for bringing it for me.'

'Saved up a bit this trip, Bets. Thought we could look out for some empty rooms here at Portsmouth. And we'll buy a table and a few bits.'

She stared at him, wondering what quiet, odd thoughts were wheeling slowly through his head, what had prompted him to buy her a tea-set; and what, six years ago, had prompted him to buy her the crimson silk.

'Well, that would be nice, Math,' she said slowly. 'But it doesn't seem practical really, does it? While I'm working and keeping a place here in Portsmouth, I might just as well be helping out at home when you're at sea.'

'Ah, yes,' he said cheerfully. 'But I won't be on long services any more.'

She was surprised, then suddenly afraid because she knew he had something new to tell her, and she had grown to distrust things that were new. Usually they were unpleasant things, involving money and hard work.

'You . . . What have you done, Math?' she asked nervously.

He smiled and nodded confidently. 'Transferred to submarines,' he said. 'No long services. They're for defending the coasts, and we'll be popping in and out of Portsmouth every other day.'

'Submarines?'

'The Frenchies have them. The Kaiser's got them. And now we're going to have them. And I've transferred to the Submarine Service – meaning I'll be home a lot and we can set up house in Portsmouth.'

She wasn't sure quite what to think. The submarines were new and crazy like the automobile and the zeppelin. They were things one heard about but quickly forgot because no one had time to take them seriously. She distrusted them because they were new. But if Mathew's information was correct, it meant . . . it meant a house with the tea-set unpacked and seeing Math all the year round and not worry and counting the months until he came home again.

'Is is dangerous?' she faltered.

He shook his head, and made one of his quick, startling changes of conversation.

'Hurry up if we want to see the Fleet, Betsy. They'll put the lights out before we get there.'

Later that night, lying on his back staring, he turned and she could tell he was lying on his back staring up at the ceiling.

'Was you all right that time?'

'What time?' She felt her heart pounding, suspecting what he was going to ask.

'On your own that time. Just after I left. Bunts wrote to me.'

She could think of nothing to say except 'Oh'.

He reached his hand across and felt for her fingers. His hand was small and warm and the fingers very smooth considering he was a seaman.

'You should've told me, Betsy. You should've told me before I left.'

'You were going off, Math. It wouldn't have helped . . . no point in making things worse.'

He squeezed her fingers in the darkness and then lifted her hand and held it against his cheek so that she felt the silky stiffness of his beard against her palm.

'Well, I'll know next time,' he said quietly. 'Because I'll be here, won't I?'

'Yes, Math. You'll be here.' She curled into his side, not thinking about anything for the first time in nearly three years, and then she fell quickly asleep.

She found two nice rooms in Portsmouth, basement rooms, but one of them had a huge iron stove that threw out so much heat that the other room was warm as well. There was brown linoleum already on the floor and she bought a bed and a table and two chairs from a junk yard at the back of the harbour. The table and chairs didn't look much after standing out in the rain, but Betsy, used to working in houses where the furniture was good, had an eye for wood and design. When she had rubbed linseed oil into the table and chairs and then waxed and waxed and waxed them, the wood began to come up a warm, mellow golden colour. The legs of the chairs were bowed in a graceful curve and each foot of chair and table ended in a claw and ball. The top of the table was inlaid with mahogany shells and scrolls. When she had finished polishing the top, she unpacked the china tea-set and spread it carefully out on the gleaming surface, gloating in the reflection of each cup and saucer on the polished wood.

The most expensive item was the mattress. If she had been at home she could have made her unbleached calico mattress-cover and then, after the Christmas poultry pulling, have filled it with feathers and scraps of fleece. Living in Portsmouth she was forced to pay seventeen shillings and sixpence for a woollen flock mattress and it cost more than the table, chairs and iron bedstead put together. Mrs Bunts lent her a small bed for Peter – 'Bless 'is little 'eart!' – which she set up in a corner of the kitchen. She bought a kettle, a saucepan and a pail, and then she went home to fetch her linen, which was packed in the box under the bed.

She went on a Saturday, knowing that Jonathan usually came back to the village on Saturdays and thinking it right that he should see Peter when he could. She was excited, planning how much she could carry back with her on the following day and wondering if her mother would give her a few old cups that she and Math could use for everyday mealtimes, the china tea-set being a special piece, coming out only on ceremonial occasions. On the train, walking up to the village from the station, she felt as elated as the small boy at her side.

'Just wait till we tell Auntie Pritchard about our new house,' she said, and Peter chuckled and threw a stick at a herd of cows.

She was lifting the latch on the back door when she heard a voice she had not heard for more than a year.

She paused, and then opened the kitchen door. When she went inside Anne-Louise was sitting at the table in front of a large basket of exotic fruit – oranges, bananas and grapes. She was talking to Daisy, the next to youngest of the Pritchard girls, and she stopped to look up when Betsy came in.

'Hullo, Betsy.'

Betsy slowly removed the pins from her hat and placed it on the table. Then she went round to kiss Anne-Louise on the cheek.

'Hullo, Annie.' She stared at the basket of fruit. 'That must have cost something.'

Anne laughed, a trifle uncomfortably, and dabbed fussily at an orange. 'Well I thought with Will being ill, and Ma and the children not having much in the way of nice things, I'd treat them all.'

She glared at Betsy, defying her to say anything about not sending money when they needed it.

'Will's not ill now. He's working again. So is Frankie, and Daisy will start soon. We're all working so that we can pay the doctor.'

185

Anne jumped up from the table and began to fidget with the kettle on the stove. She looked slim and elegant. She was wearing a pink cotton dress that was completely unserviceable. It was strapped and stitched with pink of a lighter shade and had two rows of flouncing round the hem.

'Well, actually that's why I've come home,' she said confidingly. When she said the word 'actually' she gave it a long drawn out sound as though emphasising that she was a Londoner and spoke differently. 'You see I've decided to come home and get a job in the village. Then I can help ma and Will.'

'I thought you were supposed to be courting,' said Betsy stonily. Anne shrugged and made a small grimace.

'Oh, he wasn't much really. They were a very vulgar family and not good Christians at all. I told him – Maxie, his name was – told him it was my duty to come home and help the family and that nothing would make me change my mind.' She laughed gaily, and when Betsy didn't answer her smile faded and she snapped. 'Oh, for goodness' sake, Betsy! Stop looking so grumpy and cross. I don't wonder your Math rushes off to sea whenever he can. And honestly, Betsy, don't you ever look in a mirror? You look terribly frumpy! Why do you always wear brown or dark blue? You know dark colours don't suit you.'

'Where's ma?'

'Gone to a lying-in,' said Anne irritably. 'Daisy and I are getting the dinner.' She opened the drawer of the table and pulled a cloth out, and then she looked up to see Peter standing just outside the door staring in at her. For a moment she didn't move, then she swept the basket of fruit and Betsy's hat off the table and flung the cloth over it.

'Is that Jonathan's boy?' she asked casually.

Betsy, still stinging from the comment about her clothes, pulled Peter towards her and began to unbutton his jacket.

'Yes,' she said. 'And I suppose you're going to tell me that's another reason you've come home. To help look after poor Myra's children.'

'I shall help where I can,' said Anne serenely. 'Are you

186

going to take him to see his father after dinner?'

The scheming, the planning, the unexpected arrival of Anne-Louise became transparently clear to Betsy. Astounded, she realised that her sister hadn't changed at all, not in any way, since she had first stolen the money to buy herself a silk dress. She had gone to any lengths at that time to attract Jonathan Whitman. In six years she had learned nothing, her only ambition being once more to pursue him.

'Anne-Louise,' she said slowly. 'That's why you've come home, isn't it? Not to help ma, or to earn money for Will's leg. You want to try and get him again, don't you? You want to get Jonathan Whitman. To take the place of his dead wife.'

Anne didn't answer. She flung a handful of cutlery on the table and began to saw savagely at a loaf of bread. Betsy was suddenly sorry for her, in spite of the pink dress, in spite of living in London and spending her money as she chose.

'He doesn't want you, Annie,' she said gently. 'I've seen him since he's come back. He doesn't want anyone. Not even the children. He's not like he was before. He's been sick for a long time. He lived with the Boers for months. They found him when he was nearly dead and they looked after him and now he's changed. He doesn't want anyone. If he can't have Myra, he won't have anyone at all.'

Anne's face was bent over the stove. When she turned round she was red and cross.

'Don't be stupid, Betsy!' she snapped. 'Good gracious, can't I come back to my own home without you making a fuss about everything? I can go and see him without wanting to marry him, can't I?'

Betsy thought of Jonathan, silent, reserved, staring most of the time into the middle distance, and wondered why Anne-Louise, sharp, spoilt and self-willed had settled on this particular man for her life's obsession.

'Oh Anne!' she said wearily. 'Why don't you go back to London? Go back to your Maxie and your dresses and baskets of fruit. You don't like it here, you know you don't, you never did. Leave Jonathan alone and go back to London.'

Anne slapped a ladle of hot stew – it would be stew on a

187

boiling August day – into a bowl and banged it down in front of Betsy.

'Eat your dinner,' she said tersely, and with a rapid change of expression she put a smaller plate in front of Peter.

'There you are, dear.' She smiled at him and patted his head as she walked back to her chair.

When they got to the Misses Vincents' house, Betsy told Anne to wait round the corner with Peter.

'They go potty if they think he might run into the house. They don't even allow me inside. They wait until I'm at the gate and then they send Harriet out of the door.'

'What about Jonathan?'

'He's not allowed in either.' She pushed Anne-Louise and Peter ahead of her and stood by the gate. There was a rustle at the curtains and then the door opened and Harriet walked slowly down the path. When the child had reached the gate, Betsy took her hand and followed Anne-Louise down the lane.

Anne, staring back at the house, saw her sister with a squat, odd little creature in a ground-length dress, a style of dress that children had not worn for at least twenty years. Her mouse-coloured hair was strained tightly back from her face and she walked in a stooped, curious way, staring down at the ground all the time.

'What – ?' exclaimed Anne-Louise, and stopped when Betsy warningly shook her head.

'Give Peter a kiss then, dear.'

The little girl raised her hand to her face and rubbed her eyes. She kissed Peter under cover of her hand, as though worried that he might see her face. Betsy took her hand again and left Anne to follow with the little boy.

'That's Auntie Anne behind. She's walking with Peter.'

Harriet darted a quick look over her shoulder and then stooped back, shuffling along through the grass and letting the hem of the long dress trail on the ground.

'I'll go with Peter,' she said suddenly, and waited.

'All right, dear. Go and walk with Peter.'

In the same odd, shuffling gait, she slid back and put her

arm round her brother's neck. Anne-Louise came forward and joined Betsy.

'What's the matter with her, Betsy?'

Betsy looked distressed. 'She's just a funny little girl, I think. They dress her in their old clothes cut down.'

'Not just her dress. Bets. There's something odd about her.'

'She misses her mother, I expect. And they were alone in the cottage for a day and a night before anyone discovered there was something wrong. Peter was too young to understand, he was just hungry. But the little girl had sat all night in the dark and the fire had gone out. It's a wonder they didn't freeze to death as well.'

'What does Jonathan think about her?' she asked slowly.

'I've told you, Annie,' said Betsy wearily. 'He's not interested in anything. Not anything at all.'

They came to the cottage and went round the back. When Betsy opened the door, Jonathan was on his hands and knees scrubbing the kitchen floor. Anne-Louise stared round at the rooms. They were spotless and shining, the stove gleaming with black-lead, the tables and chairs and desk polished to a mirror-like surface. In the corner Myra's sewing-machine stood with the cover off and an oil-can standing close by.

'Hullo, Jonathan.' Betsy pulled the children in behind her and shut the door. 'How are you feeling?'

He stared at Betsy, then at Anne-Louise, and then at the children. He stood upright and Anne suddenly wanted to cry because he was so thin, so transparently, haggardly thin. A deep weal went from his left temple down the side of his head leaving a white flesh mark in his hair. His face was more secretive than it had ever been.

'Hullo,' he said slowly, then turned round and stared at the kitchen floor. 'I've finished the floor. It looks nice now. Everything's polished and the machine's oiled.'

'I've brought the children.'

He nodded, not looking at any of them, but staring again at the floor. It made Anne feel uncomfortable and reminded her of the way Harriet walked.

'Yes, yes, of course. And I must give you the money for

189

Peter. And perhaps you'll give Em her money at the same time.'

He fumbled in his pocket and brought out an envelope that he handed to Betsy. 'They look fine, Betsy, they look fine.'

'Wouldn't you like to take them for a walk? Take them up to Tyler's meadow and play with them for a little while?'

He frowned and the white scar of flesh moved across his forehead. Betsy hurriedly pushed Peter towards him.

'You should take them, Jonathan. It's not right otherwise. You're only home at week-ends. You ought to spend some time with them.'

Suddenly he smiled at her, and Anne-Louise was jealous because it was the old smile. The smile that she always wanted him to direct at her, but that he rarely did. He smiled at Betsy as though they were old friends, as though they understood one another.

'Good lass, Betsy,' he said quietly. 'I'll take them for a walk. Good lass.' He patted her on the cheek and smiled again, and Anne thought she was going to die of anguish because it was plain, dull, frumpy old Betsy he noticed instead of her in the pink dress.

'Take them for a walk and then bring them back to our house for tea,' she said quickly, hoping to remind him that she was willing to help as well as Betsy.

'All right, yes, I'll do that. Then I'll have to go. I promised to be back with the flocks tonight.'

He walked dreamily out of the door, the two children holding to his hands, but not taking any notice of him, nor he of them. Anne-Louise watched them across the yard. When he had disappeared she burst out, 'It's terrible, Betsy! It's terrible what they've done to him! How could they be so cruel!'

Betsy turned and looked at her sister's face, seeing the delicate skin and the concern in her eyes for the man who had just left.

'It was terrible for a lot of men. It was terrible for Myra too. It was a bad war and a bad winter for a lot of us.'

Anne-Louise had the grace to flush, and she walked out of the kitchen stiff-necked and uncomfortably silent.

At tea-time – bread and margarine tea – the strangeness of Harriet was even more pronounced when compared with the rest of the children. She sat next to Sophy, the youngest and last of the Pritchard children, and Anne noticed that she didn't appear to eat, not when anyone was watching. She waited until everyone's attention was elsewhere and then she furtively stuffed bread into her mouth, glaring round the table in case anyone had seen her. The rest of the time she was bent almost double looking down at the floor. When the time came to take her back to the Vincents, she stood waiting in a corner with her back to the room. Anne-Louise was puzzled and wondered if she was as strange as she appeared to be.

'Shall I take her back, Betsy?' She was curious and wanted to find out if there was something wrong with the child. Betsy shook her head. 'Come if you like, but I think I'd better go.'

They were at the bottom of the lane when Anne felt the child's hand begin to tremble in hers. Her eyes met Betsy's, each of them admitting silently that they could feel the tiny, quivering body fluttering between them. At the Vincents', Betsy led the child away, put the envelope of money into her hand, and watched her walk slowly up to the door. She paused in front of it and Anne-Louise sensed a shrivelling in the child. Then the door opened without anyone showing themselves and Harriet disappeared inside.

Anne-Louise, returning to the village was – superficially – a calmer and more controlled person, able to look back on her past attempts at securing Jonathan's attention objectively, and to feel annoyance at her stupidity and lack of tact. She was disgusted with the way she had handled the entire affair. She still wanted him as much as she ever had, but she returned from London – leaving a hurt, angry Maxie and a family of disappointed Dances – knowing that she could get any man she wanted providing her behaviour was neither as gauche nor as unsophisticated as last time. Intensity and a fear of losing Jonathan had made her act precipitately, but now straight from the arms of an adoring Maxie, she felt secure and supremely confident of her ability to win the man she had lost six years before. Maxie and the Dances had pampered her, spoilt her, doted upon her, and their worship had been sufficient to feed her obsessive vanity and sustain her through a long and difficult courtship of Jonathan. She knew she would have to act differently – to behave quietly and contrary to her erratic temperament – but she knew – this time she knew – that she would not fail. This time Jonathan would turn to her and at last she would completely possess him.

She found no difficulty in securing a position. She was a local girl with a London training and she went as second parlour-maid – and very quickly moved up to first parlour-maid – at the Fawcetts'. She settled to work, and to wait, in a quiet and confident fashion.

Every Saturday afternoon she went to the Vincents' cottage and waited, as Betsy had done, at the gate to the dark, overgrown garden. Whoever watched from the window was apparently satisfied that she was a trustworthy connection of Betsy's. The door would open silently and Harriet would shuffle down the path in her weird, bent little way. Sometimes Anne took her to see her father and sometimes she took her back to the Pritchard cottage to have tea with the rest of the family. It seemed to make no difference to Harriet. She followed obediently wherever Anne-Louise took her and the only animation she ever showed was when Betsy came home with Peter.

Anne-Louise, who had initially begun using the child as a means of access to Jonathan, became puzzled and finally confused about Harriet. As late summer gave place to autumn, and autumn to the beginning of winter, she found she had grown no closer to the child and that whatever happened when the Vincent cottage door closed on Harriet each Saturday remained a silent, inscrutable mystery. Once or twice she caught a quick glimpse of Emily hurrying across the fields from the shop, and she ran after her, calling and shouting, anxious to speak to Emily and find out if there were something wrong with Harriet. She was sure Emily had heard her, but she never managed to catch up with the gaunt, severe figure. Emily increased her pace so quickly it was obvious she did not wish to speak to Anne.

'Do you like living with Aunt Emily?' she asked the child one dreary Saturday afternoon in mid-November. Harriet hunched her shoulders together and pulled her chin down on to her chest.

'Little girls are bad and must do what they are told,' she said tonelessly.

Anne hesitated. The child was only repeating some grumble of Emily's, a scolding that probably meant nothing. 'You must be good then, Harriet.'

Harriet stared at the ground. 'It's dark in the cupboard,' she said, without moving her head.

Anne-Louise felt the first prickle of alarm touch the back of her neck, not because of what Harriet said, but because of the sombre, withdrawn look on her face and the way her eyes never ceased to stare dully at the ground.

'Does Aunt Emily put you in the cupboard when you're naughty?'

Harriet didn't answer. She shuffled her feet slightly, then became still again.

'Harriet?'

She began to walk away from Anne, wandering down the lane hunched stolidly in the ugly, long dress.

Anne-Louise was not Betsy. She lacked tact, and when she thought it was time to interfere she did so immediately without wondering and worrying if it was the right thing to do. On the following Saturday, when Jonathan was home, she spoke to him bluntly about his daughter.

'There's something funny in that cottage of the Vincents. You ought to take Harriet away from there.'

Jonathan was forking the heavy clay soil over in the garden. It was the first time it had been turned since Will Pritchard had been able to help, and the ground was thick with bind-weed and mandrake roots. He didn't answer her and she had to touch his arm with her hand before he looked up.

'Emily knows how to look after children. She's cared for enough in her time.' He swung the fork back and broke up the rich, loamy soil with the prongs. Anne felt irritated at

193

his dreamy disinterest, but she managed to answer him calmly.

'There's something wrong, Jonathan. I tell you there's something wrong. Have you looked at your daughter lately? Have you looked at her since you came back from the war?'

He was faintly surprised. He looked at Anne and frowned. 'Of course I've looked at her. I see her every week.'

'Well, look at her now!'

She pointed up the garden. Harriet was standing beneath the walnut-tree, her squat, small body hunched and defensive. Something must have penetrated Jonathan's abstraction. He called to the child, as though noticing for the first time her curious clothes and the unnatural stillness of her body.

'Harriet! Come here, Harriet.'

She walked slowly towards them.

'Harriet. Does Aunt Emily give you enough to eat?'

Harriet stared round the garden, at a tangle of dead raspberry canes, at a robin pulling at a reluctant worm. She nodded.

'Does she smack you?'

Anne-Louise felt she couldn't stand the useless inquisition any longer.

'Ask her if Emily locks her in the cupboard,' she burst out quickly. Harriet suddenly jerked away and raised her head to stare at her father.

'It's dark in the cupboard,' she said as tonelessly as she had the first time. 'It's dark – like when mumma went away.'

Anne saw Jonathan's face screw into a mask of pain. She felt her chest hurt with watching him and only some of the hurt was jealousy. The rest was because of his agony that was somehow nothing to do with Myra. She began to chatter noisily, hoping to dispel the image of the frozen ghost who stood between them.

'I know the child must be punished if she's naughty, and if Em shuts her in the cupboard, then that's her way, although I don't think it's right and I certainly wouldn't do it to any of my children – that is if I had any. And it's not only that,

194

there's something else wrong in the cottage, something nasty about those old women. You ought to find out what's happening there. You ought . . .'

She heard herself, heard her voice getting shriller and louder, and she stopped because she knew Jonathan wasn't listening and in any case she wasn't being careful enough. She was behaving foolishly and was in danger of antagonising him. He was forking the soil at a furious speed and there was a thin film of moisture over his forehead and cheeks.

'What shall I do about Harriet?' she asked quietly.

'I'll speak to Em and see if there's anything wrong.'

She dared not say any more to him because his face was so white. She took Harriet's hand in hers and led the child away, back to the Pritchard house for tea. She wasn't satisfied with what had been agreed upon, but she did not know what else to do.

When she saw him on the following Saturday, he said dully, 'I've spoken to Em. She says the child imagines things and makes up stories. Em knows how to look after children. I've told you that.'

He wasn't interested. He treated the whole affair – and her – as an intrusion, a tiresome, irritating intrusion on his absorbing grief, and Anne's carefully planned composure tore a little.

'You're not interested!' she said angrily. 'You're so wrapped up in self-pity you don't care what happens to your children!'

Astonishment creased his face into a startled protest. 'That's not so, Anne! That's not so at all!'

'You just wandered off down to Romney, not giving a thought to Peter and Harriet. So busy grieving for yourself that you're just not interested in what happens to Harriet.'

'No!'

'Well, it's a good job Betsy and I *are* interested. You needn't trouble yourself any more. We'll find out if there's anything wrong!'

She snatched Harriet's hand and flounced out of the cottage and across the yard. Jonathan, amazed at her assessment of his preoccupation, tried to call her back, but she was gone.

For a moment he considered, wondering if Anne was right and he was, in fact, indulging a grief for Myra that excluded everything and everyone else. He had never thought to reflect on how his behaviour must appear to the village. He had never thought that his separateness, his sense of isolation would be interpreted as sorrow and self-pity.

He was lonely. He felt apart from the people about him, but he did not think he grieved to the point of despair — because he did not believe that Myra was dead. He had not seen her die — therefore he could not imagine her dead. Every time he came home to the village he expected to see her walking across a field, shutting a gate and pulling brambles out of her skirt, or coming out of the cottage where she had lived before their marriage. For it was not Myra, his wife, he remembered, they had had too little time for that — it was Myra, his cousin, the smooth, smiling girl he was in love with, the girl who had pushed him into a hawthorn bush the first time he kissed her, the girl he had partnered at Betsy's wedding.

And then a piercing agony would shout in his heart, 'She's dead! Myra is dead! You'll never see her again, never, never again!'

He didn't believe it. It wasn't true. He would see her again, watch her smile, touch her hair, see her in the faded blue dress. He had not seen her during the years of the war, but she had been there. He had known she was there, waiting for him, knowing he would come back and see her again. And he had come back, back to a community where there was no Myra, where he was not needed — where there was no gap for him to fill, no one whose life was richer because he had come home.

If there had been one, just one person who had needed him, he would have tried to settle back, would have wanted to settle and take part in the village again. But his cottage was cleaned and orderly — all traces of Myra packed into cupboards and boxes and the bedding neatly rolled into a sensible but unwelcoming sausage on the naked spring of the bedstead.

His children, two small strangers who aroused nothing in his heart, were already settled in lives and households of their own and demanded nothing more of him than financial support. His sister had seen him once and was obviously uncaring. A brother on the other side of the country had written, wishing him well and offering consolation for his bereavement – and that was all. No one had needed him, had asked him to arrange his life around a new necessary pattern. If he left the village it would not matter – and so he left the village.

Nine

HE SOUGHT his father with the Romney flocks because the old man, too, was apart from the community, had been apart for many years, but did not seem to mind. He settled to the isolated living on the marsh, finding in the grey mists and windswept stretches of grass a curious resemblance to the peace and isolation of the veld.

At night, staring up at the Plough and feeling the damp sea wind touching his body, he would forget where he was, forget who sat by his side, and he would turn to his father expecting to see the dark, waiting figure of a Zulu guide. He wished, more than anything else he wished, that he knew if he had dreamed the field of marigolds in the desert. He had asked the Boers who found him if there had been flowers at that place, orange flowers. The taciturn Boer farmer had shrugged and said in his thick, guttural English, 'You was near water. Where there is water on the veld, sometimes there is flowers.' The man was not interested, and probably did not remember anyway, and Jonathan, grateful that the farmer had carried his dried-out, emaciated body to a house where no harm had come to him, had remained silent. Obviously the Boer did not think the question of flowers was important.

To Jonathan it was important, strangely, overwhelmingly important. If the hill of orange flowers had really existed, then he was glad he had lived to come home, even though Myra was dead, even though there was no place for him.

His father was a silent companion, by day wandering round the borders of the herds watching for ticks and sickness in the flock, and by night sitting in the small shepherds' hut spinning the stray tufts of sheep's wool into hanks of yarn beneath the lamp. When he spoke it was about lambing or the dipping and shearing of the sheep. Sometimes he told stories of his boyhood in the village – of his prowess as a wrestler when he had thrown the sixteen-stone son of a pig-farmer into the midden. He chuckled when he told the story, describing with relish the smell and sight of the unhappy giant pulling himself out of the muck. Jonathan, who had always considered his father a serious, reserved man was surprised to find that the old man – who somewhat resembled a mischievous gnome – also on occasion behaved like one. Once when they went to the farm for their wages they were invited into the kitchen for tea and the farmer's eldest girl, a stout, square creature, had offered an irresistible temptation to the old man when she bent over the stove to lift the kettle. Peter had patted her smartly across the behind and, when she spun round red-faced and affronted, he had shaken his head disapprovingly and glared at Jonathan.

'It's my youngest boy,' he said apologetically to the girl. 'He's a bad one for the girls. Can't keep his hands off them.'

She had flounced out of the kitchen, giving Jonathan a backward, speculative glance and the old man had winked at Jonathan.

'Wicked old varmint,' said Jonathan good-humouredly.

When they brought the flocks back for the winter, the farmer said they could stay and wait for lambing if they wanted. They slept in the upper part of the barn on two canvas beds, and with the night sounds of cattle rustling beneath them. These were the times he tried not to think about Myra, or about the veld, or about anything other than lambing and whether it would be a good yield. One night, long after he had thought the old man was asleep, Jonathan was startled to hear his voice in the darkness.

'Jonathan?'

'Aye?'

'Jonathan, thee should get home to thy children, lad.'

Jonathan looked across to the sound of the voice.

'They're fine, pa. One with Betsy Pritchard, and one with Em.'

The old man was silent for so long that Jonathan thought he had drifted off to sleep. Then he heard Peter say, 'Emily ain't bad, no, not bad. She's sick. She's a sick woman and she's been sick since she were born. You should go home, son. Go home and see to your children.'

The old man was warning him, as Anne-Louise had warned him. He shifted uneasily on the canvas bed.

'Emily's all right, pa. And the children don't need me. They don't know me. I might just as well stay here.'

Peter whistled, a high-pitched fluted sound, and the cows in the barn below rustled fretfully at the disturbance.

'You can't stay your life with the flocks, boy. You must go home. There's things for you to do. The flocks is fine for an old man who wants time to think. Your thinking time hasn't come yet.'

He wondered if his father was right – if the very slight awakening of restlessness in him was the sign that he should move away from the flocks and try his hand at something else. He had no one who wanted him to go anywhere or do anything. Provided he earned enough to pay for his children's board, it did not matter what he did.

The restlessness grew in the weeks ahead. It was partly a rebellion against his loneliness, it was also a tiny concern about Harriet – a concern introduced by Anne-Louise and fostered by his father's words. He wondered if perhaps they were both right, if it would be wise to ask someone else to take the child.

When lambing came, his restlessness swelled to frustration. He tried to crush it, then, failing, he tried to reason why he was so angry. He found his answer one night when he was holding the wet, hot body of a new-born lamb in his hands. The birth had been a difficult one and the ewe – only young herself – had grown frightened and not known what to do. He had severed the cord that held the lamb to his mother, and then broken the sac round the small, struggling body. The ewe bleated painfully and then licked the lamb when he placed it close to her, and he was suddenly reminded of a wood in April, of a Romany fire and a man who had envied him his wife, and whose wife in turn he himself had desired. Despair, greater than any he had known since his return from the war, filled his breast. A sense of desolation knotted itself tightly round his stomach and loins and he heard himself groaning.

'Why aren't you with me, Myra? Why aren't you here with me? I need you so much, Myra. Why did you die? Why? Why?'

His hands were covered in blood and he placed them over his face, rocking slightly to and fro, his heart and his body aching with loneliness and desire. He remembered waiting downstairs when their child was born, the fear and anxiety he had known because she might die. And now she was dead. She was dead and he wanted her, wanted her so badly it was a sick, physical agony in his breast.

He swayed backwards and forwards, his face stained with blood and he wondered how he could bear the rest of his life, the useless, meaningless years, so many years until he died. He wanted to walk away, leave the sheep, and the village, and the people he knew but who cared nothing for him. He wanted to go away and leave them all while he searched for Myra.

The sheep bleated again and he took his hands from his face, knowing he could not leave. There was lambing and he had to earn money for his children. And Myra was dead. She was dead and he would never see her again.

He opened the barn door and whistled to the dogs. When they came he set off across the field to see that the rest of the flock were well.

The next time he came home, he walked up to the village to wait for Anne-Louise and Harriet. They came along the lane, slowed to the tempo of Harriet's pace and Jonathan tried to see his daughter as though she was the child of someone else. Slightly alarmed he realised that she *was* strange, her gait was unnatural and she did not behave like a child of four.

'Hullo, Jonathan,' said Anne, surprised.

'Anne.' He nodded a greeting and then tried to catch hold of Harriet's other hand. The child looked up startled and then let her hand rest acquiescently in his.

'I've decided to stay overnight, Anne,' he said slowly. 'So I think I'll keep Harriet with me until tomorrow. What do you think?'

Anne-Louise paused, wondering if it would benefit either of them to spend the night together in the lonely rather uncomfortable house.

'Suppose she stays the night with us,' she said suddenly. 'And I'll bring her round early tomorrow morning and you can spend the day with her.'

'I just thought it might be an idea to keep her with me for tonight,' he muttered. Anne-Louise smiled.

'You haven't any bedding or anything ready, Jonathan. Betsy packed it all away when . . . It isn't aired, and anyway ma sold some of your blankets to pay the rent when they thought someone else was going to live there.'

The cottage had remained empty after Myra's death solely because no one else had asked if they could rent it. On the one occasion it had been suggested, Mrs Pritchard had hastily stepped in, paid a couple of weeks, and averted a new tenancy.

'All right . . . yes . . . perhaps that would be best. I'll bring her up to your house tonight.'

Anne sensed she was being dismissed. She felt annoyed, then angry, but she knew she must show nothing of what she felt.

'I'll leave you then, Jonathan. Good-bye.'

She let go of Harriet's hand, smiled at him, and turned back the way she had come. He watched her walking away and thought, idly, what a good figure she had for such a small woman. Then he settled to a heavy and silent afternoon with his strange daughter. He tried to interest her in the garden, in the animals on Tyler's farm and, finally, in her mother's sewing-machine. Nothing seemed to touch the little girl, nothing appeared to break through her withdrawal. He began to tell her about South Africa, about the flowers and the animals and the sky at night. She was quiet and he didn't know if she was listening or not. But eventually he didn't really care, he just remembered things about the veld and talked softly to himself. When he took Harriet up to the Pritchard's house, Anne-Louise was nowhere in sight and he handed Harriet over to Mrs Pritchard.

'Don't worry,' she said cheerfully. 'I'll put her in with Daisy, and Annie will bring her round first thing in the morning. She'll be all right with us.'

When Anne-Louise came round the following morning she carried a basket with a cloth over the top. She wouldn't come into the kitchen. She stood at the back door and handed the basket to him.

'I thought, as it's a nice day, you might like to go off on your own with Harriet. There's some bread and cheese and apples, and a bottle of tea in the basket.'

'It's very kind of you,' said Jonathan unenthusiastically. He had found Harriet difficult on the previous afternoon and evening, and he didn't find the idea of a whole day alone with her particularly attractive. He looked at Anne-Louise. She was wearing a cream alpaca suit – very unpractical for the April day – but she looked clean and attractive and her neat figure was well outlined in the tiny-waisted, full-skirted suit.

'Can't you come too?' he asked suddenly, thinking how much easier it would be with Anne-Louise there. When she flushed he thought he was probably being a nuisance and he hastened to add, 'But I expect you're busy. And you'll be going to the Meeting too.'

'It's at our house this evening,' she said quickly. 'I'll come, by all means. Harriet's used to me, I think.'

She took the basket from him and led the way across the yard. She was exultant because it had worked out the way she had planned. She was so excited she wanted to shout, but she kept her voice and her face under rigid control and, when they reached the gate, she turned right, up to Fawcett's estate, taking good care that they were not going anywhere near Sandy Bottom and the meadows where Myra had died.

It was fresh and bright, and from the hills to the north the breeze had collected a faint scent of flowers and spring grass and blew it softly through just-budding trees. Whitethorn, hawthorn and pussy-willow showed siftings of green in the tangled hedge. Clumps of primroses, their leaves muddy from a recent shower, hung precariously to the sides of the ditches and, when one looked closely under the grass and leaves, the first violets showed tiny, scentless heads.

She had the sense to remain silent, although she was longing to chatter and draw Jonathan into conversation. She let him walk behind with Harriet, and whenever he stopped to point out a bird or a flower to the little girl, she waited, forcing herself to relax and smile at him.

They found a sheltered place in the wood, and Anne-Louise took the cover off the basket and placed it on a fallen trunk before sitting down. She had risked her cream suit and the ruse had been successful. She did not, however, intend to relax to the extent of staining her skirt.

She looked charming against the soft green of early buds. Her hat was yellow and she blended perfectly with the spring morning. She gave Harriet a piece of bread and cut her a slice of cheese. Jonathan watched her, and remembered he had never said thank you – not seriously – to either her or Betsy.

'You've been very good, Annie,' he said awkwardly. 'The way you've helped. You and Betsy. I shan't forget.'

She smiled, because if she spoke she would not be able to stop and then everything would be ruined.

'There's no reason why either of you should help with my children,' he said slowly. 'No reason at all.'

'I'm fond of Harriet,' she answered.

He looked at her and tried to remember what she was like before. He had a hazy recollection of a rather irritating girl whom he didn't especially like. The years and whatever had happened in London appeared to have changed her.

'I thought you would have married by now, Anne.'

She wanted to shout and stand up and tell a dramatic story about Maxie and Mafeking night and the whole adoring family of Dances who had begged her to stay with them. She glowed with frantic excitement because it was the first time, the very first time, Jonathan had directed a personal remark to her, a remark about her, a remark showing interest in what she did and why. She choked the hysteria back and answered as calmly as she could.

'I don't suppose I shall marry now, Jonathan. I'm twenty-five. Everyone that we grew up with got married long ago.'

'I thought you'd marry a Londoner,' he said.

She shook her head. 'I wouldn't care to leave the village.'

Instinct told her what answers she should give, and instinct told her when not to answer at all. She knew one wrong thing would spoil it completely, and she held tightly to her self-control, willing herself to play the right part.

'Jonathan.' She hesitated. 'Jonathan, I'm sorry if I interfered about Harriet – you know – about there being something wrong with Emily. It was none of my business and I shouldn't have said anything.'

They both turned to look at Harriet, who was leaning against a tree with her back to them. The sight of the strange, small figure made Anne forget her calculated plans.

'Just the same, there is something wrong!' she blurted suddenly.

He didn't answer for a moment and she was furious with herself for spoiling everything. She was relieved and surprised when he did speak.

'Maybe you're right, maybe you're right. I'll try to find someone else to have her.'

'Betsy would, I suppose,' she faltered, 'but she'll be having her own baby soon and . . .'

'I didn't know that,' said Jonathan surprised. His face changed and he looked worried.

'Does that mean she won't be able to look after Peter?'

Anne didn't answer, but she let her face register doubt and uncertainty.

'I'll work something out,' he muttered. 'I'll think of something very soon.'

They went home again, to Anne's home, and that night Jonathan attended the Meeting in the Pritchard front parlour. It was the first time he had gone since his return from the war, and he didn't have time to remember that last time he came it was with Myra. He was too busy wondering what to do with Harriet and Peter.

Although Anne-Louise never for one moment lost sight of the fact that Harriet was the invaluable weapon in the battle of winning Jonathan, she was, nevertheless, fascinated by the queer, half-sensed connection between the child and the strange women in the Vincent house. She knew – as only a Pritchard with a Pritchard's all-consuming preoccupation in other people's lives could know – that there was something unpleasant, something uncanny in the life of Harriet at the Vincent house.

She found she was developing an obsession about the cottage and, even when she wasn't going there to collect Harriet, she would walk past the half-hidden house, sometimes making a journey twice as long because she wanted to go round that way and look over the high hedge at the dark, withdrawn building. Once she saw a curtain move, but no hand, and she wondered if someone was staring out at her or if it was only one of the cats swaying the hanging fabric with a silent body. She tried to recall when she had last spoken to Emily, or when she had last seen the Misses Vincent. It was years ago, before she had gone to London. She began to ask around the village had anyone seen the Misses Vincent? did Emily ever speak to anyone or go to the Meeting any more? People were vague and hazy in answering. The Misses Vincent had always shunned the company of people, and no one really bothered to notice when they had last been seen.

She waited until Betsy came home. When Peter had gone out into the garden, she called her back into the kitchen and asked her about the Vincents.

'How long since you saw those women in there, Betsy?'

Betsy frowned. 'I used to see Em in the shop sometimes.'

'But when did you see the old Misses Vincent?'

'Why . . . why it was when I took Harriet there to live. Just after Myra died. They came out and . . . no . . . no, it was only one of them came out. The fatter of the two. The one called Miss Aleen.'

She stared at Anne-Louise, sensing something in her preoccupation with the Vincent house. Then she said nervously, 'What's wrong, Annie? Why are you asking these questions?'

Anne swallowed and wondered just how foolish she was being. If she was foolish it might jeopardise her progress with Jonathan.

'Nothing . . . nothing really. Only . . . there's something wrong, Betsy. Can't you feel it? There's something wrong in that house.'

Betsy looked out of the kitchen window. Harriet was standing beside Peter, whispering into his ear.

'Perhaps. Perhaps you're right. But there's nothing we can do. You said you'd spoken to Jonathan. What more can we do?'

'We could go and see Emily,' said Anne-Louise decisively. 'We could ask her to let Harriet come out of the cottage sometimes to play with the other children. You know, she never lets her come out at all unless Jonathan or you and I are there.'

'Go and see Em?' Betsy felt her stomach turn suddenly and she sat down quickly on the wooden mangle-top, frightened in case it was the coming child that jarred her body. Anne did not seem to notice.

'Next time you come home we'll leave Peter here and we'll go in the morning as soon as you arrive.'

Betty nodded and wondered why she was, so uncharacteristically, allowing Anne to take the lead. Usually she made the plans and, most frequently, executed them as well. This time Anne was pulling her along in the wake of her own suspicions. And then fairness forced her to admit that she was not without suspicions herself. She had forced herself not to acknowledge that there was something wrong in the Vincent household. In the face of Anne's determination she could ignore it no longer.

It was two weeks before she came again. She wrote in advance and, when she walked into the kitchen, Anne was waiting with her coat already on. She stood up briskly.

'Shall we go now? Before you have a chance to settle down?'

Betsy would have liked a cup of tea to fortify her for whatever lay ahead, but she nodded. She knew her face was white and she was secretly relieved to see that Anne too was pale and rather bright-eyed. Betsy sat Peter on the sofa and told him to wait until they came back. Then she followed Anne out into the lane.

'I expect we're being silly,' she panted, hurrying behind Anne. 'We're letting our imagination catch hold and we're probably interfering in things we shouldn't.'

Anne didn't answer. Her speed along the lane increased until it looked as though she was skimming along on wheels. She was feeling the familiar sense of taut elation that always accompanied any kind of unusual action on her part. She was nervous, a little afraid, but beneath the fear was drama – a knowledge that she could play her part, and play it well.

The Vincent house looked, as it always did, overgrown, dark and depressing. Anne swung the gate open and led the way up the path. Something rustled in the evergreen hedge and Betsy caught a quick glimpse of a furry creature vanishing into the shrubs.

There was no answer when they knocked on the door. Anne banged again, very loud, and called through the letter box.

'Emily! Emily Whitman! It's Anne and Betsy Pritchard. We'd like to see you for a moment.'

There was another long silence, and then the door opened slightly and Emily peered through the crack. Anne, who had not seen her close-to for several years, moved back in alarm. Emily was still tidy, still severe and neat, but there was undoubtedly a curious change in her, a too-brightness of the eyes, a wary withdrawal like a wood animal.

'What do you want?' she whispered.

'Can we come in Emily?'

'No. You come this afternoon as always and wait by the gate. Go away now. Harriet isn't ready for you.'

She went to shut the door sharply in their faces but Anne put her hand up and held it open.

'We won't take a minute, Emily. We just want to talk to you about Harriet.'

'Come this afternoon.'

'We want to come in now, Emily.'

She was strong again, supreme and powerful because Emily was trying to stop her from coming in and she was, in turn, determined to get in. She was challenged and excited. Emily could not stop her.

'We're coming in, Emily. You might just as well stop trying to close the door.'

Abruptly Emily let go of the handle and Anne lurched forward where her hand had been pushing the door. Emily's face was contorted into almost a snarl. She stood back and let them edge slowly into the room.

Betsy had seen it before, but Anne, prepared for unknown horrors, was startled and dismayed. It was a quiet pleasant room. A little dark, but warm and pink and tidy.

'What do you want?'

'We've come about Harriet,' said Anne lamely.

'Well?'

She wondered suddenly where the child was, and where the two Misses Vincent were. She stared at a door on the other side of the room, sensing there was someone listening behind the door.

'Well?' said Emily again.

She spoke sharply, in a bullying, aggressive way, and Betsy, silent until now, tried to explain their precipitate entry into the house.

'We're bothered about Harriet, Emily. She seems such an odd little girl.'

'I can't help that.'

'Of course not,' said Betsy quickly. 'But we wondered . . . perhaps, if you would let her out to play more often . . . out with the other children. It might help to make her a little . . . less strange.'

Emily scowled and moved across the room to stand in front of the door.

'She must stay in and help as she's told. Children are spoilt nowadays. Everyone worries about the children, always the young, always the young. They must learn. They must learn that they are not important, learn to look after the old and subdue themselves to serious things — bad things. The old need attention as much as the young . . . and they have more right to it . . . more right.'

Her voice dropped to a whisper and Betsy could hardly hear what she was saying. Anne stared at the far door.

'Where are the old women, Emily?'

'Upstairs . . . no, in the other room. They don't like you. They don't want to come out.'

'Where's the old one? The one called Miss Thalia. Why has no one seen her for a long time?'

The room was quiet; heavily, oppressively quiet. Betsy was afraid that Anne had gone too far, had pushed beyond the bounds of concern for a child and now could not draw back. She was aware that there was not even a clock in the room, but when she looked round she saw there was one, but it had stopped, offering a contribution of silence to the room.

'Why are you afraid, Emily?' whispered Anne. She whispered because she was suddenly afraid herself. She had asked her questions unthinkingly, not taking them seriously and not expecting an answer. When she saw Emily's face she felt something crawl up her spine. She began to wish she had never come to the cottage. She moved closer to Betsy, wishing that Emily would stop staring at her.

And from the other side of the door there was a dull, creeping noise, the heavy sound of something dragging across the floor.

'What's in there, Emily?' She was shivering, but she had to ask.

Emily's face grew whiter and stranger. 'Go away,' she growled.

'Where's Harriet?'

Betsy heard the noise again, the ghastly noise that made the back of her neck grow cold.

She felt Anne move beside her, saw her leap quickly past Emily, who shouted 'No! No!' and tried to pull her back. She saw Anne dodge Emily's arm and throw herself against the far door, twisting the handle at the same time. She saw the door swing open and – and framed like a picture – she saw Harriet, Miss Thalia and Miss Aleen.

The old one – Miss Thalia – was sitting in a low chair. It was low because the legs had been sawn off so that the old woman could not fall from it. She wore a nightdress and her hair – what was left of it – was uncombed and hanging spikily about her face. Her arms were tied securely to the arms of the stunted chair and Betsy, even in that one brief glimpse, saw that it was important that she was tied to the chair, saw from the blank, wild look in the woman's face that it was necessary. Miss Thalia stared at them, but did not see them. Then, sensing something was different, she put her feet out in front of her and tried to move the chair along, and Betsy heard the dull, muffled noise that had sounded from the other side of the door.

Harriet was standing beside the chair, holding a dish in her hands, and Miss Aleen – now weeping – appeared to have been spooning liquid from the bowl into the mouth of the woman tied to the chair. White gruel ran down the side of her chin and into the nauseous rivulet on her nightgown.

She saw everything, the whole room, the mad woman, and the unhappy one. And the distorted, frightened figure of a child who lived in a nightmarish world of disciplined madness. Then Emily pushed Anne-Louise violently out of the way and shut the door.

'Are you happy now? You can tell everyone in the village now, can't you? You can all have a good laugh at the mad old women living in the cottage! The mad old women who keep themselves to themselves! Are you happy now, you prying busybodies, you interfering Pritchards who can't leave anything alone? Why don't you keep out of other people's affairs? Why did you have to come and push in here?'

The skin of her face was transparent. Her hands, clenched by her sides, were trembling, and Betsy was suddenly ashamed for her.

'We didn't know . . . ' she began slowly.

'There was no need for anyone to know,' shouted Emily. 'But you had to come. Prying and poking in here, fussing about that wretched child who's lucky to get a home at all. Get out! Get out, will you!'

211

Betsy backed nervously against the wall. For the first time since entering the cottage she thought of her child and prayed it would come to no harm because of the wildness of the morning.

Anne took a step towards the closed door. 'We'll take Harriet with us.'

'Why?' Emily suddenly laughed, a harsh raw laugh that filled the room with ugly sound. 'Don't you think Auntie Em is good enough for her now? Auntie Em isn't fit to look after children any more, is she?'

Betsy began to feel ill. She knew if she didn't get out of the house very soon, away from the cats and the old women in the next room she would faint.

'Em,' she said weakly. 'You can see that Harry can't stay here. She should never have come here at all. You know that. You should have told me about . . . about that poor woman.'

Emily glared at her, then she slumped wearily against the wall. 'Get out,' she said dully. 'Take the child and get out.'

Anne-Louise opened the door of the other room. Miss Thalia had turned the chair over on to the floor and was lying whimpering on her side. Anne-Louise went to enter the room and then held back when she saw the pathetic but unpleasant figure of the elder Miss Vincent.

'You get Harry, Bets,' she said quickly, and she held the door open for Betsy to push past and bring Harriet out.

The Pritchards said they'd have her until he could find someone else. They took her because it always was the Pritchards who, having precipitated a crisis, stepped in and prepared to stand by the consequences of their actions. They took her as a temporary measure, but Jonathan knew he must eventually find some other way of caring for his family.

Every week-end Anne-Louise came to meet him with Harriet, and sometimes Peter as well. She always smiled when she saw him and very occasionally she was able to make him laugh. He knew that she spent all her spare time with Harriet and he was grateful, but he was aware that something had to be done, he must find a way of bringing up a family without

212

a wife. He wrote to his two brothers who lived across the county. They must have consulted together because they agreed to take one child each for a short time, until he could come to some other arrangement. A temporary home was no good, and in addition he was now loath to take Harriet from her brother. Peter seemed to be the only link she had with normality and the memory of her mother.

He sat, one Saturday evening in the Pritchard kitchen, watching the two children together on the sofa. Harriet, ready for bed with her hair combed into braids, looked more like a normal child, but the stillness, the strangeness, had not completely gone. Anne came in to take them to bed, and when she came down again he was slumped tiredly over the table, his hands resting loosely in front of him.

'I shall have to do something, Anne,' he said wearily. 'I've trespassed on your family long enough. I'll have to do something.'

She wanted to reach out and touch him, to stroke the back of his neck and feel his arms go round her. In the old days she would have stood close beside him and made him conscious of her presence. Now she turned her back on him and began to trim the lamp.

'Don't worry. We can manage. She's a quiet little girl. And Peter seems happy with Betsy and Math.'

She brought the lamp over to the table and set light to the wick. The flame leapt up and made Jonathan realise that the evening had grown dark without him realising it. She placed the globe over the flame and it settled to a gentle golden glow softening her face in the light and making the black hair shine thickly where it was swept and piled high on the top of her head.

'You've pretty hair, Anne,' he said abstractedly. He saw colour come up in her face and her bright blue eyes stared directly into his, asking him, pleading with him, inviting him. Startled, he gazed back, refusing to believe that his casual compliment had fired the strength of emotion showing in her face. Her mouth moved slightly and he saw her throat pulse above the white neck frill of her dress.

'Why, Anne. . . . ' he said slowly.

Her tongue delicately showed between her lips and moved moistly along the lower one. He was aware of her throat, of the soft swell of her breast and the fall of her skirt resting against his leg beneath the table. She moved back in her chair, leaned away from him, and he saw how small her waist was, how tiny and neat, and how full she was at breast and hip. Rich, hot need for a woman boiled up suddenly inside him, setting his body on edge, making him frantic with carelessness and the urgent need of the moment.

'Anne,' he said hoarsely.

She didn't speak or move her body. She turned her head slightly and her white neck creased the ruffles of lace. The light framed her body in a gentle suffused glow, and she was, at once, a warm, terribly desirable woman.

'You should marry again, Jonathan,' she said slowly. 'If you married you would have no need to worry about your children.' She stood up and came round the table to stand beside him. She was faintly scented, a mixture of oil from the lamp and of lavender water. The smell jarred his senses and he held his hands tightly together, fighting the desire to reach up and pull her down on to his lap.

'You should marry anyway, Jonathan,' she continued softly. 'It's wrong for a man to live alone.'

She leaned back again, and the thrust of her body, the glow in her half-closed eyes, was an invitation, a somnolent erotic invitation that drove directly to the core of his senses.

'Would you like to marry me?' he said angrily, and then he felt her hands touching his neck and he stood up and wrenched her close to him, pressing her body fiercely down the length of him. He felt her slacken, felt her hanging to him and then heard her say, 'I'll be a good wife! I swear it. You'll never regret it Jonathan, never! I'll look after the children for you. You won't have to find anyone for them. I'll come and live in your cottage and you won't have to worry again. We'll marry as soon as we can, won't we? We'll marry as soon as the Rector will let us?'

The desire went from him and he was only aware of relief

that the problem of Harriet and Peter was solved.

'You're sure it's what you want?' he asked. 'Don't do it unless you're sure. You're young enough and pretty enough to marry someone without ties if you want to.'

She gripped him tightly by the arms. 'If I don't marry you, I shan't marry at all.'

He thought she was taking her age and spinsterdom a little over-seriously, but he was too tired to make her change her mind. She was kind and pretty and she liked the children. If she considered him her last chance of marriage, then he was grateful to her. He smiled and patted her shoulder.

'All right, Anne-Louise. We'll marry as soon as we can.'

She made only one mistake in the six weeks before their marriage, one unguarded mistake that she withdrew from as quickly as she could. Everything else, everything that she thought would be difficult to handle, she managed with superb calm and self-control.

She moved her few things into Jonathan's cottage and stamped her personality quickly on a home that might still remind him of Myra. She put the sewing-machine which she could not and would not use – into a cupboard and moved the bed round against another wall. She mixed Myra's china and linen carefully with her own so that it was impossible to separate them. For two weeks before the wedding she slept with Harriet in the house so that a family pattern of some kind was established before Jonathan came there. She coped, as best she could, with Peter's miserable howling when he first said good-bye to Betsy and Math. He had lived with Betsy for eighteen months, and the wonderful, exciting, navy-blue Uncle Math was the first man in his small life. Anne soothed him, pampered him and promised he would see Uncle Math every month if only he would be good. She bought him a miniature sailor-suit, a replica of the clothing worn by the omnipotent Uncle Math, and he subsided into grudging forbearance.

She pressured her mother, Betsy and Will into silence, daring them to voice to Jonathan the doubts they felt about her suitability to be his wife. She was confident and careless when she made her mistake.

Three weeks before the wedding she met him at the station and let her news bubble rapidly out on the way home.

'I've spoken to Mrs Fawcett about your job,' she said in a business-like way. 'I'm a favourite of hers and I waited until I thought she was in a good temper and I asked if she could find something for you back on the estate. She's going to see what Mr Fawcett can do for you.'

She was bouncing along the track from the station, swinging a little ahead of Jonathan, and she could not see his face.

'I told her the sooner the better. And I said you're not fussy about what you do so long as you can get something quickly. She was a bit highty at first, but then she said, as a favour to me, she'd try and find something.'

She was aware that Jonathan had fallen back behind her. When she looked round he was walking very slowly and he had the reserved look that she remembered and hated on his face.

'You shouldn't have done that, Anne-Louise,' he said quietly.

Even then she didn't realise what she had done. She thought he was querying her decision as to the choice of employer.

'Well, there's nowhere else,' she said impatiently. 'Magistrate Wilkins has his farms all filled. The Rector only takes a gardener and a game boy, and all the rest of the farms only need men at harvest. It'll have to be Fawcett's.'

'I'm not working for Fawcett or Wilkins.'

'What do you mean?' she said sharply.

He stopped and placed his hands on her shoulders.

'Anne,' he said, 'I am never going to work for Fawcett or anyone like him ever again. I've had enough of fools. I've had enough of lazy men who give nothing to life except a sense of their own importance. I've had enough of men who are not strong enough to earn their own bread and, fortunately for them, do not have to. I've had a lifetime of the Fawcetts, first the old man and now this one, and I want nothing more of them.'

216

'You've been reading all that radical nonsense,' she said uncertainly. 'You're talking like those trade-union men who hate everyone rich.'

'No, Anne.' He shook his head impatiently. 'I don't care how rich they are. It isn't important. But it's important that they're weak and stupid – or at least Fawcett is – it's important to me that a man – who is no man – should tell me what to do when I know better than he.'

She began to grow flustered and angry as she saw how she had miscalculated, how she was handling him in the wrong way.

'So what do you intend to do? Start running Mr Fawcett's estate for him?' she said spitefully. He shook his head again.

'I'm staying with the flocks for a while. I'll come home week-ends, and then next year I shall leave the marsh and start new work.'

'And what is this new work!' she demanded shrilly. 'This new job that only the high and mighty Jonathan Whitman can do. Do you want to run a farm? Or be a doctor? Or the schoolteacher perhaps? That's fine! The great Jonathan Whitman with twelve years of schooling is going to run the country and tell other people what to do!'

She saw then that she had gone too far, and instantly screamed inside at her useless, dangerous taunts. His face whitened and became even more withdrawn. She hoped he would hit her and shout like Maxie would have done, but he remained silent for a long, terrible moment. Then he said quietly, 'No, Anne. There's no way that I can jump to be a teacher or a doctor, no way for a man who knows only farming and the land to pretend to be a scholar. But I can be more – just a little more – than a groundsman or a gardener. And I can move up one step, then Harriet and Peter can move up one more.'

She didn't understand. It was confusing and muddling, and she only knew that she had nearly ruined everything. She wanted him to come back all the time and work on the Fawcett grounds like he had always done. She didn't know what this new job was, but she was jealous because it was something

217

he had planned without her. She wanted him to do what she told him to do. To come back to Fawcett's and spend every night with her.

'Well, what is the job?' she jeered.

He raised his hand and slowly touched her cheek with one finger.

'You don't have to marry me if you don't want to, Anne,' he said softly.

Panic tightened the skin on her back and arms. She dared not lose him again because there would be no third chance. She had three weeks, three more dangerous weeks to get through before she could relax and know he was hers for the rest of his life. She bit her lower lip and forced herself to grow calm.

'I'm sorry, Jonathan. I'm sure you have everything planned. I only thought it a good idea to ask Mrs Fawcett about the position.'

She hated saying it, hated apologising to him, but she could think of no other way of undoing the damage, the nearly irrevocable damage her thoughtless tongue had provoked. When he smiled she nearly sobbed with relief. 'Only three more weeks,' she thought. 'Only three more weeks.'

She was sure that, once married, she would be safe, secure in the knowledge that nothing would make him go away, and she counted the days to her wedding with feverish haste, checking each one off as yet another obstacle from her Holy Grail.

She made no further mistakes. She was careful and quiet and tried to behave as she thought Betsy would have done in the same circumstances. When she went to her wedding she was even more careful, not trusting herself even on the morning of her marriage in case it went wrong again.

She married him quietly, she took the children straight back to the cottage and entertained her mother and brothers and sisters at a wedding tea of her own making. She put the children to bed. She went up and waited for Jonathan, knowing she could rouse him as she could rouse any man. Just once, briefly, in his arms, she was happy, believing she possessed

218

him, but when the morning came she could not understand why the feeling, the nervous, strained feeling, of wondering how to hold him was still with her. She was his wife, she looked after his children, she kept his house, but the fear of losing him had not gone, the anxiety that he might one day walk out and never come back.

The torment stayed with her, through the autumn and winter it stayed with her, guarding her behaviour, making her act with wary caution when he came home at week-ends. And not until the spring did the fear leave her. When her child was born she knew she need never worry about losing him again.

Ten

THE CHILD was Myra; some accident of genes, some strange passing of physical cells from the grandparents that he and Myra had shared, resulted in the child of Anne-Louise resembling, exactly, the smooth, beautiful girl who had been his cousin and his first wife.

He had felt no undue anxiety about the birth, not because he was uncaring – Anne-Louise was his wife and deserved his loyalty and affection – but because he sensed that the forceful, self-willed Anne would not allow any disorganisation in the birth of her child. He went in to see her almost as soon as the little girl was born, and in the first moment of the child's life, the brief moment when it resembles an entity instead of a child, he saw with sharp, jolting pain, the face of his dead wife.

The shape of the face was as Myra's had been, high-cheeked and wide across the brow, the eyes as huge and smiling were blue – but the darker flecked blue that shortly turns to hazel, the soft warm hazel of Myra's eyes. To Anne-Louise the child owed nothing but the colour of her hair. It was soft and thick, but the colour was black; strong, silky black like Anne's.

He held the child in his hands, the small, downy head feeling like an apple in his huge palm, and he knew a delight in this child that he had never felt for his two first-born children. Later he was to wonder why he loved this daughter of Anne-Louise's so much, when the children of Myra aroused no more in him than dutiful tenderness and a pity for their motherless condition. But Sarah – he named the child after his mother – was his Benjamin, his Joseph, his Myra all rolled into one. He knew such pleasure in watching her, in holding the tiny struggling body that he could not bear to leave her when the time came to return to the flocks. Again and again he reminded himself not to show favour for this child over the others, he must give Harriet and Peter the same attention as he gave to Sarah, he must carve a ship for Peter, a doll for Harriet at the same time as he smoothed and polished a wooden lamp for Sarah. And with an instinctive, unrealising skill, he carefully disguised from Anne-Louise the extent of his love for her child.

Three months after Sarah was born, he made his final plans for the work that would bring him home to the village. Anne-Louise, since their friction about his mysterious work, had tried never to mention it again, pretending that it was some pipe-dream of his that she considered to be of no account. She was not always successful, there were times when she could not resist flinging his great ideas at him, demanding when the mighty work was going to begin. Her milder taunts he answered with a grin and 'It's going to be a surprise.' Her infrequent but virulent attacks on the subject he ignored altogether.

She knew he was writing letters. He took paper and envelopes from the desk one Sunday evening and carried them with him when he went back to Romney. She discovered accidentally that he had borrowed an atlas from the doctor's house and presumably this went to Romney too, along with the paper and envelopes.

And then, one Wednesday evening, he returned unexpectedly to the cottage and asked if she would press his braid jacket.

'Where are you going?' she demanded fractiously, torn between fear and a desire to prove that she didn't care what he was doing. Jonathan grinned.

'Tomorrow I'm going to London,' he answered. 'And if everything goes right I shan't be going back to the flocks. I shall stay here with you and the children.' He got the blacking out of the boot-box and carefully began to rub and smooth the blacking on his boots. Anne-Louise was impressed in spite of herself. It must be something important for him to go to London.

'Are you going for the day?' she snapped, lifting the flatirons and crashing them on to the top of the kitchener.

221

'Uh-huh.'

'What time will you be home?'

'For supper, Annie. For supper.' He looked up at her and grinned. 'Contain yourself, lass. Tomorrow evening you'll know all about it.'

He spoke teasingly, in the same way that he sometimes spoke to Harriet and Peter, and she was annoyed. Her annoyance kept her haughtily silent for the rest of the evening, and when Jonathan came up to bed she lay with her back towards him, registering disapproval. She managed to hold her fretfulness until he was actually walking out the door on the following morning.

'I'll tell Mr Fawcett he'd better start looking for a new estate,' she gibed childishly, and wanted to scream when Jonathan only smiled and then walked out into the yard.

She spent the day irritably working at things she had no need to do. She took the flues of the kitchener down and achieved some kind of release in crashing the pieces carelessly together. She broke two basins, slapped Peter once and Harriet twice because they were in her way when she was flinging herself across the scullery. She handled Sarah so roughly that the child cried, and when Jonathan walked in that evening she was ready to scream with vexation.

'Well, I hope you're satisfied!' she said tearfully. 'Leaving me to look after everything while you go gallivanting off to London for the day.'

Jonathan looked puzzled, then dismissed her nonsense with a shrug.

'Don't you want to hear what I've been up to?' he asked aggravatingly.

'I'm not interested.'

'All right,' he said. He had a large envelope in his hand and he took a paper out of it and began to read quietly to himself. She stood it for a few moments and then could bear it no longer.

'Well, what have you been doing?'

He folded the piece of paper and placed it back in the envelope.

'You know they're having a branch post office over at Longley Green?'

'Of course I know,' she said irritably. 'Everyone knows.'

He grinned. 'I'm the new postman.'

She was shocked. She had imagined many things, but not this.

'But you're only a shepherd,' she said slowly.

'I was a shepherd. Now I'm a postman.'

She tried not to let him see she was surprised because somehow that would mean that he had won. But she was surprised, surprised and curious to know how he had obtained the job.

'Why did they choose you?'

Jonathan unlaced his boots, took them off and wriggled his toes.

'I've been helping over at Marshfield post office,' he said, 'helping with the rounds when they were short. The postmaster there, he gave me a letter to take up to London, and they gave me a test, I got a reference from the army, and a reference from the farmer at Marshfield.' He walked over to the baby's cot in his stockinged feet and lifted Sarah out. Anne-Louise, against her own inclination, was fascinated.

'What happened in London?'

'I had to answer some questions – on a form – like a test it was. Then I had to do a lot of things, sorting and reading the forms and addresses.' Suddenly he laughed. 'Couldn't say some of the places on the envelopes. They gave me a big bundle of foreign mail. I knew where most of the places was, but I didn't know how to say them.'

'What happened?' she breathed.

'I gabbled them so quickly, and shuffled the letters over at such a speed they didn't notice properly . . . I think.' He held Sarah high in the air over his head and she gurgled down at him.

'Your pa's a postman, missy,' he said to the Myra/Sarah face above his own. 'No more waiting on Fawcett's good will. No more having to say "Yes, sir" and worrying in case you forget and let them see what you really think about them. From now on I depend on no one but myself.'

He brought the baby down and laid her across his shoulders. Anne-Louise felt a stab of jealousy at the way he was speaking to Sarah, as though she were old enough to understand him.

'I don't know why it had to be such a great secret,' she said derisively. 'Just because you think you'll look fine in a stupid uniform with a hat and a leather bag, we're all supposed to think how clever you are.'

Secretly she was impressed. In five generations of wood-cutters, ploughmen, shepherds and farmhands, Jonathan was the first to achieve the status of a government official. It was no more than she deserved.

The miracle of the twentieth century began.

Mr Orville Wright 'effected a landing' in his heavier-than-air machine. The landing 'effected' was shakily and warily on one wing – but nonetheless the great moth had landed. Female suffrage, which had smouldered for more than fifty years as no more than a gentle philosophical discussion, suddenly flared into militancy. British gentlemen found themselves vastly amused at the sight of aggressive females in the London streets. The ladies – in Holloway being fed through a rubber tube jammed into the nostrils and down the throat – failed to see the humour.

In 1906 Jonathan, who was now in a position to buy himself a daily newspaper, voted in the election. Brigadier Whithurst-Benson, who had represented the village and its environs for the past seventeen years was returned once more, but Jonathan felt a savage delight in knowing that this time the Brigadier's party was overwhelmed by an astonishing liberal majority. At the same time he wondered – uneasily – if things were becoming unstable when the returns also registered twenty-nine labour members.

The unspoken feud between Kaiser Wilhelm and his uncle, the King of England, began to take a more positive form. The German navy, like the German ambition, could no longer be ignored. Feverishly the outdated British navy took a realistic look at itself. The look was disturbing. The resulting action culminated in the mightiest battleship ever built — the *Dreadnought*.

Young Peter, who under the tutorial eye of Uncle Math had followed the progress of the great ship with all the enthusiasm his six years could muster, waited with agonised anticipation for the launching. The launching to which he had been invited — by Uncle Math — about which he spoke all day and every day and which was the greatest event in his sea-starved life.

Two days before the launching he experimented with some pine cones in the kitchen-range. The explosion that followed fetched him a blow round the ear from Anne-Louise and the news that he would not be allowed to go to Portsmouth to Math, Betsy and the *Dreadnought*.

When Anne-Louise saw his small horrified face she wished she hadn't said anything about the trip to Portsmouth. She was irritably pregnant again and found that the children, her own Sarah as well as the other two, annoyed her. Harriet was slow — too slow — and seemed impervious to her threats, punishments or bribes. Peter lived his life counting the days between visits to Betsy and Math, and she was increasingly aware of a growing resentment towards her daughter, Sarah, who was too serene, too beautiful, and too beloved by Jonathan. She was angry that the children should have lives that did not centre about her. Harriet appeared not even to notice her, and Peter's untactful preference for Betsy was both stupid and infuriating. And they took Jonathan away from her. Time that he should spend with her he devoted to his children. She was resentful and hurt.

When Jonathan came home that night, Peter burst into a passionate plea for the restitution of his ship-launching. Jonathan upheld her discipline before the boy, but she knew, by the way he looked at her, by the way he paused before saying 'You must do as your mother says' that he thought she was spiteful and mean. She wanted to withdraw the punishment, but couldn't. Her pride refused to let her confess that she had been unfair. And when, in bed that night listening to Peter's miserable sobbing in the far bedroom, she tried to draw Jonathan into an argument upon the subject he listened quietly to her simulated anger about Peter, said, 'The boy is punished. There is no need to discuss it any further', and went to sleep.

She wanted to discuss it further. Not discuss it, but quarrel and shout about it and if she lost the fight that wouldn't be as important as the fact that they had had the fight.

She lay, trying not to hear Peter, and finally she reached across to Jonathan, brushing his neck with her hand, pressing her body close to him, firing him – as she always could – with the excitement of her own body. He tried to stiffen against her, but she knew, in this one way she knew, he could never win. However impervious he was to her during the day, at night his body betrayed him. These were the times, the only times, she knew she possessed him. He shuddered once, then turned and seized her roughly between his hands. Exultantly she answered, fired, and encouraged his increasing brutality until the noise of Peter crying was no longer noticed by either of them. She took no physical delight from the embrace, but her vanity was appeased for just a short while.

When Peter awoke the next morning he knew something nasty had happened. He thought for a moment and then the full weight of misery descended on him. Tomorrow Uncle Math, Aunt Betsy, Aunt Betsy's two baby girls, and King Teddy would launch the *Dreadnought* all on their own and he, Peter Whitman, would not be there to see it was done properly. Despair swamped over him and he slipped out of bed, his toes curling icily on the cold lino, and went into the bedroom that led off his. Sarah was sitting up in her cot. She cooed amiably at him and smiled toothily, but he was too miserable to go and speak to her.

He pulled back the covers of Harriet's bed and slipped in beside her. Harriet didn't open her eyes, but she reached for his hand under the covers.

'I shan't see the king,' he said quaveringly. 'Uncle Math will take everyone but me.'

Harriet squeezed his hand. 'Aunt Betsy's nice,' she said irrationally. 'I like Aunt Betsy. I like Aunt Betsy better than ma.'

They lay taking warmth from each other's bodies, sharing a

sympathy with each other that slightly soothed Peter's disappointment. The bed was jammed against the window on one side and Peter reached over and drew a pattern with his finger in the frosty whorls that were beginning to melt. Harriet lay quite still beside him, her eyes closed, her body moving only with the rise and fall of her breathing.

'I don't suppose I shall ever see the king now,' he said mournfully. 'Not the king, and the *Dreadnought, and* Uncle Math. Not altogether at Portsmouth.'

Sarah pulled herself up and dangled amiably over the bars of her cot.

'Aah!' she said sympathetically, not understanding the misery, but sensitive gloom in the air.

Suddenly he knew that he wouldn't be able to bear it if he couldn't go – life would just be over for him if he couldn't go.

'Harriet,' he said thinkingly, 'I'm going anyway.'

He got out of bed, thought some more, and then went back to his own room.

Harriet opened her eyes and stared at the ceiling.

'Aunt Betsy's nice,' she said, but Peter was already out of earshot.

He was up early next morning and into his fine, Sunday-best sailor-suit with the hat just like Uncle Math's. He went into Harriet's room and woke her.

'I'm off to Portsmouth, Harry.'

Harriet nodded, then reached down into the bed and pulled up a handkerchief with some money tied into it. When she opened it there were lots of pennies and a sixpence as well. Peter gaped and stared at the money.

'Where did you get all those pennies, Harry?'

She smiled, sorted out eight of them and handed them to him.

'Did you steal them?' he asked with approving curiosity. Harriet only smiled again and closed her eyes. Peter climbed over her, pushed the window up and stepped out on to the shed roof.

'Good-bye, Harry,' he whispered cheerfully. 'I'm sorry you

can't come too.'

He slid down the slope of the shed roof, held his breath and dropped on to the frozen ground, rolling and bouncing up again like a small puppy. He looked up once to see Harriet quietly closing the window and he hurried across the yard and into the lane. A few yards away from the gate he paused, aware of a serious and grave omission.

He was a child of the village and knew the laws of village hospitality. One did not visit relatives unexpectedly without taking a gift of some kind. It was imperative that a visit to friends should be sealed with a jar of homemade marmalade, a cake, a honeycomb or some delphinium roots from a garden. He turned round, went back through the gate and considered.

At the top of the garden, seven stout cabbages stood in a row. He selected the largest, sawed away at the stalk with a piece of stone and finally tucked the cabbage under his arm.

'That will do very nicely for Aunt Betsy,' he said, gratified with his own generosity, and then once more he was on his way.

He had done the journey, with Betsy or Math, more times than he could remember. Over the fields to the station – the train to Brighton and then another to Portsmouth. He was vaguely aware that Betsy and Uncle Math had something to do with tickets, but as no one ever troubled him about such things he presumed it was an odd formality restricted – like so many things – solely to adults.

The morning across the fields was sunny and clear, so sunny that the white powder of ice across the grass was already melting. A thrush standing on a black branch was illumined against the pink morning sky. Peter saw the bird open its beak and then soar swiftly into the air. He was filled with an exciting sense of liberty – a knowledge that he could do all the things he was unable to do with his father or Anne-Louise or even his beloved Uncle Math.

He walked through the side-gate of the station, stumped up and down the platform a few times, and then mounted the steps that led over to the other platform. There he stood stiffly to attention as befitted someone who was going to see the king, and then he got cold and bored and began to roll the cabbage along the platform. He hoped that Mr Watkins would come out of his ticket-collector's office on the opposite platform. He enjoyed shouting across the rails to Mr Watkins, but the door of the office remained firmly closed and the smoke from the chimney indicated a large apple-wood fire that Mr Watkins probably didn't want to leave.

When he heard the rails move and the distant sound of the train along the tracks, he picked up the cabbage, rubbed some of the platform dirt from it with spit and then dried it on the front of his jersey. The train grew from a moving grub into a panting, belching iron paper-chain, stopped, and the door immediately in front of Peter was thrown open, thereby obliterating him from the sight of the guard, and from Mr Watkins who was trundling hurriedly over from the other platform. From the open carriage descended Mr and Mrs Colley, Grandfather Colley, Great-Uncle Ned Colley, Cousin Maud Colley, and the seven young Colley sons and daughters. The platform was swamped.

Uncle Ned Colley saw Peter waiting with the cabbage in his arms.

'Haa, young Whitman!' he said wheezily. 'Watching the trains come in, eh?'

He began to explain about the *Dreadnought* and taking the cabbage to Aunt Betsy, when suddenly the youngest Colley, climbing down from the carriage, fell face first on the asphalt surface. There were shouts, screams, cries of, 'I told you to hold her hand, Reuben!' 'Let me have your handkerchief, father!' 'She's torn her stocking right through!'

Peter waited politely to see if Uncle Ned Colley wanted to hear about him going to Portsmouth, then, realising that none of the Colleys were interested, he climbed into the carriage and sat down. The door slammed – hastily shut by one of the panicking Colleys – Mr Watkins blew the whistle and the train was off.

The fields and woods, familiar to him from many train rides with Math, were strange and somehow clearer and more vivid now that he was on his own. He counted to see how many big

229

plough horses were in the fields, and then to see how many he could count up to while the train was going through the tunnel. The spit had dried on the cabbage and it was looking shabby again.

When the train slowed down he could hear – some long way back in the train – the sound of someone singing. He stood up, went out into the corridor and followed the noise back up the length of the swaying passage-way. He was surprised to find that, as he went farther back in the train, the carriages were full of people. The singing was traced to a coach bulging with passengers, two sailors, three ladies in navy-blue coats and feather-brimmed hats, three little boys, each in a sailor-suit exactly like his own, and quite a lot of small girls with their hair tied back in red-white-and-blue ribbons.

Peter pressed his nose against the glass and stared in with interest. A small boy on the other side of the glass stared back, then the door was opened and one of the fine big sailors stuck his head out.

'Hullo, young-un!' he said jovially. 'And where are you off to?'

'I'm taking this cabbage to my Aunt Betsy.'

The sailor turned his head back into the carriage.

'Hear this,' he guffawed. 'He's taking a cabbage to his Aunt Betsy!'

The ladies giggled, the other sailor laughed. One of the little girls offered him a bag of humbugs and he said 'thank you very much' and picked the biggest he could find.

The boy who had stared at him through the glass stuck his tongue out. Peter put the humbug in one side of his mouth, looked furtively round the carriage and then crossed his eyes at the boy.

'What are you doing out in the passage on your own?' said the sailor kindly. Peter moved the humbug over to the other side of his face.

'I heard you singing. So I thought I'd come to see who it was.'

They all laughed again and one of the ladies took a mouth-organ out of her bag, shook it and began to play. When everyone started to sing again Peter wriggled excitedly and tapped his feet. He didn't know the words, but the general air of happiness communicated itself to him and he felt it was the happiest day of his life.

'Are you going to Portsmouth to see the king?' he asked breathlessly in the next pause between songs. One of the ladies nodded.

'The whole train is going to Portsmouth!' she said. 'I've never seen so many lovely sailors on one train before!' They all laughed again and Peter said proudly, 'My Uncle Math is a sailor. He's taking me to see the king.'

They sang some more songs. Peter had another humbug and wished he had something to offer all the jolly people in the carriage. When the train began to pull into Brighton all the ladies straightened their hats and the sailor opened the door into the passage.

'Now you get back to your uncle, young-un,' he said. 'He'll be wondering where you got to.'

Peter started to explain that Uncle Math wasn't actually *on* the train, but that he was travelling on his own and would see Betsy and Math when he got to Portsmouth. He'd only just begun when the engine gave an especially loud shriek, the train jolted violently and one of the ladies – the one who played the mouth-organ – was thrown across the carriage into the arms of a sailor. They all screamed and laughed. The lady's hat was tilted forward over her face and the sailor sat down quickly and pulled the lady down on to his lap. The man who had told Peter to run along said, 'Oi-Oi, George! Mind how you go then!' and the lady tried to straighten her hat again and stand up. The train lurched to a shuddering halt, the engine let out an exhausted sigh of whistle and steam and the corridor was suddenly crowded with sailors, sailors' wives, and sailors' families, all on a day's outing to see the *Dreadnought*.

Peter waited for his nice sailor and George and the lady who played the mouth-organ and all the others in the carriage to step down on to the platform. Then he got out immediately in front of yet another sailor who had a small boy and girl with him. The platform teemed with little boys in sailor-suits all clutching paper cones of winter-mixture or caramels or Sharp's Kreemies. He was swept in a surge of navy-blue humanity down the platform and through the barrier gates where a harassed ticket-collector snatched at outstretched hands offering half-fare tickets, full-fare tickets and return tickets that had to be hurriedly torn in half and then thrust back into a waiting hand. After the first swarm had gone through he gave up trying to count how many small boys in sailor suits or little girls with red-white-and-blue ribbons were passing through his gates.

Peter, who was in fact a little hazy about which platform he usually went to for the Portsmouth train, just followed the tide of trippers through yet another gate, on to the platform and into a train packed to capacity with people shouting, singing and jostling one another. He was hard put to keep the cabbage from being trodden underfoot and eventually found himself squeezed into a corner seat beside a small girl who told him her name was Agatha, that she was seven-years-old, and that her ma was sitting in the next carriage but one. By this time he had given up trying to tell people about Uncle Math and the *Dreadnought*. He just smiled at the little girl and told her his name was Peter and he was taking a present to his Aunt Betsy.

If the ticket-collector at Brighton had been harassed, the Portsmouth man was even more so and was no longer even trying to control the crowd. Peter followed Agatha and her family through the barrier, said good-bye to Agatha and then, feeling very hungry – he had missed his breakfast and the humbugs had only served to aggravate his appetite – began the longish walk to Aunt Betsy's.

Half an hour later he stood tired, dirty and victorious on the steps of Betsy's lodgings.

'Hullo, Aunt Betsy,' he said when she opened the door. 'I thought you might like a cabbage.'

They spent a little while arguing about whether or not Peter should go to the *Dreadnought*. Betsy had the letter saying he wasn't to go, an apologetic and self-defensive letter from Anne-Louise. But Betsy's claim to uphold Anne's authority

232

was half-hearted, and Math said the lad deserved to go when he'd managed the journey on his own. He couldn't take him back until the crowds had gone so he might just as well come along and see the launching. In the end she gave in. Partly because the day was a holiday, the little girls already dressed in their serge dresses with the blue sashes, but mostly because the sight of Peter's dirty, beaming face over the huge, green cabbage made her want to cry. He looked so like Jonathan. She made him wash his face and hands, sat him down to a big bowl of porridge and some bread and syrup, and then the huge, beautiful, wonderful day began. The day that shone with the magic of a fat, jolly old gentleman in a blue and gold uniform, of a huge ship with two masts and a flag flying from the highest of them, of a newspaper of tripe and cowheel, steaming and tasty, brought from a street cart by Uncle Math.

It was a day when he took turns with the little girls to be lifted up on Uncle Math's shoulders, when finally he had to walk home dragging on Betsy's arm with his eyes closed from sheer weariness because Uncle Math was carrying Mary and May, who were both asleep. And it was the day when Uncle Math whispered a secret in his ear, a secret that not even his father or Anne-Louise knew, a secret he could hug to himself, to be taken out later and gloated over when he was alone. He fell asleep in Betsy's armchair, a slice of dripping toast still in his hand. When he awoke his father was standing in front of him with folded arms and a stern face.

'He made it all on his own,' he heard Uncle Math say. 'He's a stout little lad.'

Peter blinked, rubbed his eyes and said, 'Hullo, pa.'

'Do you know what a bad boy you've been?' said Jonathan severely.

'Yes, pa.'

'Your mother's been worried, and I've had to come all the way down here to see what had happened to you.'

Peter beamed.

'And you stole a cabbage to give to your Aunt Betsy.'

Peter nodded, 'I expect you'll have to wallop me, pa, when we get home.'

'I'm afraid I shall,' said Jonathan sternly.

Peter looked cheerfully around him. The lamp was lit and stood in the middle of the table, sending out a warm, cheerful glow into the room. The fire in the range was so hot that the top of the stove was red and the kettle had been moved to one side. Mary and May, bibbed and sitting on chairs piled high with boxes and cushions, stared round-eyed at him over pieces of bread and butter. He looked at Jonathan. The matter of the thrashing being settled once and for all, his father seemed cheerful enough. And the thrashing didn't really matter at all. Not when he had seen the king; not when he knew the secret about Uncle Math and Aunt Betsy.

'The king's awful fat, pa,' he said chattily.

Jonathan turned hurriedly away. Discipline demanded he should retain an air of aloof disapproval until after the thrashing had been administered. He found the disapproval hard to maintain. Young Peter was too much like old Peter, and he wanted – very badly – to laugh.

On the train going home he tried to give the lad a small, stern lecture, but gave the task up as completely impossible. Peter agreed with everything he said and still maintained his air of affable goodwill. He offered several comments on the events of the day, on his journey to Portsmouth, on his fellow passengers, on the size of the *Dreadnought* and the size of the king. When they reached the village and began to walk home across the fields he said conspiratorially to his father, 'I know a secret about Uncle Math, pa.'

'Do you, now?'

'No one else knows except me.'

'Ah-ha,' said Jonathan.

They trudged on in silence for a while, then Jonathan, aware of the small boy pulling wearily at his arm, said, 'Come on, lad. I'll carry you the rest of the way.'

As he lifted him up Peter said off-handedly, 'Pa, shall we get the walloping over tonight?'

'That might be as well.'

Jonathan climbed over the last stile, walked down the lane and into the cottage yard. Anne-Louise, who had been taut with anxiety all day because she feared Jonathan might blame her for the boy running away, opened the kitchen door. When she saw Peter her anxiety vanished, absorbed into furious anger.

'Just wait, my boy! Just wait until you're inside! I'll teach you to go running off like that! You're a bad, wicked boy, and you're a thief too.'

'It's quite all right, ma,' said Peter serenely. 'Pa's going to thrash me.'

She saw Jonathan grinning at her across the boy's head. It was a grin that asked her to share his humour at the boy's cheekiness, to take part in the pretend of being cross about the escapade. It was a grin that should have joined her with Jonathan, made her part of the adult conspiracy. She wanted to smile back but couldn't. She felt he should have cared more for her than to laugh at the way Peter flouted her discipline. As he put the boy down on the floor she spun out and hit him hard across the back so that he stumbled inside and tripped over the scullery step.

'You'll get a thrashing all right!' she spat vindictively. 'And you'll go to bed early for the rest of the week. And you won't have any more trips to Portsmouth for the rest of the year!'

Peter hiccoughed noisily and turned to face her. He was trying not to cry because the blow across the back had hurt him. Her furious face made him step back a pace and then he remembered the secret and he threw caution to the winds — knowing that the news would divert her attention as nothing else would.

'I won't have to go to Portsmouth!' he choked defiantly. 'Uncle Math is retiring from the sea. And he's coming back here to live! So there!'

He had underestimated the effect of his news. Just in time he managed to duck, miss the blow she aimed at his right ear and run round the other side of the table to where she could not reach him.

Eleven

ANNE-LOUISE was surprised – and a little indignant – at both the quality and the size of Betsy's home. She had never bothered to visit Betsy at Portsmouth, largely because she was too busy and couldn't afford the fare anyway. Now she was astonished to see that Betsy boasted, among other things, a brown leather button-studded settee, a carved mahogany side-table, two cabriole-legged chairs and, of course, the china tea-service.

It was the tea-service that moved her to final indignation. It wasn't right that Betsy should have things like egg-shell delicate cups and plates brought all the way from China. Betsy was the plain one, the dowdy one, who, by the very virtue of her plainness was constrained to accept second best in everything. Her husband, small, quiet, self-effacing Mathew, was a shadow of a husband beside the powerful figure of Jonathan. Her life, one of useful village work and constant separation from that same insignificant husband, was dull and colourless beside Anne's. And when Mathew, returning to the village, found it impossible to get work, it was right and natural that it should be Jonathan, the husband of Anne-Louise, who managed to find him temporary work, with the post-office, with the harvest and with odd carpentry and building tasks about the village. But the china tea-service in Betsy's corner cabinet was all wrong. It had no place in the make-do, secondhand life that was Betsy's.

It became an obsession with Anne. Every time she popped into Betsy's cottage she had to go and open the cabinet and take the china out, as though holding it, feeling the smooth, delicate texture in her hand, would somehow make it hers. And when she had a letter from Florrie – a letter that brought a wave of nostalgia for evenings at the Brixton Empress and fish-and-chip suppers with Maxie afterwards – she knew she must borrow the tea-service for when Florrie came to see her.

She called into Betsy's on a hot, scented July evening. She was expecting the birth of her second child at any time, but her preoccupation with the tea-service had driven her nearly due confinement to a place of unimportance in her mind. She hurried in and threw herself hotly into a chair by the open window. Betsy was ironing and the heat of warm linen and burning soap made the air scorch in the tiny kitchen. Mathew was washing one of the little girls – Anne was never sure which was May and which was Mary – and he looked up and nodded when she came in.

'I'll borrow that tea-service of yours, Betsy,' she said briskly. 'I've a girl I was in service with coming to see me tomorrow, coming down from London she is, so I could do with it very nicely.'

Betsy looked uncomfortable. She knew Anne's way with china, careless and rather erratic, but she didn't wish to seem ungenerous to her sister. Mathew dropped a cotton nightie over the head of May – or Mary – and said pleasantly, 'I'm afraid you won't borrow it, Annie.'

She was startled beyond measure. Mathew spoke so little she had almost come to accept him as a mouthless adjunct of Betsy. She had certainly never expected him to contradict her.

'Well . . . ' she said, bridling up swiftly.

'That's Betsy's tea-service. It's a very special one I bought for her, Anne-Louise. You can borrow anything in the house except that.'

She waited for Betsy to say it was all right, that she could have the china after all, but Betsy only looked down at the wooden table and pressed her iron harder on the nightshirt.

'How could you be so selfish, Betsy?' she asked piteously. Betsy flushed and looked uncomfortable.

'Ah,' said Math wagging a finger in the air. 'But you see it's nothing to do with Betsy. It's me. Betsy does what I tell her to do.' He smiled at Betsy suddenly, a neat, gleaming smile and he put his hand up and pulled at a tendril of her hair that curled out from the back of her neck. 'You do as I say, lass, don't you?' he said gently.

Anne felt a pain leap violently between her thighs. She thought for a moment the child was coming, but the pain, a sharp, searing one, moved up to her breasts and spread out in a glow of misery that was nothing to do with the tea-service. She didn't know why the pain hurt so much, except that it was something to do with the way Math looked at Betsy, the way he pulled teasingly at the curl of hair. She was overwhelmed by loneliness.

'It doesn't matter,' she choked. She got up and went to the door.

'If there's anything else you want,' said Betsy hurriedly. 'A tablecloth, or a cakestand, just say.'

'No, thanks.' She blundered heavily against the door, feeling big and clumsy. When she got outside she wanted to cry, but realised there wasn't any point because Jonathan wasn't there to see her. By the time she got home she had pushed the pain away and managed only to remember that Betsy had refused the loan of the china tea-service.

Florrie was fatter, more blowsy, and more expensively dressed than Anne remembered her. She had a fur tippet – a ridiculous extravagance in view of the warm day – and a frieze dress with tucking down the front. She swept through the door, filling the kitchen both with noise and a skirt that was far too full for a country room. She took in Anne's size and condition in one glance and said vulgarly, 'My! You don't waste time do you? And the little girl only just gone two! When's it due?'

'Any time now.'

'Well let's 'ave some tea first, dear!'

Florrie pulled off her gloves. Her hands were just as red and swollen as Anne remembered. She followed Anne about the cottage, admiring and allowing herself to be impressed, and slowly Anne began to thaw. At least she was mistress of her house, not running at the beck and call of a mean-spirited employer. Graciously she poured tea into cups that were pleasant enough – if one hadn't seen Betsy's china – and pressed Florrie to help herself to a generous meal.

'I expect you're hungry,' she said cheerfully. 'Do you remember how we never had enough to eat? When you said you were coming I thought the least I could do was give you a tea that would last a couple of days.'

Florrie ladled gooseberry jam generously on to a slice of bread.

'Well, of course,' she said, 'it's not quite as bad now. I still get the fish from the market.'

'After all this time?' said Anne surprised. Florrie's face turned a hot, sticky colour and she took a large bite from her bread.

'Well . . . as a matter of fact . . . well, I know you won't care now, being as you're married and all, but the truth is that Maxie Dance and me are walking out together.'

She felt the pain again, the pain she had felt last night when Math had refused to lend her the china. A foolish, inconsequential pain that was nothing to do with Maxie and Florrie walking out together any more than last night's pain had been because of the tea-set.

'That's nice,' she said dully.

Florrie considered a plate of cakes and finally took a slice of a chocolate sponge.

'I told 'im you wouldn't care now. But 'e 'ad some funny idea that you ought to know before we finally decided. 'E was very cut-up at the way you treated 'im – rushing back 'ere and all, and saying you'd never really bin serious wiv 'im. But, o' course, 'e's over it now – I mean it's four years since you come back 'ere. I don't expect you even remember what 'e looks like.'

'No.' She couldn't remember in detail. But she remembered the evenings at the Dances, she remembered the presents and the flattery and the quarrels that she and Maxie used to have.

'But I told 'im I'd come. And I thought it would be nice to see you. To see' ow you're getting on and that.'

'I'm getting on fine,' she said. 'You can see that.'

Florrie looked relieved. 'You seem to be managing all right. With your own and the other two as well. And you've got everything very nice 'ere too.'

Anne-Louise suddenly straightened herself in the chair.

'I'm fine,' she said again. 'You'll have to hurry up, Florrie, if you want to get the evening train.'

She said good-bye, waved Florrie off across the fields and then went to clear away the shattered remains of a ravaged feast.

She wondered what it would have been like if she had married Maxie Dance. If she had stayed in London and settled to a life of outings and fun and violent quarrels with Maxie that ended in equally violent reconciliations. She couldn't envisage it. She had waited seven years to win Jonathan and nothing else seemed to matter except that now he belonged to her. She began to wash up, and the pain in her breast still hurt and she wondered if she would ever be happy again.

This time she had a son; and in the following year another. Nature, creating her a bad mother, also created her a prolific one, but she never – to her relieved satisfaction – had another daughter. After the initial mistake of Sarah, her children were all boys.

She wanted no more women in her life, not even – especially not even – her own daughters. Men she could handle, she could answer them, cajole them, bully and blackmail them. But women, any kind of women, were a threat to her supremacy. And as her sons were born, as the cottage began to be filled with her own male children, she began to resent, and finally to loathe the slow, dull, stolid figure of Harriet, her stepdaughter.

Things she had once accepted about the girl now infuriated her. The way Harriet stood, with her shoulders hunched and her head on one side. The way she moved, so slowly that Anne wanted to scream with annoyance. The fact that she had to be told everything several times, to be nagged, and shouted, and scolded at before she would do any task about the house properly. It enraged Anne even more that no one else in the house seemed to notice there was anything wrong with her. Peter apparently communicated with her in some strange way

240

of his own. Small Sarah treated her as an equal — and sometimes as though Harriet were a younger sister. 'Come *along*, Harriet.' 'Don't dawdle, dear.' 'Here now, Harry, let me do that. I'm quicker.'

Jonathan, when she tried to draw his attention to Harriet's stupidity, refused to answer, but she noticed that each time she complained to him he would take Harriet out with him, sometimes on his rounds, more often to the meadow at the top of the garden.

The rambling, overgrown meadow was now the driving force in Jonathan's life. He and Mathew had rented it from the Tyler farm. It was a large, unfertile field, crowded with gnarled fruit-trees at one end and left to the waste of nettles and foxgloves at the other. The fruit-trees were old and gave very little fruit and the soil was thick with sour weeds and the roots of trees. He and Math had begun the back-breaking work of clearing the ground. Every minute of leisure they had was devoted to the meadow, to the staking out of raspberry, black-currant and gooseberry canes. To the erection of chicken-runs and fresh hives. When the summer came, Mathew, who frequently had days without work, packed as many combs and punnets of fruit as he could manage into a deep shoulder-basket and walked eleven miles to the nearest market town. He returned nearly always with an empty basket and a full purse. Once, when they were wrapping eggs in newspaper late at night, Math said thoughtfully, 'It's not the people in Grinstead who want these things. It's folk up in London, or Portsmouth, or those places. They're the ones who want fresh honey and eggs.'

The following week they got Betsy to pack up a special basket. She lined it in her best linen and set the raspberries carefully in rounds of lime-tree leaves. She packed eggs round the fruit and combs of wax-wrapped honey over the top. Mathew bought a train ticket to Victoria — the money lent by Jonathan — and set out with a list of shops that Anne-Louise remembered from her service days.

He returned exultant.

'The first shop, Jonathan lad! The very first shop I went

into! They took the lot and want more, as much as I can carry.'

'I could go with you next time,' said Betsy quickly 'I can carry as much again. And we must do it now while the soft fruit is in.'

The following week they both went – and returned with empty baskets. Jonathan began to plan for the winter and fetched in some geese to try and catch the Christmas trade. They began to experiment – not always successfully – but whatever else failed the Lambeth grocer would take eggs, poultry, fruit and honey when it was in season.

They bought two goats – bad-tempered creatures that delighted in chasing Peter and young Sarah round the field – and endured the torment of milking the creatures and fermenting the milk to make cheese. The process was an arduous one and in the final stages demanded the assistance and kitchen skills of Anne and Betsy. The cheese scheme failed because Anne's patience refused to cope with dripping curd and the scalding of the cheese pails. The goats were sold and they tried something else.

There was, slowly at first, but it came, more money to spend. Money to spend on books, on a second-hand harmonium, on music lessons for Harriet and Sarah. Anne was furious at the waste of the extra money.

'It's trumped-up nonsense!' she raged. 'What do we want books for? And the girls learning to play the piano? It's a piece of foolish nonsense they'll have to forget when they start work. Harriet will be going into service in a couple of years and what good will playing the piano do her then?' She paused and added spitefully. 'That is if we can find someone stupid enough to take her.'

Jonathan ignored the gibe.

'Harry's not going to work in a couple of years,' he said. 'And when the time comes neither is Sarah. They, and the boys as well, are staying at school until they're fourteen.'

'Whaaaat!'

She was surprised rather than enraged. But she argued on principle about his decision. She didn't mind about the boys

242

staying on to school, but if Harry and Sarah did too, it meant they had something that she hadn't had.

'They're staying,' he said firmly. 'Maybe it won't make any difference to them when they go to work. But they're staying. And the girls are having music lessons and there'll be money for books if they want them.'

'It's stupid,' she spat. 'Sarah's too young anyway, and it's wasted on Harriet. You know it's wasted. You just won't admit it!'

He pushed past her, resisting the temptation to strike out and hit her as he went through the door and out into the yard. She was right – in a small part she was right – Harriet was slow; at school she had mastered the elements of reading, writing and adding, but her progress had stopped there. She was backward, but that was as far as his admission about her would go. He refused to consider anything else. She would get better as time went on. Even when Miss Chamberlain, the village organist who also taught piano, called him in and told him it was pointless trying to instruct Harriet in the rudiments of music, he would not believe that there was anything more than unhappiness and fear at the root of her slowness. He ignored the things he could not bear to see.

Finally there occurred an event he could not ignore. An event that was fired by the return of old Peter – Peter the shepherd – to the village and the home of his youngest son.

He came in the spring of 1909, his round, gnome-like figure striding across the field with the black-and-white sheep-dogs circling and wheeling round him as though they were guiding him back to the pens. He came up to Jonathan and stood over him, watching him clear out the runnels between the fruit bushes.

'Be a good crop this year,' he said ruminatively.

Jonathan straightened up and grinned at the old man.

'Hullo, pa.'

'Are the bees well?'

'Aye.'

Peter nodded and sat down on the top of a hen roost. The dogs flopped at his feet and spread long, thin noses across their paws.

'It was cold on the marsh this winter,' he said slowly.

Jonathan felt the familiar pang of guilt and concern for the old man. He looked at Peter and realised suddenly that his father *was* old, very old. His face had the innocent, gentle look that spreads over features right at the end of life, the look that is the outward sign of a mind concerned only with simple things and simple desires.

'You should have come back, pa. Why didn't you come and stay here?'

The old man didn't answer. He picked at a loose piece of wood on the top of the run and stared out to the hills that showed over the distant tree-line.

'They tell me there's a new law passed by the king?' He watched Jonathan carefully like a small round bird waiting to fly away at the first signal of alarm.

'That's right, pa.'

'About giving us a few shillings every week. That Mr Lloyd George, he says there's a few shillings for a man when he's old.'

Jonathan nodded gently, beginning to see the way of the old man's mind.

'It's the new law, pa. Pensions for the old. Not like the Union or going on the Parish. It comes out of the taxes and . . . ' He stopped because he realised that Peter wouldn't care about the economics of the scheme. If he had got to the point of asking if the scheme was true, he would be over the hurdle of accepting government charity.

'I could give you my shillings,' said the old man simply, 'and I could stay with you. I would be a boarder in your house.'

He had to turn away because of the pain in his heart, pain that was pity and love and respect for the old man's pride.

'You could have come before, pa. We wanted you to come.'

Peter shook his head. 'It's all right now,' he said. 'Now I've got my shillings.'

A thousand foolish ideas flashed through his mind at the same time, ideas that ranged from how they could reorganise the bedrooms to whether Anne-Louise would accept the old man in the house.

'Wait here, pa,' he said gently. 'And I'll go and tell Annie.'

He hurried down the garden, remembering many things; the old man at his wedding, waiting for him and Myra to come out of the church; the two years he had spent with him on the marsh. He tried to recall what his father had looked like before the war, and before he had run away to join the Hussars. He had been younger than he was now, of course, but in Jonathan's mind remained an image of an old man. He could not remember his father as young, or even as middle-aged.

'Pa's in the meadow,' he said to Anne. 'He wants to come home. Someone's told him about the old age pensions and he's decided he's no longer a burden on us.'

His youngest son tried to crawl up his leg, but he didn't even notice. He was warily watching Anne's face, wondering how much he was going to have to fight. He watched her stiffen, then flush and tighten her mouth.

'I never said he couldn't come before,' she said sharply. 'Don't put it about that I was too mean to have your father here.'

He sighed. 'It's nothing to do with you. He wouldn't come before because he couldn't pay his way. He's seen too much of it, families crippled by an old one living on them and not bringing any money in.' He paused to see if she would answer, but she dried her hands on the towel and turned away from him.

'He can have the girls' room,' she said, her face expressionless. 'Sarah can go in with the boys and Harriet will have to sleep down here on the sofa.'

'He won't mind going in with the boys, Anne.' He didn't like the way she spoke about Harriet sleeping on the sofa. It was as though she were glad of an excuse to push Harriet out of her room.

'He's your father. He's entitled to a room of his own. Go and get him in and then we'll get Harriet's mattress turned and the other bed put in the boys' room.'

He waited for the sting to come, the fight to rage about

whether or not old Peter would stay, but nothing else was said. She unwound her thick, damp scrubbing apron and went up the stairs to move the beds.

Peter was still sitting on the hen-run picking at the piece of wood.

'Come on, pa,' said Jonathan gently. 'Come into the house.'

'I'll give you my shillings,' said the old man fiercely. He stood up and followed Jonathan slowly down the garden. The dogs went as far as the kitchen door, then stopped, afraid of the small enclosure within and the noise of children over the scullery floor. Peter turned and looked at his dogs.

'They'll miss the flocks,' he mumbled. His hand, dirty and deeply grained, dropped to caress the heads and muzzles of the beasts.

'They'll be fine, pa,' said Jonathan quickly, frightened lest the old man changed his mind again. He had a disturbing vision of his father lying dead for several days among the flocks, with no one knowing, no one going to help him. 'They can stay in the shed at night, and probably Tyler can use them sometimes on the farm.' He pushed Peter gently through the door. The dogs wanted to follow, but ingrained suspicion of enclosed spaces made them hold back.

He had just persuaded the old man to sit uneasily at the table when Anne suddenly burst into the kitchen, her face raging with excitement, and holding a small cloth package in her hand.

'I told you!' she shouted at Jonathan. 'I told you that girl wasn't normal! Just look at this . . . look what I found under her mattress . . . this . . . and this . . . and this brooch belongs to Betsy. She took that from somebody else's house! Just look what she's stolen!'

Dully he watched her spread the things across the table, several coins, handkerchiefs, a pair of Anne's gloves, a purse he recognised as belonging to Miss Chamberlain, the music teacher, one or two brooches and a spoon. The things were all stolen and the booty was all the more pathetic because it was jumbled up with dead flowers and stones and pieces of old twigs that had, for some reason, taken Harriet's fancy.

'It's only a child's secret hoard,' he said desperately, knowing it wasn't true.

'It's stolen!' she cried. 'It's money. And Betsy's brooch and Miss Chamberlain's purse.'

'Perhaps Betsy gave her the brooch,' he said weakly.

'And perhaps she didn't.' Anne snapped. 'And Miss Chamberlain certainly didn't give her the purse. You know very well she was asking if she'd left it here.'

He couldn't dispute the purse. No amount of reasoning could dispute the purse. The other things could have been the result of an idle, dreamy collecting. But the purse meant that Harriet had crept up behind Miss Chamberlain – probably when Sarah was practising her scales on the harmonium – and taken the purse from her leather case. The purse was stolen.

'I'll punish her. I'll talk to her,' he said heavily. Anne snorted.

'Talkin's no good, or punishing. She's stupid! She's more than dull, she's stupid!'

'Stop it, Anne.' A small throb of pain pierced the left side of his head beneath the old scar of the Boer bullet wound.

'I've told you! I've told you time and again that she's not normal! I tell her to do something and she doesn't understand . . . And when she does she just takes no notice. She's not right in the head! Why won't you admit it? Why won't you see that she's stupid?'

The pain beneath the scar throbbed heavily and he held his head stiffly on one side to try and ease the discomfort. A slight blurring of vision in his left eye cast a haze over everything on that side of the room and he was suddenly reminded of stumbling over the African veld with a black mist sealing one side of his vision.

'Be quiet!' he shouted, and then quickly controlled himself. 'She's slow. She's quiet and not as bright as Sarah. The years with Emily and the Vincents didn't help – and you don't help either, Anne!'

Anne-Louise gasped, and then swung her head back angrily.

'There's only one thing wrong with Harriet,' she cried. 'She's the child of first cousins! If you hadn't married your

247

cousin she might have been normal!'

The room was quiet, so quiet he could hear the dogs pattering outside, trotting up and down the yard. The pain in his head vanished, disappeared and was replaced by a dull soreness that spread down into his breast.

It was said. The tiny core of disease, the spark of rotting suspicion that no one had ever admitted before, hung heavily in the air between them. The dread that had festered in his mind for years and years, the anxiety, the speculation about Harriet was torn open and left for him to weep over.

He stared at Anne, a white, silent stare of hate and disgust, and then he turned and pushed past old Peter and hurried out of the house.

'Jonathan!' She tried to call him back, frightened at what she had done, but knowing there was nothing she could say to put it right. He was gone, and she was left staring at the gnarled, round face of her father-in-law. The old man puckered up his mouth and stared at her.

'You planning on getting Harriet taken away to the Colony?' he asked mildly. The Colony was the home, two villages away, for women and girls who were subnormal. They were frequently to be seen walking out in a long blue-and-brown-clad crocodile, their forms and faces the dull, distorted shapes of the mentally deficient.

She was not sure if he was serious or trying to gibe at her. She turned round and began to climb the stairs. 'You'd better come and help me with the mattress,' she said sharply. Old Peter grinned and followed her.

'You've upset him,' he said informatively. He watched Anne's body swinging from side to side as she moved up the stairs ahead of him and his head nodded appreciatively in admiration.

'He'll get over it.'

But she wasn't sure. This time she wasn't sure that she could coax and persuade him with her body when they were alone at night. She fretted and worried at her foolish, thoughtless words for the rest of the day. She was nice – especially nice – to Harriet. She packed up a slab of bread and jam and told

248

five-year-old Sarah to take Harriet out for the afternoon. She waited for Jonathan to come back, for tea, for supper. He came for neither and not until she was lying in bed did she hear him come into the kitchen and remove his boots. He sat talking to Harriet in her made-up bed on the kitchen sofa. She could hear the soft rumble of his voice and the occasional slow, disjointed reply that came from Harriet and then he came heavily up the stairs.

When he climbed into bed he lay right on the far side, away from her, not touching her and she had to curl her hands hard into her side to stop from crying. She moved over and felt him stiffen and his back turn flatly against her. When he spoke his voice was curt.

'Go to sleep.'

She forced herself not to cry, not to let him know she was afraid. It was the first time she had failed to wheedle him away from anger, to beat him in the battle that was their marriage.

He did not touch her for three weeks, three weeks of icy terror that he might never come near her again. But in the fourth week she won. The persistence of her body achieved what she thought to be her victory. And in the pleasureless frenzy of that victory she had to hold hard to stifle the sobs of relief that shook her body.

The joyless reunion brought her another pregnancy, a pregnancy that took its part in the pattern of the house, along with old Peter trying to settle gently to a life indoors, and with Jonathan in an agony of mind that seemed to hurt him physically, watching his daughter Harriet.

She stole – repeatedly stole – and all he could do was try to see where she concealed her magpie hoard. Reasoning with her proved futile, she sat quietly while he tried to explain what she must and must not take, and he knew from the curve of her body, from the apathetic dullness of her eyes that she did not understand. And finally he settled for a searching out of her hiding places and a dividing of the treasures he found there – returning the coins, the tiny ornaments, the doilies and lace mats to their rightful owners, and carefully replacing the pebbles and blown shells of bird's eggs for Harriet to gloat over again.

He watched when she and Sarah were walking and working together, and saw how Sarah at five treated her as though she were an infant, holding her hand, scolding her gently and pushing her along in the tasks they were supposed to share between them. He saw the bright, healthy body of Sarah, his younger daughter, his favourite child, and then the white face and hunched shoulders of his first-born, and the pain in his heart grew so much that weeping did not help, nor anger, nor gentleness. The only relief was work, work starting at half past four in the morning and finishing at ten at night. Letter rounds, farming, gardening round the village when he could get it, mending shoes, making shoes, work that he had to do because the growing size of his family demanded it, but work that he was pleased to do because it eased the frenzy of Harriet within his breast.

He took the news of another child without any tangible emotion. He loved his children – mildly – but there were too many for him to identify himself with all of them. Sarah was the child of his heart. Peter belonged to his Uncle Math, and Harriet – now it was that Harriet became his child.

He took her to see the doctor, but the money was wasted because he was told what he already knew. What he knew, what Betsy had known for several years, and what Anne-Louise told him whenever her fury with Harriet aroused her tongue to indiscreet accusations. She was always irritable during her pregnancies and Harriet was the butt, the whipping boy, for her unhappy frustration. She hated her, she wanted her to go, but lacked the courage to suggest it. Now that old Peter had put her wish into words, she pushed and nagged at Jonathan as hard as she dared.

'She's bad for the others,' she scolded him. 'They see her stealing and not doing any work and they'll do the same. She's in the way every time I'm in a hurry and she's a burden . . . '
She stopped because the tirade ended as it so often did with Jonathan walking straight out of the cottage in the middle of

her speech. She thought he just wished to infuriate her. She did not know that if he had stayed he would have knocked her to the ground.

There was a time, in the summer when the raspberries hung thick and red on the canes and he and old Peter were knocking away the wasps as they picked the fruit, when he suddenly said to his father, 'What can I do, pa? What can I do about Harriet?'

Peter set his basket on the ground and spread grass over the top of the fruit to keep the wasps away.

'I think you should let her go,' he said slowly.

'She's not that bad, pa! She's not like the rest of them in the Colony!'

Peter lifted another punnet and began to pick and fill.

'She'll be better there. She don't have much of a life here. Annie keeps at her all day, don't she? And it's Annie what has to care for her – remember that, lad, next time you want to hit her – it's Annie that has the children and the work with the children.'

Jonathan felt a tiny twinge of startled surprise, astonishment that his father should be able to read him so well.

'Am I unfair to Anne?' he asked, keeping his face turned away from the old man.

'Annie hasn't very much to give,' said Peter mildly. 'I thought you knew that when you chose her out. She's smart – or she was then – and she's a lively, good-looking woman. But she don't see things like you and me do and you expect too much from her.' He paused for a long, long while and then, in exactly the same tone of voice said, 'That black pig has rooted under the fence again.'

They hurried over to the pen and pulled the porcine Lucy out of the trench she was digging by herself. They never spoke about Harriet or Anne-Louise again.

He tried to remember what his father had said every time Anne's vitriolic temper grew insufferable, tried to remember her as she had been, a smart, vivacious girl in a cream alpaca suit on an April Sunday. He wondered if it was the children or the hard work or the struggle with money that had slowly

251

changed her, but he hardly considered any of these suppositions seriously. Every woman in the village had a big family and worked hard and had trouble with money. It was the pattern of village life. And if the women had more trouble with the children, then the men had to work harder and longer to provide for those children. There was no advantage or disadvantage between the sexes, and if the women appeared to age early, then it was usually the men who died first. The harshness of their lives allocated its penalties equally between them.

Throughout Anne's pregnancy he tried to understand her, tried to see if, in fact, he did demand too much of her, expecting her to find her happiness in the way that he found his — assuming that children and work and the gruelling routine of every day were the things that had to be done, but were not the things that gave beauty or hope or serenity of some kind. He saw, for the first time, how she had changed in appearance since their marriage. The vivacity of her face had thinned to sharpness, her sparkle to spite. She was still smart — when she and her pregnancies chose — but the smartness had become a trifle too keen. But he saw, too, that she did what she was capable of. The love she gave her children was the most she could manage, the joy she brought to her home was the best she could provide.

The child, her fourth, was due in January, and that Christmas he made a point of assembling the family around her, making Sarah and old Peter look after the children and house and taking Anne to Meeting with him alone and then on to see Betsy and Math as though they were a young couple without children. She became better tempered, quieter and not so sharp, and the day following Boxing Day she was so affably inclined towards Harriet and Sarah that she agreed to let them make toffee on the kitchen stove.

The little boys clustered close to the sticky, sweet smell, waiting hopefully for largesse from the culinary queens. The toffee bubbled and hissed, and Harriet, under Sarah's instructions lifted the saucepan off the stove to pour in more treacle. Anne-Louise, already beginning to regret her unaccustomed

252

laxity, fretted irritably at the heat, the smell, and the sight of too many small faces waiting greedily by the stove. Harriet lumbered back to the fire and placed the pan on the hot metal.

'If it's not ready in five minutes, you'll have to take it away anyway,' Anne said crossly. 'I shall want to come there and set the bread.'

'You've not even started the bread!' said Sarah indignantly. Anne – purely as an automatic gesture – reached out and smacked her round the ear. 'Don't answer back,' she said without interest. Sarah was used to her mother's irascibility, but today, made careless by the threatened disappearance of the toffee, she was moved to protest.

'That's not fair!' Her small, high-cheekboned face was flushed with heat and with disappointment. 'You said we could make toffee, and now you say we can't!'

'That's it!' said Anne-Louise, completely losing patience and interest. 'Take the saucepan off. I'll use it in the pudding. I'm not having defiance in my kitchen.'

Sarah's huge, hazel eyes brimmed lavishly with tears. Anne looked at the child and felt jealously resentful of the beauty in the small face. Even in tears Sarah's smooth, high cheekbones were graceful and arresting. Anne was suddenly aware of her heavy, unattractive body.

'You're mean! You promised and now you won't let us make toffee! You're mean and hateful!'

She was astounded. Sarah never answered her back, never defied her, and indeed usually seemed nervous and a little cowed by her mother's discipline. Anne felt surprise – and then anger. She took hold of the child's ear and pulled her to the door.

'Up to bed!' she shouted. 'Up to bed for the rest of the day and no supper either!' She slapped her once round the head and shut the door. When she turned round she saw molten toffee streaming down the sides of the saucepan and on to the stove.

'Take it off, you stupid girl!' she shouted to Harriet. She tried to get her clumsy, swollen body round the table quickly and she reached out over Harriet to snatch at the saucepan.

It happened so swiftly that she saw the saucepan jerk violently to one side shooting the contents over the covered swelling of her waist, and over her bare arms, before she felt either alarm or the searing pain of scalding liquid. Then she began to scream.

He heard her from the top of the meadow and he knew the scream was something serious, not just one of Anne's rages. He threw down the swill pail and began to run, arriving at the kitchen at the same time as Old Peter. He saw Harriet, white-faced and whimpering in a corner of the room, the little boys crouching sobbing on the floor, and Anne bent double, brown liquid bubbling over her forearms and covering the front of her dress – and screaming – a high, jerky, non-stop scream that had an inhuman sound about it.

'In water! Put her arms in water!' he shouted to himself. He tried to push her out into the scullery, but she was bent double with pain and couldn't move. Finally he lifted her knotted body and stood her over the scullery sink. Old Peter began to undo the side of her skirt and rip it off before the liquid soaked through.

He plunged his wife's arms into the sink of icy water and saw the toffee harden on her flesh, puckering it round the edges. She stopped screaming and began to whimper softly and the colour blanched suddenly from her face.

'Send Sarah for the doctor,' he snapped at the old man. 'When you've got the skirt off, tell Sarah to run, and on the way back she's to get Betsy. Quickly.'

He felt her body go limp suddenly and he took her arms out of the sink and carried her into the kitchen and on to the sofa. Harriet was in exactly the same place and stood with apathetic fear on her face.

'Go upstairs and get a blanket and a pillow-case, Harry,' he said. She didn't move, or answer. She stared dully at him.

'A blanket, Harry. Go up and get a blanket to keep her warm. Hurry, there's a good girl!'

She turned round and faced into the corner of the room, hunching herself defensively against the wall. He was choked with frustrated exasperation and for the first time appreciated

Anne's complaint about the child.

'A blanket, Harry,' he said desperately. 'I want a blanket, and a pillow-case to cover her arms.'

Anne began to sob. The lower part of her body looked somehow ludicrous in the long, blue drawers and black stockings. He heard the front door slam and Sarah's feet running up the lane and then Peter came in with a clean towel and a woollen blanket in his arms. He laid the blanket across her unclad body and carefully stretched her arms across the towel. When he moved them she screamed again.

The toffee was hard on her arms and round the edges it curled over swollen, puckered skin. She was crying and her body moved rigidly against the pain.

'Shouldn't we try to get if off her arms?'

The old man got a piece of clean sheeting and Jonathan washed his hands and then, using the rag as gently as he could, tried to lift the scale of brown sugar from her flesh. It came up fairly easily, but she screamed so much he couldn't bring himself to carry on. He covered her arms with the towel and turned to his father.

'We'll have to wait until the doctor comes. I'm making it worse.'

Peter nodded. He stared down at Anne's writhing body with a shepherd's practised lambing eye.

'She's starting labour,' he said bluntly. 'Best get her upstairs away from the children.'

Jonathan lifted her in his arms and carried her upstairs. He tried to undress her and she was crying all the time, helplessly, making him painfully aware of his own impotence, his complete uselessness in the face of her pain.

'You'll be all right, Annie. You'll be all right.' He was worried about what the doctor should do first, see to her arms or wait for the child to be born. He began to pray, a sincere, devout prayer that simplified itself to 'Oh Lord, let the doctor come soon. Oh Lord, let the doctor come soon.'

Betsy came, bringing young Peter, whose guilt at being absent from home in an emergency showed in his face. Mrs Pritchard came and Will Pritchard came. The doctor was absent on a call. When he did come, Anne was well into labour.

He was not the doctor who had attended Myra. Jonathan had seen him only once professionaly – when he had asked him about Harriet. He was brusque, big and impatient. Jonathan, wondering what he would do first, was asked to hold Anne-Louise tightly in his arms while the toffee was pulled off. He didn't know if the doctor was a good one or a bad one, but when he saw Anne's arms, when he heard her screaming and felt her struggling against him, he wondered angrily if there was need for the doctor to be so cruel. Anne moved violently and wrenched herself away from his hold.

'For God's sake hold her still, man!' the doctor snapped.

It was too much like the other time. The time when Myra was in labour and the doctor had spoken to Jonathan and to Betsy and Betsy's mother as though they were illiterate children who did not need courtesy or subtlety or good manners. It was like the other time when Jonathan had hidden his anger because he was young and afraid of what the doctor might do to Myra. He was older now.

'And if it was Mrs Fawcett,' he said harshly. 'If it was Mrs Fawcett, would she get treated the same way?'

The doctor's eyes widened in astonishment.

'I'm paying money – like Fawcett pays, and Magistrate Wilkins, and the Major. I'll pay the same money as them. I'm not a village pauper in need of your charity and I'll pay the same as them. So give my wife the same treatment as they would get. Understand?'

The doctor's hands stopped suddenly over the bandages and a dark, ugly flush spread up from beneath his collar.

'What the hell are you implying?'

'I'm implying nothing,' he answered doggedly. 'But I want you to treat my wife the same as you'd treat Fawcett or any of those in this village.'

He watched the colour recede from the doctor's face and then the man turned away to wash his hands in the basin on the marble stand.

'You can go now,' he said impersonally to Jonathan.

'Understand, I want the same treatment for her as you'd give to anyone else!' He opened the door and was about to step outside when he heard the doctor again, politer, gruffer and slightly apologetic.

'It's very unlikely the child will live, postman.'

'I know that.'

The doctor wiped his hands and hung the towel over the metal rod at the front of the wash-hand-stand.

'All right then. I'll call you when you can come up.'

He went downstairs and into the kitchen. Harriet, Sarah and the three boys were sitting in a solemn row on the sofa. He began to ask questions, trying to find out how the accident had happened. He never really understood properly, he only knew that it had something to do with Anne-Louise pushing Sarah out of the room and Harriet holding a saucepan of toffee. And with a sinking heart, recalling Harriet's helplessness when he had asked her to perform the simplest errand, he wondered how much had been Harriet's dull slowness and how much the violent temper of his wife.

The child, a boy, was dead. Perfectly formed but six weeks premature, it stood no chance against the shock of Anne-Louise's burns. The doctor called him in as soon as the child was born, so soon that Betsy had not yet had time to pull a shift over the small body, and it lay, alabaster white, curled on a piece of sheeting spread over the chest.

Anne was crying piteously and uncontrollably, partly from the pain in her arms, partly from the sight of the tiny, dead figure of her son.

'Oh, Jonathan! It hurts so! It hurts so!'

He slipped his arm under her shoulder and held her against his chest, rocking her gently to and fro, feeling her pain and grief in his own body.

'It's so bad! I don't think I can bear it!' She didn't know if it was the agony of her burned flesh that was unbearable, or the terrible, wasted sorrow of the dead child. She didn't know and he understood her pain and bewilderment. He kissed her face and tried to comfort her with strength from his own flesh, contact from his unharmed, whole body. Her cheeks streamed with tears and she was ugly, white and drawn with a ravaged face, but he had never loved her so much, had never understood her so well or felt so closely aligned with her. Every fresh sob jerked the length of her body into a fresh jarring paroxysm that sent yet another surge of agony through her burned flesh. She turned her face into his chest, gasping with the violence of her grief.

'What can I do, Jonathan? Tell me what to do!'

'Annie. Hush, Annie. I've got you now. The pain will go. I promise it will go.'

'He's dead,' she wept. 'He's small, and my son, and now he's dead. What can I do! Jonathan, help me. Please help me!'

He wanted to take the pain from her, to absorb her grief into his own. If weeping with her would have helped he could have done so easily. He held her tortured, sore body in his arms and offered her what he could.

'I promise it will be all right, Annie. I promise! You'll feel better. The pain will go and you'll feel better.'

She groaned and twisted her arms, trying to ease them over the top of the sheet and he was suddenly furious with the doctor again. His arms, holding her, were gentle, but the face that he turned towards the doctor was resentful and bitter.

'Can't you give her something to make her sleep? She'll die if she goes on like this.'

The doctor turned round from the small side-table and Jonathan saw that he already had a glass with a small measure of liquid in the bottom.

'Give her this,' he said gruffly. 'She'll sleep until well into tomorrow and I'll come back first thing in the morning.'

He left the room at some point, but Jonathan wasn't sure when. He was holding the glass, persuading her to sip the liquid between sobs, soothing her, rocking her, holding her in his arms, finally, she drifted into sleep. He felt the pain go from his body when her face relaxed and the swollen lids fell over her eyes. He was able to turn to Betsy, to watch her clothe his son in a small nightgown and wrap the body in a white sheet.

'I'll take him downstairs until the coffin comes,' said Betsy prosaically. He nodded. 'I'll make you up a bed on the parlour floor. You'll need to get some rest, Jonathan. Mother says she'll stay during the day.'

He smiled across at Betsy. Good, kind, sensible Betsy. Sensible on the surface, delicate and hurting underneath.

'I'll stay here tonight, Betsy. I'll bring the chair in from father's room and sleep in that. I'll be here if she wakes.'

Betsy took the small bundle in her hands and left the room. He heard her bumping down the stairs and opening the parlour door. Carefully he lay Anne's shoulders back on the pillow, trying not to jar her bandaged arms and leaving them over the top of the sheet. Then he went to get the armchair from his father's room. He heard the little boys and Sarah come up to bed, trying to walk softly and speaking in whispers because Betsy had explained that ma was very, very ill. There were the sounds of a house quieting for the night and then everything was still.

He looked at Ann's wan, exhausted form and felt more pity for her than he had ever felt for anyone before; more than for Myra or for the soldiers he had seen die in the war or the Boers trapped by the River Modder with their women and children. More than he felt for Harriet or his sister Emily or himself when Myra had gone out of his life. He felt pity because now he knew that Anne-Louise was unable to bear pain, to sustain and stand against a deep and wounding grief. She had never had to endure a real sorrow, never a death or a parting or a task that involved day after day of endurance in the presence of unhappiness or pain. She had no strength. No spiritual reserves to bear her own Gethsemane. She lived in a world believing that, if she wanted something strongly enough, it would come to pass. The shock of finding that life sometimes defied her was more than she would be able to bear. And Jonathan did not know how to help her.

She woke for a brief while very early in the morning, while it was still light and only the reflection of the snow outside

259

cast a gloom into the room.

'Jonathan?'

He bent over her and placed his hand on her forehead.

'Go to sleep again, Annie. It's not time to wake yet.'

Her eyes were dark, the pupils enlarged to twice their usual size, but she had regained a little of the alertness he had come to associate with her.

'She'll have to go now, won't she? She burned my arms and killed the baby. She's dangerous and she'll have to go. You'll send her away now, won't you, Jonathan? You'll send her away?'

Only for a second – just one small second – he hesitated, fighting the despondency welling up within him. He tried to think of a way around the dilemma, knowing it was useless; Anne and Harriet together would destroy his family. She sensed his indecision and moved her body fretfully and painfully in the bed.

'She can't stay now,' she said, the first note of hysteria in her voice. 'You can see she'll have to go. Otherwise she'll have to be watched the whole time!'

He leaned forward, controlling the hopelessness in him and stroking the braid of thick, black hair that lay across the pillow.

'All right, Annie,' he said gently. 'Harriet will go.'

She fell asleep almost at once. He took the chair back to his father's room and then went downstairs and up through the snow to the meadow. It was early, but he began to clear out the pig-pens and put fresh water in, not because it needed doing, but because he needed to do it. He felt heavy and old and wearily tired, tired of his body, tired of working, tired of emotion. His head ached on the left side and he put his hand to the pain and tried to press it away. Then he shut the pig-pen and went down to the shed, he could put in at least an hour's boot-making before it was time to start on his early rounds. He was going to need every spare moment for work. The doctor's bills were going to cripple him.

*

He took Harriet away in the summer. He waited until then. Until Anne-Louise was well and about again. Her arms had healed, leaving violent and bad scars, and the combined shock of childbirth and burns had turned her hair white at the sides. She spent a lot of time crying about that. She nagged and worried at him about taking Harriet to the Colony, but when it came to it, he couldn't put the child in there. He found a 'Home', a semi-charitable organisation for backward and retarded girls and women and, by paring his expenditure to near-frugality he managed to provide the part-payment towards Harriet's keep.

It was called The Park. It was in the northern part of the county and it was semi-charitable because – as well as the dependants' relatives paying something towards their keep – the inmates, wherever possible, were put out to small daily cleaning tasks in near-by houses.

It was July when he took her. A Sunday afternoon because, for the rest of the week, he was working. They sat through a heavy, oppressive Sunday lunch that Anne-Louise had tried to make more extravagant as a parting sop to Harriet. She had opened a tin of peaches, an unaccustomed luxury that no one could remember eating in the summer before – only at Christmas time. The little boys ate them, but to the rest of the family they had lost their special holiday appeal. Anne didn't stop talking. She chattered on and on about the Home where Harriet was going to have such a wonderful time, about how lucky she was, and how many girls there would be to talk to, and what marvellous times they would have. Her voice grated and pierced and suddenly young Peter burst into tears and ran out of the room.

'Well, what's the matter with him?' she snapped uneasily. 'He hasn't eaten his peaches or anything. Sarah, go and fetch him back.'

'Leave the boy alone.'

He thought she was going to persist in arguing about it, but one look at his face and she subsided into irritable muttering.

Harriet's bag stood by the door. It was a new one, a blue

261

carpet-bag, and it was filled with new things, new under-clothes, new stockings and even a new face-flannel. Anne-Louise, having got her way, had put herself to the utmost pains to see that Harriet should have the best. The kitchen door was open and the hot smell of a summer Sunday wafted into the room. The sunlight picked out the blue threads in the carpet-bag and made the red bricks of the kitchen floor breathe with life.

Harriet made patterns with her spoon in the peach juice.

'Don't you want your fruit, Harry?' he asked gently. She shook her head. She knew she was going away. She knew she was a lucky girl, but she was afraid and the feeling of depression around the rest of the family had communicated itself to her.

'Shall we go, then? Say good-bye to gramp.' She went round the table and stood meekly by the side of old Peter's chair. He mumbled something vague, and patted her on the cheek. 'I've got a penny for you,' he muttered, fumbling in his pocket. He pulled it out and pressed it into her hand. In the ordinary way she loved pennies, not because of their monetary value, but because they were bright and round. She held it in her palm and the penny didn't ease any of her dread.

Anne-Louise kissed her, tweaked the collar of her dress straight and tried to push her shoulders upright. 'You behave yourself now. Your father's paying good money to send you to that place.'

The little boys giggled and held up peach-stained faces to be briefly touched. Sarah threw her arms round Harriet's waist, sobbed once, and then dashed out into the garden to find Peter.

'I don't know what's the matter with everyone,' said Anne sharply. She was uncomfortable – as though the family were all united against her when she really had done her best. She wished they would hurry up and go and let things settle down again.

Jonathan picked up the bag and took Harriet's hand in his. 'I don't know what time I'll be back.' He stepped through the door and had the strangest feeling he had done it all before.

The misery in his heart was familiar, the ache of parting, and even the blue on the canvas bag reminded him of something he had done before. The sun poured hotly on to his head and shoulders. He was already warm in his thick Sunday jacket and high stiff collar and by the time they reached the station he was unpleasantly hot.

He sat opposite Harry in the train, watching her face and telling himself that it would be better for her in the Home. She would be free of Anne's ceaseless scolding, of the tasks that she was made to do and could only do badly. At the back of his mind beat the hope that perhaps she would get better one day, get better and come home. He tried to think why she was like she was – because of being left alone in the cottage when Myra died? Because of the years with Emily and the Vincents? Because of Anne's impatient treatment? Or because – because he and Myra were cousins and Harriet the child of cousins.

Was she bad? Was she really as sick and unstable as Anne said? She sat opposite him staring out of the window, her eyes were dull and frightened, her face white and pinched in spite of the balmy summer and the hours spent outdoors. He closed his eyes quickly as a wave of pain assailed him at the sight of her smallness, her dullness, her apathy.

The Home was at the end of a long tree-lined drive. There were gardens and flowers stretching out on all sides and the girls and women were walking about in the sunshine. He began to feel better. It was like the Fawcett house, only bigger with more flowers and trees and greater expanses of grass.

The front door was open and he led Harriet up the steps and towards a tall, raw-boned woman in a navy-blue uniform.

'My name's Whitman, ma'am. This is my little girl. You're expecting us.'

The woman beamed and held out her hand. It was cold in spite of the warm day and Jonathan was uncomfortably aware of his own sticky palm.

'Welcome to The Park!' she said heartily. 'I am Sister Cameron and I'm sure we're going to be very happy here.'

She swung round and led Jonathan through into a small

office at the side of the hall. There was a girl waiting inside, a girl with a round face and a completely hairless scalp. She had the same hunched shoulders and dull eyes as Harriet and suddenly he was worried again.

'You don't have bad cases here, do you?' he asked. 'You see my little girl lived with a mad old woman when she was young and . . . ' He stopped, realising how ridiculous he sounded. The sister held up her hand and tutted.

'Now then, now then!' she chided. 'Elsie, why are you waiting in here?'

The girl with the bald head giggled and then rushed out of the room. 'Such naughty children,' Sister Cameron said benignly. 'They think it's daring to hide in my office.'

He felt sick. He looked out of the window and stared hard at the women walking about on the grass. Some of them were dragging their feet in an abnormal way, a few sat apathetically in wheelchairs. He could feel Harriet clinging tightly to his hand while the sister consulted a folder and a card in a small wooden box. Then she rose and held her hand out to Harriet.

'Come along now,' she said cheerfully, and then in a loud, dramatic whisper to Jonathan. 'We like the parents to go as quickly as possible on the first occasion. It gives us time to get settled down, doesn't it? Visiting day is the first Sunday in the month – from three until four – and please don't bring any food – it makes them sick at tea-time.'

She took the carpet-bag from Jonathan and he felt Harriet's hand pull on his for a second as she resisted the attempt of Sister Cameron to take her away. He looked down at her.

'Be a good girl, Harry,' he choked. 'I'll come to see you soon and bring you something from home.'

Suddenly he saw Harriet's eyes light with sane realisation. Her small white face crumpled and she began to sob.

'Can't I come home, pa? Can't I come home?'

He knelt and held her shaking form against him, feeling her frightened, quivering body in his arms. He had a struggle to speak, but he no longer cared if the sister saw him cry.

'You'll come home for Christmas, Harry. And we'll have a tree and a goose and presents like always.'

He heard the woman behind him tut disapprovingly and when he stood up she trotted Harriet out of the room with a scolding backward glance at his overwrought face.

'We're not helping a bit! Are we now?'

He could hear Harriet crying as she was led up the stairs. She looked tiny beside the towering figure of Sister Cameron. He waited for ten minutes and then the sister came back.

'Well! We're settling in beautifully now. And there's no need to get ourselves into a condition, is there?'

'Will she be all right?'

Sister Cameron permitted a faint frown to cross her brow. 'Mr Whitman, we have three hundred girls here. We are accustomed to settling in. It is really better if the parents go as quickly as possible.'

He took the rebuke as it was intended and hastily stood up. 'Good-bye, Sister Cameron. You'll . . . you'll see she's all right?'

'I look after all my girls. We have no favouritism here.'

She came to the porch with him. He looked back up the stairs, wondering if he might see Harriet coming down, but everything was still, the stillness of a hot Sunday afternoon.

He walked slowly down the long drive, feeling strangely empty and missing the pull of Harriet's hand and the weight of the carpet-bag. He tried not to look at the women on the lawns, but every so often something would catch his eye – someone laughing or crying foolishly – and then he would have to hold tightly to himself so as not to run back in the house and fetch Harriet. When he got on to the train his head was beginning to ache again – the left-hand side and he was heavily, ponderously depressed.

The air from the open train window was scented with hay and hot grass. The warmth, the sun on the fields and the sight of birds hovering lazily in the sultry air added to his acute misery. He kept seeing Harriet's small, white face, remembering her as she had been when they took her from the Vincents. A surge of hate against his sister Emily, still incarcerated with the surviving Miss Vincent, boiled suddenly in his heart.

'How could you, Em? How could you!' And then truth

265

shamed him with the knowledge that he had done nothing, had let Betsy and Anne-Louise find out the truth and take Harriet from the mad cottage. He tried to remember Harriet before he had gone away, a quiet, still baby and an even quieter little girl who had sat alone in a freezing cottage for two days waiting for her mother to come back with milk.

When he started to walk up from the station the pain in his head was blinding, again the left-hand vision was blurred, but he hardly noticed it because he was picturing a little girl in a dark room, holding her brother's hand and waiting for a woman who had frozen to death.

'I should have looked after her better. I should have taken special care of her, Myra. I should have loved her like you loved her, taken care of her . . .'

He couldn't face Anne-Louise and the amorphous faces of his family. He walked over the fields, disturbing the crickets and ants with his feet until he came to the meadow at the top of his garden. He sat down on the grass and put his hands against the agony of his aching head. He tried to blot out the bright sun from his eyes.

There were marigolds at the edge of the meadow, growing thinly along the poor soil where nothing else would grow. He could see them through the blurred haze of his pain. He thought he was back on the veld – he saw again the great molten expanse of golden flowers leading up into the sun, the flowers that meant more than work or pain. The bright, iridescent vision that he had never understood, but that had promised something beautiful, something different and dream-like. The pain thumped dangerously in his head and he remembered Myra walking towards him through the flowers and it was somehow confused with saying good-bye to her in the cottage kitchen. And then that too became confused with Harriet saying good-bye and the blue of a canvas bag being the same as the blue of a cotton dress. The pain swelled and grew black and he had the good sense to lay his head down on the grass before he fainted.

It was cool when he opened his eyes. The sky had changed to a thin, pale blue and, though the sun still shone, there were long shadows stretching out from the feet of the trees. Myra was staring down at him, her smooth face and hazel eyes concerned and worried. But her hair was black. How had she done that, he thought, how had she made her hair turn black?

'Pa! Pa! Are you all right, pa?'

Myra's face became younger, rounder, more troubled and turned into Sarah's face, blotched with crying and unhappiness. He sat up slowly to avoid jarring his head, but the pain seemed to have completely disappeared.

'You've been asleep for a long time, pa. I couldn't wake you. I tried but I couldn't.' Her voice was choked and broke tremulously when she spoke. He was aware, suddenly, of her misery about Harriet – the misery that was not his – but misery just the same.

'That's all right, Sarah, lass. I had a bit of a pain, but it's gone now.'

She reached up and put her arms round his neck.

'I wish Harriet hadn't gone away,' she mumbled. 'I didn't want her to go away. And Peter's been gone all the afternoon. He went to Uncle Math's and he said he hates ma and he's never going to forgive her for making Harriet go away.' He watched tears well into her eyes again and saw that, even in distress, she was beautiful, even with her hair scraped back into one of Anne-Louise's time-saving braids, she was still beautiful.

'We'll go to see her next month,' he said quietly. 'We'll take her something nice. We'll think about it and then decide what to take.'

She couldn't answer because tears were embedded too thickly in her throat, but she nodded and finally managed to say, 'I thought you were dead, pa. Why were you lying so still?'

'I had a pain, lassie. A little pain in my head.'

He saw two small red spiders scurrying across the ground. and he lay flat and pulled her down beside him.

'Look, Sarah. If you put your head low and look through the grass you can see the world as though you were a spider.'

They pressed their heads close and he saw Sarah squint and turn herself into a spider.

'The big one keeps pushing the other one out of the way,' she said suddenly. 'Let's call that one Anne-Louise.'

Idly he supposed he ought to rebuke her, but he felt too peaceful and rested. And she was scolded enough by Anne. It was nice to enjoy a few moments alone with Sarah.

She lost interest in the spiders and she peered through the grass at ground-level and then said dreamily. 'If you look at the marigolds from here, pa, it looks as though they go on for ever. Wouldn't it be nice if they went on for ever, pa? Right to the end of the world.'

'But then we shouldn't have any room to grow potatoes or corn. And the pigs would have to go, and the hens and geese.'

He looked along the ground with her and tried to see with her child's eye. Two or three flowers stood against the sky from this angle and it was possible to imagine that the flowers stretched away into the distance. Sarah quickly sat up.

'Pa, could we plant marigolds round the edge of the meadow? Not to interfere with the pigs and raspberries,' she added hastily. 'Just around the edge. Then it will look as though it's full of flowers.'

'I don't see why not. You'd better collect some seeds from the dead flowers, hadn't you?'

She grinned and clutched at a dead head growing near by, crumbling the curled, nutlike seeds in her small, fat hand. Carefully she began to plant them in a line along the edge of the ditch.

Jonathan stood up and brushed the dust from the front of his trousers. On the way back to the house he idly picked a few of the seeds and scattered them along the edge of the field.

Twelve

SHE'D HAVE been lonely if it hadn't been for gramp.

With Harriet gone there was no one to look after and take out on walks, at least not in the same way. She could take the little boys out, but they weren't quiet and nice to talk to like Harriet was. Harriet listened, and she knew when she had said something to please Harry because she'd smile and hold Sarah's hand a little tighter. Peter was fun – when he was there, but mostly he was away with Uncle Math or helping pa and Uncle Math up in the meadow. He only came in for meals and a scolding from Anne-Louise.

And she was frightened of Anne-Louise, not of the smacks and punishments, but of Anne-Louise's sharp voice, the cruel, unkind voice that said horrible things. It was Anne-Louise who had first told her she was ugly – a big fat lump of a girl, she said, and Sarah knew her ma was right because since that time she had *felt* big and awkward and clumsy. Sometimes Anne would look at her and snap, 'I don't know how I came to get such a big, galumphing daughter. All the Pritchards have been neat, small women and now look at you! You're a Whitman, that's the trouble. And what's the right size for a man isn't the right size for a woman! I don't know what we're going to do with you!'

She worried about it herself, imagining that she would grow up to be the size of Mrs Jenkins in the village shop who was so huge that once, at a Meeting Supper, she had stood up with the chair still fixed to her behind. When she couldn't bear to think about herself and her enormous size any longer, she would creep into gramp's room and say, 'Are you awake, gramp? Are you awake?' and if he wasn't she stayed there just the same, making small fidgety noises and sighing until at last gramp woke up.

It was gramp who showed her where wicked Emily lived – wicked Aunt Emily who had shut poor Harry up in a cupboard and made her look after mad Miss Vincent before she died. Gramp would wait round the corner of the lane and tell her to knock loudly on the door of wicked Aunt Emily's cottage. Then she would turn and run as fast as she could to join gramp and they would hurry off down the track laughing until the tears flowed down gramp's brown cheeks. It was gramp who told her about the king dying and took her up to the village to see the picture of King George and Queen Mary in the window of the village shop. Mrs Jenkins had draped them all around with red, white and blue ribbons and set them up between a stack of Epp's Cocoa Powder and some packets of Benger's Food.

It was gramp who – when Anne told her she couldn't go to the coronation party in the village because of letting the milk boil over the stove – went himself and brought her back a bag of cakes and a coronation mug with 'God Bless Their Majesties' printed round the handle. Gramp told her about the Kaiser, and about the English navy being bigger and better than any other navy in the world, and about the flying machines and the suffragettes. It was gramp, too, who showed her how to wrap a farthing in a piece of silver paper and rub it until it blended right into the face of the coin.

'Haa!' he chuckled. 'Now you get up to Mrs Jenkins's shop, Sary, and see if you can catch her out.' She knew it was wicked, but gramp was chuckling so hard she felt she had to try. She bought four gob-stoppers, a coconut bar, and a hank of liquorice bootlaces and received fivepence-halfpenny change. As soon as she was outside the shop she realised what she had done and an enormous anxiety about what would happen if Anne-Louise found out made her legs tremble and a horrible pain came into her stomach. She got half-way home and then threw the money and the bootlaces and the gob-stoppers into a ditch. She kept the coconut bar because that was a farthing anyway.

One morning she went into gramp's room and he was lying

on the floor, very red in the face and with his legs sticking straight out from his nightshirt.

'Can't stand on me legs!' he huffed. 'Got out of bed and me legs went funny. Go and get yer ma, Sary.'

She was frightened then and ran downstairs to get Anne-Louise. Betsy was in the kitchen, on her way back from getting the milk, and they both hurried up the stairs to see what was wrong with gramp.

'Got no legs,' he grumbled to Betsy. 'Like pieces of wool they are. Come on now, girls, help me up.'

Betsy and Anne-Louise tried to pull him upright, but the offending legs wobbled and crumpled again. Finally Betsy gripped him round the waist and Anne gave a mighty heave and shot him forward on to the bed.

'Mind how you go, me girls,' he said chuckling. 'You'll have me out of bed the other side.'

When she saw gramp was laughing she felt better, only gramp didn't get up any more after that. Each morning she would take his plate of porridge and a mug of tea up to him and ask, 'How do you feel this morning, gramp? Do you think you'll be getting up?' and gramp would stir his porridge and shake his head.

'Tomorrow, lassie. Perhaps I'll get up tomorrow.'

When she had time, from looking after the little boys – there were three now – and going up to the shop, and taking her turn at black-leading the stove, and cleaning, and tidying and dusting, she liked to read to gramp. Usually he would go to sleep in the middle of *Alice's Adventures in Wonderland* or *Gulliver's Travels* or *Pilgrim's Progress*, but she didn't mind that. It was being with gramp that she liked, feeling that he and she shared something that the boys couldn't intrude upon. She liked to hurry up to his room as soon as she got home from school and tell gramp what had happened at school and in the village.

'Mr Masters said we're going to fight the Kaiser, gramp,' she remarked informatively one day.

'Shouldn't be a bit surprised,' muttered gramp. 'It's no more than he deserves.'

'Does that mean pa will go and be a soldier again, gramp? Will he have to get his red coat out of the box?'

The red coat was a feature of every Christmas in the cottage. Each year Jonathan would get it out and then go outside and knock on the door and say he was a poor old soldier come to see if they could spare him a bit of Christmas goose. The thought of Pa in the red coat made fighting the Kaiser a bit like Christmas. Gramp shook his head.

'I shouldn't think so, Sary. No, I shouldn't think so.'

Sometimes gramp began to talk to himself, and once, on the evening before she went in, he was sitting up in bed holding his arms crooked in front of him.

'Take this, for goodness' sake, Sarah,' he said impatiently, holding out an invisible burden to her. Timidly she reached her hands up.

'Not like that, not like that!' he said crossly. 'You'll never be able to hold it like that. Put your arms right out.'

'What is it, gramp?' she asked nervously.

'A lamb, of course,' he snapped. 'Quickly, take it now. I've a lot more here to pass up. The poor old ewe is caught in the drift as well. We'll have to get her out last.'

She sat with gramp for twenty minutes, taking the wet, snow-bound lambs from his arms and putting them on the floor.

He was all right, though, on the day she ran in from school and pounded up the stairs shouting her news. She wanted to be the first to tell him.

'There's a war on, gramp! We're going to wop the Kaiser! Everybody says so and they've sent for Uncle Math to go back on his submarine. Mr Masters says it won't take us more than three months to teach the Kaiser a lesson.'

'Eh . . . well now,' said gramp thoughtfully. 'Called Mathy up again have they?'

She sobered a little because Aunt Betsy had looked unhappy when she came to tell them about Uncle Math. She had told Aunt Betsy what Mr Masters had said, about the Kaiser being whipped in three months, but Aunt Betsy had continued to look unhappy, not crying or anything, just sad and very quiet.

'Ma says they won't want pa. Because he's too old and because of the mark on his head.'

Gramp said nothing, but thought for a while.

'Better watch young Peter,' he said slowly. 'Better watch that young brother of yours. I've an idea he might decide to do something a bit saucy if he's not watched.'

She was about to blurt something out, but then she remembered and reddened and held her tongue. She could tell gramp most things, but Peter had made her promise not to breathe a word of this to anyone. They only spoke of it to each other last thing at night – when the boys were asleep and she could slip into bed beside Peter and whisper to him under the sheets. That night she told him that gramp suspected something.

'How much money have you got now?' she breathed to him.

'Not quite enough. I need threepence more, and then I've got it.'

'Will you still go?' she asked diffidently. 'I mean, now that the war has come, wouldn't it be best to wait?' She felt Peter stir and fidget restlessly beside her.

'I'm not waiting any more,' he said fretfully. 'I'm not staying with *her* any longer. She sent my sister away and she hates me. I'm going to leave as soon as I've got the last threepence for the fare.'

She didn't answer him for a moment because she felt somehow guilty about *her*. Anne-Louise was her mother and she felt she ought to apologise in some way, to try and atone for what Anne had done to Harriet and would have liked to do to Peter.

'I don't think she hates you, Peter,' she said timidly. 'No more than she hates me.'

'Yes, she does,' he said bluntly, and he spoke so loudly that one of the boys turned restlessly in his sleep and whimpered. 'I'm going. As soon as I've got the fare to Chatham, I'm going.'

She wriggled closer into Peter's side and hugged him tight. She never saw very much of Peter, but now he was going for good he was infinitely more precious to her.

'Do you think you'll go on the same ship as Uncle Math?'

she whispered noisily.

'Don't be silly,' he scoffed. 'There are *thousands* of ships in the king's navy, *hundreds* of thousands. I expect I shall be given one of my own.'

'Supposing they send you back,' she said nervously, filled with dread for him.

'How can they? I'm fourteen aren't I? They take boys at twelve if you're lucky. And now they're going to knock the daylights out of the Kaiser, they're going to want me.'

He was supremely, arrogantly confident, and she was suddenly envious of him, because he was a boy and because there was a way for him to escape from Anne-Louise.

'Won't you miss pa?'

Peter paused and picked at the end of a goose feather that was sticking out of the pillow.

'I'll miss pa,' he said slowly. 'But I can't stay here, with her. And I don't mind too much.' He waited for a long time and then said, 'Pa's got you. Pa loves you most. He don't have very much time to spend with you, but he loves you most, better than me, and better than Harriet.'

She felt guilty again, but in a different way from feeling guilty about Anne-Louise. And in an odd way she knew Peter was right. Pa never gave her more than the others, or spoke to her more, or spent the tiny amount of leisure he had with her alone. But she belonged to pa. She loved gramp and gramp was fun to be with. But she belonged to pa. She and pa were the same.

'So I don't mind too much,' he finished carefully. 'And beside, when I'm a sailor I shall be like Uncle Math.'

He went away three weeks later, when he had saved the last threepence. She covered up for him until the afternoon and then, when pa and Anne-Louise found out he had gone, she said she didn't know where to. She felt guilty when she saw pa setting out for Portsmouth at the end of a long, tiring day, but she had promised Peter she wouldn't tell, not until four days had gone by and he was officially a sailor.

At the end of the week Peter wrote to them, and by that time there was nothing they could do.

Dear Pa, (he refused to put *her* name, even on a letter)

I'm a sailor now. I came to Chatham and they gave me bread and margerine and a cup of cocoa. It took three days to make me a sailor and I had to wait to see all the doctors and the officers but they said I was a fine strong lad and will be a good sailor. I am going to the training ship *Northampton*, and I will come to see you as soon as I am on leave.

Give my love to Gramp and Sary and the boys, and Harriet next time you go to see her. Please tell Aunt Betsy what I have done and ask her to write to Uncle Math. When I have done my training I am going to go on the submarines, like Uncle Math. I am writing to Aunt Betsy as well, in a few days.

Your loving son,
Peter

She told gramp what was in the letter and then she went out to see if pa was all right. She knew where to find him. Up in the long meadow, at the edge where she had planted the marigold seeds. And when she saw pa's face she wished she hadn't kept her promise to Peter, she wished she had told pa where Peter had gone. Pa had been crying.

Suddenly gramp was very ill. It was funny at first because he kept on passing up the sheep to her and talking to her as though she were one of the dogs that lived outside in the yard. He stopped eating his porridge in the morning, and she had to stand by him and hold the spoon against his mouth as though he were one of the little boys. Every day Betsy and Grandmother Pritchard would come in and wash him because he couldn't do it for himself. Pa shaved him on Sundays, but the rest of the week he just grew whiskers all over his face.

He started to wet the bed. She knew because there was a whole lot more washing and ironing to do and she was for ever pressing sheets with the heavy flat-irons on the kitchen stove. One day Grandmother Pritchard brought in a funny white chamber-pot that was the queerest shape Sarah had ever seen. Anne took it up to gramp's room and everything was suddenly very quiet. Then she heard gramp say, 'I'm not going in a teapot, Annie! I've never gone in a teapot in my life and I'm not starting now!'

She wanted to laugh because that was exactly what the funny chamber-pot looked like, a teapot, and she decided that gramp must be getting better. Then Annie came down the stairs and said, 'He's gone, Jonathan. Your father's passed away.'

She couldn't believe it. A moment ago gramp had been making them all laugh (only not out loud because what he said was really very rude) and now Anne-Louise said he was dead.

She shouted, 'No! He can't be dead. Gramp can't be dead!' and she ran across the room, past Anne and through the door up to Gramp's room. His hand was hanging down by the side of the bed and his eyes stared up at the ceiling.

'Gramp!'

Anne came up behind her and suddenly pushed her out of the room.

'Gramp's passed away,' she said, not unkindly. 'You go down and get the boys' tea and then fetch Grandma Pritchard up here.'

She went slowly downstairs and began to put plates round the table, spreading them unseeingly on the bare oilcloth without first spreading a linen cover. Suddenly Tommy, the next boy down from herself, started to cry and the tears spread to her own eyes.

'I didn't want gramp to die,' she said unhappily. 'I didn't think he would die for a long time.'

When Anne came downstairs she gave her a penny and told her to take the boys up to Mrs Jenkins's and buy them some sweets.

'You can go and see your Aunt Betsy if you like,' she said mildly and, because she was so unusually kind, so quiet and almost gentle, Sarah realised properly that gramp had died.

And the following week she was put into gramp's room, the first time she could remember having a room to herself. Ma told her that from now on she wouldn't sleep in the boys' room any more. She was ten years old and it was time she slept apart from the boys.

Alone in gramp's small back bedroom, with the window that looked out on the garden, and the pear-tree spread flat against the outside wall hanging its fruit almost inside the window, she was miserably aware how empty the house was, without Peter and without gramp.

Thirteen

SUDDENLY all the young men were gone from the village.

Uncle Math and Peter were the first, then Uncle Will Pritchard, then Mrs Jenkins's two boys. A week later Uncle Frankie Pritchard (who was really too young to be called her uncle) followed his elder brother. The four Tyler boys went and then the doctor left to serve in a field hospital and they had to walk over to the next village when anyone was sick.

At first it was exciting, seeing the men and boys she had known all her life marching through the main street to the station in the care of a bristling recruiting sergeant. And then she became aware how empty the village was, how thin and reedy the Sunday hymn sounded without the husky, off-key tenors and basses, how empty the fields were, how strange Aunt Betsy's house without Uncle Math.

Pa became even more tired and had even less time to spend at home. He was now the only man left among the three families – among Betsy, Grandmother Pritchard and Anne-Louise. There were three lots of logs to bring in, three lots of milk to fetch, three gardens to tend and three families who needed the occasional presence of a man. He looked weary and walked with the perpetual stoop of an old man.

Ma was in bed again, having another baby boy, and Sarah, getting pa's breakfast in the morning, packing up his apple and bread and cheese for his midday piece, began to share his tiredness. She wasn't sure if it was because she loved pa so much and wanted to take his fatigue from him, or if it were that caring for the three boys and running up and down the stairs before she went to school – to see to ma and the new baby – made her tired too.

School became, as it always had been, a refuge and a haven

from ma, from the continual scolding and household chores. School was quiet and orderly and one was made to sit still at a desk and think about things, or write things, or sometimes just read. She hated the week-ends and she hated, even more, the long summer holidays which were one long toil of house-work that she never seemed to do to ma's satisfaction. The days were work, incessant nagging, and what Anne called 'home truths' that were mostly comments on Sarah's size, the way she spoke, walked, held her shoulders and ate her food. More often than not the day ended with a slap around the ear. She usually got through the holidays by marking each day off on a chart hidden under her mattress.

She had been back at school only a week in the term after gramp's passing away, when Mr Masters told her to remain behind in school one afternoon.

Mr Masters was a flint-faced man with black hair and huge, bushy eyebrows. Three of the fingers on his left hand were paralysed and he had the habit of walking up and down between the desks and suddenly jabbing the stiffened fingers into the neck of an idling pupil. It was such a poke, sharp and startlingly unexpected, that aroused her one afternoon.

'You! Sarah Whitman!'

'Yes, Mr Masters, sir?' She wasn't really afraid of him. She was used to Anne-Louise, and Mr Masters was a watery comparison of sharpness beside the intimidating figure of her ma.

'Stay behind! After school.'

'But, sir . . . ' She dared not be home late because that meant another drubbing from Anne-Louise – in addition to the one she was going to get from Mr Masters.

'You heard . . . to stay behind!' He swung his hands together at the back of his tail coat, glared at her, then proceeded up the line of desks. Anxiously she began to watch the school clock, trying to calculate how much the delay would affect her arrival at home. When the bell rang at the end of school Mr Masters called her to stand by the raised dais.

'Haa . . . Hmm, Sarah Whitman,' he glowered, stroking the smooth side of a tin ruler. 'Now then, how many brothers have you, Sarah Whitman?'

'Four, sir.' She wasn't surprised at the apparent oddness of his question. Mr Masters always led up to his punishments in a succession of devious questions.

'Four, eh? And does your pa bring his money home regularly? Not spend it at the Prince of Wales? Spend it on drink?'

'Oh no, sir!' She was indignant, but beneath the outrage was a sense of annoyance with Mr Masters. He knew very well how many brothers she had. And that her pa was the village postman, and that they were Meeting folk who did not spend family money on drink.

Mr Masters rapped his three hard fingers on the desk.

'Send your pa along to see me,' he ordered abruptly.

She was really worried then. Not about Mr Masters, but about pa being upset about some imagined naughtiness of hers; about Mr Masters wasting pa's time when he had to work so hard.

'My pa don't have much time, sir,' she said coldly. 'He's looking after my Aunt Betsy and my cousins and my Grandmother Pritchard as well.'

'Hrrmph!' barked Mr Masters. 'Want to see him. See him about you working for the scholarship.'

Clouds of hazy astonishment whirled in her head. Ribbons of thoughts twined and floated and detached themselves to knot again in a confusion of ideas. There was the worry that she would be home late, and the worry of pa being bothered by Mr Masters, and the worry of Peter and Uncle Math, and the hurt because gramp wasn't there to talk to any more. And now there was the scholarship – the scholarship!

'Me, Mr Masters? Me work for the scholarship?'

'You're to send your pa up, young Whitman. Tell your pa Mr Masters wishes to talk to him about the scholarship.'

She knew about the scholarship. Everyone knew about it. Five years ago, just after she had started school, David Herbert had spent a year studying and then been sent up to take it, and finally had had his name put on the Roll of Honour in the hall. Since that time no one had ever been recommended for the scholarship. An excited drumming began in her chest, she felt herself soaring up over the classroom, over Mr Masters and his three fingers, over the figure of herself standing breathlessly by his desk.

'The scholarship, Mr Masters!'

'Shan't talk until I've seen your pa. Leave now.'

'Oh yes, sir! I'll speak to my pa, Mr Masters. I'll tell him what you said. I'll ask him to come and see you . . .'

'Get along now, young Whitman,' said Mr Masters impatiently.

She smiled brilliantly at him, turned and managed to walk with controlled dignity to the door. Once it was shut she raced along the passage and out into the road, tearing along the track, ripping her stocking and catching her dress in brambles and thorns. She swept past her cousins, Mary and May, without stopping, pounding across the fields and down the lane until she came to the cottage. She prayed that for once pa would be inside, not at Aunt Betsy's, or gardening, or working anywhere else. And as an extra gift on this incredible day she flung open the door to see pa sitting at the table his tea in front of him.

'Pa! Pa! Mr Masters wants me to work for the scholarship! He told me. He says I can work for the scholarship! He wants to see you, pa! He's going to tell you about it!'

She paused, gasping for breath, and she saw pa slowly put his cup back into the saucer and lift his face to stare at her. Then he started to grin.

'It's true, lassie? He really told you that? He's going to send you up for the examination?'

'He wants to see you. You'll go soon, won't you, pa?'

The smile on Jonathan's face grew wider and the smile made him seem not so tired, younger and more like he used to be.

'I knew,' he said softly. 'I knew we could do it. There was Harriet, and then Peter, but I knew we could do it. And the next time it will be easier, the next time it will be even better.'

'I'll work so hard, pa, you won't know me! I'll do everything Mr Masters says. I will, pa, really I will!'

She clasped her hands fervently together and pa suddenly

stood up and lifted her into the air. (She wasn't *so* big, was she, if pa could still lift her?)

'Sary!' he said exuberantly. 'Sary girl! You're going to be a teacher or a nurse or a hundred and one things that you want to be. You're going to be somebody, Sarah. You're going to be someone who's as good as anyone else in the world.' He hugged her quickly, something he never did in front of Anne-Louise, and then they heard, very dimly as though she were hardly there at all, the voice of Anne-Louise.

'Stop this ridiculous shouting! And telling her she's going to be somebody! How do you think she's going to study? What time is she going to have?'

They both turned to face her, surprised because they had not even remembered she was there. Her words only vaguely pierced their delighted pride in each other. Their pleasure was sufficient without any interruption from outside.

'And what about the money? Suppose she gets the scholarship – not that she will, she's a great stupid lump – but if she did, where would we get the money for her to ape her betters and go to a fancy school and forget how to earn her living?'

Neither of them answered. They just went on staring at her with their arms still intertwined with each other's.

'She's a cottage child,' snapped Anne, furious at the faces so alike and so withdrawn in front of her. 'There's no point in stuffing her up with a lot of foolish notions about bettering herself. She's an ugly great thing, but she can learn to run a house. At least I can teach her to do that and then she can go into service.'

'But, Anne,' he said slowly, 'don't you understand? They want her to take the scholarship. The first time in five years, Annie, and they've chosen Sarah.'

'Well, more fool old Masters! And I'll have a word with him next time I see him! Putting ideas in a girl's head when there's not the slightest chance of her taking the scholarship.'

'Oh, but there is, Annie,' he said quietly. 'There's every chance of her taking it, every chance indeed.'

His stern, forbidding voice made her resentment flare into open temper.

'Well, she can't!' she shouted. 'I need her to help me. There's seven of us and a daughter is put into the world to help in the house. Your sister Emily had to help – and so will Sarah.'

Jonathan frowned and thrust his hands perplexedly into the air.

'She's your daughter, Annie! What's the matter with you? She's your own daughter!'

She bent forward, leaning her weight on the table and shaking with rage and unhappiness.

'And why should she have what I never had!' she cried. 'She'll have to live like I did. Why should she have more than me?'

He had never looked at her with so much contempt and disgust before. Sometimes he looked as though he hated her, mostly he ignored or didn't even notice her complaints. But now he looked sick, as though she were loathsome and stupid and it was more than she could bear.

'That's not the reason she can't go,' she muttered foolishly, trying to retrieve her words. 'She's just not bright enough. Old Masters has made a mistake and there's no point in her being disappointed.'

'I'm going to see him now,' said Jonathan, rising abruptly from the chair. 'I'm going to see exactly what it will mean, in money and in time.'

He was gone so quickly from the kitchen that Sarah was frightened – partly at the speed at which things had happened – partly because she was left facing her mother across the table. Anne, terrified at the reaction she had unleashed in Jonathan, turned thankfully on the child.

'You're nothing but trouble in this house! You're a wicked spiteful child! And you're late home too.'

'It was Mr Masters, ma. He kept me late to talk about the schol – '

She wasn't quick enough to dodge Anne's hand.

'Don't answer back! And I don't want to hear any more about Mr Masters either. Eat your tea and then you can get on with the socks.'

It was unfortunate for Sarah that she had a certain ability as a needlewoman. Anne-Louise, who had boasted proudly for many years that she didn't know one end of a needle from the other, had relinquished the entire family mending to Sarah with the air of one conferring a favour.

Sarah waited with gloomy dread through the bread and margarine tea, through the evening of a mound of woollen, mutilated socks. Finally Jonathan walked in with the bootlast in one hand and a half-sewn lady's boot in the other. He sat down by the kitchen range and began to fit the boot over the iron mould.

'It's settled,' he said tersely. 'Two evenings a week she'll stay late at school to work with the master. The other evenings she's to study here at home.'

'And what about the money?' snapped Anne. 'If she passes how are we to keep her at school?'

Jonathan waxed his thread and began to stitch the sole.

'We'll find the money. When the time comes we'll find it.'

Anne looked once at his face and dared not argue further. She contented herself with a muttered, 'It's a stupid waste of time. She'll never pass', and then she assumed a sulky silence for the rest of the evening.

She knew all along that the scholarship was only a dream. She knew that when ma shouted that she'd never manage it, somehow ma would be proved right. For a while, when pa had been so pleased because she had been chosen, she believed that perhaps she would, after a lot of hard work, manage to go up for the scholarship and get her name on the Roll of Honour.

It was all right, too, working late with Mr Masters. She could never remember spending her evenings so pleasantly before, so quietly – sitting down – scratching away with a pen and Mr Masters going over everything she did with pedantic and scrupulous thoroughness. But the evenings with Mr Masters were completely overshadowed by the evenings at home.

When pa was there it was fine. She could take her books into the parlour, put her coat and gloves on because it was cold, and begin reading and writing. But pa was hardly ever there. Pa worked until ten o'clock most nights and then she was left to the undiluted venom of Anne-Louise.

A pretext of study was made, a play of putting the books on the kitchen table. ('You're not sulking away in the parlour. You can keep an eye on the baby out here while you're messing about with those books.') But after ten minutes Anne would find her something that needed to be done, the darning, the lamps to be cleaned, the brass polished, pa's shirt to be ironed. Impatiently Anne would bear with the books for a short while, then frustration would break into, 'Haven't you finished yet? There's work to be done, you know. I'm not here to slave for a stupid great lump who just wants to sit reading all evening.'

She tried. For a little while she tried, but then the fusion of Anne's nagging, banging and constant presence, the noise of the small boys getting ready for bed, chasing round the table and upsetting the ink, the smallness and hotness of the kitchen with Aunt Betsy and Grandma Pritchard and Mrs Jenkins and everyone constantly popping in to talk about the war, about the bomb that was dropped on Dover, about the food shortages and the nastiness of the wartime margarine, all became unbearably confused and she finally gave up trying to read through the noise. And ma was so much to her nicer when she didn't even get the books out at all.

She cried only once – and then in private – when Mr Masters told her she wouldn't be ready to go up for the scholarship. She cried when she saw pa's face. She wanted, so much, to please pa, to make him proud of her. But she couldn't do it – because Anne-Louise was right after all – she *was* stupid and Mr Masters had been wrong about the scholarship. They should all have listened to ma in the first place. Ma was usually right.

Liège, Mons, the Marne, Ypres. They thought it would be a war of juggernauts, of charges and decisive victories. It turned into the war of the machine-gun, of the submarine and the rat.

The names were the same – to Jonathan it seemed incredible that the names should be the same. French (tired horses and tireder men grinding over the dusty veld?) commanding the blood-bath of Mons. Kitchener (lying in the sun without water, waiting for Kitchener and the infantry to arrive on the other side of the Boers) staring out from posters and hoardings – YOUR COUNTRY NEEDS YOU.

Once or twice he found himself nearly caught into the enthusiasm of war fever, regretting his age and the skull injury that prevented him from dashing off to the furore of trumpet and flag. But the fourteen-year-old memory of the war with the Boers remained fresh in his mind – the thirst, the smell of dead bodies floating down the River Modder, horses screaming, severed arms, severed legs, severed heads. It would be no different this time.

It was a war of 'firsts'. The first time lungs were filled with poison gas. The first time one million men were killed in a single battle, the first time a machine-gun was able to cough out death efficiently and speedily as well. And the first time in one thousand years that the English were attacked on their own soil – albeit from the air.

They were woken in the night by the sound of someone hammering on the door. When Jonathan went down he saw a fat, florid-faced woman with four children. She had been crying and the youngest of the children was still crying.

'I'm Florrie,' she said noisily. 'Florrie Dance. It's the Zeppelins. They've knocked us out all over the East End.'

He stared blankly at her, not understanding for a moment and bemused by the sight of five people late at night.

'I was in service with your Annie,' said the red-faced woman again. She was shouting nervously, and, when she saw that Anne-Louise had appeared behind Jonathan, she began to sob again.

'Oh gawd, Annie! Can we come and stay with you for a bit. Maxie's in France and I can't stand the bombs no more! They sent a load of us off tonight – come down on the last train we 'ave. All the street next to me is blown up, Annie . . . ' She

286

lost control of her voice and began to shriek and sob at the same time.

They quieted Florrie with cocoa and the children with bread and honey. They slept the children head to toe, the girls with Sarah, the boys in with Tommy, Billy, Bertie and the baby. They awoke next morning to find the village had been invaded by East Enders, noisy, frightened – of the country as well as the Zeppelins – hungry, and in some cases lice-ridden. They stayed for three months.

1916: Verdun and the Somme. Will Pritchard came home on leave and spent the first three days in bed. When he got up his hands were shaking all the time. Everyone noticed, but was too polite to say anything. At the end of his leave his hands had stopped shaking, but then a barn rat ran out in front of him and he started to scream. When he stopped screaming his hands were shaking again.

The four Tyler boys were killed within six weeks of each other. Mrs Tyler shut herself in her bedroom for two days and when she came out she never referred to her sons again. The younger Jenkins boy came home with a yellow face and a voice thick with lung poisoning. He was a semi-invalid, but he was lucky – his brother never came home at all.

Food was scarce – or it would have been if it hadn't been for pa and the meadow. Every month Florrie Dance came down and went back with a sack of potatoes and eggs and whatever else they could find for her. Maxie was still alive, but two of the Dances boys – those big, blond giants – had died at Verdun.

Mrs Fawcett, in deference to the troubled times, took up her charity visiting again. At sixty she was as thin, mean and sallow as she had been at forty. She sat in Betsy's front parlour and complained bitterly about the deprivations of the war.

'It hardly seems fair,' she said resentfully. 'They've taken two of my horses. We only had four, as you very well know, and now the Government has requisitioned two of them.'

The century and the war had done much to remove tribal deference from the village. Betsy, along with Jonathan and the Jenkinses and the Tylers, no longer lived her life in the shadow of the Big House. And she was impatient of spoilt, petulant women.

'That's very hard, ma'am, to lose you're horses. But they've taken my husband, and that's worse, ma'am. That's much worse.'

Mrs Fawcett looked surprised, then faintly superior. She considered.

'Well, yes. I suppose so. If he was a good husband. Was he a good husband, Mrs James?'

Betsy reddened, stopped herself from retorting and rose from her chair to signify that it was time Mrs Fawcett left. Watching the older woman's back — in fluted, seal-backed musquash — climb up into the trap, she doubted her own ability to be civil to the old woman ever again.

The Battle of Jutland : They said the 'lads', the boys under eighteen, were too young to die, eighteen was soon enough. They battened the boys down below decks before the action started — away from the danger, the guns, the falling debris. They were all there, safe amidships, when the shell blew straight through the body of the ship and killed them all.

He had just delivered the letters to Fawcetts' when the Jenkins' errand boy flashed past him on a bicycle. 'There's a telegram come from the Admiralty,' he shouted and was gone before Jonathan could call him back.

He began to run, fighting the pain in his head and eye, the pain that was there all the time now, feeling his heart lurch as the words sank down to the pit of his stomach.

'My son,' he breathed, pounding along the road, the bag jogging heavily against his side. 'Oh, God, please don't let it be my son ! Please, Lord, don't let it be Peter !'

He ran faster, wanting to know about the telegram and sick with fear of whatever news it contained. When he finally burst into the room at the back of the post office he could hardly speak.

'The telegram . . . the telegram from the Admiralty . . . is it my boy? Is it Peter?'

When Jenkins shook his head he had to bend forward over the sorting table to ease the knotting pain in his stomach. He wanted to be sick, but he was ashamed for letting Jenkins see him like this. Jenkins' elder boy had died — he should have had more control in front of the man. When he looked up Jenkins was staring at him uneasily, in some kind of distress.

'Not your boy, Whitman,' he said slowly. 'It's your brother-in-law, it's Mathy James.'

Jonathan's relief dissolved slowly and was replaced by disbelief.

'Mathy?'

Jenkins nodded, 'He's dead, Whitman.'

He sat down on the sorting stool, staring at the telegram lying unopened on the table. Quiet, neat little Mathy. Navy-blue eyes, good with bees, working hard on the meadow to make it a profitable success, five children but still able to fill the place he had made for himself in young Peter's life. Smiling, marrying Betsy — though no one could ever understand why — Mathy . . . killed.

'Mathy . . . ' he said again.

Jenkins looked uncomfortable and coughed.

'Will you tell your sister-in-law? You being one of the family and all. It would be kinder from you.'

He nodded and picked up the telegram without seeing it. He felt faintly guilty, because he had prayed to God not to let it be his son. Foolishly, he wondered if God had spared his son and taken Math in his place.

He hid the telegram in the bag and walked to Betsy's cottage. The children were playing in the lane outside the house and two of his sons were with them. When he walked into the cottage Betsy was rubbing a sheet against the washing board. He recognised it was a Fawcett sheet, it was cream with lace along the top hem.

'Betsy,' he said heavily.

He didn't have to tell her. She looked at his face and then began to cry. It wasn't a sad crying, just a nervous, silly noise as though she were saving her grief for later and this was just to get over the bad moment of first knowing.

She came into the kitchen and sat down at the table, her hands were soapy and she let them lie uselessly on the table in front of her. It was odd to see Betsy with idle hands. Then she stopped crying and wiped her sleeve roughly across her face. 'My poor Mathy,' she said thickly. 'My poor, poor Mathy.'

He couldn't watch her. He stood up and came clumsily round the table, pulling her untidy head up against his side, wrapping his arms round her shoulders, rocking her against him and feeling the tears in his own eyes.

'It's like my ma all over again,' she whispered. 'I used to watch my ma and think how well she managed, six children and a husband dead while the youngest was just a baby. I used to think how clever she was, how strong to manage without him. I never thought about how she must feel, how lonely without him. I thought we were enough for her. I've got to do it all over again, just like my ma, lonely, just like my ma.'

He brought his face down against her hair, smelling soap and bread and grief, remembering the way Math had smiled his neat little smile, tweaked the curly tendrils of Betsy's hair, given her five children.

'You won't want for anything, Betsy. I'll promise you that. You'll have just the same as Anne-Louise. I'll see you're not wanting for anything, Betsy.'

'He gave me things,' she said tightly. She was holding her hands clasped together against her mouth. 'He gave me seven yards of silk when we were married. Did you know that? Seven yards of silk and he couldn't really afford it. And a fob watch. And a china tea-service. And a brooch and . . . No one ever gave me things before.'

He was overwhelmed with compassion and love for her, seeing how much he took her for granted because she was always there, had always been there, but how he had never thought of her as a girl, or a woman like Myra or Anne-Louise. She was just Betsy.

'I'll get up to see my mother,' she said softly. 'I want to see my mother.'

He got her coat from the peg at the back of the door and helped her put it on. When she went out he began to walk with her, but she shook her head and brushed her hand over her eyes again.

'I'll go on my own. Will you take the children up to Annie's? Give them their tea?'

He nodded and watched her walking slowly along the lane. She kept stopping and looking at the sky or a tree or across an open field. He had never seen Betsy walk so aimlessly before, and suddenly she looked small and helpless and not capable any longer.

He wanted to take on the whole of mankind, the whole of the terrible war and tear it apart with his own two hands.

'Come on kids,' he shouted to the playing children. 'You're coming up to tea with your Auntie Annie.'

And still it was not the end. There was Ypres again – the third battle – and Passchendaele, and again, Verdun. It was rats and mud and machine-guns. And soldiers who came younger than before, and older than before, and with less training.

Frankie Pritchard (young Frankie, too young to be an uncle) came home for good with his left eye missing from his face. Magistrate Wilkins's son was in a Kent hospital. Magistrate Wilkins hurried off to see him and came home crying, weeping all through the village on his way back from the station so that everyone could see.

No one was ashamed any more. No one minded if men wept, or shouted or, like Will Pritchard, shook the whole time. In some miraculous way Will came through with no more than the permanent trembling of his limbs and a twitch on the right side of his mouth. In time, a few years, the shaking and the twitching got better, but he never ceased to shout whenever he saw a rat. He bought himself two ratting terriers when he came home, and killing the vermin became an obsession with him. No one ever asked what had happened to make him loathe rats so much.

The shortages got worse. There was honey-sugar from Australia – rather nice – and synthetic sweets that didn't taste of sweets at all. Two girls, members of the Women's National Land Service Corps, appeared without warning on Tyler's farm. They were a novelty for a few days, then faded into the general tiredness and apathy of the village.

Peter came home on leave — a tall, brown-skinned young man who spent most of his time with his Aunt Betsy. Sarah was suddenly fourteen, soft-skinned and gentle. Her black braids were twisted up into an unsightly knot at the back of her head and she went to work as fourth chamber-maid at the Fawcetts'.

And then it was over. The war was over, but everyone was too tired to feel anything more than relief and sorrow. Of the village community, eighteen men had died and seven came home with permanent mutilations, poisoned lungs, or chronic sickness from the trenches. Will Pritchard counted as one of the whole ones although he couldn't hold a cup in his hands.

Betsy had a widow's pension of twenty-two and sixpence a week. She set aside her six shillings rent and prepared, grimly, to rear her children on the remaining sixteen and sixpence.

Florrie Dance still came down for potatoes and eggs, but now she was able to pay for them, and Jonathan — thinking of Betsy, and ma Pritchard whose two sons weren't able to work yet, accepted the money. Maxie had come home all right — without his right arm — but he had come home.

The men began to trickle back to the village, slowly and unrecognisable as the men who had left five, or four, or even three years before. Their presence only lent emphasis to the cottages where the men didn't return at all.

There were still shortages.

Women had the Vote.

The war was over.

Fourteen

SHE HATED working at the Fawcetts'. She hated Mrs Fawcett, who was bad-tempered and peevish and threatened to tell Anne-Louise every time she caught Sarah out.

'You haven't dusted this ledge, Whitman . . . I looked behind the wardrobe today and you haven't swept there . . . the vase on the escritoire is chipped, you will have to pay for it out of your wage . . . '

Even more than Mrs Fawcett she hated old man Fawcett. He was old and smelt unpleasant and once – when she was standing on the library steps to dust the top shelves, he tried to put his hand up her skirt. She wanted to hit out and push him violently out of the way, but she dared not because it would cost her her job. And every time he pinched or squeezed her she had to control herself and try to get away from him without making him annoyed. She dared not tell Anne-Louise. It was so humiliating and shaming that she didn't want to talk about it. And she had the feeling anyway that Anne-Louise would somehow think it was all her own fault.

She wanted to tell pa how much she hated it at Fawcetts', but then, when she saw how tired he was, how his hair had turned grey, how hard he was working to help Aunt Betsy, she just couldn't worry him with her misery over the Fawcett house. Each morning she would drag slowly up the drive and round to the kitchen, dreading the day ahead, looking forward to going home in the evening and starting work again for her ma.

But even though she hated Fawcetts', she was quick to see – and to take advantage of – the assets of the house. And of course the biggest asset was the library. Pa had told her about the library – about the walls lined with books that no one ever read, books that continued to come down from London every month, that were filed, dusted and admired – and never read. She didn't have much time, but whenever she could she opened a book and read for five minutes, ten minutes, in bed at night, walking home in the evening. She discovered, as her father had done more than twenty years before, the incomparable rich delight of a profusion of books. Once, when she was walking across the fields with her eyes and mind lost in *Vanity Fair*, she crashed straight into Mr Masters. He hrmmped and grumbled and then darted a sharp look at her from beneath his black brows.

'Ha, Whitman! Still dreamy and inattentive, eh?'

She grinned at him. She had never been afraid of Mr Masters, even when in his school, and she remembered with nostalgic longing the quiet evenings spent studying with him.

'What are you reading, then?' he growled. She held the book out for him to see.

'Hrmp.' He took it from her and leafed quickly through the pages, glancing sharply at her again. 'You still reading, girl?'

'Oh yes, Mr Masters,' she said fervently. 'You should just see the books up at Fawcetts'. Hundreds . . . thousands of them. I've never seen so many in my life. All the ones you told me to read, all the ones on your list, and hundreds more besides!'

He handed the book back to her and paused.

'You read what you can, girl, read what you can. Try to find time. And read some history as well. It's important you know. Read history as well.'

'I will, sir!' she said grinning.

He stared at her as though considering – and then turned his back and stumped away. He was ugly and grey and bad-tempered, and yet she liked Mr Masters. In an odd, inexplicable way he was like her pa, and even a little bit like gramp.

When she started to read *The Brothers Karamazov*, she found it unbelievably difficult. She plodded stubbornly through the first hundred pages and then she called in to see Mr Masters after work one evening. He opened the door of the schoolhouse and snapped, 'What on earth do you want at this time of night, Whitman,' but she had seen, before his usual grumble, a quick flash of interested pleasure on his face.

'I don't understand this book, Mr Masters,' she said cheekily, holding the 'borrowed' *Karamazov* out towards him. He glared at her, at the book, then grunted, 'You can come in for a few seconds if you want. How I'm supposed to explain Dostoevsky in half an hour is something only a mind as stupid as yours could expect, Whitman.'

'Yes, sir.'

He led her inside – to a room that was unbelievably disordered – and flung himself down in an armchair with torn upholstery.

'Well, what's the matter with *Karamazov*? What's Dostoevsky done that you don't like, Whitman?'

'I don't understand the people,' she answered. 'It's not just the words they use – I don't understand those either – but they don't seem real people.'

Mr Masters put his feet on a stool. He was wearing a pair of tatty slippers with the toes hanging out.

'Did you like *Emma*?' he barked. 'Did you like Jane Austen? *Pride and Prejudice*? Eh?'

'Oh, yes!' breathed Sarah. 'They were people like us. Rich, of course, but like us inside – you know, irritating and bossy and domineering, and nice too. They had nice manners and talked about their health – just like we do.'

'You're stupid, Whitman!' he snapped again. 'You don't know anything about it at all. You know why you like Austen? Because she's English, that's why. You're like everyone else, can't understand a temperament of any other country. Here.' He spun round suddenly and snatched a huge, broken-backed book from a shelf piled high with papers, books and dirty cups. 'Read that. That's a history of the Russian people for the last two hundred years. Read that, then try to work out what sort of person you'd be if you lived in Russia. You're too young to read Dostoevsky anyway,' he finished illogically. 'You shouldn't read books like that. Put it back on Mr Fawcett's shelf – from whence you should never have taken it in the first place – and don't dare read it again until you're twenty-five.'

'No, sir.' She grinned again. They both knew she wouldn't take any notice of what he said.

'I'll have to go now. My ma will be cross if I'm not home soon.' She opened the door.

'Whitman!'

'Yes, sir?' She turned round and faced him again. He was staring hard at the toe of his mauve slipper.

'Whitman, would it be possible for you to live in at the Fawcetts? Get away from your mo – Spend a little less time at home. If you lived in at Fawcetts' you'd have the evenings for reading.' He glared at her. 'If you wanted to come and ask me your stupid questions in the evenings, I'd put up with it.'

She knew he meant well, but the thought of staying all night at the Fawcetts', within easy reach of old man Fawcett and his horrible poking hands, made her flush suddenly. 'No,' she said vehemently. 'No, I wouldn't want to stay there. Not at night. I'd sooner go home and help ma. I don't like it at Fawcetts' – apart from the books,' she added, not wishing to seem unappreciative.

'Huh!' grunted Mr Masters. 'Is it your mistress? Or is it the old man? Or don't you like hard work, Whitman? Is that the trouble? You don't like hard work?'

A flash of resentful temper flared briefly in her face, then she saw that Mr Masters was deliberately baiting her – baiting her because he was interested and wanted to help.

'It's him,' she blurted, feeling suddenly relieved because she had told someone. She didn't understand why she could tell Mr Masters all about it, but in some strange way she wasn't embarrassed or worried. She told him about the old man, and about Mrs Fawcett who seemed to pick on her for a reason of her own, and about ma threatening her with what would happen if Mrs Fawcett gave her the sack. When she saw that Mr Masters was listening, was interested and observant, she began to tell him about the funny things; the time she had discovered a sixpence under Mrs Fawcett's wardrobe, a sixpence that had obviously been put there to test either her honesty or her thoroughness in cleaning. She had – indignantly – thought of a way round the bait. She had polished the sixpence with silver polish until it gleamed beyond any possible doubt of having been found – and then carefully placed it on a saucer in exactly the same spot under the wardrobe. She had been tempting providence – and risking her post – but was too angry at the time to care. And some latent sense of shame had kept Mrs Fawcett quiet. She had never mentioned the sixpence to Sarah.

Mr Masters listened attentively. He didn't laugh or even smile, but she knew he was interested. She was half-way through another story – about Mr Fawcett hiding the port bottle in the chamber-pot under his bed – when Mr Masters's grand-daughter clock began to chime. She broke off in the middle of a sentence, her face turning white.

'It's late,' she whispered. 'I should have been home an hour ago. Ma will kill me.'

Mr Masters got up, wound a scarf round his neck and put his high, black homburg on his head.

'An exaggeration, Whitman, like all your statements. An exaggeration. However, to alleviate your anxiety, I shall accompany you home and offer my excuses to your mother.'

'Oh, don't do that sir,' she said quickly. 'That will only make it worse. If she knows I've been here talking about books and things like that, she'll be furious.'

Mr Masters opened his front door and stumped out. 'I have been known – in my time, Whitman – to possess a little tact. Please refrain from insulting me with your inanities.'

He walked down the lane so swiftly she had a job to keep up. She was worried about what she would say to her ma, and every so often she would begin a sentence, only to be interrupted with 'Quiet, Whitman! I am thinking.'

When she walked into the cottage she knew, from one look at her mother's face, that she was in trouble. Anne had her hand raised already to strike her when she suddenly realised Mr Masters had followed Sarah into the kitchen. She flushed and quickly dropped her arm back to her side.

'Mrs Whitman,' said Mr Masters gruffly, 'I must apologise

for detaining young Sarah. I encountered her coming home this evening and asked if she would assist me in clearing the sink waste of my small house. It is a task I always find completely beyond me.'

Sarah stared hard at the floor, amazed not only at Mr Master's blatant untruth, but at his skill in selecting exactly the right kind of untruth. Anne-Louise appeared slightly mollified.

'She's handy for housework,' said Mr Masters loftily. 'Indeed, Mrs Whitman, it prompts me to ask a favour of you. I live roughly, as you know,' Anne-Louise nodded, then fearing she had been impolite shook her head.

'I wonder if your daughter could come – say two evenings a week – and tidy my rooms. I could manage only a modest payment – say a shilling a week. But it would be quite a help to me.'

Anne was gratified. For her daughter to go and clean up the schoolmaster's house was a kind of compliment to herself, and a shilling was always handy. She was, in spite of her indignation at him suggesting some years ago that Sarah should take the scholarship, aware of the respect due to his professional status. She liked the idea of Sarah unstopping his sink waste.

'Well, I think that would be all right,' she said graciously. 'She'll come on Tuesdays and Thursdays, if that is convenient with you.'

Neither she nor Mr Masters looked at, or even considered, Sarah, who was still staring hard at the floor. She was confused and embarrassed by Mr Masters's suggestion, knowing exactly what he had in mind. He would give her the shilling, as promised, and she would spend the evening talking and reading with him, getting her money for nothing, merely for spending a wonderful evening working with him like she used to when she was going for the scholarship.

'That's settled then,' said Mr Masters abruptly getting to his feet. 'I'll expect her on Thursday.'

He walked towards the door and Sarah suddenly noticed that he had come to see her mother still wearing his mauve, tatty slippers. She stifled a giggle, seeing how funny he was in

slippers and black homburg hat – and feeling at the same time
a wave of tolerant affection and gratitude towards him.

'Marm!' he said, swinging the hat back on his head. 'I wish
you good night.'

He disappeared and Anne-Louise said affably to Sarah,
'You'd better get yourself some supper. You'll be hungry after
helping him out with his sink waste.'

Guiltily Sarah helped herself to bread and cheese. She had
expected a scolding and a slap round the head. Instead she
had supper and the promise of two evenings a week off.

Surprisingly he didn't spend as much time with her as she
had thought studying the book from Fawcetts'. He made her
do arithmetic and geography, saying that she could manage to
read history and novels in her own time. And somehow –
because he took her co-operation for granted – she managed to
do the extra reading in her own time. The two secret evenings
a week made a difference to her, made her feel there was a
purpose in Mr Masters's mind, a plan that he was trying to
work out and that she must try her very best to bring to
fruition. And this time Anne-Louise knew nothing of what
was happening. The study was secret. Anne couldn't prevent
it because she didn't know it was happening. The only time
Sarah felt bad was when Mr Masters gave her the shilling at
the end of the week. She felt guilty and miserable, but knew
she had to accept it – otherwise Anne would wonder what was
happening on Tuesdays and Thursdays. Sometimes she would
catch Mr Masters looking speculatively at her. 'Haa, Whitman!' he would snap. 'And just what are we going to do with
you, eh? What are we going to do with you?'

In April, when she had been working with him for five
months, he made her sit one evening answering questions on
a printed form. He had his fob watch in front of him and he
gave her four question papers to answer. When she had
finished – or when he called out for her to finish, he sent her
home he told her he would look at the papers before she came
the next Tuesday. She spent the intervening days in a frenzy
of worry, knowing that the papers had been a kind of test as

to whether the plan – whatever it was – should go on. When she arrived on the following Thursday Mr Masters glared at her.

'Quite ridiculous, some of your answers, Whitman,' he growled. 'And you don't know how to spell Dardanelles. We shall concentrate on your European geography for the next two weeks.'

She was relieved, happily, glowingly relieved because she knew he was pleased with her and the 'plan' could go on. Everything else became second to the 'plan', to the evenings with Mr Masters, to the quick, snatched minutes with books during the day. Nothing else seemed to matter any more. Not Fawcetts', or ma, or being huge and fat and ugly, only the 'plan' was important.

Sometimes she longed to tell pa because she knew how happy he would be, how it would give him something important too, something to excite him when he was tired or ill or had the pain in his head. But she didn't tell him because the last time – the scholarship time – she had failed and she couldn't bear the thought of hurting pa like that again. She must wait – until Mr Masters was ready – until she was ready.

'Will your mother permit you to go away from home?' Mr Masters asked suddenly one evening. 'You're fifteen, aren't you? Do you think she'll allow you to go away?'

She couldn't answer, and the first doubts about the success of the 'plan' gnawed at the back of her mind. Sooner or later Anne was going to have to know what was happening. Instinctively Sarah knew her mother would fight it, would try to prevent her from taking advantage of the reading and the evenings with Mr Masters. And Sarah had grown to respect her mother's self-willed objectivity. Whatever Anne-Louise wanted, she got. She had wanted Harriet to go away – and it had happened. She had wanted Peter to leave – and that had happened too. She had said the scholarship wouldn't work – she had been right. Anne-Louise was infallible. And even if pa stood against her – still she would win.

'I'm not sure,' she faltered when Mr Masters pressed his

300

question a second time. 'I'm not sure – but I don't think she'll like it.'

Mr Masters glared. 'We'll have to know soon,' he said. 'We'll have to know soon.'

'I'll ask her . . . I'll tell pa . . . after the Armistice party,' she agreed nervously. 'We'll tell her then – after the party. After July . . . and see what she says.'

She began to feel it was hopeless, that she had been living in a dream from which Anne-Louise would brutally wake her. Once Anne knew what had been happening, there was not a chance she would allow Sarah to go away from home. The dream would end; Anne-Louise would begin.

She put the thought away from her, tried to take the same amount of enjoyment from the lessons that she had done until now. She told herself she wouldn't think about it until the Armistice party was over. Until then everything would be as it was, absorbing, exciting and anticipatory.

The Armistice party, settled for the second week in July, was the most important thing that had happened in the village for longer than anyone could remember. It had been planned and discussed for six months and – socially – it combined and united the religious, tribal and economic groups of the village into one huge, universal celebration. The village was echoing – as was every village and town in the country – the relief from a war that had been over for nearly a year. The initial grief of bereavement was over – the Armistice party made a pretext that the grief had been worth while.

The whole day was to be a holiday. In the afternoon, games, races and tea for the children. In the evening, dancing – for those whose religion permitted such extravagances – supper and a brass band for the adults. It was to be such an event that relatives who had long since left the village were coming home just to join in the Armistice party. The East Enders who had fled to the village from the bombs were coming. The Dances, Florrie, Maxie and the children, were coming. Even the land girls who had worked on Tyler's farm were coming. The party was the first event of magnitude that had occurred since the celebrations for the Battle of Waterloo.

At first she wasn't going to be allowed at the adult party. Anne said she could go to the afternoon games and help with the children, but then she would have to leave.

Two days before the party Anne discovered that Betsy was allowing her two elder daughters to stay for the evening – and that she had made shantung dresses for both of them. Anne-Louise, stung to revolt by the appearance of her widowed sister's generosity, lent Sarah her own black, silk skirt and said she could join in the supper in the evening. She was furious with Betsy for not letting her know sooner about the shantung dresses. Betsy – on an infinitesimal pension – was gaining the admiration and help of the whole village, and Anne-Louise was tired of hearing what a wonderful mother Betsy was, how good she was to her children, how brave and generous and how amazingly well she managed. Now, by the secrecy of the shantung dresses, she had ensured another evening of admiration. Anne-Louise knew exactly how it would be – everyone admiring Mary and May in their new dresses and remarking how wonderful Betsy was to buy the material and to make the dresses when she had so little time and money.

She couldn't afford to buy Sarah a dress, and there wasn't time to make anything over for her. She flung the black silk skirt irritably at her and said, 'You can wear that with your cream shirtwaist. And I'll give you the money to get yourself a band for your hair. For goodness' sake try and look less frumpy, stand up straight and don't slump when you're sitting at the table. And try to talk to people too, not sit there dreaming the whole time.'

Sarah, tormented by the knowledge that soon her mother would know about Mr Masters and the 'plan', paid scant attention to the customary admonishments. She knew Peter was coming home on a brief leave and she wondered if she could confide in him, and perhaps enlist his support for the shattering disruption that was shortly going to occur.

When she saw him, she suddenly realised she couldn't talk to him any more, not like she had talked to him when they were both children. He was a tall, quiet, brown young man who said very little and looked rather like pa. He had the secret smile that pa had. He was even a little bit like Uncle Math to look at – or maybe that was because of the quietness and the blue sailor's uniform.

He spent nearly all the time with Aunt Betsy and went, twice, to see Harriet in the Home. The rest of the time he was so very reserved and withdrawn she didn't like to mention her problems to him.

Nervously, without pleasure, she dressed herself for the party in the cream shirtwaist and Anne-Louise's old silk skirt. She didn't bother about trying to look pretty – she was too big for that – but, in spite of her perpetual anxiety about Mr Masters and her mother, she felt a faint twinge of excitement at the thought of the party. She heard, from downstairs, the arrival of Florrie Dance with her husband and children, and when she went down she saw ma was looking very flushed and bright-eyed, talking to a big, fat, fair-haired man whose right jacket-sleeve hung useless and empty from the shoulder.

'Hullo, Aunt Florrie,' said Sarah without enthusiasm. Florrie's enforced stay with them during the war had left Sarah with a memory of too much noise and too many tears and hysterics. Florrie flung herself forward and embraced Sarah to her huge, upholstered bosom.

'My! What a young lady you've grown into! You'll be having a fella next, won't she Anne? If she's anything like you and me when we was girls, she'll be a fine old one for the fellas! Won't she, Annie?'

Anne-Louise smiled icily.

'And this 'ere's your Uncle Maxie,' said Florrie pulling Sarah over to the one-armed fat man. 'Maxie says 'e'll never forget what you done for us in the war, 'aving us down 'ere to stay, and then sending us all that extra food when it was so short. "I'll never forget Annie and her husband," he said to me only the other day. "Real Christians, that's what they are, helping out like that".'

The big man laughed and put his remaining arm round Florrie's shoulder.

'Never thought,' he boomed jovially, 'never thought when I used to bring you two girls the fish from the market all

303

those years ago, that one day Annie would be sending me something back!'

'It was me you brought the fish for,' snapped Anne suddenly.

'Was pleased to do it, pleased to do it,' said Maxie heartily. 'My, but you two were a pair of skinny rabbits in those days, weren't you? You certainly needed feeding up. We had some right old times, didn't we? You two girls, and me and Bert.' He sobered suddenly. 'Bert got 'is ticket, you know. Went down at Ypres. Poor old Bert. A good mate of mine, 'e was.'

'I can't really remember him very well,' said Anne haughtily. 'If you remember, he didn't come with us very often.'

'Don't remember Bert?' said Maxie teasingly. 'No, well, o' course, 'e was keen on Florrie to start with, wasn't 'e? Then we all 'ad a change round and sorted ourselves out for the best.' He suddenly shot Anne a quizzical, perceptive kind of look, and Sarah decided that he wasn't quite so noisy or insensitive as she had thought. 'My, Annie,' he said teasingly. 'At least Florrie's put a bit o' weight on since then. You don't seem to have fed yourself up much!'

'I've tried not to let myself go,' said Anne. Her face was white, and Sarah knew – from long experience – that her mother was about to lose her temper. 'Just because one gets older, there's no need to get fat and bloated.'

Florrie's face went a slow, dull red, and Sarah was suddenly terribly ashamed for her mother, ashamed of the way she was behaving, ashamed of her rudeness to Auntie Florrie, ashamed of the way she prinked and talked too much in front of Aunt Florrie's husband. The room was very quiet and the uncomfortable, ugly silence grew longer and longer. Sarah stared out of the window.

'There's someone outside the back door,' she said, thankful for something to break the atmosphere in the kitchen and take people's minds off the way her ma had behaved.

'Struth! I forgot,' said Maxie with enforced jollity. 'I 'ope you don't mind, but we brought my youngest brother. I don't suppose you'll remember 'im either, Annie. If you don't remember Bert, you won't remember Charlie, will you? 'E was only eight when you knew 'im. 'E's a real masher now. Only got back from France four weeks ago and 'e asn't found 'is feet properly yet. Thought you wouldn't mind us bringing 'im down.' He didn't wait for an answer. He went straight to the back door and called, 'Come on in, Charlie, do. There's no need to stand out there waiting to see if you're welcome.'

A young, fair-haired man with wide shoulders and blue eyes stepped uneasily into the kitchen. The Dance children began to make a noise again and Sarah felt the atmosphere ease, relax and grow normal. Anne-Louise, her hospitality appealed to, said of course she remembered Charlie and they must all have a cup of tea before they went to the party. She chattered gaily around the kitchen, putting the cups out and appealing to Florrie to remember what a mischievous child Charlie Dance had been.

Sarah, making the tea in the best teapot, was suddenly aware that Charlie Dance was staring at her, staring hard, and she wished she'd taken more trouble getting ready, had done her hair differently, or had had time to alter her ma's black skirt.

Anne-Louise and the children, between them, were making so much noise that the room seemed fuller than it was. Anne poured tea and passed biscuits. Florrie and Maxie Dance were finally won over by her efforts at welcoming them and the unpleasantness was – nearly – forgotten.

The young man continued to stare at Sarah and she grew uncomfortably hot, feeling both embarrassed and pleased at the same time. He was really rather nice to look at, not as handsome as Peter, but . . . different. Peter was tall and thin and had soft brown hair and eyes. And he was quiet. Charlie Dance was big and blond, and looked as though he could be boisterous.

'Well,' said Annie, when several cups of tea had been poured and consumed, 'I suppose we had better get up to the hall if the children are to go in for the races. Jonathan's been up there all the morning helping to get everything ready.' She paused and added grandly. 'Jonathan's usually the one who does all the arrangements for anything like this.'

They filed out of the house and up to the village, Anne, Florrie and Maxie walking ahead with the children and leaving her to follow behind with Charlie Dance. She glanced swiftly at him once and saw he was still staring, so for the rest of the journey she didn't look any more.

She was aware – the whole of the afternoon she was aware – that he was never very far away. He helped her with the children during the games. He wiped her skirt down when Maudie Dance spilt lemonade down it. In the middle of the afternoon, just before the egg-and-spoon race, he suddenly said, 'You're staying for this evening, aren't you. I mean, you haven't got to take the children home or anything?'

'Of course I'm staying,' she said haughtily. She was worried in case he thought she was a child who had to do what she was told. She had worked out that Charlie Dance must be at least twenty-five, and he obviously thought she was more than fifteen. She wondered if she would have time to run home and do her hair for the evening.

She didn't have time, but she managed to borrow Aunt Betsy's comb and mirror and she went into the privy of the Institute Hall and combed it out looser at the front with the bun higher on the top of her head. She left the band off because she looked older without it.

There were sausage rolls for the supper, and fish-paste sandwiches and cheese and lettuce and rock cakes and tea or lemonade, whichever you preferred. They sat on wooden benches at trestle-tables covered in red, white and blue *crêpe* paper and Charlie Dance sat beside her, passing her cakes and sandwiches and spooning out jelly on to her plate.

'Go on, have another cake,' he urged. 'You know you'd like another one.'

She felt excited and happy. For the moment she had forgotten Mr Masters and telling ma about going away from home. Just for now everything was wonderful.

'I'll burst my waistband if I eat any more,' she confided. 'You see this isn't my skirt. It's my ma's. And she's nice and slim you see, not fat like me. If I eat too much the skirt will be spoilt for her.'

306

Charlie looked at her and the smile on his face changed, became odd and a little strained.

'I don't think you're fat at all,' he said slowly. 'I think you're beautiful. You're the most beautiful girl I've ever seen. When I was in France in the trenches, I used to make a girl up for myself. I used to imagine what sort of girl I would like and then imagine her walking along the trench towards me, all through the mud and everything. I knew exactly what she'd look like.' He turned and stared at Sarah again and she felt tears well into her eyes, because she had thought it was all fun – just excitement and laughing and having him pay attention to her – and now she realised that it was the war again. The horrible, terrible war that had taken Uncle Frankie's left eye and made Uncle Will shout and tremble. The war that made Mrs Tyler stay at home mourning her four sons when everyone else had come to the party. The war that made Aunt Betsy – sitting at the top of the table trying hard to smile – a tired, determinedly cheerful woman whose gaiety deceived no one. She couldn't drink her tea because of the lump in her throat – the lump that was the war, the unhappiness, the loneliness of Aunt Betsy.

'Hey, come on,' said Charlie Dance quickly. 'Don't look like that. I shall stop telling girls they're pretty if they look like that.'

The brass band arrived and seven florid-faced gentlemen began to unpack their instruments. The trestles, the benches and plates were removed, and cakes, broken sandwiches and crumbs were swept up from the floor. Sarah went and sat at the side of the hall to listen to the music. The evening once more glittered with excitement and breathless suspense that she didn't quite understand. The music, the eyes of Charlie Dance, the couples jigging up and down on the Institute floor made her feel that something wonderful was about to happen, something grand and splendid that had never happened to her before.

'Come and dance with me,' said Charlie suddenly.

She looked worried and shook her head.

'Oh, no! We're not allowed to dance. We shouldn't really

307

come to this kind of thing anyway – only that it's the Armistice and the war's over and everything. But we're not allowed to dance!'

'It won't hurt, just once.' He was sitting beside her and his arm was stretched along the back of her chair. Once he accidentally touched her cheek with his finger and then he did it again, deliberately, smiling at her, never taking his eyes from her face. Beside him she felt small and slender, not the great galumphing thing that she knew she was.

'Please, Sarah. Dance with me.'

She looked round the Institute Hall. It was crowded and she couldn't see her ma anywhere. She was probably in the kitchen talking to the other women. Aunt Betsy was at the other end of the hall with Peter beside her. She could see her pa as well, but she knew pa would understand.

'Dance with me, Sarah.'

Feeling that the world was about to collapse on her, she stood up, smoothing her skirt out at the back. 'I can't dance,' she faltered, knowing it was a poor excuse because no one in the village could dance and yet they were all prancing about the floor in discordant joviality.

Charlie put his arms round her waist and she was glad she was such a big girl because her face was just at the right height, and she was able to look up into his face and see – however much she pretended otherwise – how much he liked her. He swung her round to the music. They were out of time and sometimes she trod on his feet, sometimes he on hers. Then she suddenly fell into step and began to twist round and round with him, her steps blending with his, her body swaying against his arms, her eyes shining and smiling, staring up into his.

She had forgotten everything but Charlie and the music when she felt the blow on her shoulder and the slap across the face.

Anne-Louise had not enjoyed the party. The sight of Maxie with his empty sleeve had upset her, and so had meeting Florrie, who was expensively dressed and obviously not in need of money. At the back of Anne's mind fidgeted a tiny speculation of what would have happened if *she* had, after all, married Maxie instead of Jonathan. She was surprised and annoyed to find that Maxie was still a handsome man. He was fat, but the strong body and energy were just as she had remembered them. His hair was as thick and he had the same boisterous zest for life that had always attracted her. She could see he was still ready for a fight, ready to dump Florrie – or Anne-Louise if it had been her – in an argument. A strong, forceful, noisy husband and father. Quick to row and quick to get his own way, if he thought it was right.

With a rare and unusual gift of perception – usually she was completely insensitive to what anyone else thought or felt – she saw how she looked in his eyes. She was no longer Anne-Louise, adored and pampered by the blond Billingsgate fish family. She was a petulant, shrewish woman who had got her own way and still was not satisfied. He seemed happy. That was what annoyed her. He had married fat, vulgar, unexciting Florrie, and he seemed happy instead of always regretting that he had been jilted by Anne-Louise. If he had given any sign at all of sadness, just one quick glance of lingering regret for what might have been, she would have exerted every effort and charm to see that both he and Florrie went away adoring her. As it was, she was still smarting over his carelessness and over her own rudeness, which reflected badly on her.

The afternoon had been bad, but the evening was worse. Everyone had admired Betsy, as she had known they would. The shantung dresses were fingered and praised. Betsy was called from this table to that, to sit with this person, to talk with that family.

But she could have borne even that if it hadn't been for Sarah. Sarah was the final, hurting irritant of the evening, an irritant that finally became so painful she felt sick with impotent anguish. For Sarah, in the passed-on skirt and the old cream blouse, had suddenly turned into a beautiful young woman – not just pretty – not just a flushed, delighted young girl at a party – but a young woman, whose face, carriage, posture and behaviour was something that had not been seen in the village before, something vivid and delightful and completely enchanting. People began to come up to her and remark on Sarah, asking where she'd been hiding such a beauty in the family, noting how well she sat, how charming she was when she smiled, how she seemed to be smiling all the time. Even the women complimented her on Sarah, and with each piece of praise, each flattering comment, she grew angrier and angrier — so angry that she began to feel really ill and had to step outside into the night air for a moment.

When she came back in she saw Sarah dancing. Dancing with Charlie and — in the background — Jonathan standing in a corner, watching his daughter with such fatuous, transparent love on his face, such pleasure and delighted smiling pride, that her control finally snapped completely.

She pushed her way violently through the couples on the floor, knocking people aside with strength lent to her by misery. When she reached Charlie and Sarah, she pulled the girl's shoulder viciously round and smacked her across the face. The blow contained everything in her heart — all the frustration of Maxie, of Betsy, of Sarah, of Jonathan — of Mathy looking at Betsy on a summer evening and tweaking her hair, of Sarah and Jonathan planting a silly row of marigolds round the edge of the meadow, of Jonathan planning to be a postman and not telling her about it, of Peter running off to Portsmouth because he liked Betsy and Math better than he did Anne-Louise. The blow across her daughter's face said everything that Anne-Louise did not know how to say.

'You slut!' she shouted, forgetting, and indeed not caring, where she was or how many people were listening to her. 'You sly, wicked, little slut! You get home at once, you hear? You get home and when you get there you're going to get the thrashing of your life! You cheap — sly — wicked — little — slut!'

With every word she struck the girl on alternate sides of her face. Sarah's face swung violently back and forth. The music from the end of the hall stopped, the couples ceased to move and stared, at first amazed and then embarrassed at the scene of humiliation at the centre of the hall.

Sarah began to cry. Her face was marked red and white and

she was shaking. Charlie Dance looked astonished and then agonisingly ashamed – not for himself – for Sarah. 'It was my fault, Mrs Whitman . . . ' he began, but she didn't hear him.

'You've been nothing but trouble to me since the day you were born! One thing after another! A spoilt, wicked child and now you're a slut! A sly – wicked – slut.'

Her hand came down again, hard and viciously. She swung it back in the air and then felt it held in a sharp, angry grip.

'That's enough, Anne!' shouted Jonathan. 'That's enough!'

'Leave me!' she shrieked wildly. 'It's none of your business. You never correct the girl! You spoil her. You've always spoilt her! She's a slut! A slut! You hear me? Your daughter's a spoilt little slut!'

He suddenly twisted her arm behind her back and pushed her, roughly and unceremoniously, towards the door. His face was controlled and furious. At the door he looked over his shoulder and shouted to Betsy.

'See Sarah comes home, Betsy. Bathe her face and see she gets home all right.'

He pushed Anne roughly through the door, still holding her arm behind her in a vice-like grip.

Betsy ran over to Sarah. The girl was weeping piteously, her face buried shamefully in her hands. Her hair had come unpinned with the violence of Anne's slapping and her bun hung lop-sidedly over one side of her face.

'Come along, dear,' said Betsy quietly. 'Let's go home now.'

'In front of everyone!' the child sobbed. 'Everyone's looking at me. They're all looking at me.'

'Come home, dear.'

Some kindly inspiration set the band quietly playing again. People pretended to talk to one another, looked away from the embarrassing figure of Sarah with her Aunt Betsy.

'What will he think? He said I was beautiful and he thought I was grown-up! In front of everyone, Aunt Betsy . . . How could . . . ' She began to walk down the hall, choking and stumbling with misery, not looking at anyone because of the humiliation. Betsy led her out of the door.

'Oh, Annie,' she said tiredly into the night. 'Will you never learn?'

He knew then that it was the end of trying. The end of hoping that one day Anne-Louise would find some kind of love, some kind of compassion in her heart. Beneath his anger and frustration he was dimly aware of pity – because she could never have what she wanted – and if she had it she would still not be happy. But now he would not try any longer – now Anne must live with her own frustration.

With a profound sense of grief he reconciled himself to the knowledge that he must send Sarah, his best-beloved child, away before Anne completely destroyed her. He remembered what plans he had had for the child – plans once fostered for himself that had been worn away by hard work and poverty. Sarah's chances, like his, were still-born, but at least if he sent her away she would live her dull, unexciting, overworked life without the additional burden of Anne-Louise's bitterness. He had wasted her life for her. He should have stood against Anne several years ago – when the child was first born. He had tried to compromise – to build a marriage on reason and hope, and instead all he had done was destroy the talent, the embryonic, gifted beauty that could have been his daughter Sarah.

Bitterly he set about finding a place for her in service far, far away from the village, away from Anne-Louise, away from him. It must be a good place, with a fair employer and a chance of friends and pleasure. Sarah had had too little pleasure in her life so far.

He read all the advertisements he could find and wrote letters, more and more letters because he wanted – indeed he must – find just the right place for her. When the letters and the advertisements failed, he began to make inquiries about the village – did anyone have a cousin, a relative who knew of a good post. He never thought to ask the schoolmaster, who was a bachelor without friends or family. The schoolmaster would be unlikely to know of domestic vacancies.

He was surprised and puzzled when Mr Masters ran after him in the street one day. He caught up with Jonathan outside the post office and he was panting and out of breath.

'Postman! Postman! I've got to talk to you. Pouf! Wait a minute now. Pouf!'

He leaned on the wall of the general store and waited a moment.

'It's about your daughter. I just heard you were planning to send her away. Into service. Away.'

Jonathan nodded.

'Be fatal, utterly fatal!' said Mr Masters snappily. 'She's got brains that girl of yours. She's got brains *and* imagination. Put her into service again . . . utterly fatal.'

Jonathan felt tiredly irritated. 'What else can we do?' he asked wearily. 'She's had her chance and she lost it.' He paused and then discarded his last loyalties to Anne. 'We both know why she lost it.'

Mr Masters hrumphed and glowered at the ground.

'She lost her chance,' Jonathan continued. 'But, perhaps – away from home – in domestic work of some kind, she'll be a little happier.'

'Stuff!' snorted Mr Masters rudely. 'She won't be happy at all. Now listen to me. I've got a plan. Been working on it with her. Every evening . . . Tuesday and Thursday, been working with her, studying, making her take tests, reading, everything. Got a plan for her.'

Jonathan watched Mr Masters's face and then realised vaguely what the old man was saying. A small excited hope began to thump in his breast.

'Not going to be easy,' growled the teacher. 'Not like if she had taken the scholarship – but it's a way – and she'll work hard – she'll do that all right. She might just manage it.'

'What?' he asked eagerly. 'What can she do? I'll help all I can, every way I know, if you can think of something for her. Something that will give her a chance, help her to be more than a servant.'

Mr Masters moved his black brows vigorously up and down

over his eyes.

'I've arranged for her to take a small test, nothing much – she'll pass it easily, I've seen to that – I've written to a friend in Stepney – not the best area, but all I can do. She'll go as a pupil-teacher – have to give a hand with everything – children, housework, everything – hardly any money – just her keep for a couple of years. If she's satisfactory – works hard – she'll be able to get a grant for a training course. The Government will lend her the money and she'll have to pay it back when she's working as a teacher. It'll be hard for her. Lots of study – no money – paying off debts for a long time – but she's worth it. And she'll do it, too,' he suddenly said happily, not growling, or grumbling, but looking thoroughly pleased with himself. 'She'll manage it, that girl of yours. She'll be a school-teacher or she'll know the edge of my tongue!'

Jonathan had to close his eyes suddenly with the relief. Something wonderful had happened, something wonderful and surprising that he didn't deserve. A chance that Sarah had won for herself with the help of this funny old man. He felt ashamed because he had done nothing – because he had let tiredness and pain and poverty drive the fight from him – destroy the energy that he should have used for Sarah – the energy that had dragged him up one infinitesimal step from labourer to postman, a nothing along the line of progress that he had wanted for himself.

'Oh, God. Thank you,' he muttered, and then laughed when he heard Mr Masters grunt, 'It's not God you should thank, man. It's me, and my friend in Stepney and the Education Committee.'

'I'll do what I can,' said Jonathan. 'If we can get some money together it will mean she won't be so long paying back for her training. We'll manage somehow to save a bit. We always manage somehow – when we have to.'

'You'd better come up to Stepney with me,' said the schoolmaster. 'Bring her on Saturday and she can take the little test at the school while she's there.' He paused and glowered at Jonathan.

314

'The sooner she goes the better.'

He knew what Mr Masters meant. He knew and didn't care who else in the village knew as well. He cared only that Sarah had a chance – a last-minute unexpected chance. He was content.

She went in September. Flushed, excited and feverish with hope and anxiety. He'd brought her a new case – it was an extravagance, but he wanted everything to be wonderful for her – a new life, a new suitcase, a new chance.

He carried the case up to the station, holding each moment of her presence tightly against him, knowing this was the last time she would be 'his' Sarah, his very own beloved Sarah, his daughter who thought and was as he himself was. She could be different from now on – climbing up – thoughts that were new, ideas more complicated and deep. She wouldn't be 'his' Sarah any more.

'Go to Meeting on Sunday, won't you, dear?'

He didn't really care if she went or not. He just wanted this last chance of being her father, of knowing that she would do what he asked without question, would love and adore him blindly because he was her father.

'Oh, I will, pa,' she breathed fervently. She was silent for a moment, then said hesitatingly. 'Auntie Florrie wrote to me. She said I can go there whenever I like. Is that all right, pa?' She blushed slightly and he knew she was thinking of Charlie Dance. For a moment he was worried – then forced himself to throw off the worry – to let her take things as they happened – to learn to control her own life.

'That's fine. You go and see her whenever you're lonely or in need of a good meal. She'll always give you a good meal. Just make sure you don't grow to look like her.'

She grinned and hugged him.

'Pa,' she said hesitating. 'I won't forget. Not anything. I'll remember everything you told me – whatever happens I'll remember the way you want me to be.' But already the gulf was there. The gulf that would widen and grow.

When she was sitting in the train he felt as though a piece

315

of his body were being taken away from him. She kissed him and looked slightly tearful – feeling the pain of leaving him in the same way that he did, but already excited and looking forward to whatever was going to happen to her. Then the train pulled out and her face was anxious and afraid from the window – the hazel eyes were questioning, the soft mouth trembling slightly. He waved and she leaned out of the window until the train was a tiny maggot on the distant track.

He strolled slowly back across the fields, noting the rowan-berries already forming and the hint of gold in the air about him. 'It's going to be a long winter,' he thought. 'I'd better get Betsy an extra supply of logs just in case we're busy when the bad weather comes.'

He crossed the lane and walked down to his own house. Anne-Louise was watching him from the window. She saw him coming back from the station – without Sarah – and felt relieved and happy for the first time since the terrible Armistice party. Sarah was gone now, and she had him to herself. Just him and the boys in the cottage – no one else to demand and want him, no one to take him away or distract his attention.

'Now he's mine,' she said gloatingly to herself. 'Now he belongs to me and there's no one to interfere or take him from me. Now he's mine for the rest of his life.'

Bobbie, their youngest son, was sitting on the grass outside the cottage. He held his hands up to Jonathan and pulled himself up on plump, four-year-old legs. Jonathan reached down and swung the child high up into the air and on to his shoulder. He waited outside the house, looking about him, and then he felt Bobbie reach his hands out into the air.

'Flowers. Flowers for Bobbie!' cried the small boy pointing to the marigolds along the grass verge.

She saw him laughing at the small boy on his shoulder – saw him reach down and pick a handful of marigolds for Bobbie, who buried his face in the flowers and grinned at his father.

Then she saw him raise the child high into the air again,

smiling and talking to him. When he put Bobbie back on to the ground they didn't come inside to her after all. They went walking off together across the fields opposite – towards Tyler's woods and the hills beyond – talking together like two old men and stopping to look at the flowers or point up at the sky.

A SELECTION OF FINE READING
AVAILABLE IN CORGI BOOKS

☐ 552 08073 X	THE PRACTICE	*Stanley Winchester* 8/–
☐ 552 08391 7	MEN WITH KNIVES	*Stanley Winchester* 7/–
☐ 552 07116 1	FOREVER AMBER Vol. I	*Kathleen Winsor* 5/–
☐ 552 07117 X	FOREVER AMBER Vol. II	*Kathleen Winsor* 5/–

War

☐ 552 08487 5	SIGNED WITH THEIR HONOUR	*James Aldridge* 7/–
☐ 552 08512 X	THE BIG SHOW	*Pierre Clostermann* 6/–
☐ 552 08410 7	THE DEEP SIX	*Martin Dibner* 6/–
☐ 552 08528 6	MARCH BATTALION	*Sven Hassel* 6/–
☐ 552 08496 4	JIM BRADY—LEADING SEAMAN	*J. E. Macdonnell* 5/–
☐ 552 08536 7	THE SCOURGE OF THE SWASTIKA	*Lord Russell* 6/–
☐ 552 08470 0	UNOFFICIAL HISTORY	*Field-Marshal Sir William Slim* 5/–
☐ 552 08527 8	THE LONG DROP	*Alan White* 5/–
☐ 552 08448 4	BRAVE COMPANY	*Guthrie Wilson* 5/–
☐ 552 08511 1	DOWDING & THE BATTLE OF BRITAIN	*Robert Wright* 7/–
☐ 552 08537 5	THE KNIGHTS OF BUSHIDO	*Lord Russell* 6/–

Romance

☐ 552 08515 4	THE HEALING TIME	*Lucilla Andrews* 4/–
☐ 552 08452 2	NURSE IN THE HILLS	*Irene Roberts* 4/–
☐ 552 08477 8	A STRANGER IN TOWN	*Alex Stuart* 4/–

Science Fiction

☐ 552 08499 9	REACH FOR TOMORROW	*Arthur C. Clarke* 5/–
☐ 552 08516 2	NEW WRITINGS IN SF 17	*John Carnell* 5/–
☐ 552 08453 0	DRAGONFLIGHT	*Anne McCaffrey* 5/–
☐ 552 08401 8	A CANTICLE FOR LEIBOWITZ	*Walter M. Miller Jr.* 6/–
☐ 552 08478 6	LOGAN'S RUN *William F. Nolan and George Clayton-Johnson* 4/–	
☐ 552 08500 6	THE INNER LANDSCAPE	*Peake/Ballard/Aldiss* 5/–
☐ 552 08533 2	EARTH ABIDES	*George R. Stewart* 6/–

General

☐ 552 98434 5	GOODBYE BABY AND AMEN *David Bailey and Peter Evans* 25/–	
☐ 552 07566 3	SEXUAL LIFE IN ENGLAND	*Dr. Ivan Bloch* 9/6
☐ 552 08403 4	LIFE IN TH E WORLD UNSEEN	*Anthony Borgia* 5/–
☐ 552 08432 8	PUT-OFFS AND COME-ONS	*A. H. Chapman, M.D.* 5/–
☐ 552 0 7593 0	UNMARRIED LOVE	*Dr. Eustace Chesser* 5/–
☐ 552 07950 2	SEXUAL BEHAVIOUR	*Dr. Eustace Chesser* 5/–
☐ 552 08402 6	SEX AND THE MARRIED WOMAN	*Dr. Eustace Chesser* 7/–
☐ 552 07400 4	MY LIFE AND LOVES	*Frank Harris* 13/–
☐ 552 98121 4	FIVE GIRLS (illustrated)	*Sam Haskins* 21/–
☐ 552 97745 4	COWBOY KATE (illustrated)	*Sam Haskins* 21/–
☐ 552 08362 3	A DOCTOR SPEAKS ON SEXUAL EXPRESSION IN MARRIAGE	*Donald W. Hastings, M.D.* 10/–

☐ 552 98247 4	THE HISTORY OF THE NUDE IN PHOTOGRAPHY (illustrated)	*Peter Lacey and Anthony La Rotonda* 25/-
☐ 552 98345 4	THE ARTIST AND THE NUDE (illustrated)	21/-
☐ 552 08069 1	THE OTHER VICTORIANS	*Steven Marcus* 10/-
☐ 552 08010 1	THE NAKED APE	*Desmond Morris* 6/-
☐ 552 07965 0	SOHO NIGHT AND DAY (illustrated)	*Norman and Bernard* 7/6
☐ 552 08105 1	BEYOND THE TENTH	*T. Lobsang Rampa* 5/-
☐ 552 08228 7	WOMAN: a Biological Study	*Philip Rhodes* 5/-
☐ 552 98178 8	THE YELLOW STAR (illustrated)	*Gerhard Schoenberner* 21/-
☐ 552 08456 5	COMPLETE BOOK OF JUKADO SELF-DEFENCE (illustrated)	*Bruce Tegner* 6/-
☐ 552 98479 5	MADEMOISELLE 1+1 *Marcel Veronese and Jean-Claude Peretz*	21/-

Western

☐ 552 08532 4	BLOOD BROTHER	*Elliott Arnold* 8/-
☐ 552 07756 9	SUDDEN—TROUBLESHOOTER	*Frederick H. Christian* 4/-
☐ 552 08451 4	THE OWLHOOT	*J. T. Edson* 4/-
☐ 552 08400 X	THE RIO HONDO WAR No. 60	*J. T. Edson* 4/-
☐ 552 08531 6	BACK TO THE BLOODY BORDER	*J. T. Edson* 4/-
☐ 552 08514 6	ALIAS BUTCH CASSIDY	*Will Henry* 4/-
☐ 552 08270 8	MACKENNA'S GOLD	*Will Henry* 4/-
☐ 552 08475 1	NO SURVIVORS	*Will Henry* 5/-
☐ 552 08485 9	THE FAST FIRST DRAW	*Louis L'Amour* 4/-
☐ 552 08476 X	GALLOWAY	*Louis L'Amour* 4/-
☐ 552 08484 0	GUNS OF TIMBERLAND	*Louis L'Amour* 4/-

Crime

☐ 552 08530 8	THE PROBLEM OF THE WIRE CAGE	*John Dickson Carr* 4/-
☐ 552 08498 0	WARN THE BARON	*John Creasey* 4/-
☐ 552 08529 4	HERE IS DANGER	*John Creasey* 4/-
☐ 552 08316 X	FOUNDER MEMBER	*John Gardner* 5/-
☐ 552 08513 8	A COOL DAY FOR KILLING	*William Haggard* 4/-
☐ 552 08472 7	THE INNOCENT BYSTANDERS	*James Munro* 5/-
☐ 552 08520 0	KISS ME, DEADLY	*Mickey Spillane* 4/-
☐ 552 08425 5	THE SHADOW GAME	*Michael Underwood* 4/-

All these books are available at your bookshop or newsagent; or can be ordered direct from the publisher. Just tick the titles you want and fill in the form below.

CORGI BOOKS, Cash Sales Department, P.O. Box 11, Falmouth, Cornwall.

Please send cheque or postal order. No currency, and allow 6d. per book to cover the cost of postage and packing in U.K., 9d. per copy overseas.

NAME ....

ADDRESS ....

(OCT. '70) ....